Holyrage
Chronicles
Book 1 – Vivication

Written by: Jonathan C. Socha

Cover artwork by Steve Goad
http://stevegoadart.com/

For my beautiful wife and creative other half, along with my energetic sons. Thank you for your endless patience and support for the many years this took to write. Also my friend of Ancient times, Michael Bloome whose ideas and input have helped shape this novel. Thank you.

CHAPTERS

I...7

II..11

III...19

IV...23

V..29

VI...37

VII..43

VIII...49

IX...57

X..61

XI...71

XII..79

XIII...89

XIV..99

XV..109

XVI...119

XVII..127

XVIII...141

XIX...147

XX..151

XXI...159

XXII..165

XXIII...171

XXIV..181

XXV...189

XXVI..199

XXVII...209

XXVIII 223

XXIX 235

XXX 251

XXXI 271

XXXII 287

XXXIII 301

XXXIV 317

XXXV 327

XXXVI 333

XXXVII 347

XXXVIII 357

EPILOGUE 375

I

The boy panted, the sun beat down mercilessly onto him. He wiped away the sweat from his brow before putting a hand up to ward the sun away. He scanned the horizon looking for his quarry. He had his bow with him and, as always, the dagger that his father had left him. It was a remarkable dagger, made by an elven blacksmith, he stroked the pommel out of habit. It had become a thing of comfort to him lately since his father Narkta departed with a strike force of elite warriors to engage the demon dragon Daemalai.

That was a little over a year ago now, he missed him tremendously. His mother warded away any dark thoughts he had about his father not being alive. She assured him weekly and sometimes daily that his father was still alive. She felt it in her heart, more importantly her faith kept it alive. She served Antul'aman the god of the forest and mountains. It was him that supposedly won the heart of Mother Nature herself, as a gift to her he created the great mountains in the world. His father served the Nameless One, there was some contention between each other at times on how to raise him, so they decided to teach him about both and left it up to him to decide what god he would follow.

There was truly a great love between his father and mother, it was made more solid in the fact that his father was elven and his mother human. The differences drew them close, as they were outcasts to both their peoples, so they had to fend for themselves, from what he understood times had changed in the recent years and it wasn't as bad as it once was. Part of that he knew was for the great renown his father had earned while serving in the nations numerous wars.

Movement caught his eye, he quickly came to his senses and caught sight of the object moving and found it to be a great big fat rabbit. He licked his lips thinking of it being spit and cooked. His mother always made the best rabbit and it was good eating. He carefully drew an arrow and knocked it. He drew it back and collected his aim. He was just about to let the arrow loose when the town bell rang off in the distance. It set off his concentration and when the arrow was loosed it went flying off into the woods completely missing his target. Frustration gnawed at him but the bell kept going off. That could only mean trouble.

He turned and began running towards his home. As he broke from the woods he saw his town burning. Smoke filled the air with dark clouds, the heat of the fire could be felt standing hundreds of yards away. Panic struck him and all he could think about was getting home to his mother where he knew he would be safe, so he did just that. He took off sprinting as fast as his legs would allow. It was only a few moments before he was staring at the door step to his home. He felt the intense heat from the flames that were consuming his home. He went up to the door which was smashed open and observed a strange thing hovering above his mother. It had a dark slimy body. Spikes protruded from its elbows and knees, it smelled of brimstone. His mother was lying on the ground at its feet bleeding from the head, her clothes were torn and she wasn't moving. The unknown creature licked its lips as it reached down for her. The boy drew his blade and ran at the creature fury erupting within him.

The sound of his footsteps drawing near caught the creatures attention and as it turned he jumped up with all the strength he could muster and plunged his dagger deep into the things head. The collision was enough to knock the unbalanced creature over. He held onto his blade on the way down, when they had hit the floor he yanked his dagger free and stabbed several more times with zeal and ferocity. Soon he was covered in black blood. As he stared at the wicked thing tears began pouring forth streaking his dirty stained face.

He was no longer that boy he thought to himself as he stood looking out over the battlements of the great wall known as Fenrir, taking in the sights across the sea of snow and ice in the uncharted lands of Vin Ara Talv. The moonlight danced in the reflections of the ice making it seem like the land was alive.

Many people believed that was true, for it did indeed shift and change with each day. So it remained as an uncharted land due to the complexity of keeping an updated map on record.

He breathed into his hands to warm them. It was always cold on the battlement but he didn't mind. The cold was always crisp and clean to breathe in. So he rather enjoyed it. It also always gave him time to think. He did a lot of that each day, things of his past. How his life was and is now. He had come a long way ever since he was 9 and that horrible incident that began shaping him into the person he was now. The thought of it never strayed far from his thoughts. The picture was always so vivid. He tried to put it out of his mind but it never truly left, it sat in the corner of his mind shrouded in darkness waiting for a moment to pounce.

"Zarron, hey Zarron." A voice brought him back from his trance. He shook his head to clear his mind and turned and saw one of his captains. He rendered a salute.

"My apologies Captain for not hearing you. I was thinking of my child hood and became lost in my thoughts." He said in a quiet voice.

"It's fine soldier that happens out here on the Fenrir. It is a hard place to be assigned to after your graduation from the church. I am just confused as to why you were assigned here. They must either really hate you or think you are quite good. So which one is it?"

"Well sir I would say that is a decision you can make yourself," Zarron replied as a smile crept across his face.

"Good answer soldier. I think you are going to blend in here quite well." The captain said in a cheery voice. He patted his shoulder as he walked past him.

"Carry on Zarron, carry on."

II

The sun was just starting to creep over the horizon when Zarron's relief showed. He was relieved he was on the night shift. It harbored more danger with the bitter cold but the sun light reflecting off the ice and snow was hard on the eyes he thought to himself.

"Anything to pass onto to me soldier?" The man who was relieving him had asked dryly, more out of duty then actual curiosity. Zarron turned to look at his relief and a massive man stood there. It took every ounce of his self-control to not have his jaw drop. The man stood heads above him, easily 9 ft. tall. His massive arms were thicker than a mighty man's leg. His chest was deep and barrel like, heavy with muscle. He wasn't convinced that the man would even bat an eye at a horse ramming him full speed. In fact, it would likely be that the horse would be worse for wear. He had a commanding presence that permeated through every action he made. Scars etched here and there across his exposed skin and face, it did little to take away from his handsome features. He had a strong jawline with a well groomed beard. His eyes were a bright blue that seemed to glow with predatory instincts, with a touch of mischief. He was a dangerous man to be certain.

"Nothing to pass on. All was sound and peaceful last night. I haven't met you here before what's your name?" he asked the man inquisitively.

"It is Partaxis, soldier of the Black's army, and you?"

"I am Zarron of the church of the Nameless One. Pleased to meet you Partaxis that is a name I will be sure not to forget especially if you are from the Black's army, I haven't met many of those in my years of existence. I had thought the Black's army was disbanded and scattered to the winds since the Black war but good to see it might not be true." Partaxis grunted in reply.

"Zarron you say? You are the one that came out here after a woman if the rumors are true." Zarron winced at hearing that. Partaxis took note.

"My apologies if I caused offense, it was not my intent. She must be a pretty important gal to have someone seeking her out in such a dangerous land."

"Indeed she is, my apologies for my reaction, it is an uncomfortable feeling having people know your business. She is a treasured friend of mine, and daughter of the Hand of the Nameless." He paused for a moment before speaking again.

"There is no limit to the distance or danger I would go to find her." He was surprised by the hardening of his words and the unshakable resolve. As he thought about the letter that drove him out here, he felt a hot anger boiling up just below his skin, it seeped to every corner of his body, warming every inch of him. Just as he thought it was about to boil over a hand touched his shoulder. The heat of rage immediately subsided, he looked around briefly and saw that no one was near him, but the eyes were on him.

"Zarron, are you well?" Partaxis asked his voice a whisper. He was surprised the big man could speak so softly. He shook his head in the affirmative, gathered his thoughts together and smiled.

"I am well, thank you. I am going to be off now, will get some rest while I can. May the Nameless One bless you, I will see you around." He nodded his head to the man.

Zarron turned and headed off towards the castle of Korilith. Partaxis spoke his good bye, his mighty voice rolling away as thunder fades. His thoughts were briefly put on pause as he walked back to the keep, the view was always an impressive site to behold. Aside from castle Korilith the main wall was a keep in itself. There were passageways in the Fenrir that could make quick travel and safer travel between two points possible and every so many yards there would be an extension in the Fenrir where ballistae's were posted.

Anyone who thought these parts weakened the fortification were sorely wrong for it was reinforced by steel and layers of hardened ice. And if the extension would be blown down or it became a hazard there would be a lever that one could pull and it would cover the port in a 9 ft. thick wall. Protecting the interior and giving it more strength. The main wall also connected to the second wall and the castle Korilith. Massive bridges connected the two walls. The bridges, in the unlikely circumstance enemy succeeded in throwing ropes or getting ladders up to the top, could be blown in an eye blink leaving the enemy force to fall 548 ft. to the bottom of the keep. The lifts on the main Fenrir could also be severed and cut down to prevent enemy troops from making it to the bottom. The top of the main wall would be a graveyard to them. Or so that was the plan.

The second wall was not as amazing as the main but it still stood an impressive 225 ft. Longer range siege equipment along with ballistae's were posted on the second walls wide girth. It connected to the main keeps high level then from there would be a maze of stairs. In between the walls was also called the last man's stand. Should the enemy break through the main gate or find the scouting gate, they would have to contend with the army of the north and many traps and oil fields. Before having to breach the second wall and take the keep itself. Zarron couldn't help but wonder how anything could breach it but everything has its weakness and the Fenrir wasn't made as it was to protect it from a normal army. It was made to stop things that are unknown to the world. The thought of that sent chills down his spine as he approached the top level of the castle and began winding his way down the stairs and passageways to the barracks.

Within a few minutes he found himself in the barracks. The barracks themselves were several. They had put them below the level of the ground to be warmer and they were smaller than the normal barracks he would reside in when he was with the Church. Each room was large enough to sleep 17 and a large fireplace was at the center in the room. The warmth from the fire and the room eventually was too much for him to handle and he found himself sweating in a matter of moments. He threw his heavy white cloak with a dark black wolf emblem sewn into the back side onto the peg and next he took off his white Yeti fur boots. His gloves were seal skin and were white as well. The only thing that had any color outside of white was his leather chest piece. Yeti fur lined the inside and the exterior was black with silver outlining the dark blue emblem of the Nameless One. It was a fine piece of leather, one that was granted to the few that graduated at the top of the class. Small runes that were nearly invisible were etched into the silver lining. It made the armor to be blessed and those that had been at the top of the class knew runes well and could change and alter them to what they need.

His runes were simple he had just put the winter heart rune on it. It allowed him to be up on the Fenrir and keep his main core warm and it kept the wind from going right through the clothing. Mixed with the Yeti fur he was always warm on the wall. He felt bad at times when he looked around and saw so many warming themselves by the fires or covered in so much fur they might as well had been wearing plate armor by the weight of it all. There was little he could do for them though for the runes were self-runes he learned as being a body of the Church, the physical working when the church needs them. The minds of the Church were the casters and they learned the runes to help many, but with time and rank he would learn them. Before he went to sleep he ate some of the bread and drank the water that was in the barracks before he re-drew his runes. He prayed to the Nameless One and within moments after his head hit the pillow he was fast asleep.

He had only slept a few hours when the Commander of Korilith Keep barged into the room. Waking everyone as the door slammed open. "Wake up Night Wolves!" His voice echoed loudly in the room. Zarron along with his companions were quickly out of their beds standing at attention.

"Who feels like being a hero today? We have an important scout party heading out and they happen to be short a man. So who feels like going beyond the Fenrir today?"

"I will go sir I have always wanted to see beyond the Fenrir." Zarron volunteered himself.

"Excellent, good for you, the rest of you go back to sleep. Zarron grab your things and report to the courtyard in 10 minutes." The commander spun and left after he issued the last command.

Zarron quickly dressed himself and donned his long sword and equipped the Elven dagger he has had since he was a child. He looked at it for a couple seconds before sheathing it in his boot. The cloak was tossed on and he was outside in the courtyard within moments. As he got there 3 men were there equipping their horses. Commander Froth was there as well.

"Here is your new recruit from the Night Wolves. His name is Zarron and he comes with the highest honors a new recruit can achieve from graduating from the Body of the Church of the Nameless One. He will do a fine job with you and I don't think you will be disappointed. Durakon be sure you report back to me as soon as you enter this castle upon your return. Don't even put away your horse just come right to me. I wish you all the best of luck." The commander saluted them all and took off towards his high tower.

The one that the commander called Durakon spoke first. "Hail Zarron we have quite the task to do, I hope you are prepared for combat and set for a long ride into the uncharted lands. I myself am Durakon the other two with me are Partaxis and Tombah. Mount up we leave in 10 minutes."

Just as Durakon had said they were gone and out the scout gate within 10 minutes. They put their horses into a gallop and within moments the great Fenrir vanished slowly into the distance. As soon as they were well beyond the Fenrir and couldn't see it anymore Durakon signaled them to slow and dismount. They stopped at what seemed to be a small pond with several trees growing around it. The water was miraculously un-frozen and it gave time for the horses to drink.

"Zarron watch the front and Tombah watch with him. Partaxis you are with me in the rear guard. We will stay here for just a few more minutes."

Zarron nodded his head in acknowledgment and went to the front with Tombah. They sat there peering out across the icy wastes. Not much moved from their perspectives except windblown snow. Within moments a sharp whistle came from Durakon.

"Brace yourselves we have company." Durakon yelled as he knocked an arrow and let loose. Far out in the distance you could hear a roar of something. Zarron snuck a look and sure enough a large yeti was running towards them. Durakon kept letting loose arrows and soon the yeti had dropped but it wasn't the end. As if from nowhere they were soon surrounded by snow orcs. They popped out of the snow a stone throws distance from them.

Zarron unsheathed his sword and prepared himself as the first one charged in with a low stab. He riposted the attack down and swung up with his sword catching the beast in the chin and splitting its lower face in half, he turned and dodged another one that came in with a middle jab he grabbed the orc by the forehead as he went past stabbing his sword down into the creature's heart.

Tombah saw the first orc running at him and smiled. He opened his hands wide and slapped them together in front of him sending a fire blast that completely burned it in half. The immense power of the spell tore right through him and ended burning itself part way into another orc, spilling its insides from him.

Durakon had pulled off firing a few more arrows into the orcs that were charging before they were upon him. Luckily one had hit its mark and the other orcs' clumsiness worked in his favor as he slipped on the snow and fell as the arrow passed over his head. He growled to himself as he realized he had missed. He pulled his spear from the horse and turned in time to lower it as an orc rushed him, it found itself at the fate of the spear as it was unable to stop before planting himself onto the end of the spear. He slid the body off to the side and rushed to the orc that had tripped. The creature had recovered with just enough time to stare into the blade of a spear as it ripped through his eye, bursting through the back of his head.

Partaxis had only one orc to deal with and he made quick work of it. As the orc rushed him he let out a loud roar with his arms spread out holding his two massive battle hammers. As the orc closed in he swung the hammers together crushing the beasts head between the two mighty pieces of steel.

Tombah and Zarron were standing there breathing lightly from the fight when all of a sudden a tingling sensation went throughout their bodies. "What is that Tombah? You feel the tingling sensation right?" Zarron asked.

"Oh No! Not Now! Everyone grab their belonging and horses the land is about to shift." Tombah yelled out to everyone.

III

As Zarron rushed to grab his horse the land rapidly began to alter. The snow and ice around them melted away as rocks and boulders grew in their place. Tree's sprung up out of the ground. He had to move several times as some trees burst through the surface of the dirt. The watering hole they were by had stretched itself into a long flowing river that disappeared into the distant horizon.

As things were happening around him he felt a strange pulse move through his body. He felt the essence as being magick and he reached down to grasp holf of it as they had taught him to do in the church. He felt it as a wound in his body and he thought to himself what would happen if he was to cast a healing spell on it. As he did this, a strange thing happened as the land around him temporarily froze its alteration. Soon the sensation was past and the ground continued to change around them.

Within moments the whole land around them had changed. It hardly felt like a winter land after it was done. An abundant forest grew around them and a large river flowed through the land. The ground had no more sign of ice or snow and large boulders were scattered around the woods.

"Well I was hoping that we wouldn't find ourselves in the forest before night fall." Durakon spoke.

"Well we best get moving then if you don't want to be sitting here at night." Partaxis piped in as he hung his hammers from his back.

"With these changes Durakon how is it we will know what way to go?" Zarron asked.

"Simple, I have been doing the tracking business for so long I have developed a sixth sense for direction. I know exactly what way is what and where we came from. I also leave something like a magick trail that I am attuned to. That is why I can track and scout beyond the far reaches of the Fenrir." Durakon smiled. "This way is where we need to go." Durakon pointed down the river.

The whole group started moving out. Even though the land had changed and looked much warmer it was still far colder than an average winter day for the rest of the north land. The sensation Zarron had felt kept bothering him and apparently his pondering had been quite noticeable.

"So Elite of the Nameless One you seem to be pondering over something. Care to share what is on your mind?" Tombah asked.

"When the shift happened I felt that sensation of magick deep inside of me. The feeling was like that of a wound, so in return I cast a heal spell and the area around me froze temporarily in the change. How do these barbarians keep all their homes in one place and not have it change constantly on them scattering them?"

"Hmm you say it was a wounding spell of sorts? Very interesting, do they teach any of you in your church order about circle spells? They teach us that in the Mage Academy. What happens is you carve runes or make a circle of something inanimate and imbue it with magickal essence to create a protective barrier of sorts."

"I remember something about circle spells. But that is something the Mind of the church deals with not the Body. But, to make those spells would require great time and a large amount of energy, most particularly, a large amount of energy if they are keeping a whole camp under its protection."

"You have a point, even we are taught the extreme amounts of energy that is required to keep a circle of protection up, especially a large one. Now if that is a case then they have the help of a god or...there is someone with them that has incredible power. If that is the case then we might find ourselves in quite the bind should he use it for destructive purposes."

Before they could continue Durakon placed his hand up and pointed towards a large amount of boulders stacked up. Immediately Partaxis followed his command and headed there hiding his horse then himself within the rocks. Within moments all of them were hidden among the rocks each one tending to their horses to keep them still and silent. Lucky for them, the horses they had were the most elite horses the castle held. It was said that they were trained by Hislanderlings, the horse-folk of the world. They had the most elite cavalry division in the known world. They pledged allegiance to no one except their own and whoever had the most amount of gold. Because of this there is large division between all the tribes of their land.

As they watched through crevices in the rocks they saw what Durakon had seen and understood why he put them into hiding. Before them out only 100 yards was a war party of large mammoths with giants riding on them. Their march shook the earth and caused small rocks to tumble down on top of Durakon and his party. Amazingly the horses stood perfectly still and didn't make a noise. Among the mounted mammoths many men marched all wearing furs of familiar and unfamiliar animals. Some had basic fur hats but a few had their fur hats adorned with bear heads, wolf heads, antlers and some with ram horns. Towards the middle of the procession they had several poles being carried between two of the mammoths and attached to them hung men. Most of the men were unconscious and they were hung wearing nothing but a strip of fur hanging around their waist. Many were wounded and blood dripped to the snow below. A few held consciousness but they had a look on their face of sheer terror. Some of them cast worried looks towards the back of the war party where the females were marched.

Towards the rear of the war party long ropes tied the women who were captured in the party together. Their hands were bound and their legs were tied to the one behind them. Many of them had faces that were cast towards the ground. A few who tried to be brave for the others held their heads high and faced forward. Many of the women were battered and bruised; their clothes were ripped and tattered. Several of the conquering armies' barbarians stood around them licking their lips and whipping them occasionally. Every once in a while one of them would take a grab at the females. The worst part was the females were so beaten down many of them didn't react when one of the barbarians would grab them. Finally at the very end, a group of 15 dark robed creatures walked with one person in the front leading them. The one in the front practically floated and a dark red aura formed from him and reflected the blood red hue on the snow below making it seem he was constantly above a puddle of blood. It was hard to tell what they were but Zarron knew immediately and his blood began to boil.

Those aren't barbarians or human they are a group of vampires and worse of all it was a lich that lead them and one he knew well as Fervver, a Lich that was supposedly defeated many years ago in the Black War. Zarron thought to himself.

IV

The thought of Fervver being alive bewildered Zarron. He couldn't believe his eyes but the fact still remained that it was Fervver there with the war party. Rage started boiling in him; he clenched his teeth together and balled his hands into a fist. *Oh Nameless one please bless me with patience for I am lacking it right now, my rage to destroy this evil is trying to get the best of me.* He prayed to himself and within moments his body relaxed. As they concentrated on the main party they had forgotten the fact that scouts usually would cover the rear flanks of a party this size and that was the group's mistake.

In the corner of Durakon's eye he caught sight of the scouts moving in the woods down from them but it was too late. They had eyed the party first. Durakon drew his bow and loosed an arrow into one, the other reacted immediately. He lifted his horn to his lips and let out a burst of noise. Durakon cut it short as he struck the scout down with an arrow but it was enough for the war party to react.

It was Fervver himself who noticed the group hidden in the rocks first. He waved his hand and the 14 Vampires with him threw off their heavy robes in near synch and they drew their weapons all at once with an ear piercing grind as they yanked them from the scabbards. Fervver then threw his hand in the direction of Zarron and the others. The vampires struck out running at incredible speed. Fervver waved his hand at another handful of barbarians who in a much more chaotic way drew their weapons and charged at the party letting out a loud war cry. The rest of the army continued forward as a few took a glance at the action, the rest proceeded to act like nothing was happening.

"Get to the Horses!" Partaxis's voice boomed. Within an eye blink Durakon and Tombah were on their horses and taking off. Zarron and Partaxis then followed shortly behind. The horse's immediately reacted to their rider's urgency and took off with great speed. As they were riding off Partaxis had the rear. While they thought they were getting away a grunt was heard from Partaxis. A harpoon had been launched at him imbedding itself in the thick fur he wore and with a quick yank he was flying backwards off the horse. Zarron who was second to the rear reacted first. He spun his horse to see Partaxis get pulled off his horse as one of the dark ones pulled him in with the rope that was attached to the harpoon.

"Keep riding Durakon and Tombah. Tell the commander that Fervver the Lich king is a part of the enemies' host. Now Ride!" Zarron's voice was filled with such command that Durakon and Tombah listened and kept riding hard. As he turned to look back at the enemies' one of the harpoons flew by him, he dodged it by inches but the vampire that threw it yanked it back with such precision it caught him on his backside and threw him from the horse. He landed on his face, before the creature could pull him closer he cut the rope and yanked the harpoon from his shoulder. There was a sting of pain where it had pierced his flesh but with a quick spell he healed the minor wound and charged at the vampires that were closing in on Partaxis.

As Partaxis was yanked from the saddle his horse continued off in the direction it was going. He heard Zarron yell something as he fell from the saddle. He hit the ground hard but recovered himself to his feet after he tumbled a little bit. He found a foot hold and planted his feet down. He grabbed the rope that had the harpoon attached to it and with his great strength he easily was able to pull the unsuspecting dark creature off its feet and to him. As the vamp was pulled close it realized it couldn't stand up to Partaxis's strength. It attempted to release but it was too late. Within a second Partaxis grabbed the creature and slammed his head into it causing it to take a step back stunned.

Partaxis utilized this time to snap the wooden shaft of the harpoon and drive it deep into the heart of the vampire killing it instantly.

Just as Partaxis finished killing the first one off and as another was about to attack him from the side. Zarron rushed in and with a quick slash he easily took the creatures head.

"Here Partaxis, take my two-handed sword. You need it. Hammers aren't too effective against vampires. Take heed, it is a blessed weapon that is runed to slow them down if you strike them, continue to aim for the head and the heart." He said to Partaxis. Partaxis who easily stood taller than him reached into his baldric and yanked the two-hander free just in time to cleave another vamps head into two pieces. Its head melted away and it slumped into the ground.

Zarron engaged and parried another vamps attack as it came in towards his front with another right behind it. As he parried the first ones attack the second one slashed downwards in an attempt to finish him off quickly. But, Zarron saw it coming, he side stepped the slash and thrust his sword into its heart as it fell forward from the velocity of the downward slash. He pulled his sword free with enough time to block the attack from the first one that had rushed him. He riposted and slashed it in the stomach, as it keeled over he quickly took its head.

Partaxis rushed charging the vamps. As they were about to cross paths Partaxis slashed out and the dark one parried the blade. The weight and force of the two-handed weapon drove the creature's blades deep. Deep into its own neck nearly severing the head as it hung from a couple strands of muscle. It wasn't enough to kill it but it would definitely not be moving for a long time. The parry from the creature didn't stop Partaxis's forward velocity. As he closed on the next one he changed his direction last minute and was on the other side of it. He thrust the two-hander deep into its chest catching it on the rib cage. The speed Partaxis held was enough to rip the blade from its chest cleaving the rib cage open and cutting its heart and organs open. But, his charge was stopped at that one. "Damn!" Within moments he was surrounded by the vamps with the barbarians close behind.

Zarron looked up from the vamp that he just took the head of and saw Partaxis start rushing them. His focus was soon gone from him as another one lunged at him. He blocked the high attack and jumped out of the way with just enough time to keep his stomach from being split open. The creature attacked one more time with a sloppy slash which he stepped away from. In a defensive maneuver he slashed at the vamp's hand getting a lucky strike and cutting it off. The vampire let out a screech then with his other hand he extended his claws and jabbed them into Zarron's leather piece. He smiled at the creature as his hand was burned from the armor. But the fire didn't stop at his hand and soon the whole body of the dark one was burned up in holy fire. Zarron quickly gained focus again looking for his next target and found the remaining ones turning their focus on Partaxis. He rushed towards the now surrounded Partaxis.

As the vamps all lunged to attack Partaxis he whirled himself into the air into a full circle and as he finished he slammed the sword into the earth sending out a giant shock wave that sent the vampires flying out to the side. As Zarron rushed to Partaxis's aid he saw what he had done and rolled underneath a vamp as it flew over him. He popped back up and was at Partaxis's back just as the barbarian horde began to surround them.

Partaxis breathed in deeply and let out a loud roar at the horde as he readied himself as the first one closed in on him. He easily slid underneath the man's guard and spilled his stomach open. He felt Zarron behind him moving his shoulders as he parried, cut and slashed at the relentless adversaries that approached them. Partaxis held his own for a long while as well, it wasn't long before bodies were soon piled up in front of him and to his sides. The fatigue of battle though, was setting in and within a moment he felt a sharp pain strike his temple and stars explode from in front of his eyes.

Zarron was holding his ground as bodies littered the earth around him as well, the ground greedily consuming their blood. It was then that he felt Partaxis's large mass fall behind him, he turned in time to see the stone fall to the ground. He turned again and jumped out of the way as a slash came at him but he was a little slow, he felt the sharp bite of pain as the steel caught him from above the eyebrow and sliced him to just below the eye. He felt the hot sticky blood run down as it interrupted his vision. He then felt another bolt of pain to the back of his head driving him to his knees and his world started dimming around him. In front of him the circle parted and he could see Fervver enter it. He said something and pointed at him as darkness consumed his mind, soon the world became no more and silence reigned supreme.

V

It had been two years since he witnessed his mother's death. Ever since that day Zarron had the conviction instilled in his soul to destroy evil and set his heart on doing what is good. He spent his time in the city simply known as Citadel Heights. The city of the Nameless One's church of both the Body and Mind of the Nameless. They would train here and live here. Through the years he had lost many meals and rest for the night choosing to do what was good. Sleep wasn't a common thing for him for he lived on the streets, and it was a dangerous thing to do. Not the ideal situation for a growing boy of 11. In the past year he had had his moments of getting beat up, robbed and spit on. It never wavered his spirit though whenever he stood up to the older boys, usually to save some other kid or person from being harassed or robbed. He almost drew strength in knowing he was doing something good.

He would win fights as well. Eventually, he found that he was making a name for himself even though he was young. People would refer to him as the "Light Stalker". He had heard stories of himself being a 7ft giant that would stalk after those that would cause trouble. He smiled to himself when he thought of it as he worked occasionally in a tavern here and there for food and board, these stories would warm his heart. He never thought of himself as being something to make stories of because he knew he didn't always win the fight but he always saved the person being harassed from further harm and injury. Most of the time they would listen to the little boy and surprisingly run not seeing the outcome.

One night though had stood out above everything else. It was the night his life changed forever. He was finishing up his nightly cleaning and decided to take a walk down to the Light Bridge before he rested for the night. He had been given a sweet tart for his work during the day and he wanted to enjoy it. He loved the sweet tarts and how they tasted. Treats like that were rare. Only the wealthy could afford them. Once every other month he would get one for his hard work and cherish every moment of the delicious treat.

He was almost done with his treat when he heard a scream for help come from close by. He sighed as he looked down at his almost finished treat and was sad that it couldn't be finished because the scream for help sounded more urgent. He threw the treat down and ran towards the sound of the troubled voice. Upon turning a corner he saw 4 men throwing a girl around. They would toss her amongst each other whistling at her and saying crude things. Anger boiled up in him as he saw this. He stepped out into the alley and put his fists at his hips.

"Hey leave her alone!" His voice piped and cracked. The men looked at him and laughed before returning to their bullying. He looked around and found a stone laying close by, he picked it up, judged its weight, and then chucked it as hard as he could. It hit a man square in the face. Blood burst from his nose as the rock crushed his nose.

"I said leave her alone!" Zarron's voice broke as he yelled at the men again.

"Get that little bastard!" The guy that he had hit with the stone ordered the other men as he clutched his nose with his hand blood pouring freely between his fingers. One of the men threw the girl to one of his companions who detained her as the other two engaged him. He picked up another rock that was close by and spoke to the men again.

"I said leave the girl alone. That means you let her go." He said this time with a clear concise tone, he was shocked at the strength and finality of his voice. However intimidating and impressive it sound he realized the man was not going to listen to him so he heaved the stone and nailed him in the forehead causing him to release his grip on the girl giving her enough time to run. He tried grabbing her again but he wasn't fast enough. She took off running and he could see her past the men turn to look at him again. He gave a smile to her and she took off around the corner. He returned his focus on the men around him who appeared to be incredibly angry.

"You bastard child! You will pay for what you have done." One of the men said.

"Pay for what I have done!? I have only stopped a girl from being harassed when she didn't ask for it. She was minding her business going wherever she was. No one asks for that, you guys are just big dumb bullies." he said resolutely as he stood in front of them with his hands now balled up into fists setting on his side.

"I get it he must think he is the Light Stalker, big talk for such a little boy. How about we beat you into knowing that we are right and you are wrong." One of other men said to him.

"You guys are dumb, how can you think what you say even makes sense." Zarron replied back to them. All the last comment did for him was to cause more anger in the two men in front of him and soon one lunged at him. He knew he was smaller than the guys but he was faster. He proved that effortlessly as one of the two men that hadn't been hit by rocks tried hitting him with a punch. He ducked it quickly and punched him in the shin. As he fell over to grab his hurt shin he kneed him with his bony knees to the head. The man fell back stunned into his companion, who in turn fell. As the two in the front fell he saw the man he had hit with a rock in the head start running at him. He looked around and found another rock. He quickly judged the weight, then threw it at the guy as he ran towards him. Same as the first time it nailed him in the head but this time hitting his temple causing him to fall unconsciously into a heap on the ground. He turned his attention to the two men that fell before him and found them nearly on top of him giving him no time to react. One of them grabbed him and easily lifted his light frame up off the ground just enough to throw him hard upon the rock road below. The wind burst from his lungs as he hit the ground hard.

The other man came up and picked him up again with one hand and slammed a large fist into his face causing blood to erupt from his nose and also causing his lips to tear open. He threw Zarron against the wall of the building next to him and he slumped to the ground. The men deciding he wasn't any fun after not moving too much turned to recover their unconscious friend.

Zarron pulled himself to his feet wiping blood from his face.

"I am not finished with you big bullies." He said wiping blood once again from his face.

"Little baby hasn't had enough of his milk to teach him a lesson." One of the thug's spoke to him.

Zarron jaw dropped, he couldn't believe the stupid remark that came out of the thug's mouth. He set himself just as one of the men rushed him attempting to finish him fast but it was his mistake being so clumsy. As the man rushed him he threw his arm out wide attempting to do a complete power house punch that would finish him off with one blow but it left him wide open. So he reacted, he lunged into the opening the man made and buried his small fist into his stomach causing the man to almost throw up. As he doubled over, he moved to his side and kicked him in the head causing his head to hit the building hard. As the man was on his knees with one hand clutching his stomach and the other holding him up on the building Zarron jumped up and landed with his knees sharply on the man's back causing him to collapse to the ground completely. The other man that was helping his unconscious buddy dropped him on the ground and bull rushed Zarron who couldn't get out of the way fast enough. The full force of the man and his weight crushed into him, falling on top of him breaking some of his ribs.

The man who had the small boy squished under him put his knees on either side of Zarron and landed several brutal punches to his face. The pain was nearly unbearable and his vision became more blurry with each blow. After several punches the thug got up again and spit on Zarron's bloodied dirty tunic. As he got up he turned and went to gather up his two unmoving buddies.

Zarron breathed out a little bit and found it was incredibly painful to do. Something in him gave him a sick feeling that if he didn't get up to try to stop the last guy, they would continue to harass innocent people and perhaps even murder. His one thread of hope was to at least hold up long enough for the town guard to come around on their patrol. So in great pain and slow movement he forced his body to stand. Breathing was painful to do and his face was so swollen he could hardly see. But it was enough to see the only thug left standing and undamaged. He was attempting to pull both his unconscious friends under each of his arms dragging them down the alley. He clutched his ribs with one of his hands and the other hung loosely at his side. With great strength of willpower he managed to come up with a voice.

"I won't let you leave. You are a monster." His voice was small and he could barely hear himself but it was enough for the thug to drop his friends and turn to face the boy who remained defiant. As the man rushed him, he knew he had nothing left in him to fight the man and he knew the man wouldn't stop this time until he was dead. He brought one of his fists up and entered a weak battle stance. As the man was about to reach him he all of a sudden stopped in his tracks as a javelin pierced through his back spilling out his front rib cage. Blood splattered the walls around him as the man spun to the ground.

Behind him came several armed men all wearing the symbol of the Nameless One on their surcoats. Several of them wore the blue and silver plate armor glowing with bright golden runes common of the high ranking Paladin's in the Order of the Nameless. Their great helms donned angelic feathers' on both sides and a golden cross marked the front of the helm. Long white capes flowed from their backs. With them were two others that wore beautiful robes of blue and white. Silver thread created amazing designs common of the high clerics of the Nameless. Same as the Paladin's, golden runes etched the sleeves of the robes and bordered it. A chain with the pendent of the Nameless hung from their necks. Their faces were covered by the hood of their silver cloaks.

The party of the Nameless Ones men went among the wounded and they couldn't believe the damage that was bestowed upon each one. Finally one man appeared who stood out above all the others. His armor glowed like the light of the sun. His helm was similar to the Paladin's helm but there were much more intrinsic designs on it. The wings that donned the helm on both sides were angel wings as well, but they burned like fire. In the eye slots of the helm was a dull glow of blue light as if it were his eyes. His white cloak was drawn across one side of his body and was clasped to the other side by a hand. Zarron knew then that that person was none other than The Hand of the Nameless the highest achievable rank in the body of the Nameless. They conferred amongst one another than he saw the girl that he had saved come out from behind the party. She smiled at him as she pointed a finger towards him.

"He's the one that saved me Papa." She said in a sweet voice that was calmed from being harried earlier. The Hand nodded his head and ruffled his daughter's hair as he walked up to Zarron. Zarron attempted to stand tall and be brave for The Hand but weakness overcame him and he collapsed to his knees, before he could fall The Hand of the Nameless caught him in his strong grip and pulled his weakened body off his feet cradling him in his arms as a father would do for his son. His eyes finally closed as fatigue caught up with him, his adrenaline had drained from him and he felt strong warmth overcome him.

The sun peered through the curtains falling upon Zarron causing him to flutter his eyes open. He found himself awake in a large feathery bed wrapped in fluffy blankets. He wiped the sand from his eyes as he peered around the room and found it to be an incredibly large room. His awe of the room overlooked the fact that the little girl who he had saved was staring at him from the foot of his bed.

"I brought some crumpets and tea with some fruit to you." The girl's voice pulled him out of his reverie. As he focused on her she lifted the tray up that was hidden from his view. She placed it up on the bed and crawled into the mighty bed with it, shuffling it towards him.

"Thank you…" Zarron stopped mid-sentence as he remembered what had happened with the thugs, he felt his face only to find it feeling normal.

"My daddy fixed your wounds up. He knows how to heal people. He says usually little wounds are good because it makes you strong but you were really beat up. You looked like a squash. Your face was puffy and you were bleeding a lot. Daddy said you had broken bones in your ribs and your arm was limp like unbaked dough." The girls smile faded a little bit. "But good news is you are fixed now and daddy says you won't hurt from them anymore." Her smile returned and he couldn't help but laugh. She picked up a piece of fruit and ate it.

"You were really brave. What is your name?" The girl asked him.

"Well I am Zarron. Don't know my last name but I know I have one because everyone has one. What is yours?" he asked the girl as he picked up a crumpet and ate it down quickly.

"My name is Mary Ashen."

"Mary is a nice name." He giggled while Mary blushed.

VI

The sharp rank smell of filth brought Zarron out of his dream. He slowly fluttered his eyes open and found that it was in the afternoon just as the sun kissed the earth good night in vibrant colors of orange, yellows and reds. He was in a camp and had an overly large barbarian guarding him. He reeked of cheap liquor, his furs that covered his body were matted and tainted with blood and dirt. He smelled as though he hadn't washed himself off in years. He couldn't see much of what he was doing but, he knew that the barbarian was drinking and he could hear the sharp sound of a whet stone against his weapon. He would only pause long enough to pick up his flagon of ale to take a deep swig of it.

Zarron tried moving and found his hands were bound and when he moved his foot he felt chains grow taut as he found himself bound to another individual. He turned his head to get a better look and found his partner was Partaxis. *'Glad to see he is still alive and that they were dumb enough to pair me with him'*. He looked down to find they had only taken his sword from him but his armor was still in place. Partaxis was not so lucky as to keep his armor. He was stripped down and given a nasty looking fur jacket along with a loin cloth. Barely enough to keep anyone warm. Zarron winced in pain as he peered around at his surroundings. He then remembered the sharp blow to the head and the cold kiss of the blade that struck him in the eye. He reached into himself and brought forth his healing magick in an attempt to heal the wound only to find that it had felt like someone was burning it with a hot iron rather than fixing them. The pain was unbearable and he could do nothing more than to stop.

He was pulled from his trance as he heard the all too familiar voice of

Fervver speaking to the giant barbarian in a tongue he was not well versed in. Partaxis seemed to know it well as it stirred him from his rest. He gradually drew to his feet and pulled Zarron to his as the barbarian moved out of the way showing Fervver standing there. Zarron couldn't help but scowl.

"Fervver you should have died your second death back in the Black Wars. To see you still here disgusts me." Zarron spat between clenched teeth.

"Well I agree with your disgust, I had not planned to run into another member of the church here. If it was up to me, Body of the Nameless I would have you killed by now, but, I know someone that would rather appreciate seeing one of you." Fervver's voice sent chills down his spine.

"You are an evil disgusting monster *Lyckendune.*" The last word Zarron spoke was said like poison and it held some power causing Fervver to step back in pain.

"Your power is weakened here soldier of the Nameless. My power is the one that rules in this area, HERE you are nothing." Fervver said those words to Zarron as he stepped closer; his face was merely inches from him. Zarron peered at him with hate. He smiled at Fervver then leaned his head back and with great force smashed it into Fervver's face. Black blood burst from the Liche's face. Fervver stepped back and started laughing.

"What is your name soldier of the Nameless?" Fervver asked as he wiped blood from his nose.

"I am Zarron ra Holyrage." He said unable to stop a smile that was forming.

Fervver's eyes widened and his mouth dropped a little as he mentioned his last name. *'It can't be the Holyrage house'*.

"That's impossible that name was destroyed." With a roar Fervver turned and left in a storm.

Partaxis couldn't help but stare at Zarron not understanding. Zarron watched Fervver till their big guard returned. He turned his attention back towards Partaxis and met his bewildering gaze.

"I suppose you are wondering why that happened?" Zarron sighed. Before he could talk more their guard grabbed them. They were shoved towards the rest of the prisoners. Something had happened in the camp and they were starting to move. Horns blared around them as it summoned the war party into action. On the fading sky Zarron could see the giant's getting their mammoths ready for marching. Their big forms were a dark shadow on the horizon. The prisoners were being formed back up in their proper location. The men were hung again from giant poles between the mammoths. The women were put towards the back. That is where Zarron and Partaxis wound up at. They were strung in the back and surrounded by the few remaining vampires they hadn't killed. A few barbarians surrounded them but Fervver was nowhere to be found.

"Zarron to think they decide to put us with the women I would say they have us underestimated." Partaxis whispered to Zarron. Zarron barely heard Partaxis as he concentrated on praying to the Nameless One. Almost instantly he heard the familiar voice of the Nameless One. *'Zarron my son I hear you I haven't left you in this time of trial. Just remember that your power is merely nothing where you are. But my power is limitless and no land or space will stop me from helping you if I see that it is needed for you. Right now Zarron, concentrate on the initial problem before you, the hex the Lich king put on you'.* Zarron once again summoned his healing spell and found it burned more than helped. He continued to push the healing spell; finally he found the one piece of the power that surged within him that was alien to him. The pain started becoming unbearable, so, Zarron feeling the part of the spell that was not his honed it to his memory so he knew exactly how to recall it when he needed it.

They seemed to be walking for hours. The moon was now completely full in the sky, it cast an eerie glow on the forest around them. Wolves could be heard close by and as Zarron looked around with his enhanced vision he could even point out the shadowy shapes as they followed the war party. He knew they were waiting for an easy meal to be tossed to them. The men that were hung between the mammoths towards the front were in rough shape and several of them wouldn't make it through the night.

The cold was continuously taking a heavy toll on the injured and just as he suspected it wasn't long before some of the injured men had died on the poles. The barbarians cut their bodies loose and let them fall to the ground. The rest of the army would step on it, over it, or around it. It wasn't long before Zarron and Partaxis were walking over the dead themselves. Zarron looked back as he stepped over one of the men and within a matter of seconds the wolf pack was on top of it. Their growls and bickering on who can eat first was a haunting noise that did little to break the new tension that was forming in the air.

Durakon had warned the party about being in the woods at night and he had no doubt that Durakon was absolutely correct. He could almost cut the tension with a knife. The war party had fallen silent, even the elite force of vampires around them seemed to be on guard. It wasn't long before he understood why. As he listened to the woods around him the howls of the wolves that were usually calm and serene had become eerie and twisted. He looked up at the moon and sure enough it was completely full, he knew then and there that the party was on the watch for werewolves who were at their peak power during a full moon. He saw flashes of gray in the woods around them. He smiled to himself as he knew vampires and werewolves were arch enemies.

"So vampires, the werewolves have picked up on your scent and I think you all are in a terrible position being in the back unguarded." Zarron taunted the vampires.

"Shut up Nameless Ones puppet." One of the vamps responded back to him in a vile tone.

"Well I think one of you could easily be picked off and no one would be able to react. You would fall prey to the enemy you hate the most."

One of the vampires smashed a fist into his face. He spit some blood out but proceeded to put despair in the vampire's evil hearts.

"Well you can hit me all you want but my blood is going to draw the werewolf's attention on us even more. You all know that they are at their peak power in a full moon. The worse time to be fighting them is when there is a full moon. Sure at quarter moons they would be an easy kill but not now." He spit a glob of blood to the ground. Another vamp told him to shut up and this time they hit him in the stomach. It would prove to be a fatal mistake. As the vampire's hand slammed into the armor he wore it burst into flame, quickly consuming the vampire, turning him into a pile of ash. That was all that was needed to cause the werewolves to burst into a feeding frenzy.

VII

Zarron my son it is time. You have acted well in doing what you have. Even though it was playing with fire you acted wisely. Your time is short, within minutes the werewolves will attack. They have smelt the blood of yours and that of the vampires. Your chain's by my power have been weakened you will defend the prisoners but you must not run after I release you. You have a greater purpose awaiting you at the enemies' encampment. The Nameless One's voice came to Zarron catching him slightly off guard.

I Understand. Zarron thought to himself in reply to his god's command.

"Partaxis I would prepare yourself for some rough times. As I was putting fear in them I had been backed the whole time by the Nameless One. He was working in me and even though my magick is weakened the Nameless One's is limitless." he said with a smile then wiggled his hands to show that the chain links had been terribly weakened. He nodded his head towards Partaxis and he in suit found his chains were incredibly weak.

"Now when these werewolves attack which is going to be happening in nearly no time we have to act fast. Grab a dark ones weapon and guard these prisoners. We have to make sure we don't run though." The last comment caused Partaxis to take a step back.

"I know it doesn't seem to make sense but the Nameless One's got a plan that is beyond our control. He needs us to see where they are taking us. Just prepare to be locked down further after this though. We may not have known each other long but, please trust me on this one Partaxis."

"Well I do trust you, your relationship is odd with your god, and I will make sure the women are safe, after all, I do love them." A big smile widened across his face.

It was then that the first vampire was taken. Within an eye blink a werewolf dropped down from the trees around them, it snatched one of the wicked ones up and jumped back into the tree. There was the loud snap as the werewolf broke one of the bones in the vamp and a sickening crunch as its teeth bit down into it. The rest of the vampires quickly dropped into fighting stances as the werewolves started to close in on them.

"Now would be a good time to act Partaxis." Zarron said as the nervous vampires turned their attention away from them. Partaxis easily snapped the chains that bound him. With one fluid motion he grabbed a vampire around the neck with one hand, with his other hand he reached down and took control of the creatures arm with the weapon and guided it into the heart killing it. Partaxis yanked the weapon free and severed the vampires head before moving his mass towards the group of women.

Zarron took a little bit longer to break the chains. Even though they were weakened he didn't have the enormous strength Partaxis had. He looked down as he broke the last link, as he looked back up a large mass dropped down in front of him. It had landed on its feet and had one arm planted in the ground. Its muzzle turned up to face him and its yellow eyes peered from underneath dark gray fur. Just blood lust was to be seen in its eyes. He took a step back as the werewolf erected itself to his full height and let out a fierce howl. It easily towered 9ft tall when it was stretched to his full size. The height dropped to about 7 ft. as it lowered its body to their normal fighting stance. Long claws and sharp teeth were its weapons.

It quickly lunged at him in an attempt to cleave his head. He had ducked and rolled as a vampire moved in to attack the werewolf. The attack had missed him, but it hit the vampire square in the face sending it into the ground hard. He took advantage of the situation and grabbed the vampire's weapon as it fell from his grip. The werewolf not caring about him jumped on top of the vampire and bit down on its face. With great strength it launched itself into the trees again to enjoy its meal.

Only 4 Vampires were alive and however tempting it was to kill them he knew they would be a good fighting force for helping them out. So he did as he was ordered and moved to the protection of the women prisoners. Partaxis had the left flank and he the right, they knew that this situation would be tough to pull off.

The whole party was now aware of the werewolves. Their large dark masses could be seen all around them, there was another howl from somewhere and that is when the pack of werewolves launched an all-out attack on the war party. Sounds of battle quickly filled the air. Zarron waited restlessly as he watched the 4 vampires doing their best to hold off two werewolves. It wasn't long before a third then a fourth entered the fray with them. The two that had joined watched and lunged in at the vampires attempting to get an easy meal out of it. But, they were smarter than the other two and they soon found that the women prisoners who were now all huddled together would be the best bet for an easy meal. Little did they know that they had two experienced war veterans guarding them.

As one took two bounds then lunged at the frightened women it was knocked out of the air as Partaxis flung his massive body at the creature. Catching it midair, he slammed it into the ground. Partaxis stabbed his sword into the beasts back. He stabbed one more time which cut deep enough where he couldn't pull it free. The werewolf tried desperately to get the massive man off him and as soon as Partaxis's blade was caught deep in its hide it managed to get a fist back and knock Partaxis off. As soon as Partaxis hit the ground the creature jumped on him and tried to bite his face off. He reached up and caught the monster's jaw in his hands. He had both sides of its muzzle held wide open. Spit and drool dripped on him as he held the jaws open keeping them from clamping down on his head. He let out a loud roar as he pushed himself onto his feet, with all his might he put the werewolf on its knees, yanked his arms open snapping the muzzle of the great monster. A loud whimper went into the air, Partaxis quickly went behind the beast and grabbed his jaws that were now broken and twisted the head of the werewolf breaking its neck. He pulled the sword free next and with one quick strike took the head of the beast.

The second wolf closed in a bit more cautiously as he saw his pack member get knocked out of the air by Partaxis. Zarron picked up on him and put himself between the beast and the potential victims. The beast, frustrated that his easy meal would be spoiled, swung his claws at him who parried them out of the way. Zarron swung in and barely cut the werewolf in the stomach. It was enough to let the werewolf know he was a danger though. It struck at him again with one claw but he easily ducked that one and as the beast swung with the other claw he parried. The beast kept attacking with inhuman speed and each time he had ducked or parried the attack. Sometimes he would dodge to the left or the right. He would strike the beast in the arm or leg wherever he could. The wounds he knew would eventually catch up and cause the beast to decide this meal was one not to take. For each time the beast healed a wound another would happen. It constantly caused the werewolf to focus on multiple things.

Zarron just needed to stay alive long enough for it to make a mistake. The dance of death continued on for another few moments. He continually avoided and dodged attacks going from one form of fighting style to another. Finally the werewolf slumped to the ground. It let out a little whimper as thousands of wounds weakened it to a near motionless state. The energy used in the strikes and blows had worn it down physically, the constant stress on its body for healing wounds had drained it mentally, all of these culminated to the creatures defeat. He was about to finish it off but something in him stopped him from doing so. He snarled his lips in frustration. He lifted his sword high and jammed it next to the werewolves head.

"You listen to me beast I don't know if you can understand me or why I can't kill you when you deserve it but you best remember me! That is my saying to you. Leave now if you can crawl out of here. There is nothing more to threaten you." He said to the werewolf. As if the werewolf understood it managed to shift into its feral form of a large golden dire wolf and limp off into the woods. It wasn't long after that, a howl could be heard, the whole werewolf attack party stopped and bounded off into the woods.

"Put your weapons down slaves." One of the two remaining vampires ordered Zarron. He peered at the vile creature that had spoken to him. Fire filled his soul as he had the great urge to kill the vampire where he stood but he knew he needed to follow what the Nameless One had asked of him.

He threw his weapon down in front of the vampire. Partaxis appeared at his side and followed suit. The vampire and his companion carefully approached the two standing before them. Sheer terror could be seen in their eyes as they picked up the weapons. Partaxis made a quick movement towards them causing them to step back. His loud laughter boomed as he took pleasure in scaring the creatures. Soon many barbarians appeared around Zarron and Partaxis.

"You barbarians keep an eye on these two while we discuss what to do with them." One of the vampires ordered.

"Well Partaxis since our chains our broken I would say you might get lucky and be tied up with all the women."

A Smile crept across Partaxis's face. "You know I love my women."

"I know, I know." Zarron replied.

VIII

Just as Zarron had suspected they strapped the two of them with the women. Partaxis was clearly happy about the whole thing. As soon as they tied him up he went about comforting the women. Many of them were still baffled about the attack. Zarron looked over at one of the female barbarians and gave her a little smile.

"Everything will be ok; we will make sure nothing happens to you. Partaxis and I will get you all out of here." Zarron whispered to her and mustered up the best smile he could come up with. The woman smiled back and it brought back a flood of memories from his past.

****

"Mary, my child, I will need you to leave Zarron and I for there is much I need to discuss with the boy." The Hand of the church spoke to his daughter in a soft voice as he entered the room.

"Oh, is it ok if I play with him after you are finished daddy?" Mary asked him in a sweet voice.

"Of course my daughter I will fetch you as soon as we are finished. Now go, be a good girl and run along." The Hand gave his daughter a quick hug and kissed the top of her head as she ran off.

"I hope that you have found the food good and the bed comfortable." The Hand asked Zarron.

"Yes sir most definitely your kindness is much appreciated. I haven't ate so well or slept so comfortably in a long time." The Hand let out a sigh and rubbed his chin.

"Zarron do you mind if I take a seat?" Zarron was taken aback by The Hand asking him if he could sit in his own home.

"Umm, yes m'lord...it is your home after all." He stumbled over his words a little then formed a quick smile. He picked the food tray up and set it down on a table next to him and lifted himself up.

"Thank you Zarron." The Hand went over and grabbed one of the heavy oak chairs and carried it over to the bed side.

"Zarron I have taken the liberty while you were recovering to ask around about you. I have found some interesting things regarding you. Do you have any family alive anywhere?"

"I think my father is alive but I don't know where I could find him. My mother died when I was 9. Demons got her and I wasn't fast enough." Sadness filled his voice as he spoke.

"I know of your mother Zarron, my troop came shortly after that attack. It was a shame we didn't get there sooner. That group of demon's that attacked your city was a group we had lost track of. They didn't stay hidden long though. Do you have a home yourself Zarron?"

He shook his head no. "My home is the streets or if I am lucky it is in the stall of The Pegasus Inn. I do lots of work there and sometimes he lets me sleep with the horses. But I am happy with it. It sometimes is cold or hot and it is the worse when it rains but I get lots of time to help people."

The Hand laughed at his last remark. "I have heard of your deeds Zarron or Light Stalker as some have come to call you." The Hand licked his lips and rested his hand on his chin. Silence filled the room for a little. Zarron fiddled with his blankets not sure what more to say.

"Zarron, I have a proposal for you. Now, what I am about to ask you is incredibly serious and I need you to really pay attention and think about what I am about to ask you. First off, I thank you from the bottom of my heart for saving my daughter Mary. She has taken to you quite easily. But that is not the point here. What you did was something no boy should ever do. It was foolish of you to pick a fight with grown adults. But, I am glad you did. Now

Zarron what would you think about joining the body of the Nameless? I am not wanting your answer now, but I do want you to think about it and have one for me on the morrow. It will give you time to be a child one last time and play some."

Zarron's heart nearly stopped with The Hand himself asking him to join the church.

"M'lord I don't think I can, I have no real name to go off of and I am young. I have only seen 11 winters and the age is at the least 14. I don't think I would be good for it." Zarron looked down and fiddled with his hands.

The Hand smiled at him. "You have the right attitude for it, being humble is good. The age is a significant trouble since 14 is the traditional age of enlistment, however you have proven at your young age to go toe to toe with those older and stronger. Another thing is your unique upbringing has forced you to mature at a quicker pace than those with a relatively normal upbringing. We can make an exception, you will still have to work doubly hard then the others but I think you can do it. I will admit one of the most impressive things working in your favor Zarron is that you have by far one of the most prestigious names of light. In my research I have found out more about you then your town's attacks and more than you being the Light Stalker. Zarron your bloodline is from an ancient line. Have you ever heard of house Holyrage?"

"The name sounds familiar but no sir. I don't know much about them."

"House Holyrage was one of the most feared houses by undead and demon alike. They were built bred and raised to kill and destroy evil. They were unstoppable against demon armies. There was no demon, undead or evil army around that could defeat them. Sadly one of the evil gods above realized what was happening and wasn't pleased that this house Holyrage could kill any undead or demon army one could muster. So the god stepped out of his boundaries and waged an all-out war on the Holyrage house. The god himself just known as the Uttookari came down from his heavenly throne and smashed the Holyrage house. They say he brought all the demons from hell and earth with him. But, the Holyrage house stopped the army initially. The battle was huge. There was over 1 million in the demon, undead army and a mere 144,000 in the Holyrage house. There were a total of 7 battles. In the seventh one, that is when Uttookari finally finished off the Holyrage house. It took him much longer then he wanted though to finish them off and it was enough time for an order to be established in the heavens. That is when the Nameless One, Faceless One and Shapeless One were appointed and took control as the elders of heaven. They were outraged at what Uttookari had done and he was stripped of his power, his undead and demon army were destroyed and they say Uttookari himself was thrown into what is now the abyss. It is a hell basically for gods. Nothing has been heard from him since. So you know now that there is more to you than meets the eye. We can fix your name easy enough but first you have a bigger burden to decide on and that is if you will join the Church of the Nameless and serve in his Body."

"My Lord you have no reason to wait on me I already have an answer and that answer is yes! It would be an honor and a dream come true to serve the Nameless One."

The Hand smiled at Zarron. "Very well. Tomorrow you will begin your training Zarron Ra Holyrage. Enjoy today for it will be some time before you are able to enjoy a day without intense training." He smiled once again at Zarron and as he did that his daughter came bursting into the room full of excitement.

"Daddy does that mean Zarron will be staying and not leaving us?" Mary asked looking up at her dad with her big brown eyes.

"Yes it does. He will be training here at the church so I am sure you will get to see him passing by. Now I have work to attend to, you two have fun. If you would like, show him around the citadel and Zarron I will send someone for you tomorrow." With that The Hand pulled himself to his feet and left the room.

Mary's face lit up and she ran and tackled Zarron wrapping him up with a big hug.

"This will be exciting I can show you all the cool areas and secret places. But you have to promise if I show you them to keep it a secret." As Mary warned Zarron about the secret she put her finger to her lips and said shh.

"Now Zarron get ready I will wait outside your door but be quick or you will miss the morning feeding of the fish in the Church's pond. Daddy had clothes put in your foot locker to wear. So hurry up." She ran out of the room and shut the door behind her as she waited in the hallway.

Zarron smiled after Mary then as soon as the door shut he let the flood of excitement flow from him. He bounced around on the bed a couple times and it took everything in his power not to scream aloud in excitement. Everything so far that had happened since he had got up in the morning had been great.

After bouncing around the room some he realized he was taking up too much time. Also the impatient knocking of Mary had brought him back to a more level mindset. He went to the foot locker and flung it open finding several sets of clothes available to him. He picked out a basic green woolen shirt and black pants. As he dug around more he found a suitable pair of boots to wear. He put them all on and was surprised to find they fit him wonderfully. As if they were tailored just for him. He took a look in a mirror at himself and decided he liked what he had picked out and he flung the door open. Mary stood off to the side and as soon as he came out of the room she grabbed his hand and started running down the hall way.

Throughout the day Mary had shown him everything within the church. There were passages he knew he would never have found without her that was shown. Each time one of them was mentioned she would tell him that it is a secret. Mary also showed him the feeding of the fish in the beautiful pond the Church had in one of its many courtyards. She showed him how breakfast, lunch and supper were served. She had taken him to the bakery and they had enjoyed some fresh baked bread. She had shown him many things but she also said that one day just isn't enough to show you all the cool stuff you will have to find out the rest later. Just as the sun was about to set Mary had one more place to show him.

"This is my biggest secret place ever. I want you to pinky swear you will never tell anyone of this place." As she said that she closed her hands into a fist then stuck out her pinky finger.

"You have my word Mary." He reached out with his pinky and clasped it with her pinky and they shook.

They went to the back of the church yards. In an area that had little traffic. There was the mighty wall that stood around the church protecting it standing tall. Unlike other walls of the church this one had grown thick with brush. Vines climbed and attached itself to the stonework. Even with it being old it was still an impressive structure. The section of the wall was between two large buildings that he couldn't begin to guess what they were. But they were huge buildings and there were so many windows that reflected the light of the setting sun towards the top. No guards patrolled the area either, which was eerie, but light could be seen shining through a few windows in the tallest building. Mary looked at the wall then pointed up at a stone statue that once was great but now was falling to disrepair.

"That is how you tell where to enter. You might need to take a couple tries to find the entrance but it is within three stone lengths of that statue. It used to be an impressive statue of a great angel my daddy used to always say. He said it would protect us and I have to say that I believe it. You will understand more once we enter." Mary said to him in a little voice that he had to strain to hear. With that she walked to the wall and almost instantly disappeared into the thick vines and brush. His eyes widened in amazement. He quickly ran up and pushed his hand where he thought Mary had entered and felt nothing but cold stone. He took a step back and counted the stones from the statue then tried again. This time he successfully found the entrance and walked through the vines and brush. As he emerged on the other side he gasped at the sight before him.

He had emerged into an amazingly beautiful garden. Tall trees, that reached nearly as high as the wall, created a beautiful canopy of leaves of all colors. Many of them were in bloom and countless flowers covered them of all shades, shapes and sizes. A great number of them bore fruit and nuts which were ripened to near perfection. Green grass covered the ground and thousands of blossoming flowers were delicately woven throughout, creating what looked like a masterpiece of art. Many of the trees also had higher branches and made walking through the sanctuary easy.

As he continued to walk in, amazed at the sights he didn't notice there was a tiny stream that ran through the middle of the sanctuary giving life to all the plants. Stepping in it brought him back out of his daze. He quickly stepped out of it and started to look for Mary. It didn't take him long to spot her with her dark hair and blue and silver dress. There she sat on a bench under an enormous willow tree arching over the sharp cliff side. It looked as though it was the king of the sanctuary. The sunlight seemed to catch every part of the tree and gave it a subtle orange glow. He went over and peered over the cliff edge. Hundreds of feet below him were the local farms and the luscious green valley that the city sat on. As he looked off in either direction, he could see some of the guard towers. They stood like stone sentinels watching over the valley below. The city guard had begun to light their torches for the incoming darkness. Many of them could be seen wandering the tops of the tower. As he looked down there was nothing but a sheer cliff that seemed to be polished down to a bright sheen.

"Mary, this is amazing and so cool!" He said as he turned back to her his eyes twinkling with excitement. He walked over to her and sat down next to her on the bench which was made of superior craftsmanship.

"I come here a lot to play when the other kids pick on me too much. I can run here and it is a safe place. My daddy and you are the only people I have told of this place to. So it is a real big secret. Daddy says this part of the church used to be on a great hill but during a war powerful magic created the cliff. That is why it is so shiny and smooth. The two great building next to here were towers for protection and also they were a place to grow flowers and plants. Daddy says mom used to have a green thumb for growing plants and she headed the building. Even the stream is considered magickal and it connects the two plant places and makes things grow or so I am told. I haven't been in the other building though because they are dangerous. The outside walls were partially destroyed when the big magick came and destroyed the cliff. Daddy hasn't had the chance to try to repair the building because of all the wars." Mary looked down at her feet as they dangled a few inches above the grass.

"You sure are smart Mary. I am glad I was able to save you." He smiled at her and she giggled.

"Well we best be getting back to the house." Mary said in a saddened voice.

"Don't worry Mary, I won't forget about you, remember, I will see you around the church. When I get time off maybe we can come here and play in the streams." He smiled again.

"Last one out of here is a rotten egg." He said as he jumped up and started running back towards the entrance. It wasn't long before they got back to their quarters. The morning would come quickly for him and it was only a short night's rest before he becomes an acolyte in the Body of the Church.

IX

As they trudged along with the women the cold air and fatigue was finally getting to Zarron, as was his wound that had caught him in the eye. Given the time it took to get where they were going he had time to disenchant the spell that was preventing him from doing too much of anything. His fatigue though made any actions nearly impossible. He knew that the wound on his eye was going to be a permanent scar for him to remember this ordeal for the rest of his life even if it may be short lived. What made the fatigue worse on both him and his partner Partaxis was keeping the women up and going. Countless times they had to carry the weight of one or two of the women as they were barely able to stand.

They had walked all night and finally he could smell the aroma of many cooking fires and the path they walked became more and more worn. Large wheel tracks had been worn into the ground from constant wagon traffic and it wasn't long before they crossed a line of huge totems with markings that looked all too familiar. As they continued their path they passed many other barbarians and beings in general, more of the totems appeared with all the same symbols. They were runes of healing.

After what felt like days of walking they had come to a stop but Zarron and Partaxis had no time to rest as they detached them from the women and marched them into a large wooden building. As they entered the building the decorations also seemed all too familiar to him.

****

It had been several years now since Zarron had begun his service within the church. He had progressed well and was one of the top in his class. His only competition was another young man who had excelled greatly just as he had. His name was Zeth and despite the constant competition between himself and Zeth they had grown to be great friends.

When they allowed the two of them to work together on a team they were nearly impossible to defeat. Zeth excelled strongly in jousting. Which was a pivotal skill as a member of the Body of the Church. Zarron excelled in his melee combat work. He knew he was behind Zeth in the jousting but it didn't bother him too much because he cared for Zeth like a brother. Zeth was much the same with Zarron and his melee work.

During a normal day, they would get 20 minutes a day to pray. They said the core of all the followers of the Nameless is their Faith. The stronger your tie with your god the more powerful you are and the more you empower him. The Nameless One loves taking joy in his followers. That was one part of the training Zarron excelled in, there were a great number of places one could pray but one spot that always drew him was the sanctuary he was shown years before by Mary. There he had the greatest peace, occasionally he would choose not to go there and appear at the Citadel to pray to show the Elites he prayed, for accountability purposes. He would spend much of his time in the hidden sanctuary. He would pray there, tend to his spell memorization, perfect his combat techniques and practice rune word drawings. One thing he found through the years was the sanctuary hid sound very well. Even when he had his practice dummy and was clashing steel against it, it couldn't be heard. The place was indeed a magickal place.

His week consisted of three full days of combat training. A full day plus half of another was spent with the Mind of the Nameless Ones, the Casting Order to learn the basics of rune drawing along with general magick training. Another day and a half was devoted to learning leadership, etiquette and religious studies. Finally on the last day of the week they would have the time off. That was the day he loved the most.

During the years Mary and him developed more of a fondness for one another. Soon they found themselves falling in love. Each day off he would meet Mary first thing in the morning in the sanctuary. The time they spent together was always wonderful and to both their despairs it went by too quickly. As the years went on Mary had become a beautiful woman. She had her dark hair cut short and bangs framed her sun kissed face. She had high cheekbones and a beautiful smile that would melt hearts. Her skin was dotted with light freckles but they didn't take away from her beauty. She carried herself very proper and upright. Her body was average to many people's standards but it didn't take away from the beauty he saw in her. She walked with a womanly grace. He was always awe stricken when he saw her. Her face was always the first thing on his mind when he got up in the morning and the last thing on his mind before he set himself to sleep.

****

It was her face though that was the last thing he was expecting to see sitting before him in that cabin with her eyes wide in disbelief.

X

"Za..rr…on?" Mary's voice stuttered in shock, she barely said his name.

"Mary, what are you doing?" Zarron's voice was filled with sadness as he asked the question.

"Guards, the Holy one stays here with me, take the other away." Mary had barely been able to lift her voice loud enough for the guards to hear. They had heard her though and in a flurry of motion they pulled Partaxis out. He turned to see his friend dragged away and on his face was a look of confusion and then he disappeared behind the door. His stomach turned even more when he realized that Mary wasn't a prisoner at all and was the leader of these people or someone with great authority.

"Mary…" That was all he could say as he slipped more into shock about the whole thing.

"Zarron you weren't supposed to know this. You were the last person I wanted to hurt in doing this."

"How did you not expect me to find this out? You are nearly waging an all-out war on the Fenrir and the church is part of protecting the Fenrir just as many others are." His feelings were becoming unstable. He had never felt so many different emotions at once. It was a combination of anger, love, pain and the most dominate, shock and betrayal. Tears started to roll down his cheeks.

"Zarron these people took me in after the church abandoned me when I needed them the most. Please don't cry Zarron." She walked up to him and tried wiping some of his tears away. As she got close he pulled his head back and looked at her with his eyes full of hurt. He took in a deep raspy breath.

"The church never abandoned you. Nor did I. When we had word you were well overdue on a mission to the north we immediately formed a search party to find you. Weeks of searching we came up empty. Don't you understand that the only reason I am on the Fenrir is because of you Mary. I had hopes that you were still alive. I pushed so hard to get posted here for you. I had almost been killed several times while traveling here from ambushes and thieves. You were the motivation that kept me going. Now that I see you, I wish I had died those times instead of suffering this great hurt." He said his tone wavering.

"These people are not bad it is the church that is corrupt and they are the enemy to the common people. It is the Nameless One who abandons his people and lets the wars happen. Here I am something. I keep these people safe from the shifting lands and they have blessed me with all the gold I could want and shelter. They make me feel like I am great not just a pawn."

"How dare you say that about the Church and the Nameless One? You are a foolish woman to think that. Have you even thought of how badly they have corrupted you? Your gold and treasures only last so long. The life you get for serving the Nameless One is eternal and he grants you all the riches you could need." His voice boomed over Mary's little voice. His breath became ragged and he clenched his teeth in anger.

"I don't know who you are anymore Mary. You aren't the woman I have loved faithfully and completely. You have turned into a monster that has betrayed her father and her God and the person that she supposedly loved more than anyone else." He stared hard at her as she backed off from him and sat down in her chair. Tears poured freely from her face and sharp sobs wracked her. He was only able to stand so long before the overwhelming hurt took over and he dropped to his knees weeping. His head hung low and he watched the tears he cried drop to the wooden floor. Sobs started to wrack his body as well and he turned his face up to the heavens. *I don't understand why you are having me suffer so greatly. I don't understand. I need you now.*

After what seemed like eternity the silence was broken. Mary had slowed her sobs to just tears and she collected herself some.

"Guards take this man away. Get him prepared for our entertainment." Her voice was shaky and weak but still the guards from outside the cabin heard and came in quickly to grab him. He looked at Mary one last time.

"I will pray for you Mary." That was all he could muster the will to say and Mary seemed to show the person she used to be as she nodded her head towards him seemingly agreeing with him. She smiled a half smile as he was pulled out the door, he watched her begin to cry again as the door slammed shut.

It wasn't long before he was thrown into a little cell. It was made from stone but the roof above had been made from wood and the bars were iron. Many stains dotted the floor and ceiling. He pulled himself to the rear of the cell and rested his back against it and hung his head in his hands. His mind was plagued with memories of Mary but all of them ended in hurt and he just wanted it all to stop. Tears came and went, anger would build up in him and he would slam his fists into the ground in frustration. Then when the thoughts were starting to become unbearable a loud uproar of noise brought him to his senses. He wasn't sure where it was coming from initially as he was disoriented.

He pulled himself to his feet and went over to his bars. He took a look down either way and saw several guards pulling some of the other prisoners from their cells. Many of them he recognized as being the ones the war party captured. Across from him he saw Partaxis. A little hope lit in him. He nodded his head at Partaxis too weak to talk and Partaxis returned the gesture. Soon the uproar could be heard again and he was finally able to pin point the fact that it came from above. He could hear masses of feet rushing to and fro above him and then he heard a loud thud and an uproar of hundreds of voices. As he looked at the ceiling blood started trickling down and dripped in his cell. He then knew that they were below an arena and that he was in the gladiator holding cells. He let out a sigh then went and sat back down in the back of his cell waiting for them to come and collect him.

It didn't take long for them to come. The sound of the prison doors opening brought him out of his thoughts and he was relieved for that, even if it meant he could be going to his death. *Well at least in death I can finally have peace.* The guards pulled him from his cell and he realized they were also pulling Partaxis from his. He gave a smile to his companion who saluted him back in return. The guard then pushed Partaxis and himself down the hall. The end the hall opened to a large armory with rusted weaponry and armor lying around. Much of it had been well used.

"Hurry up! Grab what you can. The people are waiting for more blood to be shed!" One of the guards ordered Zarron as he shoved him towards the weapon racks. He looked at his selection and wasn't thrilled with what it was. After some searching he finally found a weapon that grabbed his attention more than the rest. It was one that was barely showing as it was covered with the dirt of the ground. It looked like a rusty weapon but the wear on it was practically nonexistent.

"Hurry slum!" The guard yelled again in impatience. Zarron reached down and grabbed the sword. He looked at it and found it was really well made. The blade was balanced perfectly and even the bend in the blade was appropriate. It measured out to be a handle and a half sword. It thrummed lightly as he held it. He looked around but it seemed no one else realized the noise. He looked at it once again and found some words engraved in celestial and they read as "Angel Fire."

"This one will do just fine guards." He said to them nodding his head in satisfaction. They pushed him out of the room once the weapon was chose as he needed no armor because he still had his leather armor on from when he left the Fenrir those many days ago.

Soon he was joined by Partaxis who had grabbed two shoddy looking hammers, an iron breastplate with several holes in it, along with that he had fur leggings equipped. He donned an old rusted helm on his head but even with the terrible looking equipment he still looked like an intimidating foe for his size easily matched the largest of the barbarians. They were standing now at a large iron gate and beyond it was an enormous arena. Blood soaked the sands along with missing limbs from the unfortunate few. The arena walls had been coated with iron spikes and even a couple corpses were still hanging from them. Several pillars dotted the floor and they too had iron spikes on them. Around them numerous blood thirsty raucous people were seated and standing throughout the stadium rows. There was one portion that was covered and set up more like a cabin and there sat Mary along with Fervver. The sight of Fervver boiled his blood. *He will be dead by the time I am done here.*

The gates finally opened and Zarron and Partaxis casually stepped out to the arena floor as several of the opposing gladiators ran at them. With a quick duck Zarron dodged one of the men's rushing attack and flicked his blade out spilling the man's entrails. Partaxis had side stepped the one rushing him and hit him hard in the stomach with one of his hammers then he smashed the man's head with his other hammer. Two were down and only two remained. Fear could be seen on their face as Zarron and Partaxis stalked towards them forcing them closer and closer to the wall.

Zarron looked over at Partaxis and they exchanged silent communication. With a nod of their heads they rushed the men catching them off guard. Partaxis had run up and grabbed the man by his throat and threw him into the spike wall. Zarron slammed the hilt of his sword into the man he was facing catching him off balance then kicked him in the chest sending him partially into the spikes. He kicked him again causing his body to be completely pierced through. Silence filled the crowd as they stared in awe at how quickly the two of them killed their foes.

"I think we got them dumbfounded Zarron." Partaxis said to him in a quiet voice.

"Aye but the way this is going to happen is more are going to be sent so just be prepared."

Sure enough Fervver lifted his finger to some unseen person and next thing they knew seven more enemy gladiators came storming in. Zarron quickly engaged the first one as it came out the door. He parried one sloppy slash at him then stabbed his sword into the man's chest killing him instantly. Another man stabbed at him and it skimmed his armor. He attacked and took the man's hand. His screams of pain were cut short as a return strike slashed his throat. Zarron slashed at the third attacker with a high cut which he was to slow to guard. The force of the strike split the assailant's skull in half.

Partaxis easily was able to dispatch his foes as well. He had wound up hitting one in the face sending him sprawling off and then slammed another guy into the ground and dashed his head in with a quick blow from his hammer. He side stepped a stab at him and reached out and pulled the man that had slashed at him from his momentum and easily threw him into the spikes as well. All that was left was one more man and he trembled in fear as Zarron and Partaxis approached him.

"Be gone! We are finished with you here." That was all Zarron had to say to him. He quickly scrambled to his feet and ran for the door. Before he could make it there one of the barbarian guards in the crowd chucked a throwing axe at him which bit deep into the back of the man's skull killing him instantly. After the man was killed Mary got up and walked away for a reason unknown to Zarron.

Fervver stood up then. "Be prepared to face a nightmare." Fervver's eerie voice echoed throughout the arena as he started the chant of some demonic tongue.

"Zarron be prepared to leave this place, Durakon and I are about to create a distraction." Tombah's voice pounded Zarron's mind. Zarron touched his head as it happened then looked at Partaxis who seemed to have heard the same thing.

"Get the prisoners free Partaxis as soon as it happens. I will make sure Fervver doesn't do what he is planning." Zarron said.

"What about the woman Zarron?" Partaxis asked. Zarron shifted uneasily and decided it would be best not to answer at this time. Even if he wanted to there was no time as a large explosion rocked the earth from a little distance away. At that moment Zarron focused on Fervver who seemed oblivious to the noise that was happening as he was still concentrating on his chant. Zarron blinked and he was standing in front of Fervver.

"Wha…what?! How is it possible for you to use your magick? I cursed you so you couldn't!" Fervver exclaimed in shock as his eyes stared wide at Zarron.

"You forget *Lyckendune,* my power comes from a God that is far more powerful than you. Now you will face his wrath and in doing so, you will find your final death. Prepare to face the power of the Nameless One and the avenger of House Holyrage!" Zarron yelled and an enormous power surge flowed through his body. His eyes turned dark blue and runes on his body flared a bright blue and white. The power cascaded through his body into his arms and flowed into the sword causing it to shatter to pieces. The rusted pieces flew in all directions, killing those unlucky enough to be in the way of it. Lightning and fire lit the air around him. This then wrapped itself around him and raised him up as it embodied the sword, lighting it up in celestial power. He pulled the sword back with both hands and with one mighty blow swung it down with all the power he could muster. Fervver threw up a magickal shield but it wasn't enough. Zarron's power was more than enough to smash through the magickal shield scattering it. The blade cut through Fervver from top to bottom and as the blade bit into the ground the full power exploded. The light incinerated Fervver out of existence and blasted the wooden walls apart that contained the arena grounds and the former stand that Fervver watched from to oblivion. After it was done Zarron was floated down to the ground and as soon as his feet touched he rushed out the large opening. Partaxis followed behind him.

"Go now get the prisoners, I am going to cause a little more chaos here." Zarron yelled to Partaxis and the two of them split directions. Zarron ran towards the wards that held the camp in order. He found the main totem that was the key to the rest working and stood in front of it and he kneeled down and prayed to The Nameless One.

Partaxis had no problem finding the prisoners and having them escape was miraculously easy. The whole camp was in complete disarray as Tombah and Durakon rained fire down on the city. He cleared all the prisoners he could find and directed them towards the direction he thought Tombah to be at and as he was about to leave the area he heard a feint cry for help from close by. As he looked around he saw one woman pinned beneath a large wooden beam that had fallen through the roof as one of Tombah's fireballs exploded the building above. He ran up to her and found she was one of the enemy barbarians. She looked at him with large brown eyes full of fear. He considered leaving her there to burn, however his love of woman and desire to not be a total ass won over the former. He ran up and grabbed hold of the large beam and lifted with all his strength moving it just enough for her to scramble out.

"Thank you. Thank you. Please take me with you I don't want to be here anymore. Please." The woman looked up at him from the ground.

"Argh! Fine let's go now." He reached down and picked her up, throwing her over his shoulder just as another part of the ceiling dropped down. He managed to get a few more feet then another portion of the ceiling threatened to fall down on him. In quick thought he pulled the woman down from his shoulders and covered her body with his as the ceiling crashed down on top of them. After it had fallen on them he found himself still alive and the woman as well. They were covered with a good chunk of debris.

"Guard your face m'lady." Partaxis ordered the woman. Just as he did that he punched a hole through the debris and reached around finding solid ground to pull him and the woman out. Soon they were out of the debris. He once again picked the woman up and put her on his shoulders and ran out of the camp. He knew he had some serious burns but he also knew Zarron could take care of them or some other healer would care for them once he got to safety.

Zarron finished his prayer and with his God blessing him one more time he placed his hand on the totem and drew all the power in from the totem. As he felt the last bit draw itself into his body he reversed it and sent out an immensely powerful blast of energy that obliterated the totem and the runic power it once held was dissipated completely. As he looked around he found the other totems lit runes fade to darkness. Satisfied with his work he got up and ran off to where he figured Tombah and Durakon were at.

He finally found them and was happy to realize that Tombah and Durakon weren't alone as a large skirmish force were with them. He found that Partaxis and the rest of the prisoners had made it to the skirmish force as well and before they could check on people they were urged by Tombah and Durakon to get out of there fast. He agreed and the whole skirmish party and prisoners alike left the camp burning behind them. The dark smoke gave them cover enough to get a good distance between them and the camp.

XI

They had put several hours between them and the camp before the order to halt and set up camp was issued. The land had changed once over their travels and what started out as a field was changed to a heavy mountainous area that made travel a little slower than they liked. Finding a suitable camp site was hard as well but a small clearing in between several great mountains made a perfect camp area.

"Zarron what is it you are working on there you haven't looked up naught but once since we have left camp." Tombah asked him to break the silence as the line halted for camp.

"Tombah, they used simple magick runes to keep that whole camp together. I am just trying to mock what I saw. Being part of the body of the church we didn't learn a lot about major rune casting. That was always part of the Mind of the Church. Which were our heavy casters as you know and that was also what Mary was part of. If I did this right then the land should remain as it is instead of changing on us. It will keep us together but honestly Tombah I will need your help to mass produce this. If I get this one copy working I will show you how to make it work and I will rely on your capabilities as a caster to finish them out." Zarron attempted to smile at Tombah as he finished but found that smiling was too difficult to do when his heart was in such pain.

"Alright Zarron but you should finish it quickly or take a break to set up your camp." Tombah told him worry could be heard on his voice.

"Do not worry about me Tombah things will be fine I just need some time to recover from everything. You know that Mary was more than just a friend to me she was my lover and I put my whole heart into loving her." He dismounted from his horse and patted Tombah on the shoulder then he lead his horse away to an area on the outskirts of the main camp and started setting up his own camp.

Soon the last rays of the sun kissed the peaks around them and darkness fell on the camp. Many fires could be seen as they glittered and gleamed off the snow on the ground. He watched the camp from his small dark site on a little hill. He watched them for a while before looking down at the piece of wood he was carving runes into. It was almost complete, all he had was one more line to draw and as he drew it in he breathed a word and the runes all lit up with a beautiful glow. It lit up the area around him and he could feel the familiar warmth that comes with heal spells. The land around him even seemed to quiver under the power of the spell. Satisfied with his work he placed it into one of his pockets and drew forth the sword that he grabbed from the arena.

As he pulled it out from the cloth it was wrapped in he could almost feel it come to life with his touch. The blade lit up with a beautiful white glow that had streaks of blue run through it. The light constantly shifted along the blade. As he ran his hand along the edge he felt the blade to be dull to his touch. Confused by this he grabbed a log that was given to him for a fire he wasn't going to have and barely lifting the sword he cut it down on the log and cut it cleanly in half. He let out a short gasp.

"What kind of sword are you "Angel Fire"?" He asked himself and to his wondrous surprise a female voice answered him.

"I am a sword that has been waiting for you a long time. I have been in existence since the beginning. I was tied to this sword as its spirit. You are the one I was made for specifically. You have been a plan in the heavens since before you were born."

"Can anyone else hear you and do you have a name?" He asked the sword as he placed it on his knee.

"No only you can hear me Zarron and my name in simple celestial is

Angel Fire. My true name is Angeldianamanas dre Firendiija."

"Ahh I see why Angel Fire is much easier. So what happens to you if I die?"

"That should not be a concern to you at this time Zarron. Now, you should be more concerned about sleeping. So sleep now Zarron ra Holyrage." The swords voice faded and he quickly found him-self falling to sleep.

Just as the nights before his sleep was restless and nightmares plagued his mind. Haunting memories of his past constantly came up in his dreams and when they vanished they were replaced by other hurtful memories. Soon he just couldn't handle it anymore and his eyes snapped open to the darkness around him. Cold sweat dampened his brow and as he looked at the camp not a body stirred. Fires that were lit earlier were no more than smoldering heaps. The mountains around him were like dark sentinels that quietly looked over them. In some sense he could almost feel like the land was alive and watching them. He grabbed his water skin and drank in deeply the ice cold water felt quite refreshing as it slid down his throat quenching his thirst.

He stared blankly at his sword his mind thousands of miles away. He stared at it for several more minutes until a movement close to him caught his eyes. As he spun to look at the object a distortion in the air formed a figure of what looked like a man. But his face was not to be seen. It was covered in darkness and the strong feeling of magick permeated from his core. Its faceless eyes couldn't be seen but he felt them focus on him.

"You seem to be suffering from great hurt Zarron." The stranger's voice shook the ground and mountains. Or so he thought but it seemed like it was directed at just him for the camp seemed to still be in a catatonic state.

"What do you know of me? For I do not know you." He replied in a stern voice that was a bit on edge.

"You know me far more than you think. I am every face but alas I am no face. I know that you are a servant to the Nameless but it would appear

Zarron that your God has abandoned you."

His stomach turned inside out and his heart skipped a beat. He breathed in a raspy breath.

"You are the Faceless One aren't you?" He asked in a hoarse voice.

"Excellent you aren't as dumb as some of your other kin." The Faceless One said in response to Zarron, chuckling, it sounded more evil and disturbing than anything else.

Zarron quickly went and reached for his sword but before he could get his hands on it the Faceless One had him locked in a magickal grip. Pain tore through his mind as the evil magick entered him and as he fought. The grip seemed to get tighter. Finally he found himself turned and staring right at The Faceless One.

"As you can tell Zarron the more you fight me the more painful this is. You must realize or you should if your little brain can comprehend it. I could have killed you by now if that is what I wanted to do. I could destroy that brain of yours and make it where you can't respond to anything nor do anything all you could do is stare off aimlessly as your friends and companions find you seemingly lifeless and then burn you in a funeral pyre. I just wish to speak to you is all. I was hoping we could do this like men and not require me forcing you." The Faceless One's voice tore through his mind like thunder. He reached up and covered his ears in a feeble attempt to block out the god's voice. Just as he thought he couldn't take it anymore the grip was loosened, the voice subsided.

"What do you want from me you despicable God?" He asked the Faceless one his voice trembling with pain.

"Good now that you are ready to speak I just want you to do me a favor and I will do one in return for you. One I know you can't resist." The Faceless One asked and if he had a face to see it would be smiling slyly.

"What is it you could ever offer me that would be greater then what my god the Nameless One could provide for me?" He answered back in a quiet voice as the fatigue from the spell racked his body.

"It is quite simple since I serve what you consider the Evil side I am more willing to do things that the Nameless One would not be willing to do. I can take away your pain and give you back the woman you love. Imagine a clean slate with the woman you love on your side. No more pain of the hurt you suffered. The nightmares will stop and the dark dreams will no longer plague you. I know what you are thinking and that it is not possible to do these things. But it is and The Nameless One is keeping it from you." The Faceless One explained.

"Why would the Nameless One not do this? What would be his purpose?" He asked quietly.

"You really are rather stupid. Don't you realize that you serve a God that wants his people to suffer to show they are worthy? He likes seeing his people suffer and hurt. He doesn't care for their happiness." The Faceless One's voice was filled with an eerie sadness.

He stared at the Faceless One with a stern look filled with defiance for a moment or two then it faded and he stared down at his feet as his head drooped in defeat. He was far too tired and far to fatigued to be able to say anything against what the god was saying.

In some sense the Faceless One was correct that the Nameless One did demand a lot from his people. He knew that there was purpose for it all but sometimes it was tough to bear and as he was now it was too much and all he wanted was for it to be gone.

He licked his lips and was about to respond when there was a large flash of light then a large boom as the mountain around the camp collapsed to the earth. He turned around and looked at the rubble of the mountains wide eyed. He turned and looked at the Faceless One who seemed to take a step back and the camp beyond that was coming awake to the loud noises. As the

Faceless One took a step back he could feel some of his strength return and felt as if a burden was lifted off him.

Just as he was feeling that weight leave he was all of a sudden hammered again by the Faceless One invading his memory this time it seemed more hurried.

"Give me an Answer Now Zarron! I demand it of you and I demand it now!" The voice of the Faceless pounded in his mind forcing him to start forming words.

The ground shook again behind him and just as he was about to create words against his will the spell was released from him as the Faceless One dropped his focus on him. He fell to the ground as a massive boulder crushed into the evil god. As Zarron turned and looked back he saw a colossal stone golem form out of the rubble of the mountains. The face of it had a bright white crown floating around the top and its eyes glow a bright blue that was full of life and hope.

"How dare you Faceless One mess with the free will of that man. His destiny is his own choice not to be messed with by your evil enchantments." The giant's voice boomed through the darkness shaking the core of the earth.

An evil dark laughter cut through the air.

"I didn't think you would show so quickly Nameless One. I was hoping to have your little servant as mine but you always have to come and RUIN IT!" The Faceless one spewed his words filled with hate and anger. With a surge of great power he formed a giant icicle and flung it at the stone golem nailing it in the shoulder sending large boulders flying through the night sky. As some of the boulders threatened to crush the army, the Nameless One reached out his hand and cast a shield to cover the entire party protecting them from harm. The slight distraction gave the Faceless One enough time to form himself into a colossal ice golem, matching the Nameless Ones size and might.

The Faceless One charged at the Nameless one and the two massive powers collided falling to the earth in an earth shattering rumble. The ground split and stones flew everywhere, ice shards flung out every direction shattering against the mighty magickal shield that protected the scouting group. As the air cleared the two entities were gone and all that was left in their place was a large pile of frozen rocks. The shield had dropped around the camp and an eerie silence fell upon the entire camp. One of the men from the skirmish party approached Zarron slowly.

He didn't hear the man coming up on him and finally he turned just as the man was upon him his face was etched with confusion and awe.

"Who are you to have the God's Fighting over you?" The man asked in a voice that he barely was able to vocalize.

XII

Zarron looked at the man with a face that showed he had no idea the answer to the question. He opened his mouth to speak but no words came. All he could do was drop to his knees and hold his head. The millions of racing thoughts made him feel as though his head would explode and holding it seemed to be some way to keep his thoughts from bursting out and flying everywhere. There was complete silence until Tombah stepped in.

"He is a man we should be grateful that the gods are fighting over that means we cannot lose any upcoming fights. I should think though that instead of gawking at this man you should all be getting ready to break camp." Tombah's voice sounded pleasant at first but the last part of it he said with poison in his words and within a matter of seconds the crowd broke up hurriedly to their respective tents and started to break camp. All that was left standing before Zarron was Tombah, Partaxis and Durakon. It was Durakon who approached him first and offered his hand to him.

"Zarron it is ok your thoughts won't explode from your head killing you. We will have one of the men break your camp for you but we need your head back in the game for when we start moving." Durakon said to him in a calming voice.

Zarron wasn't sure what was going on he just knew that Durakon had said something to him and offered his hand to pull him up. He accepted and slowly he was pulled to his feet. The stress of everything was taking its toll on him. All he wanted was to have Mary caressing his head and holding him and speaking to him in the calm sweet voice she would always have when he had a horrible day. It never failed that she would comfort him, not once had she been unsuccessful until the past day when he saw her in that cabin. The pain of everything came back to him in a rush that sickened him to the point of wanting to throw up.

"Please give me some time to myself." He asked of his fellow companions who all nodded their head and walked off. Tombah and Durakon took a glance back at him as they walked away worry and concern etched their continence plain as daylight. He didn't care though. He grabbed his weapon then walked the opposite direction of them to a point beyond the little hill away from the sight of the camp.

When he felt comfortable he was away from the sight of the camp he slumped down on the hill into a heap. He pressed the hilt of the sword against his forehead and pressed into it to the point where he felt some pain in his head from the pressure. All he could do was to repeat the words over and over "What am I to do?" He said them to no one person in particular just to himself as if something would answer him. For once in his life he counted on anything except his God or any god. In doing that, he felt a dark pocket of loneliness, one he had never experienced before in his life even with all his losses he had been through.

"Zarron I sense your faith wavers." Angel Fire spoke to him out of the darkness.

"Is it that obvious sword or can you read thoughts?" He replied not really surprised about his sword speaking up.

"No I cannot read a thought that is for the god's to do. For they know what is in the hearts and minds of men. But I can tell you that I feel as though a piece of you was ripped away from your soul. Remember I have been linked to you for a long time. I was made precisely and exactly for you. But you are getting cold Zarron." The swords calm voice reminded him of his mothers.

"So you can't read thoughts but you can pick up on the turbulence in my soul? I don't expect you to answer that. I guess I am thrilled I have someone to talk to even though it is a sword. But I suppose you being made for me would understand me. How can I keep my faith when it does seem he has abandoned me all together? My life has been many heartaches in a row and so constantly. I have lost all that I have been close to except for a friend or two. I have been beat up, beat down, torn up, betrayed, and fought over for no particular reason and am now serving in the coldest place in the known world for what?" He said his words filled with agony.

"So because of all these trials you think that your god has abandoned you and cares not for you? It is sad to me that a man that has destroyed a great lich king by faith alone is saying his God is not there for him. A man that had the Nameless One come down from his mighty throne to do battle with an evil god preventing him from destroying your mind and twisting you against your own will. With all that it does not sound like your God has abandoned you it sounds as though he has been carefully and diligently listening for your cries of pain and help and is more than willing to help. I say it is a good thing that your God is big enough to handle your insults and even your thoughts of abandoning him, for if it was not the case, then this world would be an even colder and crueler place."

There was a long pause before he could muster up the words to continue. "Even if that was the case why would he have the love of my life betray me and even throw me in the gladiator ring to be killed by merciless thugs that rape and pillage their own people."

"Zarron, you need to take a step back and breathe. Do you think that Mary sent you to the gladiator rings knowing you would be killed? She knows you are a far better fighter then many men and few could match you. Do you think she didn't know about me? I may have been a rusty looking sword but she was a member of the Church of the Nameless and being that means she can read the celestial words. Being able to do that means she knew I was something different but she didn't understand it. All things have a plan even if they seem horrible at the time. You know this in your heart and I don't see how knowingly speaking to the epitome of evil has changed that in you. Zarron you have to know that God's in all their power and glory have one thing they all need to follow by and that is they cannot take away our right to free will. Mary made her choice but I would guess that the Nameless One did his best to try to keep her but she still made the choice of betraying The Nameless One and all those she loved. Zarron you know what is right in your heart I have no more need to speak to you about these things. What choice you decide I will always be with you the whole time." With that the sword's voice disappeared and Zarron knew that he would not hear from the sword for a while.

The sword is right I cannot believe what I have done. He thought to himself. *Oh my what have I done?* He fell to his knees and prayed aloud to the Nameless One.

"Please forgive me oh great Nameless One. I have wronged you so badly and I will not do that again in my life. I renew my vow to you and I promise you no evil will ever get a chance to corrupt me so badly. By my family name and the honor of your church I will not lose my faith in you again." As he finished his prayer he felt that loneliness in him disappear completely. The clouds in the sky burst open and light poured out from the heavens, just as the light poured out loud thunder slammed the air around them as though the Faceless One was striking out in anger knowing that his chance with Zarron was possibly gone forever. Within moments though everything went back to normal. The light that poured like water from the skies were soon clouded over again and the thunder roared off into the distance. Soon the stillness of the early morning fell upon the valley again. Within moments the silence was broken as the noise of the people breaking camp could be heard again.

Zarron pulled himself to his feet and scurried back over the hill. Just on the top of the hill stood his small group of companions; Partaxis, Tombah and Durakon. He smiled at them as he saw them.

"It's good to have you back Zarron." Partaxis spoke up first as he embraced him in a hearty handshake.

"For now I am back to whom I once was, but there will still always be the hurt of recent experiences but I know now that I will get over them it just will take time. But, right now that time needs to be spent on getting moving. Also it needs to be spent having Tombah make me copies of this talisman." He said to the group as he handed the talisman to Tombah who smiled at him and took it.

"Within a few hours I will have enough for this group made up. You have my word Zarron." Tombah replied to Zarron as he grabbed it from him. He turned away and went to get on his horse.

"Come now Zarron your camp is broke down and your horse is packed. We are ready to move and even the scouts have already headed out in front of the main body to secure our path." Partaxis notified Zarron of the situation.

"You are a good leader Partaxis and your men love you perhaps if you keep it up you to might be revered as a god." He patted Partaxis's shoulder as he went by him to mount up on his horse.

Just as Tombah had promised within a couple hours of travel he had made enough talismans for everyone in the party even the freed captives.

"Thank you for taking care of all this for us Tombah. Now we will be safe once the land shifts and we will not be torn apart from one another." He offered his hand in thanks to Tombah as he talked to him.

Tombah took his hand and gave it a hearty shake. "You are most welcome Zarron. Now do you think we will ever get out of this mountain path? Something about it gives me an odd feeling." Tombah replied back to him his voice a whisper.

"Yeah I kind of get that feeling and if you look around our freed men look a little shaken and paranoid about things as well. What do you think could be causing it?" Before Tombah could reply to him their answer happened. A loud roar could be heard from the higher points of the mountains and as he looked around he spotted the Yetis moving among the rocks quickly closing converging upon the small party.

"Everyone battle positions. You men there get these people out of here. The rest we must hold them back as long as we can." Partaxis's voice boomed over the whole party. The group he motioned to save the freed captives quickly started to push them through. The rest of the party moved towards to rear to face the incoming Yeti. Archers prepared themselves and the sound of their bow strings being pulled taught filled the air.

"Archers fire at your own free will." Durakon ordered his group of archers and the sound of loosed bow strings echoed off the mountain walls. Some yetis were hit and howled in pain as they slipped from the mountain side and fell down into a heap at the bottom. Many more though jumped and dodged the arrows.

At the sound of Partaxis's voice Zarron grabbed his sword free from the saddle and slapped the horse on the butt sending it running after the freed captives as they moved towards what looked like the end of the path. Tombah did the same in suit and both Tombah and Zarron ran towards the front line where they would do their best to hold them off. As Zarron peered at the mountain side he realized they were incredibly outnumbered as the Yeti seemed to continuously pour out from the crevices and caves that littered the mountain side.

"Partaxis they are surrounding us we need to make a circle and do our best to keep all sides secured. Hopefully they will still continue to concentrate on us and leave our retreating numbers be." Zarron suggested to Partaxis. He nodded his head in agreement.

"Alright everyone form up a circle archers in the middle, Tombah and Durakon you two in the middle as well. Zarron you cover our back side and I will take the front. Remember we must stay strong. Night is closing in fast so let's do our best to at least hold them off until then, it should be enough time for our retreating party to get to safety. If the god's are with us tonight let's hope they will allow us to be with them in safety." Partaxis's voice could be heard loud and clear above all the chaos that was happening. Within moments the first Yeti had landed on the ground and able to be engaged in melee.

One of the beastly monstrosities landed in front of Zarron towering over him. They stood easily 7 ft. on average, many taller than that, large muscles covered their frame each one was probably as heavy as two or three men. These ones were unique to him as their fur was black instead of the typical whites and tans and their eyes glowed an eerie light green color. Some had clubs for weapons but more still just used their long claws on their hands.

The one before him was one that used its claws and attacked Zarron with ferocious savagery. He ducked under the initial punch then as the other came around at him he managed to slash his sword around and take its hand. He stabbed out with his sword and it ignited in fire to help with the reach and the blade pierced through the Yeti's chest with great ease. Just as he yanked his blade free another jumped down at him from high up. Just as it was falling towards him though an arrow pierced its side and sent him flying off course, it crashed into the ground a few feet away.

Another beast attacked Zarron forcing him to parry a swing from a mighty club that nearly knocked him off balance. As the beast was recovering he stabbed at it piercing its stomach along with 4 other swords as the men around him attacked as a unit.

As Partaxis engaged the first Yeti he had his mighty war hammer and slammed it into the beasts head. With great ease he crushed the skull causing it to fall limp in its path. As another one jumped out at him he swung out and caught the Yeti in the side sending it into the side of the mountain. He caught another beasts club as it swung at him and utilizing his size and strength he overpowered the monstrosity. He pushed it aside and slammed his head into the Yeti's face forcing it to take a step back stunned, he followed up with a mighty upper hand blow smashing it into the yeti's chin. The creature's legs went limp, it crumbled to the ground. He brought his foot up and crushed the beasts head.

Durakon and Tombah constantly fired arrow and fireball at the Yeti's as they crawled down the mountain side. Their numbers never seemed to dwindle. 20 minutes had passed with them fighting the yetis and soon they found that they had beaten them back. Hundreds upon hundreds of dead Yeti's littered the face of the mountain and the path that the men were upon. Only a few of the men had lost their lives. Cheer's started to rise up from them but something still didn't feel right to Durakon and even as he looked at Tombah, Zarron and Partaxis he could tell they all felt the same way.

"It's not over yet." Durakon said in a small voice that had the impact of someone yelling at the top of their voice. The group quieted down and they all looked around at the walls with swiveling heads and cautious stares.

"Well men I would say let's head out but I think that our options our cut short at this point. If you wish to leave I would say you have a few brief moments to make some ground. None here will view you any differently and if any choose to stay back we will cover your retreat. But I must say we have not given the refugee's and the few men enough time on their retreat. But as I said go now if you want to keep your lives for I fear this next round will be our last." Partaxis voice broke the silence.

"Well what are you doing Partaxis?" A large amount of men's voices could be heard in unison asking the question.

"Doing what I feel is right and that is staying right here to cover the retreat." Partaxis answered them.

"Well then we are with you Lord Partaxis. We will not let you die alone, we would all find it an honor to fight and die by your side." The men replied back not a single one even wavered in their commitment. Zarron looked over at Partaxis and nodded his head in respect.

"It would appear your people love you as I said Partaxis and I say I am to stay with you as well. We have been through enough together and I would not be able to live with myself if I left now."

"Well if Zarron is staying then I am staying." Tombah piped in.

"And if Partaxis and the rest of you are staying I see that I have no choice but to stay myself." Durakon said lastly.

"You are all good men now let us show these yetis that the Korilith soldiers are a force not to be trifled with." Partaxis said as a last remark before he set himself into his fighting stance. Just as Durakon and the rest suspected another loud roar could be heard in the distance. The sun was now no more and the bright glow of the moon offered the only light available.

"Let your will be done Nameless One. But we do need you now." Zarron said under his breath. As soon as he concluded his prayer a motion caught his attention at the mountains directly around them where there were no yetis yet. Gray, white and black could be seen jumping down the cliff sides. One of the unknown creatures dropped down in front of him. Its large golden and white body towered over him. Immediately he recognized it as the werewolf from the first attack not to many days ago. Within moments the whole party was surrounded by them and as the party was about to attack them the one that dropped in front of him spoke.

"We wish you no harm. Please stay your weapons." The one that spoke was easily a voice of a female. Her voice was remarkably human like and if not seeing the werewolf you would expect it to be a normal human talking to you.

Zarron signaled the men to put down their weapons, after a moment the first begrudgingly lowered their weapon, the rest followed suit closely behind. A heavy silence fell over the group.

"You are the one I let live aren't you?" he asked the werewolf in front of him.

"Yes I am. I have been following you since that event. I have a debt to pay to you. One I intend to keep tonight. You all must leave now. We will stop these beasts from killing you and you will find that my pack will not attack any of you." The werewolf replied.

"You will all be killed because of it their numbers are massive. When I gave you your life back it wasn't a debt to be paid by your death." Zarron said to the Werewolf.

"Just Go! Now! Our numbers are more than you think. The moon is special tonight as well we are even stronger." The werewolf replied, flexing her razor sharp claws.

"Alright men let's go." Partaxis gave the order and all the men carefully started retreating back and soon all that was left standing there was Zarron.

"What is your name?" Zarron asked.

"My name is of no use to you for after this debt is paid you will become our foe again." The werewolf replied.

"You must give me a name even if it is one of an enemy I will face in the future." He asked again.

"Very well human my name is Sheeniaviar Forestranamas. Now go!" The werewolf replied.

"Thank you my name is Zarron ra Holyrage. I wish you the best of luck and perhaps we shall meet again even if it is being on the opposite sides." He said as he ran off after the rest of his party. He hadn't run even 100 yards before the sound of the battle could be heard. Soon he caught up with the rest of the group and the sounds of battle were eventually consumed by the still and silent night air of the cold northern lands.

XIII

Within a few hours of hard marching Zarron and the group caught up with the refugee camp. They had settled in a wide clearing that looked to be an area of woods that was clear cut. Stumps and branches covered the ground making it an incredibly hard place for anyone to sneak up on them. As Zarron, Partaxis and the others approached the camp a loud cheer rose up from within the camp as the people praised their rescuers. Partaxis was among the one most honored for his work.

Zarron slipped off into the dark corners of the camp to have time to pray. He didn't go far before he found a small area that was mostly clear of debris. A large trunk of a tree was felled there and he kneeled down on one knee and bowed his head. *Efiir* he spoke the magickal word and fire leapt to life on the stump and it floated there. He reached underneath his armor and pulled forth the last bit of incense he had. He threw it onto the flame and soon the air was filled with the sweet scent of lavender and myrrh. As he breathed it in he could feel his mind clear and his body relax. A feeling he had not felt in ages it seemed. As he felt his last muscle relax he began praying.

"So you are saying werewolves came to your aid lord Partaxis?" One of the younger boys in the group asked Partaxis his eyes wide in amazement and awe. Partaxis nodded his head to the boy as he finished his story.

"Well I would say that is best for tonight you should all get some more rest. I apologize for waking you all." Partaxis said to the group as they gathered to listen to the story of how Partaxis, Tombah, Durakon, Zarron and the rest made their escape from the Yetis. Murmurs of disappointment could be heard but they all knew that Partaxis was right and they needed their sleep. After the crowd dispersed Durakon approached Partaxis.

"Partaxis if things are right and we don't suffer too much of land change we should be able to see the Fenrir on the horizon by nightfall. By mid-evening on the second day we should be within the shadow of the Fenrir. But it won't be till the third day where we will be able to make it within the Fenrir's limits." Durakon relayed his report to Partaxis.

"Thank you Durakon you are the best tracker there is that I have no doubt in my mind about." Partaxis replied back to Durakon.

"With all due respect Partaxis what are we to do with these refugees? Do you plan to allow them to see our scout entrance and also risk the possibility of them betraying us for we do not even know where they stand?" Tombah whispered to Partaxis.

"Aye Tombah has a point but the point of stopping within the shadow of the Fenrir is to prepare for that." Durakon replied.

"You both have valid points and we can fix this issue easy enough. We give them the option to set up a permanent home base outside our heaviest defensive wall. There are not enough of them to strike us down. Also as we allow them to home themselves in the shadow of the Fenrir we can build up our trust. We might need them for soldiers someday. They need us, we are all they have left. If we leave them they will die." Partaxis said back to the two of them.

"Well I do hope you know what you are doing Partaxis for it would be a sad thing if your weakness with these people get those that you know and guard our world from the monsters of the north killed." Tombah said to Partaxis in a stern voice as fire flashed through his eyes.

"I would suggest wizard that you stay your tongue." Partaxis responded back with a deep stern voice with a scowl on his face.

"Now be gone and busy yourself with something. Perhaps rest even for I think you sorely need it." Partaxis ordered Tombah. Tombah stared at Partaxis in a cold stare. The both of them stared each other down and an eerie silence stretched between them.

Eventually Tombah turned and walked away from Partaxis. Durakon turned and watched Tombah leave then turned his attention back to Partaxis. Durakon crossed his arms and raised his eyebrow.

"I would dearly hope Partaxis that the reason for all of this is because you are quite fatigued from everything, for that is not an alright thing to do." Durakon said to Partaxis in a calm voice then he turned and walked away from him back to his camp.

Zarron felt a presence near him that brought him out of his prayers. As he looked up through the fire and smoke of the incense a figure stood there watching him. It was a woman he had not seen before. She had long dirty blonde hair and her eyes were a light green. She had a full figure of a woman grown and wisdom could be seen in her eyes. There was also a hint of wild nature in them as well. Her lips were full and her face had several scars but it did nothing to take away from her beauty. As far as he could tell she stood taller than most women. Nearly as tall as his height from what he could guess. Her body was clothed in a dark dress that accentuated her shape a slit ran down the side of her dress on her legs. She wore long dark gloves. Her arms and legs were toned of that of a fighter. As he watched her a smile crept across her face.

"Let me ask you Zarron ra Holyrage, have you ever seen a woman before?" The woman asked him.

"My apologies to you m'lady but I must say I did not hear you approach and I do not know you but you know me how is that?" He asked the woman.

"Oh, but you do know me Zarron, actually you know me quite well. How I sneaked up on you? Well that is because you were so intense in your prayer that you just didn't hear me. Not to mention you are far enough away from the camp where no guard could pick up on me. Not a smart choice Zarron I could have easily killed you." The woman laughed a little and smiled.

"No, if you wanted to kill me, you would have. Now, who are you and what can I do for you?" He asked looking sternly at her through slitted green eyes.

The woman smiled once again. "You can call me Sheen for you know my full name is far more difficult." She continued to look down at him through the fire.

He stared up at her, trying to think of who she was. He stood up and found he was a little above her height as he had guessed. He stared deeply into her eyes and then he saw who she was.

"Sheeniaviar, you are the werewolf." he said in a slightly surprised tone. "I am glad to see you are alive. But I think you mentioned to me that I would still be a foe. If that is the case at least answer me one question before you slay me or whatever it is you plan to do. How can you take a human form?"

Sheen laughed lightly. "Silly man, if I wanted you to be a target I would have done that already. No, you Zarron are different something about you is strange. You draw people to you in some amazing way. I saw that the elite gods of good and evil are after your soul. I must say up until seeing them I never believed in them. Ahh…but if I remember correctly you asked how I can take a human form as well. Well, it is simple I am not a full blooded werewolf. I am a human shape changer. There are few of us and each one of us is put in charge of one animal or another. Mine happened to be Dire Wolves and I just happened to stumble across the werewolves at some point in time and they took to me. I enjoyed the power of them and I kept with them. Good for me I found a pack of Dire Wolf werewolves. The god's smiled on me I suppose." She walked towards Zarron and phased herself past the fire and soon she was within inches of his face. She could feel the hot breath he breathed and closed her eyes taking it. Her eyes lazily opening.

"So tell me Zarron what is your story?" Sheen asked as she lifted a hand up towards his face. He grabbed her hand quickly and pulled it away setting it back to her side. Then he took a step away from her.

"Sheen my story is something I thought I knew but now I am not so sure. That is something I need to ask the church. Why you are drawn to me I couldn't tell you. But, I must be back to the camp and get some rest. I am pleased to know you survived the Yetis Sheen." Zarron turned and left with that. He paused for a quick moment and turned back to her.

"Thank you." Zarron said from the bottom of his heart. Sheen nodded her head back and gave him a little smile as she watched him walk away. As he continued methodically picking his way through the stumps he threw up his hand and waved. The fire went out leaving her in the darkness.

"Oh Zarron, I don't know what it is about you but I intend to stick by you until I figure it out." She spoke to herself. Then she changed shape and stalked off into the darkness looking back only once to see Zarron disappear into the camp.

As Zarron walked back into the camp he looked back and witnessed her change her shape and stalk away. His vision helped him watch her walk far into the woods before the brush of the trees swallowed her whole. He wasn't sure what to think about the whole incident and he was too tired to think on it too much. So he continued back into the camp only being stopped once by the guards who were on watch. They didn't keep him and let him pass.

It wasn't long before he found his camp area. To his surprise it had already been set up with his things inside his tent. It wasn't a huge tent to speak but he didn't have much use for a big fancy tent with what little belongings he had. It was actually better then what a lot of the people had. Many of them sat out in the open sky huddled with each other around a fire. As he sat down inside his tent he removed his boots and laid his head down and within moments he was fast asleep.

The morning sun pierced through the tiny slit in the tent opening bringing Zarron awake. He pulled himself up and rubbed the sand from his eyes. As he sat there pulling himself together he found that he was getting incredibly hot. So he pulled on his boots and grabbed his sword belt and strapped it on. Finally he sheathed his sword and took a step outside and found that the whole area had been changed in the night. He was surprised his magick talisman's worked so well and pretty much found the whole group all together. What surprised him more was the change that took place though.

Where they had stopped initially it was all cut down woods with many stumps and sticks and it was cold and dreary. Now the area had been transformed to a beautiful field of soft green grass. Small young trees sprouted from the ground but nothing separated the people. Some of their gear had been taken up into the higher branches of the trees and Zarron found it rather amusing watching the people try to get them down. The woods around them had sprouted up and were a bright green as if it was spring. The sun beat down and spread an incredible amount of heat in the area. A small creek twisted and turned and wound itself through the camp. None of it touching the people but once again some of their gear wound up getting quite wet. Birds could even be heard bringing life to the air with their singing. The entirety of the scene that lay before him took his breath away. In his time on the Fenrir and by the looks of all the people he was watching, never has a change occurred on this side of the Fenrir like it.

He watched the area for a few more minutes than he focused his mind and began his task of breaking down the tent. Just as he was finishing up the familiar voice of Durakon caught his attention.

"So Zarron what do you make of this?" Durakon asked from behind. He turned and looked at Durakon for a few moments then up at the sky.

"Well I am not sure to be honest. I have never heard of this before not even in stories. I guess in some sense I am kind of scared but at the same time I am marveled by it. It does give good life to everyone though it would seem. This is good for us that means we can make fast time."

"Indeed you are correct. No trudging through snow and waist deep drifts. But, at the same time I am worried about it just the same." Zarron nodded his head in agreement.

"Well I dear say we must get moving. If you wouldn't mind could you lend me a hand right quick with loading the pack horse it would be appreciated. Then once that is done we can attend to the point of getting everyone moving." Zarron asked Durakon politely who was more than pleased to help. Within a few minutes they finished and when they turned to work on getting everyone together they found Partaxis had already stepped up and was taking control of getting the camp moving. He was barking orders left and right and pointing people out to do this and that. The whole time people were following without question or delay and within 2 hours' time the whole camp was packed and moving.

"That must be a new record of some sort Partaxis. I have never seen people follow someone so well. Working on applying for your self-fulfilled divinity?" Durakon jested with Partaxis.

"I am going to move ahead and scout out what our path looks like ahead of us. Make sure there are no unpleasant surprises." Durakon said to Partaxis as he patted his shoulder before moving on ahead. Partaxis who knew his skill at scouting was unrivaled didn't question his judgment in the least bit. He just nodded his head and watched him take off. He turned his attention back to the party and got them under way.

Zarron chose to ride towards the rear of the party. Being back there he was mostly left alone and as he rode he looked up to the sky and closed his eyes soaking in the warm sun. It felt nice not having to worry about redoing his runes or anything of the sort.

"Zarron I see your talisman tricks have done well. Quite an impressive feat for an Elite of the Nameless." A familiar voice spoke to him bringing his focus back to the area around him rather than the sky.

"Why thank you Tombah I will take that in high regards coming from a master wizard such as you. But alas you did help mass produce them I had just done one and you copied them. If anything you should be the one receiving the praise not I." Zarron smiled at Tombah. Tombah gave a halfhearted chuckle.

"What are you going to do about your little incident with Mary and the god's fight over you?" Tombah asked the question in a little more of a colder tone than he would have expected.

He stared at Tombah with furrowed brows. He was rather disturbed by the tone which Tombah took.

"Well if you must know I intend to report to the Church as soon as we are back at the Fenrir and I have given my report to the Commander." He replied with a hint of annoyance in his voice.

"Are you really going to mention to The Hand that his daughter betrayed him and The Nameless One?" Tombah asked in a calmer tone then the icy one he had taken up before.

"I haven't thought that one through...I may...or may not..." his voice trailed off.

After his reply they rode in silence together for some time. It was enough time for him to forget the cold tone that Tombah had given him earlier and the silence was rather welcoming. It gave him time to enjoy the environment around him. After some time when the sun was high in the sky Partaxis called the line to a halt for a break for lunch. At that time Tombah took his leave and proceeded elsewhere in the camp. As soon as he left Partaxis approached.

"Hail Zarron how are you enjoying it back here by yourself? You are missing out on all the women and life of the line here." Partaxis said with a hearty tone.

"Just enjoying some time to myself for I know after we are back to the Fenrir I will not have much time to myself aside from the ride to the Church to report the events and take council with The Hand of the Nameless and the Voice of the Nameless. They may have an idea of what it all means and how it plays into my life. I might also be able to convince them to send more members of the Church to help defend the Fenrir for I fear a great attack is in the near future." Zarron said in response to Partaxis.

"I think you are right, well those matters aside, feel free to take some time to relax, either with us or away from us as you have been. We will be getting ready to head out and be on our way within the hour." Partaxis smiled at him then patted his shoulder before turning back to the camp.

He watched him peer around the line of people searching for something. His gaze landed on two women. He approached them in a few large strides and wrapped his arms around the two of them. The women jumped in surprise, however once they realized who it was they didn't resist, in fact they melted into his arms and looked upon him with bright, adorning eyes as he began regaling some tale or another of his adventures. Zarron shook his head and laughed to himself before heading towards a tree close by.

He tied his horse up to it and he began wiping it down. As he was out there he picked up on someone coming up from behind him and he knew almost right away who it was.

XIV

"You know Sheen if you keep sneaking up on the camp you increase your chances of getting caught and then what good would that do?" Zarron spoke plainly.

"Is that concern in your voice Zarron Ra Holyrage?" She replied in a playful voice.

"If I was to say it might be, what would you think Sheen?"

Sheen smiled sweetly at him. "The woods whisper your Holyrage name and Undead fear it why is that?"

"For someone that was supposed to be your "foe" again you sure wish to know much about me." He asked in a light tone, the stress he had been bearing melted away.

"Well there can always be a change of plans and from what I have seen I wish to know you better. The more I hear and see of you the more intrigued I am." Sheen smiled back at him and moved ever so closer. It wasn't long before she came right up to him and placed her hands on his shoulder and moved her lips close to his ear. He could feel the warmth of her body her scent of pleasant earthly smells intoxicating. He couldn't help but shiver imperceptibly.

"I know what your heart feels right now." She whispered ever so softly into his ear and then she backed off from him and stared into his face. The words Sheen said sank deep into his soul and something in him stirred. A single tear fell down his cheek. Before he could say anything more Sheen kissed away the tear ever so softly and gently and put her finger to his lips. "Someone is coming." Sheen said to him dreamily.

He looked away for a moment to identify who it was and when he turned around Sheen was nowhere to be found. To his surprise he felt a pang of loneliness. The person that approached him appeared to be one of the soldiers of the Fenrir.

"Zarron there is someone we have caught coming right into our camp. We need you at the front." The soldier reported. Zarron looked at him impatiently before scanning the woods for Sheen. There was no sight of her, he let out a sigh. The last thing he wanted to do was to go and see a camp prisoner. The soldier shifted uneasily and tapped his foot as if he were in a hurry.

"Don't tap your bloody foot at me I will go and see what it is our Lord Partaxis wants. Lead the way." He snapped at the soldier in a tone sharper than he had intended it to be. Almost instantly guilt spread through him.

"My apologies to you fellow brother of the Fenrir, I meant no offense to you, for you are just following orders. Will you accept my apology?" Zarron reached out his hand. It took a moment for the soldier to comprehend what had just happened. He accepted the abrupt and sudden apology gladly.

"This way Zarron." The soldier said to him as he took off at a brisk walk. It wasn't long before Partaxis's loud voice could be heard yelling at someone. As the view of the scene came into play he almost laughed aloud. For before him was Partaxis red in the face from yelling at another man who was smaller in frame and stature. The smaller man continued to look upon Partaxis unflinching and stalwart before the enormous and spectacular verbal onslaught. Before the smaller man was 4 of their soldiers beat up and bruised. The rest of the group created a circle around the one man with their weapons drawn.

"Now my dear giant is that the best you can offer me? Some meager soldiers? Do not toy with me giant one. You almost insult my person by sending in such weaklings to oppose me. My offer is still the same I will not follow your rules for I live by my own. But, I must say if you just asked I would have been more than willing to give up my sword and have a gentle talk." The smaller man said.

It was at this time Partaxis saw Zarron approach. It was good timing as well for he just picked up his weapons and was ready to enter the rink with the man. As with Partaxis taking notice of Zarron the smaller man did as well.

"Ahh excellent someone with some brains that I am more than willing to talk to. How fare you Elite of the Church?" The smaller man said as he attempted to get closer to shake Zarron's hand but was stopped short by the men that created the circle.

"Let him pass men." Zarron ordered much to the displeasure of Partaxis who had much anger in his eyes. But within moments he calmed down and threw his hands in the direction of him not caring about this situation any further. As the man approached him, he got a better look at him and found he was just a few inches shorter than him. His hair was dark nearly black and was down to his shoulders. His skin color was quite light, nearly pale and his eyes were a fierce green, yet overall there was a calm about him that was hard to describe. He knew the man had seen many battles and the way he carried himself showed him that he must be quite good. On the same hand he could clearly see the lack of care for authority.

He wore a black leather jerkin that was masterfully made. On his back he had a heavy cloak which was to be expected any time in the cold northern lands. His boots were worn down leather showing he spent a good portion of his time walking or running place to place and found little use for horses. On him he had many different weapons and flasks. He had at his side a fine looking sword that upon closer inspection could see it was magickal. On his other side he had another sword that was silver. Along the sword belt he had flasks of what looked to be holy water and some healing vials. There were other small pouches he had that he couldn't begin to guess what they held. Also hitched on his back was a large battle-axe.

The minute the man shook his hand he felt a strong connection to him as well. It was as if he knew him from somewhere, but not from a person in his past but perhaps a person from his future. He could tell the man felt the same way as well for an almost unnoticeable look of confusion replaced his normal passive countenance. He immediately remedied the situation and once more the passive mask fell into place.

"Pardon the men if they were difficult. These past few days have been something hard to describe and many strange things have happened. I am Zarron Ra Holyrage and as you know I am an Elite in the Church of The Nameless. The larger guy over there is our leader of sorts. He is one of the few remainders left of the "Black Army." He explained to the man in a calm steady voice.

"I am Raamok; don't ask for my last name for one does not exist. If there was one that did it died when my family was ruthlessly murdered by vampires." His voice was rough and coarse, clearly social skills were not something he pursued.

"Raamok aye? That is a name I shan't forget. I am sorry to hear about your family but I assume because of their untimely deaths you have turned to hunting vampires?"

"Yes I intend to kill every last one of them. Those damnable beasts deserve a fate at the end of my sword in which I intend to ensure they are to never rise again and be damned forever. There are not a good lot of them out there."

"So Raamok you are on a course set on vengeance. Do be careful those paths usually lead to never being happy. You wrap yourself so much up into it all you forget about little things that were happy and important in your life. You also feel more often than not, empty after the fact because you had focused all your life's energy into killing that one monster, and so once that monster is dead what more is there for you?"

"Peace that is what I want from it. Peace knowing that I sent every one of those damned beasts to hell. You have no idea what it is like to lose everything because of them." Rage flared in Raamok's eyes.

"Oh? I don't have an idea about it you say? Well I disagree my life has been very similar to yours. I have lost all that I care for because of demons and evil in general. But, I can tell you revenge is not the way to go you still feel empty afterwards."

"I want none of your preaching Elite of the Nameless. I intend to find out myself if it is worthwhile. I don't care about the feeling afterwards for I will face them than. What I want now is to kill as many of the bastards as possible."

"As you wish Raamok, now what is it you are looking for on the northern wilds past the Fenrir?" Zarron asked changing the subject knowing this man had his mind set in stone.

"I have come to find out that a great Liche has traveled on this side and with him he had many vampires. I intend on killing every last one of them." Raamok said fire flashing in his eyes at the idea of spilling more of their kind's blood.

"If you mean to say you are looking for Fervver and his clan. Look no further for they are finished off. Fervver himself was killed by my hands and the faith I possess. His clansmen died by the hands of werewolves, Partaxis and myself. His clan is no more." He said to Raamok in a matter of fact way.

"Well bloody Hell there goes some more kills to rack up. But I suppose it makes no difference if they are killed by my hand or another's just so long as they are dead. Isn't that right Zarron?" He opened his mouth to reply. Before he had time to form words Raamok clapped his hands together, brushing off the dust of the road.

"Well I guess then that is it for me here, on to the South again. I hear there is a great vampire lord that reigns there. Some say he goes by the name of Rynn Shadowlore." With that Raamok got up and gathered himself and started to head out.

"Hold on a minute Raamok, if you wish to kill vampires in large numbers I can guarantee you that in the near future there will be a great battle on the Fenrir in which many vampires will be in the enemy horde along with many other dark and dangerous creatures. We could use a good hand in keeping the Fenrir and all of the world's lands safe from the danger beyond it." Raamok paused for a moment then returned, stopping a pace or two from him.

"Perhaps Zarron, we will see I will keep an eye and ear open for those times and maybe I will meet you again there. But, in the meantime I have too much to do to keep idle waiting on a cold northern wall. I do hope we shall meet again." Raamok held out his hand for Zarron to take. He nodded his head and gladly shook his hand. As they finished Raamok turned and started to run back in the direction of the Fenrir.

"He is much faster than most men are I must say." Zarron said to himself as he watched Raamok quickly draw away.

Shortly after the visit from Raamok the party was packed up and ready to move again. Zarron went to help heal the wounded but found they had suffered no serious injuries. They were just beat up pretty good and slightly bruised. He knew that within a week they will be better, perhaps even sooner.

The party traveled at a brisk pace the rest of the day. It wasn't long before the large looming Fenrir appeared on the horizon. It stood against the bright colors of the sun set as a dark spot. It was as if the Fenrir itself was the night rushing in on the land before it's time. The party was called to a halt as it reached the limits of the magickal changing land and it was there they rested on the edge of what seemed to be two worlds.

The area they were in was still beautifully green and warm but if you took a few steps in the direction of the Fenrir the land would get suddenly very cold and snowy. Much is the usual for the Northern Lands. The camp set up in a long line along the border. There was much rejoicing for the soldiers of the Fenrir for they knew that they would soon be on the other side of the immense barrier in the safe lands curled up in their beds, with the roaring fires. They also knew it was the last they would be able to enjoy their time before having to go back to work. So the soldiers of the Fenrir celebrated. While the freed captives remained scared and worried. For they didn't know what was to become of them the following day. They had no more homes to go back to and they feared the Fenrir.

Zarron himself was eager to finish with tomorrow's journey and head for the church to ask the questions that have been plaguing him since the whole queer journey began. His mind was full of thought and wonder and as he lay down, sleep remained elusive for some time. Eventually he found it but it was anything but restful. His mind was plagued by a terrible vision. One that was sparked because of meeting the vampire slayer Raamok.

Zarron found himself staring out at a vast scene of colors and images beyond anything this world could offer. He stood in front of a mighty gate that easily could have had 33 men on horses stand next to each other and enter with no problem. In front of him spread out large rivers or what seemed like large rivers. One seemed to be flowing light with colors that no man has seen. The other seemed to be a river of blood and darkness. Finally a third appeared that seemed to be gray and dull in color. The gray one changed more colors than any of the other. It was like watching a magnificent Rainbow give birth in front of you, dies then return to life.

As he looked at the rivers more carefully he found that they didn't flow down the mighty mountain and away, but flowed up to it. As he turned to look upstream he found a magnificent castle standing there. The walls easily towered over the Fenrir. The massive towers went hundreds of feet higher and the main keep was higher yet. It was so high you couldn't see the top of it as it disappeared into the sky above. It was there that he had to guess was where the rivers flowed to. As he looked back out at the gate at the massive valley that lay before him he could see it would have been a beautiful place was it not for the massive armies that numbers were like that of the sands of the sea. The armies seemed to stretch for as far as the eye could see yet not so far to be out of the valley.

Tall pavilions and tents could be seen that had many standards of gods he had never known existed. There were monsters out there that were unlike anything he had seen in his world. Dragons and demons constantly flew above the encampment in lazy circles, every once in a while one would break away and speed off to some unknown destination. The sun itself was blotted out by a great darkness yet where he was, was one of the only sources of light. The only other sources of light was the keep behind him and the strange glow the rivers created.

As he looked down at himself he found he was covered in blood and gore. Blood dripped from the locks of his hair and his sword was covered in so much blood he was hardly able to understand how he could hold onto it. He also found that he was nearly naked except for a loin cloth. Upon further examination he realized he was armored with Light and was covered in heavenly fire. The blue glow of runes on his body could be seen trying to burst out from the blood that covered them.

As he continued to examine his body more he found he had massive Angelic wings that were made of feathers from light. His shield was a glowing cross with another cross in the middle that turned to a sword. From the cross spawned angel wings and a halo. He knew it instantly as the symbol of the Nameless. There was also a massive rune on his chest that was the same symbol. Eventually as he looked around his eye sight changed to something unbelievable. They became aglow with blue fire and it gave him a view of the field like nothing he had ever experienced. He knew with the aid of the fiery glow, what he was fighting and the individual weakness of them.

His mind became sharper and somehow he was able to gather and perceive intelligence on enemy flanking maneuvers. He even knew how many there were and his heart sank with the truth of that number. As he looked around he found one companion with him and behind him he didn't need to look but he knew that the Nameless One himself was there. Aside from those two there were no others standing with them.

He peered at his companion and found him just as strange looking. He could instantly tell that the one next to him had demon blood in him but oddly enough he could sense the good in him. He knew all of a sudden he was looking at an Aemon and he himself was an Arch Angel. The Aemon had large dragon like wings that were a stark gray color. As he looked closer though he found they changed colors much likes the middle river that flowed like a rainbow. Yet his colors were black, shades of red and blue. They always shifted depending on what power he was utilizing at the time. He seemed to be a neutral being that mainly chose to serve good but could still tap into darker powers if he needed to.

As he continued to study the Aemon he could almost recognize the face. However his mind couldn't quite piece it together, then it hit him like a hammer, he was the vampire hunter he had met earlier that day, Raamok. Pleased with himself on determining who it was he took the time to continue his examination of the impressive being.

He used two great swords that had words written in some language Zarron had never seen. He wielded them with dark black gauntlets. The armor he wore was more visible than what Zarron was wearing and looked simply diabolical. Many spikes covered the armor. His skin was similar to Zarron's in the fact that it was covered in runes, which was where the similarities ended.

His were red runes instead of the blue. His skin was a dark color as well. The closer you looked at him the more he seemed to remind you of death and Zarron looked at himself and he found he looked more like Life.

The Aemon or Raamok bowed his head slightly towards Zarron and he returned the gesture with a salute. They turned to face the great army that lay before them. The enemy came rushing at them with great fury and gnashing of teeth. They took their stand with equal ferocity. As the forces collided, he was shocked awake as a loud bang of thunder woke him from his sleep.

He was barely able to get his sense of balance and reality before a figure burst into his tent.

XV

"Mary!?" The words blurted from Zarron's lips as he was shocked.

"Here lay down. Did anyone see you come in here?" Zarron said hurriedly as he looked outside the tent and saw lightning flash, immediately after, thunder shook the earth and torrents of rain came pouring down. The only motion outside in the camp was the dark outline of people rushing to and fro getting to cover.

"No, no one saw me Zarron." Mary said quietly her voice tinged with pain.

"What's wrong Mary, are you hurt?" Zarron asked concern etching his very words. He said a magick word and created a small glow in his tent and his heart sank as he looked at the condition of Mary. She was very pale, a huge gash in her side was crudely bandaged and many smaller cuts and bruises were across her torn and battered clothing. She was drenched to the skin.

"Mary let me attend to those wounds right away." Zarron placed his hands on her largest gash and Mary reached up her hand and stopped him.

"No Zarron, my time is near. It is too late for me. I need to warn you of things." Mary stopped her sentence as she went into a coughing fit blood could be seen on her hand as she covered her mouth. Zarron remained staring at her tears filling his eyes.

"Za..rr.on be warned, Fervver was not the leader, nor wa...s I. A much str...onger being leads the Northlands...its name is Thead. Dark powers are unleashed…" Her voice trailed off as she lost strength.

"Please Mary you have said enough. Just breathe." He replied calmly holding back his tears. He brushed back her hair ever so gently and wiped away the tears that ran down her face.

"You were always so beautiful to me." Zarron said to her as he brushed away her hair and wiped her tears. Her lips quivered with the gentle touch. The two of them sat together listening to the rain fall heavily. Her eyes never left his. She licked her lips after a moment and spoke.

"You were always handsome to me." There was a pause.

"Zarron I am so sorry...I betrayed everything I had and I gained nothing out of it...You were my treasure the whole time I was just too blind to see it." Mary said as she weakly brought her hand up to his face and touched it ever so gently. He quickly grabbed her hand and pressed it to his cheek. He brought it close to his lips kissing the soft skin. His tears dropped down and wetted her hand.

"I forgive you and I know The Nameless One and your father will as well...I love you Mary." He said sniffling as he did his best to keep from outright crying. Tears still fell but no sobs came.

"Thank you…Zarron…..can you...hold me one last time?" The length of time became further between Mary's words as her life slowly left her.

Zarron brought her close lifting her up and placed her in his lap and cradled her there. She was cold, her warmth leaving at an alarming rate.

"Mary I can't handle losing you a third time." Tears freely flowed from him wetting Mary's hair as it was pressed into his chest. Mary pulled herself out from his grip and looked him in the eyes. The old Mary was seen on her face the one that he loved and cared for, for the many years he knew her. She gave him a weak smile.

"I will see you again...Kiss me please." Mary labored to say. He pressed his lips to hers and all the sweet memories of the two of them came flooding back to him; the familiar taste and the tenderness of her kisses. Her sweet laughter that he heard every day he could and even her beautiful eyes that were always so full of life and energy from the day he saved her a lifetime ago.

"I love you...Zarron Ra Holyrage I have always loved you. My priceless star in the dark world around us, you gave me life and you showed me what it was. Thank you." Mary said as she finished kissing him. Those were the last words he would ever hear from her. Her eyes drooped heavily, once, twice. They never opened after the third. The breath of life no longer was in her.

"No, please no Mary." He said between sobs. He pulled her close and held her lifeless body tightly to him. The tears poured freely now. He let out a shuddered gasp as he looked at her again, his lips quivered and he started crying ever more so. He could no longer control the intense outpour of grief. He sat there and rocked himself with her in his arms till he could cry no more and the morning sun came up.

He finally laid her down and bit his lips as he felt more tears coming. He slowly and gradually grabbed her arms and crossed them on her chest. He put her legs together, brushing away her hair as he looked into her face. She looked at peace. Finally he grabbed his cloak and wrapped her body in it, kissing her forehead one last time before covering up the face lastly. As he finished covering her, Durakon popped his head into the tent to fetch him.

"Zarr..on." He stopped before he could say more and knelt down in the entrance. Durakon knew without questioning who the person was that Zarron had wrapped.

"She is to be carried quickly to her father in the Church and with no delay. I will personally be an escort for her. Send a faster rider ahead of us to have the Church meet up with us." Zarron said exhaustedly with no emotion in his voice.

Durakon nodded his head, he quickly turned to head out.

"Durakon, if anyone asks she is to be buried a hero and as the daughter of The Hand of the Church." Zarron said to him sternly.

Durakon nodded his head once more and took off. Within minutes there was a litter brought forth and some of the fastest horses with a fine wagon. They had it all latched within minutes. Zarron went into the tent. With the help of Durakon, Partaxis and Tombah they picked Mary's body up and set it gently on the wagon.

Zarron grabbed another horse and led the team of horses along with the wagons hurriedly to the Fenrir. As he approached the massive wall he saw that the enormous gate of the fortress was open for him, something that had not been opened for at least several decades. The roads in the keep were lined up with the Fenrir's guardians all of them with their polished armor and dressed in their finest cloaks. Each one held a Rose and Firesow. Firesow was a special herb that is said to keep the body fresh for a longer period of time and ward unnatural creatures from touching the body. It wasn't long before the cart was covered with the gifts for the departed. They piled in around her body yet none touched the body or rested on the body. All that was placed on her was a medallion of the symbol of the Nameless created from magick. As he approached the last keep door before entering the open country he was stopped by Commander Froth.

"My dear Zarron, I am sorry for your loss. I." He paused for a moment.

"We, knew what she meant to you. I hope you don't intend to leave with just yourself especially with the country being covered with many bandits. I will put you together a group of soldiers that will go with you." Commander Froth said his words sympathetic.

"That cannot do m'lord, only members of the church can escort a fellow member's body. The only way there is an exception is if the one that fell was the only member of the church. If that was the case though they should be burned. Their ashes sent back to the church. I am sorry sir that I cannot accept the help. My safety and the safety of Mary's body is in the hands of The Nameless, there are no better protectors than that. What you can do is prepare the Fenrir for an invasion. Start strengthening the battlements and increase your numbers. Send riders to all the great cities and recruit as many as possible. I say you have 3 months at the most before an army will be at the Fenrir. I will be back in 2 months at most. One month for mourning and the second month for gathering what I can from the church." He replied to the Commander in a tired, drained tone. He stretched out his hand for the Commander to shake. Commander Froth took his hand and shook it.

"I say if your God protects you and brings you back with men then I say I would like to know more of him." Commander Froth nodded his head once more and Zarron continued with his journey. Zarron said a prayer to The Nameless as the great gates of the keep of Korilith shut behind him. When they shut the very earth shook and as the locks fell in place it sounded of thunder.

For three days he traveled not speaking a word and not eating a thing. The rain that had started what seemed like weeks ago on the night of Mary's death had continued constantly. He didn't care though it reflected his mood.

He tugged at the corners of his soaked hood willing it to repel the rain. The gesture was largely out of habit he realized, since the cloak had long been drenched through. Oddly enough the rain was warmer than it was cold and it actually kept his body warm. As it was he was pleased that no thieves hassled him but, that only lasted so long before he came upon a blockade on the road. Several men in ragged looking clothes and rusty weapons barred his way.

"Hail to you fellow traveler. Go no further unless you pay the toll." One of the bandits said to him. He was by far the ugliest one of the group. His face was scarred and battered, his nose was knobby and many of his teeth missing. Zarron looked at him with a scowl and disgust.

"I have no wish to fight you, nor do I have plans of paying you. Leave me be and you shall live. That, is your only option. My business is on the direct orders of The Nameless One for I carry one of his blessed children's bodies." he spit the words at him in anger.

"You think that makes you exempt from the toll of these roads? I think not. For you are in no position to make the rules. You are by yourself and carting a dead body with you, I say you pay up, or, we kill you and leave you and the body here for the beasts of the woods to eat." The leader of the bandits said back in a smart tone. He started to move in on Zarron with his group of 4 others.

"Wrong choice you worthless scum, you should know to pick your battles better and bring with you more than 4 thugs." He fired the words off at the man jumping down from his horse and unsheathing Angel Fire.

Something in him blazed to life. He felt his muscles bulge with unknown strength, his vision almost became tunnel vision yet he could still see all around him. Another odd thing that took place was the land shifted in color and hue. It turned into a bright blue field, every little motion created a cascade of different colors.

The thugs in front of him lit up in the darkest of all colors. It was as if he could sense all their evil they had committed. Yet, he could also see what good they did by a different color scope. It was as if he could reach out and touch either the evil or the good and destroy it or save it, instead of waging battle with the person he waged battle against their evil, and it strengthened him immeasurably. He felt his heart rate slow down and with it, it seemed like time itself slowed.

He took a couple steps towards the nearest man. When he got close he lunged at him sinking Angel Fire deep into his stomach. He tore it free and decapitated another with a quick stroke. He spun and disemboweled a third. He brought the blade around utilizing the momentum he gained and slashed another across the chest. On the return stroke he split the man's face in two. He stopped his blade on the fifth's man throat. All of it was over in a blink of an eye and not a single one had a chance to figure out what was going on before they were dead. The fifth bandit being the farthest back was the only one with time to react. He stopped in his tracks and dropped to his knees.

"Please don't kill me; I just need to eat is all." The fifth one begged him.

"If all you needed was food you could have gone to the Church of The Nameless One and spoke to them there. But, instead you chose a life of robbing travelers and defiling people. No doubt you have even participated in rape and murder more than once. What possible reason do I have to give you mercy?" he yelled at the man. The man remained on his knees crying.

"What reason do you deserve mercy scum?" he demanded of the man pushing the tip of his sword into his throat, drawing blood.

It was at that point that several things happened all at once. The man before him pissed himself and blubbered on spitting and asking for mercy over and over again making a sad example of him-self. There was a crack of thunder and the Nameless One spoke loud and clear to him. *This one is to be spared and given the mark for choosing to defile one of the dead that served in my church.* Then after the voice of the Nameless a human voice that was recognizable came from in front of him.

"Zarron I know little of you but I know this is not your character." Sheen spoke coming from the woods in front of him. He breathed in deeply, his body shook. His eye's twitched in anger at the unjust man in front of him but after another second he let out his breath. He removed his sword from the man's throat and sheathed it. The vision he had faded away, the earth returned to its normal colors and he felt his heart beat normal again; his extra strength had left him as well. Shaking away the feeling he grabbed the man by the tunic and tightened his grip on him.

"You shall live under one circumstance. That is you will enter the service of the Nameless One, he is more than willing to forgive beasts like you. If you enter his service in the Church of The Nameless, and if you are truly sorry for any of the horrible deeds you have done, you can survive the purifying ritual, and you will be a changed man. You will be well fed and paid. You have exactly one week to get yourself there and if I find you had not showed up there I tell you that the Nameless One will strike you down in the most horrible ways. That gives you one week to think of what you have done and beg for forgiveness of the evil you have done. For if you participate in the purifying ritual and are found that you have not repented for your evil you shall be killed. In order to let you know I am serious I am going to mark you and that will be your timer. If by the week's end you have not showed up at the Church and had the Clerics there remove it, it will strike you dead in the worse of ways." He said to the man in a cool, calm and stern voice. He placed his hand on the man's chest and burned the mark into his skin with magick.

"You can't do that! You can't make me." The man said in a disgusting weasel tone.

"But I can and I have. I warned you to pick your fights better and not to disturb me for I am on direct business of The Nameless One. Yet, you, despite all these warning continued with your attempt at robbing me and threatening to defile the body of a daughter of the Nameless One's church. You are lucky you even have a chance to live and live a good life in the service of the Church to be fed and clothed properly. Do you understand you pathetic man?" He stared hard at the man boring holes into his pathetic soul. The man's brows pulled together, his lips stretched tight. He watched him go through the whole spectrum of emotions before he finally spoke.

"Yes I understand, what shall I tell them when I get there?" The man asked.

"Say nothing; I would suggest saying nothing to any one until you get there. But, if, and when you get there you still say nothing. Just show them the mark on your chest, you need not to do more. Remember I would say nothing to any person up until that point. That way you will not have your mind changed by people. You thoughts should be your own. For you have much to find in your heart repentance for. Now be gone and I will be looking for you once I get there." He said to the man in a hard tone. He watched him run down the road and disappear around a bend before turning his attention to Sheen.

"Come; walk with me for I can't spare to lose a moment of time. We will talk more as we move." He spoke in a gentle tone to Sheen.

"I have never seen someone kill so fast in my life. What was that?" Sheen asked with great interest.

"I don't know Sheen; I think I get into these types of moods much like a berserker. But, when I go into these rages they are purely righteously driven to finish off evil people. I think the reason is because of my Holyrage blood. The Holyrage house were great slayers of evil because they could go into such rages. It was odd though it seemed like I was waging war with just the evil in them. I am going to be honest with you. I don't know what is going on with me and I don't know how to control it either." Zarron looked where he thought Sheen was. To his surprise she was not there. As he looked around in shock he spotted her as she was looking at Mary's body.

"She was your lover wasn't she?" Sheen asked almost too herself but to Zarron as well.

"Yes, yes she was."

XVI

Silence filled the air for some time. Sheen had returned to walk by Zarron. She would look over at him and would be filled with such sympathy for the holy warrior. The mysterious connection she had with him also made it so she could feel the pain in his heart. The idea of the connection still didn't make any sense to her. She wanted to ask him if he felt a similar connection but she couldn't bring her heart to do that just yet.

"Sheen, how is it you crossed the Fenrir?" His voice brought her out of her thoughts.

"Oh, uh well as you know I am a shape shifter, I may be in charge of one form but I can still change my form to what I please. However any form outside of a wolf or werewolf I can only hold for a few minutes. Needless to say when I saw what had happened from afar I knew that you would need to bring the body somewhere to bury it. So I ran to a less defended part of the Fenrir and as soon as I had a chance I turned into a fast bird and flew over. After I got to the other side I had to rest briefly in the woods to recover before I could pick up on your trail. Finally I caught up with you just as the bandits engaged you." She said proudly with her accomplishments.

"I see, look Sheen I really appreciate your company but I am afraid I will need to ask you to leave. As the law states only members of the Church may escort a body of the fallen unless there are no Church members present." Zarron spoke sadly, wishing he could have some form of company. He stopped and looked over at Sheen. He mustered up a little smile, took her hand and kissed it.

"I am heading to the city of Citadel Heights where a funeral will take place. You can find me there within the week. I warn you, I will not be great company for the month. For the first month will be of mourning. But, if you still wish to spend time with me I could show you the church grounds. Just head to the gates of the Church and ask for me." He instructed her. He looked at her for a few more seconds before mounting his horse again. "Thank you Sheen for all the help you offer, I fear I don't know how to repay you. Just be safe and maybe I will see you at The Church of The Nameless someday."

He ushered his horse onwards. He could hear Sheen in the distance mutter something about heading there and before long he was riding in silence again. The only noise to be heard was the horse breathing and the sound of the wagon clattering along. He rode at a rapid pace for the rest of the day. Soon the sun went down and the moon rose into the air casting its sullen blue light upon the world around him. Finally Frost River came into view. He slowed the horses to a stop at the banks of the mighty river. He dismounted to give the horses a much needed break. He could walk them across, it would be safer in the dark anyhow.

He grabbed sugar from his travel pack and fed each of the horses with some of it. After a moment of rest he walked them across the Frost River and decided to camp for the rest of the night. The moon was just reaching its peak by the time he disconnected the horses from the wagon and unsaddled them. He gave them all a quick wipe down and brought them to a small stream that was close by and within sight of the wagon.

He tied the horses up and drank deep from his waterskin. His stomach rumbled with hunger. He willed it to be quiet for fasting was part of the mourning process and he would not falter in that. He knew that protocol for any member except the Voice or The Hand was too fast for three days unless on the battlefield. For the men needed their strength to fight. But, he respected and loved Mary and since she was the Daughter of The Hand he chose to fast for seven days as if The Hand or The Voice died.

After drinking the last of his water he knelt down at the back of the wagon and he prayed over Mary. He didn't know how long he had been doing the praying before sleep finally took over and as he slept his dreams did nothing to comfort him. Over and over again the image of the great battle he was staring at repeated itself. It never seemed to get any longer or shorter, just the same dream on repeat. It wasn't long before the sun kissed the landscape and brought the world around him to life with brilliant colors.

Upon waking he gathered the horses and began saddling them and reconnecting the wagon. The jingling of horse reigns and the thunder of cavalry coming from up the road a little ways pulled him from his task. He pulled his sword free and went to the center of the road, prepared to meet any threat head on. He would defend her until there was no breath left. He tensed as the noise came closer, the moment seemed to stretch eternally. His body ached as he stood tensed and ready to take on this unknown threat, his hand screaming in protest at the strain of gripping the sword as tightly as he was. The slow resounding thunder of hooves drawing ever nearer.

Finally a large party of armored and mounted men appeared on the road. He peered at them for a moment then gave a sigh of relief as he recognized the bright banner of The Nameless One snapping in the wind. The group was an entire cavalry unit easily numbering in the hundreds. Behind the colors of the Nameless, he spotted the color of the unit flying in the wind as well. He immediately recognized the crimson and white colors as the Holy Hammerers. The Hand's elite cavalry unit. It was the best the Church of the Nameless had to offer, never have they been defeated in battle.

As he watched them draw close, he saw that they were donned in the traditional dark cobalt, deep gray and black garments for mourning. Leading the unit was Lord Ashen himself, The Hand of the Nameless. He immediately knelt, bowing his head as the unit approached. They halted a few feet in front of him. The dust they kicked up was settled immediately as Lord Ashen dismounted his horse speaking a word of magick. All the men in the unit dismounted as the Lord had and they all knelt as a sign of respect for the fallen.

Lord Ashen's powerful shadow cast over Zarron as he stood above him.

"Why do you bow so low Zarron Ra Holyrage?" Lord Ashen asked speaking in a calm voice. He couldn't help but notice the hint of pain and mourning on his voice as well.

"M'lord I am disgraced by the events of the past few weeks. I have doubted my faith, marked a man and I have failed you in getting your daughter back alive." He replied humbly, holding back tears as he remembered Mary.

"Rise my Son; you have done no such thing as failure. I asked you to find what became of my daughter. The mark is a sad thing to put on someone but I trust you did it with the greatest instructions from The Nameless One above. Your doubt in your faith is something we will discuss at a later time when you speak with of The Voice of the Nameless and myself." Lord Ashen replied kindly. He offered his hand to Zarron. He accepted it and was pulled up by the immense strength of the Hand.

He glanced at this man he respected and found the Hands face drawn tight with mourning, but, there was a hint of peace there as well. The Hand patted his shoulder. He pressed a hand against Zarron's forehead and laid a blessing on him.

"You have done well and shall take the second place of honor on my daughter's left side. For it would be the place of her husband had she married. None other has treated her as close to a husband as you Zarron, and none so protective over her as well. Had I my way you two would have been wed some time ago. May you always be blessed and found in favor of The Nameless for all time." He raised his voice. "All glory to him The Nameless One."

"All Glory to Him The Nameless One!" The unit along with Zarron shouted in reply. Zarron's eyes welled with tears at the blessing that was bestowed upon him and the compliments of honor. The Hand turned towards his unit.

"Burial formation men, I shall take some time to be alone with my Daughter's body here then we shall move out." He issued his order in what seemed to be a normal calm voice. By some magick in one form or another it lifted up higher than all the surrounding noises. The command could be heard all the way towards the back of the unit. Like a perfectly orchestrated performance the unit all mounted back up falling into formation in a flawless disciplined manner.

The Hand moved to the cart and removed his daughter's face shroud. He wept over her for an hour's time while the unit waited patiently. Finally The Hand finished. He signaled his men to gather up the cart and put it in its proper place. The men fell into formation around it. Zarron followed suit and placed his unadorned, common mount next to Mary's left shoulder by her head while The Hand took his place on the right. The whole unit took off at a brisk walk. An aura of silence; thick and heavy lingered around the unit.

They travelled for another 3 days before topping a hill. Below them sprawled the city of Citadel Heights in all its glory and beauty. The walls were a beautiful masterpiece of white stone; large runes that glow a bright blue adorned the walls here and there. It brought a calmness to those approaching, and was a reminder of the depth and stability of the mighty city of the Nameless.

The gates were more impressive than the walls themselves. The main gate was made of dark hardened mahogany with bright blue streaks running through it with touches of gold and silver. The main road was made from the same white stone the walls were made of. The homes and city itself was beautiful masterpieces even the "run-down" area hardly marred the beauty of the city itself. The main road wound itself up the great hill and across the large bridges that arched over beautiful rivers of water that flowed and gave life to the city. The rivers fell off the side of the great cliffs from a pitcher that a giant stone statue of an Angel held. The river itself was fed from another great statue of an Angel holding a bowl. Their wings and height almost matched that of the Cathedral of The Nameless which sat atop the hill.

The Cathedral was really the true beauty of the city. It also played as the main bastion. Its buildings were made of magickal infused marble. The tallest towers held great crystals that grabbed the colors of the sky, cascading their decadence of colors across the whole city sending the beautiful array of light everywhere. It served as a reminder to the people that the Nameless Ones ever present glory was everywhere, while also serving as a beacon to the lost that there was hope.

There was one part of the city that was damaged and was not rebuilt yet since the great wars of times and times again. It was there that the perfectly smooth surface in the cliff was created by the great magick. It was there that Zarron knew where to look to find the massive willow tree that was part of the secret place Mary had shown him. The first time they had met. Beyond the secret place and the smooth cliffs sprawled the beautiful valley that many called home and many more worked to help support the city. Zarron had wanted to continue to take in the beauty for it seemed so long that he had laid eyes on it but, the unit continued forth forcing him to move with it.

It wasn't long before they were spotted by the city guard. The massive gates swung open for the unit soundlessly, a testimate to the care and craftsmanship that went into creating it. As they travelled through the city many people were out in the streets mourning, weeping and praying over Mary.

The whole city seemed to be in mourning, amidst the mourning there was a hint of joy for they all knew she would be with The Nameless One in his heavenly realm, resting in the peace and joy of their God.

Finally they approached the keep and found The Voice of The Nameless with Silent Sisters and Brothers awaiting them. The minute the body arrived at the steps of the cathedral, the Silent ones took the body away to prepare it for her final burial which was to be in the morning. The Hand dismissed the unit before joining the Voice and the silent ones.

Zarron and one other remained in the courtyard. The person that stayed behind was one of the Holy Hammerers. He looked over at him and the first time in the past week he smiled.

XVII

"Zeth, how are you my old friend?" Zarron asked his old time friend as he extended his arm out to him. Zeth took it and they shook hands.

"Well, my heart mourns for Mary and for you my friend. I am glad you were the last one with her before her death; I know she wouldn't have wanted it any other way." Zeth replied sadly, his voice rich with compassion.

"Thank you, I see you managed to get yourself into the Holy Hammerers and even gained the rank of Crusader that is magnificent. I know it was a goal for you for some time. Come, let's walk together." Zarron replied with a sad attempt at a cheerful voice. The week of fasting was definitely getting to him now and his body ached from the hard week of travel and the weeks before that as well. Zeth fell in place next to him. The two of them walked in silence for some time before Zeth spoke.

"Zarron, what has happened to you these past few weeks?" Zeth asked worriedly as he looked at him and could see his mind was not focused on anything in this world. It was focused on something far away.

"Time will tell Zeth I know word of things will be sprouting up soon enough but, in the mean time I am going to change into proper clothing and tomorrow I would like to break my fast with you after Mary's funeral. We can catch up on things then." He stopped in front of his chambers and turned towards Zeth. Zeth nodded his head in understanding, he knew him well enough to not push the issue. He knew that soon enough he would find out about all the adventures.

"It was good seeing you Zeth, congratulations on getting into the Holy Hammerers and your rank of Crusader. May the Nameless One smile upon you and bless you." Zarron mustered up a smile and placed a hand on Zeth's shoulder before heading into his chamber.

As he entered his chamber he found nothing had changed within it since he left last. The room was cared for by the cleaners and that was about it. So it didn't take him long to dig through his belongings and find the proper clothes for mourning.

He set some wood up in the hearth and with a word, magick lit the fire. He went over to his desk and opened one of the drawers. He pulled forth some incense from its depths. He threw the incense onto the fire and knelt before the mighty hearth breathing in the smell with slow, deliberate breaths. It wasn't long before he felt its effects working on him opening up his mind.

It was then that he began praying. He prayed a prayer unlike any before, he felt the full power of it carry itself to the heavens. He had lost track of time. When he finally opened his eyes he felt an intense and great fatigue fall upon him. He was barely able to pull himself to his feet.

With a groan he stumbled toward the sink. He splashed some water on his face. As he looked at himself in the mirror he reached up and touched the scar that was given to him not too long ago. His hand dropped and he stood looking into the mirror for some time. An intense feeling of loneliness threatened to overtake his mind. Several soft raps at his door blessedly brought him out of his trance. He went to the door and found a messenger awaiting him there.

"Hail Elite Zarron I have a note here from one of the High Clerics." The messenger held the note up to him. He took it from him and thanked him for his service. He closed the door behind him, he took the letter to his desk. He broke the seal and began to read.

Hail Elite Zarron,

I thank you for your mercy and compassion on the road. I have done all you have ordered me and have spoken to no one till the yester night. The person I spoke to was a member of the church, Priest Haggard. He took me to High Cleric Daniel and I went through the purification trial. Because of your special guidance I passed it and have retained my right to live. They have placed me in the serving branch of the Church. I have enjoyed it more than I would have thought. They gave me food and shelter and treated me as an equal not as the rag tag bandit thug I was beforehand. As soon as I found out you had made it in I asked to write to you and ask for your forgiveness. I understand my errors in my way and I am so sorry for disturbing the body of the daughter of The Hand. I do hope you find it in your heart to forgive me as The Nameless One has and thank you for giving me my life Elite Zarron Ra Holyrage.

Sincerely,

Frank Roggins

He couldn't help but smile upon reading the letter. He decided to write the man back and have someone deliver the message in the morning.

Hail High Cleric Daniel of the Church of the Nameless

I received tiding from the one I sent to you. I am pleased he passed the purification trial. Praise be to The Nameless. I ask of you to put him under my care for the next two months I am here, to tend to my belongings and room as I go about my business. If it is not too much trouble and there is no great need for him elsewhere. If it is not possible than let him know that I have forgiven him and appreciate what he has done.

In His Service,

Zarron Ra Holyrage Elite of the Church of the Nameless

He read through it once and pleased with the wording he sealed it. He placed it gently on the desk for a servant to take in the morning. He let loose a mighty yawn and decided he couldn't keep himself up any longer. He changed into his night clothes and fell into his bed. He was asleep as soon as his head hit the pillows.

He rose before the sun could kiss the land good morning. He threw on his clothes for mourning and headed out to meet with the procession that would take Mary's body to her final resting place. As he approached the courtyard he found it remarkably empty with the exception of The Hand of the Nameless and The Voice of the Nameless. He stopped an appropriate distance from leaders of the Nameless and bowed his head in respect to them. He was confused that it was only the three of them.

"Rise Zarron, if you are wondering what is going on we changed the plans. Mary was mourned all night, by the time the moon was at its highest we closed the doors to the wake room. You would be glad to know many people offered their prayers for her and many more left her flowers. We are going to take her body to the place I know she would want to be buried at." The Hand spoke directly, but kindly. He was still confused by the comment then all of a sudden understanding came upon him.

"We are going to bury her in the secret garden." He replied to no one in particular, his mind already thinking of the beautiful garden.

"Yes Zarron we are going to put her there for we know that is what she would want." The Voice of the Nameless finally spoke. Her voice sounded absolutely heavenly, warmth and peace entered his body and mind as she spoke. He gave a nod in agreement.

"Come Zarron you will have the honor to carry the urn." The Hand spoke to him as she presented the beautiful Urn to him. As he grabbed the Urn he got a closer look at it. He was amazed at the beautiful make of it. Silver and gold decorations along with runes danced across the deep blue urn. It seemed to catch all the light there was to catch. The light danced and played across the surface in purposeful manner. He cradled it gently in his arms, pressing it lovingly to his chest. The three of them marched on to where the Secret Garden was. The whole time The Voice sang a beautiful tune that filled the air yet its sound was not heard by any except who she chose. In this case The Hand, Zarron and herself. As she sang the Urn's runes swayed and danced to the melodic, solemn tune.

As they approached the wall they found the hidden entrance without hassle, it was as if it moved into place exactly where they walked. As they entered the garden the Sun was working its way skyward, the few rays of light from it also danced and moved with The Voice's tune. They found the grave close to the marble bench that overlooked the valley.

He knelt beside the grave holding the urn. It was difficult to release it. Tears began to fill his eyes. He knew that as soon as he placed her in the ground that was it. She would be gone forever from this world. Her presence would only be a memory. He hugged her close, he suppressed the sobs but there was nothing he could do about the tears, they fell freely and generously. He stared at the emptiness of the grave. A strong hand was placed on his shoulder as Lord Ashen knelt beside him. With the gentle gesture, Zarron couldn't contain his sobs anymore. He collapsed to the ground in a heap, the urn cradled in his lap and he cried. The Hand wrapped him in a fatherly embrace and the two of them cried together, the immense pain of their common loss drew them together in that moment. The Voice soon joined in and the three of them cried for the loss of a young daughter, who was taken too early.

After some time the world came into focus once more. The tune that the Voice had sang earlier could still be heard. The garden itself took it upon themselves to continue it. It was incredible. The three of them listened to the sweet melody for a few beautiful moments. Zarron shoved a hand to his eyes forcefully wiping away the tears. He took a few deep steadying breaths and after another moment he was finally able to lay the urn into its place. Lord Ashen helped lift him to his feet. He kept a steadying hand on him as he composed himself. He waited for three long heartbeats before he spoke.

"I..." he faltered briefly then found his strength and continued. "I am thankful I will see you again. For you are with The Nameless One above, you shall know nothing but peace, no more pain or hurt. Death and despair will not be able to touch you. You will be missed and this world is a little duller without you. I love you Mary." He choked back a sob, and tried to continue. However words would not come, he had said what he needed to.

The three of them huddled around the grave; they offered prayers and memories until the sunrise. As the sun rose a cascade of brilliant colors lit the sky around them. A silent voice was heard among them, it brought smiles to their mouth. They felt the peace of The Nameless fall heavy on the garden. The presence of their God warmed them, they closed their eyes and soaked in his glory. When their eyes opened once more they found the grave was filled in. A single deep purple flower popped through the soil.

"Come she is at peace now." The Voice spoke and without any hesitations the rest nodded their heads in agreement leaving the sanctuary to take pleasure in the most beautiful sunrise that any had seen. As they walked out The Voice hummed another tune that was filled with hope and joy. It faded away as they approached the courtyard. It was now filled with busy people moving to and fro.

"Now Zarron come with us we have much to discuss and many questions to answer, also a wonderful breakfast to break our fasts." The Hand spoke with a smile. Zarron nodded his head and smiled back. They set off in the direction of the great tower.

It wasn't long before the three of them were walking up the endless amount of stairs that led to the great chamber. As they approached the top and entered the room Zarron's breathe was taken away by the amazing beauty of the impressive chamber. He had never been in the Great Tower in his time at the church. He had been in The Hand's tower and he was sure the Voice's tower was just as magnificent but they both paled in comparison to the Great Tower.

Richly colored tapestries hung from the ceiling, each one had a beautiful piece of art sewn into it depicting great battles. Many more were adorned with the faces of the church's Hands and Voices through time. Large crystal pillars that ended with what looked like hand's reaching up to the heavens held up the great ceiling. The great ceiling itself was nearly 20' tall. It was donned with beautiful art depicting The Nameless One's heavenly kingdom. There was one large window in the room. It was a magnificent piece of art as well. It was crafted from thousands of different colors of glass that in the end depicted the symbol of the Nameless.

The room itself also had many ancient artifacts from the beginning of time and on. A large table was set in the middle that was the shape of a cross with the inner cross that ended in a sword. The different colored marble on the floor made up the wings of the symbol and at the head of it where the halo would be was a massive throne.

The throne was made of what looked like light but it was solid and one could not see through it. Upon further examination he realized it was actually pure gold. Many runes were carved into its surface, the runes had a beautiful silver blue hue that was pure in color. A silver design was put into the back of the chair, it was a design he was unfamiliar with and did not quite understand. He felt a warming sensation in his body that made him quiver with joy as he looked upon it. From the top of the throne there was a beautiful piece of stone crafted into an angel with a sword and shield in his hand. It watched and guarded the one that sat on the Throne. The Angel's massive wings spread out to the front enveloping the would be king that sat on the throne in a protective shield. He was so awe struck by the awesomeness of it all. He didn't notice the beautiful meal laid out for the trio.

"What stone makes that Angel m'lord and lady?" Zarron asked as he continued to stare at the Throne.

"It is made of a Fallen Star Zarron, a fallen star that came from the Nameless One to wipe out a great evil near the beginning of time. The answer to your next question you are to ask is that throne is a mere copy of what The Nameless One's throne is in his heavenly kingdom. We mortals can only do so much. The next question you will ask is a simple answer and that is no mortal is to sit on that throne it is reserved specifically for The Nameless One." The Voice answered Zarron's inquiries in her beautiful sing song voice.

"The Nameless One visits here? That is amazing." He replied more to himself than anyone else. As he finally looked away from the great throne he saw on the other side of the table set high upon a pillar a mighty sculpture of a dark ebony and red dragon hiding its face from the light of the throne. One of its mighty wings covered up its face from the throne attempting to thwart the light. The sculpture was amazing just as it was terrifying. He turned his face from it unable to look upon it any longer.

"The great ebony and red dragon means the evil of the world if I remember correctly." He asked. The Hand nodded his head.

"Indeed it does, you remember much from your studies Zarron, which is a good thing indeed. Now come, sit with us and let us enjoy a meal while you tell us your tale of the past few weeks." The Hand replied. He nodded his head in agreement and the three of them sat around the center of the cross at the table.

Zarron led the prayer for the group as the Voice and Hand gave him permission to do so. The meal before them was beautiful and wonderful. It was a meal made to serve the highest of kings. It didn't take long to figure out why that was. It was simply for the reason being, if The Nameless One joined them.

While they ate, Zarron explained to the group what he had been through. The entire time The Hand and The Voice listened intently not saying a word. They would nod their head at times reinforcing what Zarron chose to do or shift their eyes, glancing at one another when something unusual was brought up. He told them everything that had happened except for Mary's deceit. He had convinced himself that it would not change anything. After all without her redemption and sacrifice the enemy would still remain unknown.

"It sounds like there is a great many troubles on the horizon. Especially if the great Nameless One himself came down to Earth to fight the Faceless One to prevent him from deceiving you. That shows us great restlessness in The Heavens and Hells. Should war break out there it will easily spill onto the mortal plane. In fact I say it has already begun. We have been receiving reports of increased activity in the sentinel zones." The Hand spoke aloud for the sake of Zarron, but his main focus was on The Voice. She chewed her lip as she thought about the new information. The Hand waited patiently allowing her time to think and reply.

"As for the God's fighting over your favor, I couldn't tell you what the reason for that is. Lore says there will be a revival of someone that was lower than low and the last in a long line. If you ask us Zarron you could be that person. As far as we can tell you are the last pure blood of the Holyrage house. You also were a mere slave to anyone that could feed you for some time after your mother's death. We will tell you one thing and that is prepare. We cannot say what for. But, I am thinking there is going to be a Great War unlike any before pouring out from the Heaven and Hell on us. You must always look to the light and never give up hope." Her voice faded away as she looked to some far away point. The Hand spoke once more, this time addressing Zarron directly.

"Our biggest concern is what Mary's last words were. She warned you of Thead being a leader. If that is the case Zarron then the war has already begun. Thead is the evil guardian of the Faceless One himself. Be wary if you see him Zarron for he is stronger than you, The Voice and myself. If he indeed does lead an army and spills the blood of protectors of the Fenrir then we know that the Heaven and Hells are at war. We are entering dark times. Don't lose sight of the light." The Hand echoed The Voices last words. He spoke in a steady flat tone with a hint of trepidation. Zarron let a moment of silence pass, he was giving time for The Hand or Voice to continue. When they didn't speak after a moment he cleared his throat and spoke.

"Before I leave my Lord and Lady I have to ask what was it that came over me on the road with the thieves?"

"Zarron you know that answer. It was your blood line awakening within you. House Holyrage was mighty and powerful against evil because they could go into a Holy Rage as the name suggests." The Hand paused a moment collecting his thoughts.

"They would wage war with the evil of the things they were fighting. It gave them such raw emotion and power because of the hate for evil they had, seeing all the evil in the people they become a near indestructible force for evil to reckon with. Or you could put it another way and say they wage war in the spiritual sense over the physical. The side effects of such a thing has a physical impact, however it is the spirit that they fight over. If you can learn to harness that power you will become the name evil fears throughout all the land. No doubt your name would be sung and remembered for all times." The Hand paused again and leaned toward Zarron, lowering his voice.

"Be warned for if you let that rage go unchecked then you could cause greater harm to innocents then evil. For however capable it is of destroying evil it is just as capable of saving good. If you let your raw feelings and emotions get the best of you and push to save that good in a person with the little evil they have you will find you are killing more innocents than anything. For everyone harbors evil in their soul but if there is greater good there, then that person are no more evil then you or I. So be warned about this Zarron." He leaned back, his voice returning to normal levels.

"I wish I could teach you more. To control it is something that is taught through the Holyrage line. Since you are resurrecting that line and I am not a Holyrage, you will need the continued guidance of the Nameless One to grow and learn. In fact I implore you to seek and learn as much as you can. For I fear that should you slip into darkness so shall the world."

Zarron shuddered with the overwhelming feeling of the great responsibility on him as he came to grips with the reality of it. He also remembered his talk with his sword and the promise he gave.

"I understand and I won't put down the Nameless One again this I have promised." He replied stoically as his loyalty and faith to the Nameless surged inside him.

"Zarron, the Voice and I have spoken much about you and your journeys already. You are young for where you are in the church and younger still knowing that you are a Half-Elf...You are still almost an infant in their time frame yet you possess wisdom and understanding over many that are years older. But, you also know that you know nothing and continue to strive to learn and serve the Nameless One. Ever so humble you are, always thinking you deserve so little but you give your everything to The Nameless One and those above you. Zarron you are about to become the first ever to gain the rank of Paladin at being so young in the church. None have achieved such rank at being not even a year out from your graduation from the church." The Hand spoke with words of sincerity and honor. He tossed Zarron the ring and pendent of a Paladin. He reached up and caught it still in shock of what was happening.

"My Lord and Lady I don't deserve such an honor, I have fell back on my faith and there are many more that have been here longer and deserve that rank more than I. I am still so new to it all I...I don't think I can take such an honor." Zarron replied his words stumbling from his mouth as he looked at the ring and pendent in his hand.

"Once more my dearest Zarron it is the reason you deserve it more than many. We have even spoken to the council and none think differently. There is not a soul in the church that will despise and be disgusted with our decision. We know that the great Nameless One smiles upon our decision. Before you take upon the rank though we just ask that you do one more thing for us. Kneel before the throne here and pray, The Nameless One and the room itself will test you. We both fear little that you will fail. We will meet you outside." The Voice paused. She lovingly looked upon Zarron. She grabbed his hand and closed it around the necklace and ring.

"We intend to see you proudly bearing the pendent of a Paladin of The Nameless and wearing the ring proudly just the same." The Voice spoke once more in her calming, sweet sounding voice that no one could feel uncomfortable with. With that The Hand and the Voice left him alone in the room.

"You know my dear Lord Ashen he will one day take your place as Hand of the Church. I think at that point I shall also step down and let the next chosen one take my place. Perhaps even with all your hurt and pain of the death of your wife many years ago and the death of your child that you can find it in your heart to love again, and love me. We could look into settling down in the valley in the wine fields and woods." The Voice spoke to The Hand, placing her hands on his. The Hand put his other hand on top of hers. He looked lovingly into her eyes, bringing his other hand up to stroke her cheek.

"I have always loved you and I wouldn't want to do anything more than settle with you. You have been a faithful and true companion through all these past years. Soon, we shall discuss this more, perhaps after my month of mourning."

As Zarron did what he was ordered he knelt before the throne and began praying. He prayed for things that were little to the biggest problems that were there before him. Tears rolled down his face and the oddest thing happened. His tears turned to blood as he wept in great grief for the events to come, and the people that would lose their life in this Great War. He wept about his past and where his life had taken him. His mind constantly warred with him about things never getting better and a hope for things to be better.

Zarron suffered and lived through thoughts that were not his own but at the same time he was all too familiar with them. Constantly he had to quell the idea of his God abandoning him. Shamefully he found himself blaming The Nameless One of all things. He rebuked those thoughts, his stomach roiling and sickened by them.

He fought himself so hard that he felt his mind was about to explode. Then finally all at once silence cut through everything and two words resounded in his head.

Be Still.

There was a sudden bright flash of light that forced his eyes open, before him on the throne sat the Nameless One in all his splendor and glory staring down at him.

XVIII

Zarron was struck dumb by the mere presence of his God. So he remained where he was, kneeling before the Nameless One on his throne.

"Zarron do not be scared of me for your future and life holds great worth with trusting in me." The Nameless One's voice boomed and shook the room as if it was too small to hold his great power. The sheer power of it should have caused him to go deaf, however by the Gods will, his hearing remained intact.

"I do trust in you my Lord. Just tell me what you need me to do and I will serve willingly." He had finally been able to find his words. The strength of his voice was not there yet, so he spoke in a weak, quieted voice.

"Zarron, you have proven to me you can be trusting of me but, you have also spent time doubting me and doubting your role in life." The Nameless One stared down at Zarron with eyes that were like light. He looked up at The Nameless One wide eyed with tears of shame. He opened and closed his mouth to speak. He found he had nothing to say in his defense. He lowered his head. He had done wrong and he deserved to be punished in some way or another.

"Your silence serves as enough of a punishment Zarron. I know that you suffer because of that event. It is also neither here nor there for you made your promise to me anew. It best be you never forget that. For there are trying times ahead. A great evil is coming, threatening to bring a plague of darkness to the lands of Vin Ara Talv. You may think I have abandoned you but, I will not. You have to carry on the light of my will. Let the people know I have not left them. There will be signs of my power everywhere, they will see it if, they take the time to look for it. This upcoming war is one this world has never seen. It will be greater and more devastating than the Black Wars and you can be assured people's faiths will be tested. In order for you to serve me properly and hold strong to your convictions you must have your soul purified."

He looked at the Nameless One quizzically. "Your purification begins now." The Nameless One stretched out a finger and touched him in the center of his chest.

He watched as the Nameless One put his finger there, nothing happened initially. He didn't quite understand and was about to speak again when an intense surge of searing pain tore through his insides. He ground his teeth together and pressed a hand to his chest trying to suppress the pain that was building there quickly. His body quivered as the pain boiled to the surface. He let out a howl of pain.

An enormous light erupted from his mouth and eyes. It lit up the great room in an incredible light that burned brighter than the sun. He let out a roar of pain and anger. He felt himself lose control of his mind and body as the intensity of the light grew. He needed to find an outlet for the rage that grew in him.

He grabbed the nearest object, the large center table, he flung it across the room, and it crashed into the wall, shattering. He continued stumbling about roaring in pain as his body fought the never ceasing agony. It wasn't long before his attention was drawn to the evil dragon that hung on the wall. He hated that dark wicked thing, he poured out all of his anger and rage on the beast. The light that tormented him obeyed his anger and rage. It leapt from his body and slammed into the stone statue of the dark beast. Snuffing the light from the room.

Zarron collapsed to the floor. He remained motionless for a moment as he assessed the situation. The light was no longer in him, the intensity of the pain and agony dissipated slightly. He moved a hand, it moved. He had control of his body once more.

He pulled himself to a knee. He kept his left hand on the ground to steady himself and hold up his weight. His right hand clasped at his chest.

As he knelt there he felt the warmth of his body leave him as the air grew cold. From the dragon he observed a dull sickly black glow begin to take shape. What hat he was observing was something of evil, he knew that without a shadow of doubt. He stared at the darkness as it crept its way into the room. He felt his blood begin to boil.

The darkness that emanated from the dragon started as a mist of sorts but soon it took a solid shape. The creature that stood before him was something utterly vile and disgusting. When it began cackling it sent chills down his spine. His face distorted in disgust. His urge to kill this wicked thing swelled in him. The creature smiled at him before rushing to engage him.

Zarron returned the smile, he would meet this foe head on. The two powers collided together. As they collided the creature swung his right arm out wide to bring in a powerful strike. Zarron blocked the attack and grabbed the creatures other arm as it swung at him. As the right arm of the vile thing recovered from the attack he uppercut the wicked thing sending it reeling backwards, not losing his momentum he brought a knee up and slammed it hard into the creature causing it to double over. He grabbed it as it reeled in pain and threw the creature into a wall. It disappeared in a cloud of dark mist.

Another wicked one took shape in front of him, the thing caught him off guard and the creatures attack slammed hard into his face sending him to the floor. Zarron recovered quickly enough to dodge the creature as it attacked him on the ground. He kicked out his feet sweeping the creature to the ground. He jumped up quickly and mounted the dark thing. He rained down punch after punch until it moved no more. Its face was nearly unrecognizable. He slammed another fist into it. As it connected with the creature he found that the creature burst into mist again.

He peered around waiting for the next attack. The next attack came from two of the creatures. As he dispatched them they were replaced by another four. Those four became eight and so it continued. It didn't matter how many formed, Zarron in his Holy Rage dispatched them each time. He became very good at killing them.

The fighting seemed endless and then as if struck by a lightning bolt the words "Be Still" pounded his head. In a matter of moments he came to, realizing the error of his ways. He regained control of his mind, the rage subsiding. In a clear concise voice he spoke to the darkness.

"Enough by the blood of the Nameless I command you to be gone." His bold voice echoed through the chamber shaking the foundations of the room. As if by some unknown magick, blood rained down on the surrounding area. The creatures of the dark writhed in pain and agony, the blood rejuvenated his body as it fell on him. He felt all the bruises, cuts and scrapes of the fighting disappear.

Once more the light of The Nameless One filled the chamber burning away the evil ones that remained until not even a speck of their presence remained.

Zarron took a moment to look around the room. The damage of it all blew him away. There was hardly a piece of the relics and furniture unbroken; the paintings that adorned the walls were covered in dark black blood, the giant table was broken to pieces against one of the farther walls. The only two things that were unscathed were the dragon and the throne of the Nameless. He was taken aback by the sheer carnage of it all. It wasn't until he heard clapping that brought him back to reality and of the Nameless One awesome presence.

"Well Done Zarron! You have done great works here and purified your soul for now. To answer your question as to what those things were, well it is simple they represented evil. Where you put down one evil another one comes up in its place and that evil that you destroyed returns. You in turn killed one evil but you killed it for the wrong reasons. Another evil came up in its place. It is what all people suffer from. It is the reason why evil is not defeated yet, too many people are focusing on their own desires and ways of killing it. In turn they create another evil out of it. It wasn't until you fought for the right reasons, the righteous cause, and lay that evil at the foot of a being that is pure good that evil was finally defeated. It is good for you to remember this test Zarron." The Nameless One's voice rumbled from deep within but came out sounding as gentle as a father's word of encouragement.

"I see my great King, but I was fighting for the right reasons wasn't I?" Zarron asked.

"Perhaps you thought you were Zarron but when you have evil in your soul just as all of us do it wasn't a pure action. You can kill their bodies sure enough, but their souls are another thing in it's entirely. That task of killing souls can only be done by pure beings. Eventually one day Zarron you will find evil has no more sway in the world. You have seen one of the events of its demise, in your dream those many days ago. It will come to a point where evil is thrown into the dark abyss never to be seen again. But, my dear Zarron that is a long ways off yet still. You have earned a break for now, much has happened in the past few weeks, as your God I command you to take a small time off to relax and enjoy yourself. The pain of Mary's loss you will find has subsided and you will feel at peace with yourself for exactly 7 days. Enjoy those days for they will be the last in this life you will feel complete peace until you join me in the Heavens." The Nameless One smiled down at Zarron and placed a hand on his head whispering a few words that Zarron didn't understand.

"I understand thank you my great King I feel a change already but what shall become of this mess might I ask? I have destroyed many priceless things indeed."

The Nameless One chuckled. "Let me worry about such things, all will be as it was." With that, an imperceptible flash moved across his eyes of light. The room snapped back to the perfect pristine location it was in before Zarron had his test. The Nameless One smiled one more time at Zarron. There was a flash of light and he was gone.

Zarron closed his eyes and basked in the wonderful gift of peace that was given to him. After several long moments he moved towards the doors. He paused for a moment, looking back at the room in wonder at all that had happened. Then he opened the door and walked outside. He smiled when he found The Hand and The Voice waiting for him.

"I see the change in you Zarron I hope what The Nameless One showed you was truly amazing. Now I know you deserve a break so being a Paladin of the Church now you are granted land. In fact a place is already built for you, a place that The Nameless One picked out for you. Your belongings have already been brought there by Acolyte Roggins. You will find a surprise or two from the Church awaiting you as well." The Hand smiled at him.

Zarron's smile widened. He bowed deeply to the leaders. He was anxious to start his week. The idea of something horrible troubled him only for a moment before feelings of complete peace overwhelmed him.

XIX

"Do you think he has stopped following us?" One person asked the other fear plain in his words.

"I, I don't know…perhaps…." The voice was violently cut short as a wooden bolt pierced through his back side, exploding out the front. The other person looked down at him his eyes wide in terror. He looked back to see the man that fired the bolt, he could see his fiery green eyes laughing at him as he loaded another bolt into his crossbow. The man turned and ran away from him another bolt slammed into a tree next to him and he could hear the man curse.

"Vampire! You will not make it far you are only delaying your death." The man shouted after his target. He looked around at his surrounding and found a little path that ran parallel to the path the vampire was taking. He drew his sword and ducked into the path running next to the creature. It wasn't long before he drew close to the creature. His element of surprise intact. He looked at the trees and found a low branch. He dove for that jumped up on it he used his momentum to somersault in front of the vampire he leveled his blade at the dark one who was looking behind him, the creature turned around only to run right into the sword. It took an immeasurable amount of strength to remain on his feet as the dark one crashed into him. He prevailed however and was rewarded with the look of fear and pain on the creatures face.

"Who are you?" The vampire asked choking on blood.

"Raamok." He said in a cold tone, he yanked the blade free and stepped to the side of the vampire bringing his sword down in one swift stroke severing the creatures head. He closed his eyes relishing the thought of another vampire killed. He didn't get long to enjoy his accomplishment as a throwing knife hit a tree close by.

He snapped his eyes open, he dropped to the ground and rolled into cover. He peered through the brush and saw another small party of 4 Vampires moving his direction. *I am quite curious about where they are coming from, perhaps this time I shall keep one alive long enough to tell me.* Raamok nodded to himself with the plan he came up with. He crept through the bushes slowly and deliberately. He got close to the middle of the party. He stepped out and punched his blade through a vampire's heart, he pulled his blade free quickly. The return slash severed the creatures head. He brought his blade up in time to parry a sad attempt at a strike on him. The sound of steel against steel ringed out into the cool night air. Raamok dodged out of the way at another strike that was meant to sever his head. On his roll out of the way he unsheathed his axe and flung it at one of the creatures. The vampire it hit slammed hard into a tree, pinning it there. Its blood dripped to the ground below. Raamok dodged another slash at him and drew his silver blade.

The two that were left circled him and they both came in to attack at the same time. Raamok parried one blow and ducked out of the way at another slash. He flicked out his blade, catching one of the vampires in the leg causing him to fall down in front of its companion, who in turn tripped over him.

Raamok brought his blades down on them with great strength, the one that had tripped managed to roll out of the way but the one that was cut across the leg was not so lucky. His swords cut clean through the vampire putting him in two pieces. Raamok recovered his blades. He attacked the dark one that rolled out of the way, to his surprise the vampire managed to parry the attack. Raamok not losing his momentum kept the creature on the defense. Each slash made was met by the vampire's blade, he growled to him-self as he ducked to the defenders side unexpectedly. He brought his leg around forcefully kicking the creature square in the stomach. The vampire doubled over. Before he could recover Raamok brought one of his blades down pinning the creature to the ground. As it tried to move his hand in an attempt to recover its weapon

Raamok stabbed his other sword into the nerves that moved the arms, he severed the link causing paralysis of the creature's arm movement.

"Now which one of you two is going to be willing to speak and give me information?" Raamok said in a stern voice. He raised his eyebrows up as he looked at either one. The one with the axe pinned in him decided to speak first.

"What do you want slayer?" The creature replied in a voice stricken with pain. Raamok smiled to himself as he got his first volunteer.

"Looks like you are the unlucky one." Raamok said to the vampire that was pinned by his swords. Raamok removed the blades and punched his magickal one through the creature's heart killing it.

He turned his attention back to the one that was pinned. He went up and yanked the axe free from it. He withdrew some holy water from his one of his pouches and poured it onto the wound causing the vampire to scream out in pain.

"There that way you can't try to heal your wound and run from me. Now speak dark one, I would suggest you speak on your own terms and not mine as well." Raamok said in almost a growl.

"Your kind's time is short, once Thead crushes the Fenrir and all those that oppose him. None can stop the Faceless One, None! Our vampiric numbers will charge from the Fenrir to lay waste to everyone along with the many other vile and disgusting creatures, we will come upon this land as a flood and who will be able to stand against it?" The vampire laughed sadistically

"Well if you get so lucky to do as you say it won't happen without me crushing your numbers and degrading your morale so low that the remaining few won't have the will to carry on. If I die then I shall take hundreds of your kind with me! You forget as well that the Nameless One will be there and I know a particular person who represents him on this land. Our time may be short but your kind's time is shorter still." Raamok spoke coldly, and with no remorse. He pulled a holy water vial from his belt. He slammed it in the creature's mouth. He forced it to bite down, shattering the vial and its contents. The vampire's head burned away as the holy water did its job. He gathered his weapons and cleaned them quickly.

"Well it seems that Rynn Shadowlore will need to wait for now. Don't you worry though Rynn your time is short as well." Raamok said to himself and to the sky as if pronouncing Rynn's death as a promise to the gods. Raamok decided the best place at hand for him to be was the Fenrir. He gained his bearings and began running back to the Fenrir.

XX

It was early when a knock came to Zarron's chamber doors. He peered over at the window, viewing the Sun in the early stage of rising. He closed his eyes tightly and rubbed the sand from them. He pulled himself out of his bed and went to the door and was not surprised to see Frank Roggins standing there.

"Good morning Lord Zarron, I have a message for you from the church." Frank's voice was quiet. Zarron couldn't help but smile at his now friend who was an enemy bandit just a month and a weeks' time ago.

"I presume it couldn't have waited till it was later. I was having the most wonderful dream." He smiled at his companion who was still standing there waiting.

"Is there something else Frank?"

"Yes sir, umm there is a visitor at the door. Quite a beautiful one if you don't mind my saying. She says her name is Sheen and said you knew, err know her. I invited her in but she is being watched by the house guards."

"No need for her to be under guard, sit her at the table, and treat her to some tea and breakfast I will be down shortly." With a subtle quick nod Frank left his quarters to carry out the task at hand. He turned back to his room and went over to his desk and sat down to read the letter that had the official seal of The Hand on it.

Hail Paladin Zarron Ra Holyrage

We have urgent need of you to carry out a task for The Church. Tomorrow at day break I expect you to be at the Church fully armed up and ready for several days of travel. I apologize for the lack of warning 24 hours was the best I could do. Further details will be given to you at day break on the morrow. May The Nameless One bless you.

In His Service, Lord Ashen, the Hand of the Nameless

Zarron set the letter down on his desk, drumming his fingers on the table. Not choosing to think on it any more he pushed back his chair and went over to his wardrobe. He dressed quickly in a simple black cotton shirt pairing it with gray cotton pants, he shod his feet in a pair of soft leather boots. Finally he grabbed his father's Elven dagger, slipping it into his boot.

He left his room and proceeded down the long hall, past several more rooms, his library and down a flight of stairs that led into the dining room. The room itself was quiet, a large fire crackled and danced in the hearth. At the long table Sheen sat towards the right side of the head chair. She was dressed in a pleasant black dress with green embroidery; the sleeves hung loosely and were made of a finer material that was green as well. Her dark golden hair was set in a braid that hung over her left shoulder. As she saw him approach she stood up and gave an awkward curtsey, he did his best to hold back a slight chuckle, choosing instead to bow, exaggerating the gesture. He grabbed her hand, kissed it then signaled her to sit down again.

"It is great seeing you Sheen how have you been faring lately?" He spoke in a soft mellow tone.

"I suppose fair enough it has been some time since I have set foot in a city, it has been rather pleasant to be honest. I went to the church the other day and asked for you but they said your quarters had been moved to a house in the forest valley. I asked around a bit as to where your place was and ran into a wonderful man by the name of Zeth who let me know the details of it." Sheen replied in a sweet voice.

He couldn't help but chuckle at this. "I suppose that Zeth thought it would be good to have a beautiful woman visit me." There was a slight pause as he furrowed his brow, putting on a show of being deep in thought. He smiled again. "I suppose he was right it is nice having company."

Sheen smiled brightly at him. "I am honored by your words. I have heard you have had an interesting past month."

"Interesting would be an understatement." Before he could speak any further the door to the kitchen flung open spitting out Frank with a breakfast of fresh bread and eggs along with a pot of tea. He served a plate to Sheen first then gave Zarron his plate before heading back into the kitchen.

Over breakfast Zarron and Sheen talked over the events they had both been through in the past month. He told her of Mary's funeral and how he was promoted to Paladin just before the test. He then went on to tell her of his first impressions of the place and how he didn't expect it at all. Sheen listened the whole time to his tale. Her eyes glistened with excitement and interest.

After Zarron finished his account of events. Sheen went into an account of her activities. She went back to Tretch and spoke with the elders of the shape changers. She didn't explain any details of what was spoken of but Zarron didn't seem to mind, nor did he press the topic. He knew that she would tell him if she chose too. There was no need to press the subject. During their conversation Frank popped in, cleared dishes and brought out desserts along with a sweet drink. It wasn't long before the sun was high in the sky and its bright rays came in through the high windows of the dining hall.

"My, it has gotten late quickly hasn't it?" Zarron asked Sheen as he peered up at his high window. He smiled to himself as he took in the beauty of the window, he never thought he would ever be in such a situation as he looked back at his child hood.

"My Zarron, are you trying to shoo me out of your beautiful home?" Sheen asked sarcastically as she let out a little giggle. He couldn't help but return the smile. He laughed along with her. It felt good to laugh.

"Of course not Sheen, that is a silly thought you are more than welcome into my home but I fear in the morning I will need to take my leave for an unknown time." The laughter that hung on his words left towards the last bit of his statement. He was sad to have to leave, he enjoyed laughing and the loneliness had left him for the moment only to return with the fact he had a duty to tend to in the morrow.

"Oh?" Sheen asked in a slightly shocked voice. "Well we best be heading into town to get you some supplies then I should say?" With that Sheen picked herself up from the table and went to the door and waited there, she raised an eyebrow at Zarron and smiled.

Zarron shook his head chuckling once more. He pushed himself up from his chair and went over to the door and with a touch of flair he opened it for her. She laughed at the ridiculous motion.

"Shall we take a carriage or ride in on horses?"

"Horseback of course, I am not a fan of the carriage thing it is too confining, I enjoy feeling the breeze on my face and the smell of the land." Zarron summoned forth one of his guards who went and gathered two horses for them. Within moments he came back with two magnificent riding horses. Zarron heard Sheen sigh to her-self out loud, he looked over at her with a puzzled look on his face.

"I suppose you wouldn't happen to have some spare riding clothing that would fit me would you?" Sheen's face looked flustered. He gave her a reassuring smile.

"As a matter of fact I do, a few of my guards are women, I am sure they wouldn't mind letting you take a pair of riding breeches along with a tunic to match. Just go inside and speak with Frank, he will take care of the rest. I will wait here and enjoy the beautiful day." His smile broadened as Sheen's face returned to its normal serene look.

"Thank you." She spun on her heels and went into the house.

Zarron talked with his guard on duty as he waited for Sheen. It didn't take long for her to return wearing a pair of light brown riding breeches and a form fitting matching brown tunic with dark brown sleeves. She smiled to him then jumped up onto her horse with grace and agility. He followed suit and led them out of the small gate to his home and onto the road that wound itself towards Citadel Heights.

"Sheen, however much I enjoy your company I don't understand it at the same time." Zarron finally asked the question that had been on his mind for some time now. She smiled timidly at him.

"Zarron to tell you the truth I am not sure why I am being the way I am towards you. There is a pulling on my heart and soul that I somehow have to follow you. Needless to say it didn't quite happen till that night when the Faceless One and the Nameless One fought over you. It was actually a strange night for me, I was approached by a man that was like the light of the sun, and his eye's had no pupils they were like pools of light. He spoke with a gentle voice, one that was filled with great peace, wisdom and care. I recognized him from earlier in my life and I didn't know who is was until the realization clicked after seeing him fight for you, that the being was indeed the Nameless One. He spoke some words to me, something in me ignited. I have mentioned it before to you but it is like I can feel what your heart is going through, I have a connection unlike anything I have ever experienced before." She sighed not exactly knowing what more to say. She felt vulnerable, which made her terribly uncomfortable. Zarron shifted his shoulders.

"I don't know what to tell you Sheen perhaps if we speak to The Hand and The Voice we can get some answers. I know with you there is something different. I apologize if I don't feel the similar feelings you have, I am not sure how to react also for it is still too soon from Mary's death. I can assure you we will find some answers once we speak to The Hand and the Voice. I promise you." Zarron gave a weak smile. Sheen shook her head, her dark golden hair bobbed back and forth. There was silence for some time on their ride before Sheen spoke again.

"I have a request for you Zarr…" Her voice was cut off as an arrow slammed into her horse. The beast kicked up and fell to the ground hard. Within a moment's time Zarron dismounted his steed. He rushed over to Sheen throwing up a magick shield protecting them from another barrage of arrows. *How are there bandits this close to the city?* He thought to himself as he strengthened his shield for another barrage of arrows. After the last barrage the bandits gave up the arrows. They drew their swords charging the two of them. He looked around, assessing the situation and determined there was at least five of them.

"Zarron let me up." Sheen said to Zarron in a calm voice even amidst the violence. As soon as he let her up she spoke a word. Wild magick poured out from her, thick and heavy. Her body began transforming. The skin fell off around her which she sped up by removing it with large tearing motions. Chunks of her skin fell away, evaporating as they were completely removed from her body. Her muscles bulged, her back arched as hair grew at an outstanding rate. Bones cracked and formed as they changed their shape to suit her transformation. She finally settled in her final form which was a beautiful golden colored dire wolf. She nearly matched the size of the horses they rode and within a moment she sprang back on her haunches and leapt onto one of the bandits who stopped short as the woman transformed.

Zarron heard the man's screams die away as Sheen ended his life. He turned his focus on the two that were approaching him and readied himself. He wished he had brought Angel Fire with him. He drew his father's Elven dagger from its resting place in his boot.

As he thought about Angel Fire he could hear the sword's familiar voice in his mind, *I am here when you call upon me Zarron.* In his empty hand that didn't hold the dagger he felt a strong tingling sensation that he easily recognized as magick. As he looked at it a vast array of little balls of light started forming in his hand creating the hilt and guard of the beautiful sword. The lights kept getting more and more numerous, soon the solid hilt of the sword rested in his hand. A bright flash of white light erupted from the hilt and guard. It formed the solid steel of the main blade, within a moment it was quickly covered in a white fire that didn't burn his hand but would prove to be deadly to any enemies he was against.

The blade formed just in time as one of the Bandits attacked him. He brought his dagger up and parried the sword of the man. He attacked with Angel Fire. The bandit made a feeble attempt at blocking the blade. As Angel Fire connected with his sword, his sword shattered. The rest of the momentum of the swing carried through burying itself into the man's side. He pulled his blade free and blocked another slash that was aimed at him from the other bandit. The man kept attacking him with great zeal. He was attempting to finish him off quickly but his anger and recklessness made his slashes wild and crazy, it left him open numerous times.

Zarron entertained the man by parrying his attacks with his dagger. When he was able to sort out a pattern he thrust Angel Fire into the opening ending his life quickly. As he pulled his sword free he turned to see how Sheen was faring. She just finished killing the last man by biting him in half with her great jaws. His heart sank as he realized a sword was sticking out her side. He ran over to her quickly. He placed a hand on her side and felt the soft fur of her that had blood matted in it.

"Give me just a moment Sheen this might hurt." He set his weapons down and grabbed the sword yanking it free. Sheen let out a howl of pain. He placed a hand on the wound. He summoned forth the healing powers need to heal the sword wound. Within seconds the wound closed itself up, the hair even grew back and Sheen was whole again.

"Thank you Zarron, I didn't need it but it was appreciated." She spoke to him in her wolf form her voice, more sultry and deep. He smiled at her. Before he could speak any further 7 more bandits burst from the woods.

Zarron picked up his weapons and switched hands. So Angel Fire was in his primary hand and the dagger in his off hand. He charged at the bandits with Sheen following beside him. As the bandits realized what they were against several of them ran at the sheer terror of Sheen in her mighty wolf form, the others that stayed were quickly dispatched. Their skills with the swords were nothing compared to Zarron's training and Sheen's ferocity.

"What is happening here, bandits never attack this close to the city unless they are backed by a larger force of some sort?" Zarron heart sank with that last comment he had said. He looked at each of the bodies he realized they all bore the same symbol, the symbol of none other than the Faceless One.

XXI

"Sheen I need you to do me a favor. Go, warn The Hand or the Voice about the impending attack on the city. You must do this and be quick about it, when you get there let them know I sent you then get yourself somewhere safe." Zarron said to Sheen in a dry voice as he held down panic.

"What will you do Zarron?" Sheen asked still in her wolf form.

"I must get back and get my guard to safety they are my responsibility and I will not let them stay there to be killed by The Faceless One's armies." Zarron said as he mounted the final horse that was alive. "Go now Sheen!" He ordered, desperation being his driving force. He turned to head back to his small keep. He looked back once to see Sheen bound off in her wolf form towards the city. He murmured a prayer for her. He hurried his horse down the road. As he rounded the final bend he saw his keep being battered by a large band of brigands who were trying to get themselves into the keep. His guard was inside the protection of the walls. He watched them pop up every once in a while shooting arrows into the group of men attacking the keep. He pushed his horse into a fast gallop.

He was upon the first man attacking the keep in no time. He leaned down from the saddle swinging his sword. He split the assailants head open with the slash. He pivoted in his saddle. He delivered another mighty blow that nearly decapitated another attacker. He cut a path through the front of the group that were attacking the gates. The risk was great with it, he relied heavily on the element of surprise. To his glee it worked in his favor. He killed many of the assailants. As he turned his mount around to perform another charge he paused for a moment. This time he knew it wouldn't be as easy because they were prepared for him. He saw little else for options at the moment, so he kicked his legs into the horse, spurring it forward at a full charge.

Sheen quickly got to the town. Her mind was focused on the task at hand. She ignored the shouts of fear amongst the people and the odd glances she got in her wolf form. By the time she got to the Light Bridge she was met by several Elites and Crusaders. They blocked her path with weapons drawn. She quickly changed out of her form. She expected them to be surprised by the sudden transformation. To her chagrin not many seemed taken aback at all. The most she got was that some of them shifted their shoulders uneasily. The Elites risked a brief glance the Crusaders. As they saw the stoic ranks remain steadfast they adjusted their equipment and turned to face her once more. *'They are indeed disciplined soldiers'*. She developed a new found respect in that moment for the soldiers of the Nameless.

"What is your business shape changer?" One of the Crusaders stepped up to her with his spear lowered and ready.

"I must speak with The Hand or The Voice immediately the city is in grave danger of an attack, Paladin Zarron has sent me, please this is urgent." Sheen humbled herself and begged of the men. It only took a second for the Crusader that approached her to nod his head. He ordered his men to stand down.

"I will personally escort you to The Hand, come we must hurry." The Crusader spoke to her. Before she could reply he pivoted on his heels and began running towards the Citadel. It was a matter of minutes before Sheen was standing before The Hand.

"I need you to sound the bell for an attack sir, the city is in peril." Sheen asked in a hurried voice. She presented one of the badges from the bandits Zarron and her had killed. The Hand's eyes widened briefly before becoming slits, his face darkened. He shook his head and grabbed a passing Knight of the Church. He said something imperceptible to her, the Knight ran off in a great hurry. Within seconds a loud bell rang forth in the town.

"Now we shall prepare this city for our defense. I can assure you the Faceless One shall not take this city. I can't believe he has gotten so bold to attack the blessed city of The Nameless. These are indeed dark times."

As Zarron charged the group again, the doors to his keep burst open. His personal guard poured out armed and armored on mighty war horses, the timing couldn't have been any better. As the brigands attacking were sandwiched between the two attacking teams many tried to hold their ground and were trampled or were met by the steel of the keep's guard. A few thought the safer route would be through Zarron instead of trying to match the number of the keep's guard but they too found that to be their death as well. The whole attack of the Brigands was obliterated. The few that managed to run didn't make it far as the guards ran them down mercilessly slaughtering them.

As Zarron looked at the bodies around him he found them all carrying the mark of the Faceless One. His fears were definitely confirmed that the Faceless One had sent and army to attack the City of the Nameless. The question was how far behind was the true force of the Faceless One. He shuddered to himself as he thought of it. His guard approached him.

"Hurry m'lord we must get you armored up, I fear that the City will need our help." It was the captain of the guard, Agrith that spoke to him. Zarron nodded his head in agreement.

"Secure the gate, remain vigilant. I also want all the horses not used by us to be released except for Thunder. I want him armored up and ready for battle. If you have any priceless items grab them quickly but do not pack anything that will be a greater burden then useful. We will need all the speed we can to get to the city as fast as possible." Zarron issued his orders, his guard went to work immediately. He flung the door open into his keep and proceeded to the armory where he found Frank already waiting for him.

"Good I am glad you are here Frank." He said in a rushed tone, his words spilling out in a jumble.

"Indeed, your armor is buffed and, uh...err well your sword had no use for it but when I picked it up to examine it the oddest thing happened." Frank paused for a moment as he walked to where the armor was on its stand.

"Let me guess it just disappeared?" Zarron finished Frank's thought. He held his sword out to him. Frank looked at it bewildered. He scratched his head. He cautiously took the sword from him, setting it aside. Then went to work helping Zarron equip his armor. They both knew that Frank wasn't needed to equip the armor however it was a great honor for him to be able to help so Zarron didn't object any. Not to mention Frank's nimble fingers got the armor on in half the time it would have taken Zarron to don it.

As the last piece was locked down in place Zarron took a moment to marvel at how amazing the armor truly was. It fit him comfortably, in fact it felt like his own skin. The armor when it was in pieces easily weighed upwards of 100 pounds but once the final piece, aside from the helm was put in place, the armor felt nearly weightless. It gave him an odd feeling of being vulnerable but so secure at the same time. As he moved certain parts of his body he found he didn't seem to lack any major motion impairments. He smiled to himself as he clenched his hand into a fist in front of him.

"Frank this will be a day of victory for The Nameless One." Zarron spoke confidently. Frank nodded his head towards him. He presented Zarron's helm to him. He adored the helm's design and look. It was a full plate helm, it covered his entire head and face. Great angel wings protruded from the side of it. The faceplate had the symbol of the Nameless placed above his eye slits. The Eye slits themselves were part of a mighty cross that extended to either side of the helm and down the length of it. He smiled again before placing the helm on his head. Remarkably he found his visibility was barely impaired. Just as the body armor was, the helm fit his head perfectly. It didn't jar or move as he moved his head back and forth and up and down.

Zarron held out his arm as Frank tightened his impressive shield to it.

This would be the first time he had used a shield in combat since he left for the Fenrir. He soaked in the security he felt with it. The first of the straps fastened the shield to the joint of his forearm and elbow. The second strap secured the shield where his wrist and hand joined together. There was also a metal handle set so he could grip it with his hand for additional strength and support. It was a requirement for frontline fighting. When not on the frontline he could flatten it down to have use of his hand for grabbing onto certain things and what not.

"Thank you Frank for your assistance. What I need for you to do now is take the rest of the house servants. Escape through the tunnel system and get yourself to safety. I would suggest you take it to the great falls. Rest there at the small defense post. That should be far enough away from the city in case it is overrun. Also, as soon as you get the rest of the servants to safety I plan on you manning the tunnels, they are one of our best defenses to get aid to the city but, at the same time it can be the downfall of the city as well." Zarron gripped Franks arm and lowered his voice.

"Frank if that tunnel should be found out by our enemies I will need you to be ready to blow it. There are magickal runes set in place already. You just need to speak one word to cause them to explode. That word is 'exposhefirr' make sure you don't forget it and use it wisely." Frank nodded his head in understanding. He knew how dire the situation was.

"Good now you should be heading out." Zarron shook his friend's hand. He grabbed a lance from the armory before exiting to the front where he found his massive war horse, Thunder, armored and saddled. He swung himself into the saddle and settled down; his guards had equipped lances and stood by waiting anxiously for their leader to speak words of encouragement and hope.

"Sheen it is time for you to get out of here, you have done a wonderful job here warning us, within minutes our defenses will be set up and we will be ready for the Faceless One's horde. What can we offer you in return for your help?" The Hand spoke to Sheen as he patted shoulders and shook hands of those heading out the churches gate to the cities defense.

Sheen had her answer within seconds. "I wish to join the Body of the Church and be put under Zarron's command." The Hand stopped what he was doing and turned to Sheen. He looked at her for a moment then drew his sword.

XXII

"Where the hell do they keep coming from?" Partaxis asked Durakon who was with him at the time of the ambush. In the past month they had to attend to the small village that was established by the refugees from attacks. This particular incident took them off guard completely and they both knew it as well. Partaxis growled as he smashed another orcs head in as it came in for the attack.

"I couldn't tell you." Durakon said between breaths as he set and loosed another arrow into an orc. The main attack had been stopped but remnants were still attacking, most of their group had been killed off in the initial attack. Partaxis ordered his men back to the crude keep that was set up in the refugee village, Durakon and himself offered to cover their retreat.

"That one looked like the last of the attackers I would say Partaxis. Now let us hurry out of here before they regroup and attack." Durakon suggested to Partaxis who in turn nodded his head in agreement. They turned and exited their circle of death they caused. They stepped over many dead orcs, as they took a few more steps the ground began to shake. They looked at each other and both of them let out a sigh. They turned to see the largest giant they had ever seen riding on a great mammoth that was equally colossal breach the horizon.

"Durakon can you kill that steed before it gets here?" Partaxis asked as he set himself for the new attack.

"I most certainly can." Durakon said as he nocked another arrow and let loose. It found it mark, penetrating deep into the mammoth's eye but it didn't slow any. Durakon nocked and let loose 4 more arrows, each one found its mark in the same eye but it still wasn't enough to down the giant mammoth.

"His brain is deeper in that big skull than normal I would say, almost like it has been altered." Durakon said to Partaxis with some worry in his voice. By now the mammoth and the rider could easily be seen, they weren't more than a 100 yards out. Within seconds the rider and his beast would be upon them.

"Well it looks like it will be to late Durakon we have to find another way." Durakon growled, he drew his spear and hoisted it ready for a throw.

"Not on my watch." Durakon said under his breath as he drew the spear back and let it fly. The spear sunk deep into the eye of the mammoth. It let out a great howl of pain, its feet wobbled. It came crashing down into the earth. Partaxis and Durakon were just able to jump out of the way as the colossal beast slid to a halt where they were standing. The massive giant tumbled over the mammoth, slamming hard into the earth. The ground cracked and the earth shook.

Partaxis and Durakon recovered quickly. To their disappointment the giant had recovered faster than expected. Durakon eyed his spear then nodded to Partaxis. Partaxis nodded back before engaging the giant. Durakon quickly ran over to the mammoth and recovered his spear. He stabbed it deep into the creature's skull just to make sure it wouldn't be getting up. When he was satisfied that it would indeed stay down he went to Partaxis side.

Partaxis engaged the giant, his massive size easily being towered over by the 30ft giant. He ducked under a mighty swing from the giant's large tree he used for a club. As he ducked the blow he spun to the side and slammed his great hammer into the beast's foot. He could hear a crack as a bone broke beneath. The giant howled in pain. It slammed a fist down onto Partaxis in attempt to crush the creature that wounded him so. Partaxis danced out of the way, missing the attack by inches, however the force of the blow put him off balance. The giant recovered his weapon and was about to slam it down onto the off balanced hero. If it wasn't for Durakon's intervention, Partaxis knew he would have surely been crushed.

Durakon let out a war cry as he jumped through the air with his spear drawn back. He stabbed deep into the giant's stomach, his weapon sunk deep becoming stuck in the process. He used the momentum of the attack to swing himself up towards the giant. As he did this he drew his sword smoothly from it's sheathe. He made an attempt to strike the beasts face. A sudden jarring impact slammed into him. The giant swatted him away like an annoying bug. The force of the blow sent him flying into the trees. He connected hard with a tree and fell to his face stunned. His spear was knocked loose in the attack as well. It landed nearby, point first. Durakon pulled himself to his knees with an intense effort. Sheer determination allowed him to get to his feet. He stumbled towards his spear. He pulled it free with a groan. His willpower and pride compelled him to pursue the assailant.

Partaxis winced as he watched Durakon slam into the tree. The attack however gave him time to recover. He delivered a savage blow to the giant's shin which caused the giant to fall to a knee. Partaxis took the opportunity to strike a more defined blow at the giant's skull but his progress was stopped as the giant slammed his mighty club straight down into the earth. Partaxis had to stop abruptly and jump backwards to avoid the attack. As he drew close to the ground he found it was lower than anticipated. The giants attack had created a crater. Unable to collect his footing he slammed hard into the ground as his feet collapsed under him. Partaxis watched as the giant righted himself. He brought his powerful weapon above his head, readying a death blow. He knew there would be no way to avoid the attack this time. He sighed as he thought about the tree crushing him. It wasn't the way he imagined dying. A sudden movement from his left grabbed his attention.

As the giant brought its mighty weapon up to deliver the death blow to Partaxis. Raamok ran up behind him, he shot several longer than normal arrows that struck deep into the giant's back. He dropped his bow and jumped up onto the arrows using them as a ladder to get to the upper portion of the giant. As he launched himself up the final section he drew his swords and drove them deep into the giant's shoulder blade. He held on as he slid down a portion of his shoulder. The blades became stuck. The unexpected stop caused him to lose his grip, he fell to the ground keeping on his feet. One of his swords fell down with a clatter nearby, the other remained stuck in the flesh of the beast. He grabbed the sword and quickly rolled between the giant's feet as his mighty weapon was dropped crashing into the earth. There was a mighty roar of pain from the giant as he reached behind seeking the sword that was stuck fast.

Durakon shook his head clear of the remaining dizziness before he charged the monstrosity. As he engaged the giant once more. Raamok came out of nowhere. He stopped in awe as he watched the precise and deadly attack. Durakon let out a whoop of excitement. He stabbed his spear into the giants Achilles tendon, he pulled it loose then twirled to stab into the other foots Achilles tendon. The attack was enough to bring the giant crashing down to his knees.

Partaxis let out a war cry and a cheer as he heard the giant roar in pain after Raamok's attack. He watched as the giant fell to the ground after Durakon's attack. Partaxis once again moved in quickly to take advantage of the opportunity. He clasped both hands around the handle of his mighty hammer to give him as much swinging power as he needed. He uppercut the monstrosities massive chin. There was a solid crack as the blow connected. He used the momentum of the attack to twirl his weapon around before slamming another savage blow to the head. The giants head jarred to one side as the blow connected. Another brutal attack struck its head. A defined line appeared moments before blood gushed forth from the cracked skull.

Instead of dying the monstrosity recovered and dealt an equally punishing attack to Partaxis. He was flung a long distance away, he skipped and slammed into the ground multiple times before grinding to a halt.

Raamok had to jump out of the way as the giant crashed to the earth after Durakon's attack. As he recovered he saw Partaxis perform his three mighty swings. He seized the opportunity and mounted the back of the giant. He some effort he pulled his second sword out of the creatures shoulder. He carefully moved towards the giant's neck. He dropped and grabbed onto the giants hair to steady himself as it attacked Partaxis. He quickly assessed the build of the giant. In a moments time he knew what he needed to do. He drove one of his swords deep into the base of the skull. He withdrew his weapon before jumping off the side of the giant. He spun mid fall and slashed out with his swords, he cut a deep line across the monstrosity's neck severing a vital vein. As he dropped to the ground he ran outside the giant's reach before risking a glance towards the creature.

He watched as the giant pulled his huge hands up in an attempt to stop the gushing blood. Within minutes the giant's struggle slowed. They soon ceased completely as the last bit of his life drained from him.

"Raamok it was a good thing you came along." Durakon presented his hand to Raamok. Raamok looked at it for a moment weighing the decision to shake it or not. After a moment he came to his decision. He took the hand and gave it a quick shake. His face darkened once Partaxis approached. He still bore an underlying hatred of the man from their last meeting. Partaxis stopped an arm's length from him. The two of them stared at one another for a long uncomfortable moment. Finally Partaxis let out a breath as he presented his hand to Raamok.

"I appreciate you coming along when you did. I still don't like you much, but, I have to say without your help this could have turned bad." Partaxis said in as gentle as a tone as he could muster. He could tell it was done with difficulty. Raamok laughed.

"It just looked like fun that is why I came along. You are right about one thing though, you two would have been totally screwed without me." He grabbed Partaxis hand and shook it. The air was soon filled with the laughter of the band of heroes. The anxiety of being close to dying, far removed from their mind.

XXIII

"My fellow brothers and sisters of the Church, this is a good day for us. It is not a day to be feared because we shall prove to the Faceless One that the Nameless One is still strong and mighty and he cannot break our spirit! We fight today not for our fellow people but for the great Nameless One. So long as we believe and hold true to our faith in The Nameless we shall come out on top as the victor. Should we lose our faith, we shall fall and fail, but know if you keep faith and die today that you have a place secured for you in The Nameless One's great heavenly kingdom! So what fear should we have?" Zarron shouted to his men, he raised his lance high into the sky and let out a mighty cheer. The small courtyard erupted with loud cheers as their spirits were lifted. One of the guards opened the gate. Zarron and his 20 guards charged out the gates. They thundered down the road a small distance before a lone rider appeared on the road.

Zarron, recognizing who it was slowed the formation to a stop. He issued the order to stay their weapons. Sheen came to a stop in front of him, his eyes widened as he saw her dressed in the colors of a warrior of the Church.

"Paladin Zarron, the Hand asked me to get to you with haste. I am to relay a message to you. The enemy is already at the gate, he asks that you fall back and send word to the outposts of the attack." Sheen reported hurriedly.

"Well I am afraid I cannot abandon the city's defense that would be against what I stand for and my role as a Paladin." He replied with a direct deadpan voice. Sheen smiled at him wickedly with a knowing look in her eye.

"The Hand thought you might say that. So he asked that you still send some of your guard to warn the outposts while simultaneously hitting the rear of the attacking party. Your mission; to cause as much chaos as possible. You will do this by forms of sabotage to the supply lines. Strike fear in their hearts."

"That my dear Sheen is something we will gladly do. I assume I wouldn't be able to get you to be one of those people I send to warn the outposts would I?" He asked already knowing the answer.

"I think not Zarron, I was put under your command that is true, but, I was put there as a guardian so I will not leave your side. You are stuck with me." Zarron shook his head and snorted. He knew there was no way to convince her otherwise. He let out a mighty sigh for show. He was actually glad to have her with him.

"Very well warrior Sheen, now fall in. Your lack of discipline is noted." He gave her a hard time, she bowed deeply playing the role of a naïve and properly scolded green troop. He thought she played it almost too well. He grew serious. He pointed to two of his men and sent them on their way. They saluted then turned their horses and shot off towards the nearest outpost.

"Alright my guard you all heard the command of The Hand. How about we go and cause some trouble for them in the back aye?" Zarron announced enthusiastically to the men. He signaled them off the road towards where he thought the main enemy force may be. It wasn't long before they came to the top of a hill giving them a clear observation point of the enemy encampment.

The camp was set up crudely with little organization Zarron realized. The numbers were massive though. Many tents were set up, all of them seemed to be scattered here and there with no apparent layout. It didn't take long for him to spot a tent that was bright and colorful. It stood close to the middle of the camp and was the only one with two guards protecting the entrance. He made note of the location before turning his attention elsewhere.

As he observed the camp details he located the great siege machines. They were loading and unloading their ammunition barraging the cities walls with mighty stones and ballistae bolts. He turned his attention to the city walls.

The enemy host was trying to get ladders to the wall, most of them failing in their actions. The few that made it to the wall were dispatched as the defenders pushed the ladders off or poured hot oil down on them, setting fire to it. The Minds of the church walked among the defenders, healing those that fell due to injuries from arrow fire or pieces of shrapnel from the wall as the siege engines chipped away small portions of the stonework. Additionally the Minds of the church fought with the enemy's warlocks. Their magick energy coursed through the air creating thunder and static discharge continuously. The small band of heroes felt the ferocity of the magick, even at their great distance from the battle. Zarron suppressed a shudder as he felt the power of it. It was intense, the power of it unbelievable.

After watching for a time a plan began to take form in his mind. He turned his horse around and left the top of the hill his guard following shortly behind. When they were a safe distance away from the enemy he turned towards his men to announce his plan.

"Alright my guard, we have orders to cause chaos and do what damage we can. As it is the enemy host hasn't sent their reserves in so I would say an attack on the camp would be suicide. For now the cities defenders are still fresh and the walls are holding up to the barrage of siege weapons, so I suggest we start hassling their supply line. It will be enough for us to decrease moral and as time goes on we shall change our course of action as we see fit." He paused for a moment to allow time for his men to speak up. Satisfied there was no additional questions he gave the command to head out.

Within 20 minutes time they spotted the first wagon carrying enemy supplies with a small armed escort. They paused their advance and sent a scout ahead. The scout came back a short time later, he reported that the supplies were ammunition for bows and crossbows. Zarron praised him for his work.

The party moved to an appointed ambush point and waited. When the enemy group came into the strike zone, he raised his sword and spoke.

"This shall be a good blow to them. Now my brothers and sisters for The Nameless One…CHARGE!" They started off at a full charge. The ground shook as their mighty war horses thundered across the ground. As they closed the distance, the first part of their line lowered their lances while the second half had their swords at ready. The armed escort was taken by complete surprise. They tried to form a defensive line but it didn't help them any.

Zarron put his shield up for the first impact, his arm jarred as a blow from a mace hit his shield. His lance punched through one of the enemies in the chest. He pulled the lance free quickly and set it again just as he collided with another assailant. This time the lance burst through the upper portion of the man's shoulder. It tore free with little effort on Zarron's behalf. He felt another man get crushed between Thunder's mighty hooves; the steed barely missing a step as it ran over the man nor did the speed of the charge decrease.

Finally Zarron was on the other side of the road, he began to wheel around, and as he turned to face the attackers he halted. There was no need to perform another charge. The group had been destroyed. He let out a loud victory cry, his guard followed suit. As he looked over at Sheen she gave him a big smile.

"Great job men this will indeed be a blow to them. I say release the horses and we shall burn the wagon with the supplies. You have done well here but our work is still far from over, now hurry I hear another wagon coming towards us a long ways out." Zarron relayed his orders. He joined his guard as they released the horses. He walked over to the wagon, his Captain and one other of high enough rank to know basic combat magick joined him. They employed their magick, willing it to form fire. After a brief moment the wagon burst into flames. They group formed up and moved to their next target. As they got closer he slowed the line. Sheen pulled alongside of him.

"Zarron this next supply is food I believe." Sheen said as she sniffed the air.

"You can smell that far Lady Sheen? I am impressed. Are you able to smell out how many are with them? Or are all the people around you setting your scents off." Zarron replied, his curiosity was piqued.

"Well of course I can smell that far I am a shape shifter of the Dire Wolf, you would be amazed at how many traits you can keep with you when not in the wolf form. They of course aren't as defined but when you talk about a wolf's smell…well we know how good they can smell. But, alas I can't pick out how many people there are." Sheen replied excitedly, she was happy to allow Zarron to learn a little more about her.

"Alright, Jonathan I need you to scout ahead and let us know what their numbers are." Zarron asked his appointed scout. Jonathan nodded his head and took off. He would head up the road a little ways where he would ditch his horse and run on foot the rest of the way. It didn't take long for Jonathan to come riding back to them quickly.

"Paladin Zarron I saw 6 defenders. I think the enemy host thinks their supply lines are quite secured. It is quite foolish of them I say to send such a small amount of guards for escort." Jonathan concluded his report.

"I couldn't agree with you more but what is foolish for them is a wonderful opportunity for us. I dear say once word gets to the main camp that there is a band of people attacking their supplies you can expect higher resistance but, until that point let us enjoy the ease of it all." He replied as the signal to fall in was relayed.

The party under Zarron's command charged down the road at the supply caravan, just as the first enemy group had done they did the same. They put up a sloppy defense as the group of the church's Body charged down at the caravan. The front row separated themselves momentarily as the second line heaved javelin's striking killing blows to the driver of the wagon. As they got close Zarron ordered the group to break. The cavalry split and crashed upon both sides of the caravan destroying the defenders with no more than a scratch done to them.

"Alright my fellow brothers and sisters grab what you think we will need for food and let us continue on. Burn the rest we don't take." Zarron ordered. The group went to work quickly. They grabbed small bags of food to keep them fed for a couple days' time. Once more they burned the cart down with magick before continuing.

When they finally stopped for the night Zarron and his group had destroyed 15 separate supply caravans. He had not lost a single person from his guard. They had routed a small band of mercenary reinforcements and killed well over 100 men of the enemy's host.

After some scouting attempts Sheen came back with a perfect place for them to set up camp. The location was deep in the woods and along a small brook. The camp was surrounded by mighty stones that created a natural barrier. The only effective way into the camp was through a tight entrance that just barely fit one of their war horses through. With some work Zarron managed to come up with some runes to put in place among the camp to have little to no noise leave the camp.

When they had all settled in Zarron ordered a fire to be lit, food to be cooked, and bread to be broken and passed around. He gave the blessing over the food. The evening was filled with celebration over their victory. The group exchanged stories of the day's events as they ate the meal and settled in for the night. Zarron located a rock that he found comfortable. He smiled to himself as he listened to the many stories and sounds of laughter. Sheen, finishing a story of her heroic deeds, came over and sat next to Zarron.

"Good evening or should I say good night Paladin?" Sheen asked him cheerfully.

"I am glad I finally have time to talk to you Sheen." Zarron replied returning the smile. She offered him a piece of bread which he gladly accepted, before settling in for a talk.

"So my first question is one you know I would ask. But, I will ask it anyhow. When did you join the church and why did you join?" He bit down into the soft bread savoring the nutty flavor of it as he waited for a reply.

"Well Zarron that is simple enough it was when I went ahead of you to warn the city. The Hand asked me how he could repay me and I asked to join the church. He pulled his sword free, set it upon the top of my head and began speaking the oath of The Nameless to me, which I repeated back and you know how it happens from there." She paused for a long moment as she listened to a story that was being told nearby. She gave a chuckle then looked back towards him.

"Forgive me, where was I, ah yes...right. I also asked to be put under your command. The Hand seemed to converse with someone I couldn't see and he allowed it to happen. Under the circumstance that I become a personal guardian to you no matter the situation. I didn't understand that when he said it, but I figure I will trust in him and know he had reason to say it."

Zarron chuckled to himself. "Sheen your main trust should be in the Nameless One, not in The Hand. I know you are to trust your brothers and sisters but, when you have a situation come upon you that you do not understand you should trust The Nameless One to give you the answers you need. I would guess he was either conversing with The Nameless One or The Voice who has nearly direct communication with the deity of our faith. So I presume since you are under my command I am to train and teach you in the way of the church aye?"

"Yes Zarron that is correct, that was exactly what The Hand spoke to me about as well." He leaned back his head and closed his eyes as he processed the information. After a moment he opened his eyes, he remained leaning back, it was quite comfortable and the coolness of the rock felt pleasant.

"So how did you gain the rank of warrior and skip soldier and how is it you can join the Church when you belong to the Shape Shifters? I haven't heard of a Shape Shifter being a part of the church since the beginning of it being established."

"Well Zarron, The Hand was good enough to be able to see my skill and capabilities and decided I need not be a soldier because he saw my wisdom went beyond that of a soldier." Sheen shrugged her shoulders. "I didn't understand that either but he said I would find out soon enough. As for the Shape Shifter thing, well as I told you I went and spoke to the council and some things were said there and done that released me from my initial duty. Now who was the first shape shifter to join the church?" Sheen asked her final question quickly to steer the conversation away from her meeting with the Shape Shifters.

Zarron peered at her for a few moments as he was deciding on the choice to press it or leave it be. After a while he decided to leave it alone, he knew she was hiding some details but, we all have our secrets. He closed his eyes once more. His brows furrowed as he tried to recall everything he knew about the first shape shifter to join the Church. After a few moments he began to tell the story. He looked around and saw that many of his brothers and sisters were listening intently. So he rose his voice to address the group.

"Well, back at the beginning, during the first war of the world that established the proper order in the heavens and hells there was a great man that appeared. Yes, he just appeared, there was no record of his birth and he claimed no real parents except for the one above." He took a sip of water before continuing.

"Well, this man had an incredible power, he could change into a massive silver dragon. He fought bravely with House Holyrage as it was attacked by the hordes of the Uttookari. He was finally struck down by Uttookari on the fourth day. The battle continued on for a few days after. Well on the seventh day Uttookari finally thought he destroyed the Holyrage house and if not for the events that followed he would have brought hell to earth and destroyed every being on it. As we should all know, except for you Sheen. It was on the seventh day that order was finally established in the heavens and hells and thus emerged The Faceless One and The Nameless One and of course the Shapeless One, however this story doesn't involve that god." He paused for a brief moment, taking another sip of water.

"Well it was a time when both the Nameless One and Faceless One worked together, probably the only time it would ever happen in all existence. As the Nameless One came down and worked on destroying the Uttookari he brought a great silver dragon with him that fought valiantly. It was that Silver Dragon that in turn fought against the first reported guardian of The Faceless One, as he turned against the Nameless One almost immediately after Uttookari was cast into the abyss. The two of them were in combat for days when finally The Great Silver Dragon struck the evil guardian down. After the fight the mighty beast turned back into the human that had fought with the Holyrage house. He was the first reported person being resurrected as well. Needless to say the people seemed to praise and worship the man who was the great silver dragon and it was then that The Nameless One realized a church would need to be established. The primary mission was to remind the people that he was God, not the silver dragon. The silver dragon was put in charge of beginning the church. He accepted gladly for he knew he was not one to be worshipped. That is the story of the first shape shifter that was part of the church." Zarron finished off his story.

"But, what was the name of that shape shifter? And did he die or did something else happen to him?" One of the men requested. He smiled at him.

"His name was Jericho and no he didn't die he lives on in this world and in dire situations he comes to the world's defense. He is quite simply this world's protector, its guardian Angel."

"Now, we should all be getting some rest I should think. We have a busy day tomorrow of destroying more supplies." Zarron announced.

Within seconds the camp stirred to life as they got ready for sleep. Fires were fed their final meal for the night, sleeping rolls laid out, food put away. Captain Agrith set up the guard rotation and within a half hours' time the camp was silent as rest settled in.

XXIV

Partaxis stood looking down at the maps laid before him. Little figurines were placed on it to represent certain armies and on a sheet of paper next to them told what the army was made up of. Partaxis rubbed his face as he closed his eyes for a moment.

"Alright so we can clearly say we facing an army of great diversity. You also say that the leader is some powerful dark sorcerer or another and they carry the banner of The Faceless One?" Partaxis asked his second in command scout, Proditor.

"Yes Lord Partaxis, I would not get such information confused." Proditor replied boldly.

"I can see that, how much time do you think we have before they are at our gates?" Partaxis requested eying him.

Proditor rubbed his chin as he thought about the answer. "Well the quickest they could be here would be about two weeks out. My guess though with an army the size they have I would say max would be a month. We might have been able to hope for slower progress but, the land has not changed in the past 2 weeks. Not even a little bit it is like someone has stopped it all together." Proditor gave his report confusion clearly in his voice about the land change.

"Very well, thank you Proditor, go now and treat yourself to some time off. I will call on you when I need you again." Partaxis ordered Proditor who bowed his head in thanks, he rendered a quick salute before exiting the war chamber. Partaxis turned towards the former commander of the keep.

"Commander Froth have we any further recruits in?"

Commander Froth chuckled to himself. "Partaxis since I put you in charge we have had people flock to our Fenrir to serve under you every day.

So yes we have new recruits in, about 40 more of them today. Under your command, Fenrir has never seen more men serving it."

Before Partaxis could respond there came a knock at his door. A moment later a servant popped his head inside.

"Lord Partaxis we have an urgent message from The Church of The Nameless." The servant notified his Lord.

Raamok turned his head sideways trying to hear the sound he heard just moments before. Raamok looked around his environment intently looking for motion of any sort. It wasn't long before the sharp sound of stone against stone pierced the air again. Raamok instantly gained his bearings before heading for the noise. Within a few minutes he came to the edge of a clearing. The clearing was speckled with a few large boulders. In addition the clearing had about 4 orcs and a creature he had never seen occupying it. He examined the creatures with great intrigue.

The unknown creature would have easily stood a few heads taller than himself if not for the major slouch. Its muscles bulged under the tight clothing that it had on. It rested a longer than normal hand on the ground. It almost reminded him of a Yeti, but something was far different with this one and he couldn't figure it out. '*What difference does it make they all die the same anyhow*' he thought to himself as he unsheathed his weapons quietly and began to inch closer.

He stopped abruptly in his path as the orcs gave a final shove pushing a massive stone away from an unexpected opening. Bright lights blasted the dying light's landscape, the colors were brilliant colors of blue, green, red, yellow and white and it took him a moment to have his eyes adjust to the sudden fury of intense colors.

The unknown creature said a few words to the orcs. They turned and started running off except for one who couldn't pull his eyes off the glowing lights. The unknown creature tightened his arm, a blade came shooting out of his skin. With one swift motion he killed the orc off with no concern over what he did. To his horror, or intrigue. He couldn't quite tell which was stronger. The creature reached down and tore an arm off the Orc. It squatted down and bit into the arm tearing great pieces of skin and flesh off it which it gladly consumed. Raamok scowled to himself as he continued his stealthy approach.

Partaxis raised his eyebrow at the servant suspiciously. "What is the message then?"

"Umm, M'lord it is carried by a person of the Church I will let him in." The servant said as he moved to another side of the door. He pushed it open presenting a man that bore the garbs of a Knight in the church. The knight entered briskly.

"Commander Partaxis we are told to report to our outposts and tell them of an attack on Citadel Heights. It is suggested you make any preparations to prepare for a siege and if possible any men you can send to help with the siege would be appreciated as well. There is a tunnel system in place to get them into the city." The Knight reported to Partaxis.

"It is Lord Partaxis young Knight, not commander I am Lord here." Partaxis scolded the Knight. The man took a step closer to Partaxis and met his glare defiantly. He lowered his voice.

"No, you are just a Commander to me no more; the only Lord's I serve are Lord Zarron ra Holyrage and Lord Ashen the Hand of the Church. The only person I swear my allegiance to is The Nameless One and I will not be intimidated by the likes of men like you. I do not respect you enough in this short time to even care to call you lord out of respect." The Knight took a step back before raising his voice to address the room.

"Now I have relayed my message and I will be on my way. If your men wish to join take the road South a short ways and there will be the city of Terrant, it is there more information will be passed on. From there, plans will be put in place to put them where they are needed." The Knight announced as coolly as he could muster, he was more than flustered with the whole encounter and was ready to be done with the entire thing. The last thing he was expecting was the loud booming of Partaxis's laugh.

"You guys are something else at the church. You say you serve under Zarron aye? How is he doing? He was here on the Fenrir not too long ago; how long ago did you begin your warning anyhow?" Partaxis asked as he wiped away tears from laughing so hard. The Knight couldn't keep his façade normal and it twisted in confusion at the sudden change.

"It was about a week's time ago. I couldn't get here faster. The roads have been swarmed with deserters from the Faceless One's armies. Along with them many thugs and bandits are trying to invest on the opportunity war can present." The Knight reported. Partaxis nodded his head at the Knight satisfied with the information. He dismissed him before turning to his battle charts.

He picked up another small figurine and placed it at Citadel Heights then looked at the many more cities on his charts that were under attack and he sighed to himself.

Raamok snuck in successfully on the unknown creature and he struck. The weapon grinded against the beast's skin as though it was wearing plate armor. It let out a roar as it swung at Raamok who jumped out of the way stunned that the blow didn't kill the unknown.

"You human dumb, die you now." The unknown said having problems forming the words. It tightened its muscles again and two bladed came out from its skin, as Raamok looked at the weapons he realized that they were actually bone not metal. He jumped back as the creature attacked.

He ducked another blow and stabbed his sword at the beast. It connected easily enough but once again his weapons did not pierce the armor skin of the beast. He rolled out of the way as the beast stabbed with his bone weapons. Raamok recovered himself from his roll in time to parry one of the bone blades just barely. He had to twist his body in some unnatural manner to avoid the second attack. He kicked both his feet out and connected with the beast's chest, sending it reeling back a few steps. He landed hard on his back and quickly gathered himself to his feet in time to prepare properly for the next wave of attacks.

The beast came at him again with a common attack of high, high, medium and finally low. Raamok met each attack with his own swords, each time he was able to riposte. The attacks that he hit with merely scratched the beasts armor skin and did nothing more. He growled in contempt. He attacked the beast with a roundhouse kick. The beast stopped its attack and bent back to avoid the kick. Raamok knowing the beast would probably dodge the kick set his foot down and lunged at the beast with a mighty two handed stab.

The silver blade connected with the beast's chest. He felt it bite into the armor a little more than his attacks had been. However the attack came at a great cost, his silver blade bent and snapped in two. The sudden shift of momentum as the blade broke put him off balance. He stumbled into the broken end. It stabbed into his leather armor and he felt a burst of pain as it pierced through completely.

The beast howled in pain. As Raamok pushed against the beast's chest to pull himself free, he noticed a small opening in the beast's armored skin under its chin. With a grunt of pain he pulled himself free of the broken blade. He dropped to the ground grabbing his side where the wound was created. As he pulled his hand away he clearly saw it was coated in blood. Scowling, he grabbed his other sword. He stabbed it up and under the chin of the beast. It burst through the top of its skull with great ease. The creature died so quickly that Raamok had just enough time to pull the sword free and roll out of the way.

He stared at the beast for a second before dropping down to his knee as the pain in his side pulsed and throbbed. He stabbed his sword in the ground and used it to help him stay upright. He reached to his side and unclasped his armor. He pulled it off dropping it to the ground. He began to examine his wound closer.

"Well that isn't pretty but I have gotten worse." Raamok said aloud. He reached towards his belt and pulled a vial from one of his pouches. He had to pause for a moment to allow a wave of dizziness and nausea to pass. As soon as he felt the nausea pass, he quickly got out the vial he was reaching for and opened it.

A strong odor hit his nose as he pulled the topper. The nausea returned as he took in a much deeper than needed whiff of the substance. As he waited for the nausea to pass once more, he felt the pain subside slightly. The medicinal rub was already working. He squeezed out a small drop of the substance and rubbed it on the wound. The cooling sensation intermingled with a strong burning, the discomfort and pain of it caused him to drop his sword forcing him to place both of his hands on the ground in an effort to keep his balance as the substance worked through the wound.

The pain of the healing substance was almost to the point of being unbearable when all of a sudden he felt the strong cooling sensation take over and the pain was nearly gone. The only feeling he had left of the deep wound was a slight scratchiness. Raamok breathed in and placed his hands behind him leaning back as he breathed in the fresh air.

"Silver seems to be more painful to heal from." he smiled to himself then started laughing.

"If it is so painful to heal from being human I bet those vampires I kill with it suffer so greatly, and the few that do get away, if they can heal, I bet they live life in such suffering. That makes my thrill of killing them that much more rewarding now." He chuckled again as he sat up. He picked up his armor and threw it on. He picked up his magickal blade and sheathed it. He also grabbed what was left of his silver blade and sheathed that as well. He turned towards the unknown beast to gather the broken tip to his silvered sword. As he looked upon it he gasped.

The armor skin it had was now dust around the beast. Raamok was surprised to see it was actually a Yeti underneath it all. The bone weapons seemed to have been made from different parts of the Yeti's own skeletal structure. A quick draw mechanism was installed underneath the fur to enable it to spring the blades forth by tensing its muscles in a particular manner. He proceed to lift the dead body up just enough to reach in and grab the second broken part of the silver sword which was sitting freely underneath it as the armor had turned to dust.

He placed the piece in his pack and looked at the beast for another second before the lights grabbed his attention once more. Raamok approached the opening.

It opened to a deep tunnel. The lights were projected from something further in. Raamok looked around the area one last time to see if he could see or hear any of the Orc's returning or any creature for that manner. Confident that nothing was around him, proceeded to duck inside the entrance. He stopped and sighed to himself as he remembered something important.

He left the cave one last time and reached into another pouch. He pulled forth a special arrow tip that was hollow but he knew something was placed in it to cause a marker to explode in the air that only the mages of The Fenrir could see. He pulled his bow loose and prepared the arrow assembly quickly. When it was fully assembled he knocked it, and launched it into the air. From what he could see it seemed like he shot a perfectly good piece of ammo into nothing and wasted it.

"It worked or it didn't, doesn't matter much to me. The help comes or it doesn't." Raamok said to himself as he ducked back into the cave entrance one more time.

XXV

The deep breathing of many men and woman echoed in the air as they finished off the remaining force of the enemy. Zarron's chest felt like it was on fire as the fighting had been long. He took a few slow breaths to balance out the burning in his lungs and within moments the feeling subsided. He knew a spell to cause it to not be there, however he wanted to save his energy for his people that would need healing.

As he looked around he saw that just about his entire force had been dismounted during the combat. He wasn't going to lie to himself, this was by far the most challenging group they had engaged in combat with.

They were a band of reinforcements for the siege at the city but something was different about this group and he relied on Captain Agrith to figure it out. He let out a quick breath of air before looking around at the damage.

As the dust settled the group's horses came back around and pawed the ground as they waited for their riders. Zarron smiled to himself as he spotted his massive war horse, Thunder. Other horses were not so lucky and he counted about 4 horses that had been killed. As he counted his men he found that there were no new losses which amazed him. He lowered his head and closed his eyes. He prayed thanks to The Nameless One for protecting them in this harrowing fight. When he opened them again he saw Sheen approaching him. His smiled quickly faded as he realized she was clutching her stomach, her face twisted in pain.

He ran up to her and just as he got close she collapsed. He was just able to pull her into his arms before she hit the ground. He removed his helm to get a better look at the wounds, his heart sank. She had an arrow pierced through her stomach and she bled freely from her chest from a nasty gash. Her arm bled profusely from a severe laceration.

"Sheen, please stay with me." He whispered to her as he laid her down. He went to work placing his hand over specific wounds. He willed forth his magickal essence and he felt it pulse through his body before it discharged through his hand. A warm tingling sensation left his hand and flowed over the wound Sheen had taken to her chest. A dull light began to glow at first and as soon as he recognized the wound in its entirety the dull light burst with a bright color, he watched as the wound healed as it would naturally but at an accelerated rate. Within moments the wound was closed, nothing remained to remind her of the wound. He placed his hands on the wound to her arm and repeated the process. Finally he got to the stomach wound. He snapped the shaft of the arrow in half and pushed it out of her. She moaned in pain, he winced as he went to work healing the wound.

'It is a good thing I have received many of these wounds before or I would have trouble.' Zarron thought to himself.

The way a person learned healing in a lot of ways was to know how the body reacts to certain cuts and scrapes. Along with knowing how to deal with the anatomy of skin, bones, blood and muscles. That knowledge defined how great of a healer one would become. It was a requirement in the Minds of the church to study those particulars fervently, in addition they always took what practice they could as well.

However the members of the Body of the church would learn their healing by wounds collected on their own body and they didn't venture to far into knowing how to heal others. They spent most of that time learning how to inflict the wounds on enemies. If needed, any person could technically apply the same theory to healing others but it was usually not advised as it would be draining to them and almost always leave a scar. In addition, the healing process would be more painful for the person being healed.

Zarron, was fortunate or unfortunate to have had lots of personal experiences receiving wounds in his short life time. Additionally he was blessed with an almost natural healing ability. With Mary's help he became a pretty decent healer, his skill rivaled those of the High Priest rank in the Minds of the Nameless.

As he finished healing the last wound he brushed a piece of hair away from Sheen's face and smiled at her. He set her down carefully before ordering some of the healthier people to create a litter and haul her back to their camp with the rest of the severely wounded. Satisfied she would be cared for he proceeded to go about tending the wounds of the others.

Within half-hour' time Zarron and a few others had healed all the wounded and transported them back to their little camp. They looked over the area once more before falling back to the camp. When he arrived at the camp he sat down heavily. He stared at his hands for several long moments deep in thought. Finally he leaned back and found a comfortable position his eyes closed from the weariness of healing and he slept.

Zarron was shaken awake in what felt like 5 minutes but as he looked up at the sky he saw the sun was low. He focused his attention on those who awoke him.

Jonathan and Captain Agrith stared at him, their faces looked like a little child receiving the best gift ever. Their eyes filled with excitement and joy. Zarron shook his head clear and pulled himself up.

"What is it that has you guys smiling like little kids?"

"Lord Holyrage the enemy we fought on the road was some of the elite forces of the army attacking the city." Jonathan reported, his eyes gleaming brightly. Zarron eyed them for a moment.

"The elite forces of the army." Captain Agrith spoke emphasizing his statement. Zarron's eyes widened as he realized what they were saying.

"Have you checked on the siege?" Zarron asked.

"Yes we have M'lord and they are using their reserves already, it would seem they thought it would be a quick siege and they would have the city under their control in no time. So, they wasted their men quickly enough. The siege machines are still barraging the walls though. I think our work back here has caused a lot of pain to them as well. Now that they aren't getting their more experienced I would say now would be a good time to strike." Captain Agrith reported.

"You are quite correct Captain. Let's get our people ready for an early morning raid when they send all their fighters to the front very few will be left in the back to defend it, would be a perfect time to strike. Tonight we shall get a good rest and enjoy ourselves for tomorrow will be a good day." Zarron announced to his companions.

The night came quickly and Zarron's groups of people were quite restless. You could cut the tension with a dagger. He did what he could to ease the men, he visited with them, swapped stories with them and prayed over them. It wasn't long before his whole group was asleep. He felt concerned for his men. For he knew that even with the army at the front there would still be much fighting and men to contend with. He didn't want to lose any of his people, it would be an eventuality, and war always claims its share of lives. He prayed them away the best he could before he laid down to get some sleep.

He got up just before the sun rose. He aroused the men and broke camp before eating a quick meal of biscuits and honey. He split his small group into teams and assigned each of them a duty. One team was to scout ahead and kill the camp guards as stealthily as possible before joining the siege team, the next team would create a distraction and his final team's job was to attempt to capture any siege machine possible, but, if that could not be done then they were to burn them to the ground. He hoped that once the people at the wall saw the main camp under attack they would form up and counter attack crushing the enemy army in between.

It took them little time to approach the camp and phase one began of his plan. His small group of men waited nervously as his first team went about killing the guards. Finally after what seemed like hours even though minutes had passed his team returned with their spirits high.

"Lord Zarron the guards have been dispatched and none made a peep. I would say with a normal camp routine we have about 5 or maybe 10 minutes to get in and get what needs to be done before they get curious about where their guards are and why they haven't received any reports." Jonathan reported to Zarron after he returned. Zarron nodded his head and smiled at him. He was proud of the skill of the group.

"Alright my brothers and sisters you heard Jonathan we have little time to get in there and do what we need to do. Remember the city and The Nameless One is depending on us to help break this siege. I would say spare no one of this group for they are all demon possessed and evil. I cannot sense one decent person among the lot of them. May the Nameless One bless you and your shields, may you strike true and destroy this serpent at our Holy Cities gates." Zarron spoke to his people and after he had finished he mounted up. Sheen and him-self led one team to the farthest side of the camp to create a distraction. Captain Agrith and Jonathan led the other team to the siege machinery.

Zarron and his team got to where they had plans of setting up the distraction quickly. He spread his people out to look as large as they could and he lifted up Angel Fire to his team before slamming it against his shield. His people followed suit and soon the air was filled with the pounding of swords and spears against shields.

"Now let us lift up our voices and let them hear our battle cry!" Zarron yelled his powerful voice echoing down the lines. Their battle cries shook the air around them with passion as if the Nameless One himself was there with them lifting and projecting their voices. A musical note came down upon them invigorating their spirits and bodies. It started off subtle then rose to a great roar of powerful moving music. The music didn't last long and as it settled down no sound was heard. However they could still feel the thrum of its power swell up inside of them. Finally after what seemed like an eternity an alarm rose in the camp. Zarron ordered the charge.

As his group of warriors burst into camp they knew right away that their ploy had worked. With even better than expected results with the strange musical hymn. The camp was in chaos, any defense they could muster rushed to engage the attackers. A few of the officers attempted to regroup their people but there was no hope in it. Their spirits had all been broken.

Zarron cut down an individual that had approached him and he looked towards the siege equipment. A great smile crept across his face as smoke filled the air from the burning siege machines. There was a strange phenomenon that occurred though and the smoke seemed to drift towards the ground rather than heading up. Zarron moved his horse out of the way as a spear was flung at him. With a spoken word he sent lightning upon the person.

Intrigued by the phenomenon he took a moment to reach out with his magick. He managed to touch what was causing the smoke to be contained. He found a powerful magickal shield had been put around the camp. It was at the moment that it all clicked. The beautiful music they had heard was actually what the Nameless One used to break down the shield to allow his people to break the siege. He knew that it was a one way ticket unless he could find the source of the shield and slay it.

He looked around for a moment before locating an exotic tent that was set up with the banners of The Faceless One. Without a shred of doubt he knew that was where the source of the magickal shield resided. He took a deep breath and charged towards the tent. He was not looking forward to combating a powerful sorcerer.

It didn't take long to approach the main tent. He was not surprised to see the evil leader there waiting for him. What did surprise him was to find it was a female, a very beautiful one at that. She had long flowing black hair with a bright shade of grey eyes. She wore very little in the way of clothing or armor and the stuff she did wear accentuated her shape, showing off her cleavage and beauty rather than provide protection.

"You seem shocked human at what you see." The woman spoke to him, her voice filling the air with its beauty.

"Pray tell me, who is this man that has caused so much trouble in my encampment?" She spoke again her voice as sweet as honey. Zarron impressed by her beauty stopped his horse and dismounted. He stared at her for some time before he spoke.

"My name m'lady is Zarron Ra Holyrage. Paladin of the Nameless One." Zarron said just audible enough for her to hear. The woman opened her eyes briefly in surprise before the smooth serene mask slid back in place.

"Perhaps Zarron, you like what you see, I would be more than willing to lay down with you, if only you can help me with this pesky little siege?" She said as she stepped closer to him. She reached out her hand for Zarron to kiss. He took it and just as he was about to kiss it his internal senses kicked in and blared a warning. He pulled away and slammed his shield into the woman sending her to the ground.

"Get back vile Temptress and prepare to meet your end." He pronounced sternly.

"So, Zarron this is how you want this to be. I shouldn't have given you an opportunity with me, I should have slain you, but who am I to think I can tempt a Holyrage. It was a mistake but one that shall not be my down fall." The woman said this time cold and heartless, the sweet, beautiful voice no more. She cast a spell and vanished only to reappear behind Zarron.

Zarron put his shield behind him and managed to block the oncoming spell blast, he spun quickly slashing out with Angel Fire but the woman dodged out of the way and threw another fireball at him. He stepped out of the way just missing it and lunged at the sorcerer. To his surprise he came in contact with another weapon that the woman had formed. She twisted her sword and knocked his out of the way as she attacked with another slash with hopes of disemboweling him. He brought his shield up and caught the invisible blade. *'Angel Fire I will need your help in tracking this sword of hers'*. Angel Fire gave him some peace, *'I will help you, but you Zarron, you have the ability to track it.'* He put his shield up as another blow was struck at him. As he swung back he just cut an illusion. He spun around again and this time he managed to bring his sword up as a fiery blast was heading at him. As it struck his blade it settled their momentarily. He swung Angel Fire at the woman and the fiery blast was redirected towards her. She cast a magickal shield and blocked the magick a look of confusion on her face.

Zarron took advantage of the moment, he cast a quick blinding spell which the woman easily recognized and unraveled it's magick before it reached her. He was expecting this. He lunged right behind the spell. As he attacked she bent backwards a ways and missed the blade as it whirred above her head. She was unable to recover in time to block the follow up kick which landed on her chin sending her spiraling off.

Zarron quickly ate up the ground and was on top of her stabbing his blade downwards. She blocked the slash. He performed a leg sweep which caught him. He slammed into the ground hard. She got up and stepped on his shield arm pinning it. She reached down and attempted to pull the shield from his hands. Despite her agility and strength he was still quite a bit stronger than her. He pulled up his pinned arm which set her off balance. As she regained her balance he pulled himself to his feet.

Anger seethed through him, his hate for the temptress overwhelmed his mind. He was tired of this fight, he wanted to be done with it so he could get back to his warriors. He let out a roar of frustration and his holy rage took over.

As he looked at the woman her beauty had all but faded. She was nothing more than an ugly hag, a tool of the Faceless One. Her spirit oozed with evil, there was not a single bit of light in her soul. Her swords glowed darker than the night could ever hope to get and was wickedly curved. He could also see when she was about to cast a spell because a dark mass came from her core and arched out her hands as she cast it. When she teleported he could follow the dark mist and know where she would reform as the mist would start to solidify.

He observed her for a while as she cast a few more spells and teleported around. Confident the he had enough insight gained on her attacks, he waited until she teleported again. As she teleported in an attempt to catch him off guard he reached out his hand as she passed close by. He grabbed hold of her neck and threw her to the ground.

As she put up her sword to defend, he turned aside her blade. He then grabbed her hand and tore the wicked blade away. She threw one more spell at him which hit him square in the hand sending his blade away as well. She pulled him close to her in an effort to destroy both of them at the same time. She wrapped her legs around him and squeezed. He made an effort to pull from her grasp but he found himself incapable of doing so as a spell he could not unravel enveloped them both. He felt his essence start to be torn from him and pain wracked his body. The woman licked her lips as a sick look appeared in her eyes.

"Looks like I got you right where I wanted in the end, it is a shame it has to be the death of us though." The woman said in a wicked coolness.

"No, woman, you are undone." He replied dispassionately as he summoned Angel Fire. As Angel Fire formed in his hand the blade burning with holy fire easily pierced her side. The woman dropped the spell as the pain tore at her concentration breaking it like a dried twig; he got to his knees and stabbed the sword into her cold heart killing her. There was a loud bang as the air tore open, the magickal shield was shattered

198

XXVI

It took Raamok a moment to adjust to the bright lights that were around him. As they adjusted he was shocked to be in a room filled with a myriad of different colored lights. Each one a separate string of color that intertwined with one another creating thick cords which in turn carried the pieces farther into the cavern.

Raamok had guessed that whatever this was, had been there for a real long time. Some of the strands had fallen away from the main strand and it created a cob web effect that littered the path he needed to take to proceed further. He stood there staring at the mess of strands and colors with his fists on his side trying to think about the next course of action.

He felt something vibrate in the air and an odd sensation of warmth flow through him. Finally there was a loud pop as a strand broke away and flew towards him quickly. He couldn't get out of the way as the strand burst through him. To his surprise though the piece seemed to heal his fatigue and wounds, as the magick faded, he took a closer look at the strand that had hit him and found that it was a bright white color.

"So white is healing, so I am assuming then that the other colors are some form of damage." He spoke aloud as he moved his hand close to another strand, this one was a light shade of yellow, and he felt a slight shock come from it. As he pulled his hand away it touched another strand that burned his skin partially. Raamok scowled and swore as the piece burned him. He felt another vibration in the air and heard the familiar loud pop as another strand broke. He managed to see this one coming from a ways off and lifted his foot as the strand whipped by him leaving an extremely cold trail that frosted part of his boot. He slammed his foot back down and shook it a little to get feeling back in it. He decided he had enough so he left the cavern.

As he exited the cavern he had just enough time to slide out of the way as an orc charged at him. The orc stumbled into the strand of colors before being consumed. The strands broke down the orc with the elements of the world. Finally the light and dark strands absorbed his body. Raamok shrugged his shoulders as he pulled his good sword free and readied himself to face the other orc's.

He quickly dispatched the next orc that charged at him and as he was about to engage a third a fireball flew past him, it exploded on the cavern entrance scattering broken rocks and pebbles. The orc he was facing quickly disengaged and ran back to hide behind several warlocks. Raamok looked at the warlocks and gave them a wicked smile as he opened his arms wide.

"So, they need magick to slay me! Well bring it on!" He yelled out to them in fierce challenge as he slammed a hand against his chest. He was familiar with casters but never had he faced so many at once. He wasn't worried about being able to slay the casters but his concern was on the many orcs that remained behind them.

He stabbed his sword into the ground and yanked his bow free as quickly as you could blink an eye he drew and loosed an arrow which killed one of the Warlocks outright. He had just enough time to drop his bow and yank his sword free before another spell was cast at him. As the spell drew closer he rolled out of the way having the spell miss him by a long shot.

Raamok stood up and readied himself for the next one that came in low; he jumped over the spell and prepared for the next volley of spells. This time all the casters started chanting all at once. It was the moment he was looking for. Rather than charge in right away at the warlocks he hung back biding his time as he watched them carefully. He didn't want to run in too soon and have them be able to lock onto him or change the spell they are casting and he couldn't be too slow as well because he would be toast. So he waited patiently and soon he saw them throw their arms forward and speak the last word unleashing all their fury at once. He seized the opportunity and rushed at one directly in front of him. He leapt over the spell and lunged forth stabbing his blade through one of the warlocks. The spells exploded shortly after that where he was standing a moment before. It sent tons of dirt, stone and smoke in their direction. He moved quickly to the next warlock. He attacked with what force he could muster. The warlock managed to get a quick magickal shield up but it was not a powerful one. With one more strong attack the poorly established shield shattered. The warlock crumpled under the might of the attack. He finished off the proned caster.

Before he could acquire another target a spell blast smashed into his back sending him falling forward. He turned the fall into a roll and popped up in front of another of the warlocks. He grabbed the hand of the warlock that held his scepter and faced it towards another one just as he finished casting a spell. The spell blasted into one of the warlocks and blew a hole through his chest. He spun to the back of the warlock slashing his sword across its neck spilling its life force.

As he finished with killing that one he saw the final warlock finish casting a mighty spell blast. He grabbed hold of the warlock he just finished killing and held it in front of him a shield as the blast hit them. The power of the spell sent him flying. He hit the ground, bounced twice before finally sliding to a halt.

He shook his head clear and looked up; he saw a wave of orcs rushing him. He breathed out before grabbing his sword. He pulled himself to his knees. Breathing in itself was laborious, there was an incredible pain in his shoulder but, he was not going to go down without a fight.

Raamok pulled himself to his feet and let out a shout of defiance. As he did that fire reigned down from above and consumed the orc line, as it hit the ground it formed into a wall of fire, a strong burst of wind blew it forward as it consumed the rest of the orc line. The remaining warlock dispersed the spell and flung another spell at Raamok, just as it was about to hit him it was destroyed in front of his eyes by a magickal shield. He felt a hand come to rest on his shoulder. As he turned he saw Tombah, behind him was Durakon, Partaxis and Proditor along with a scouting unit and a small contingent of wizards and mages.

"Why don't you handle that warlock Shaduuk?" Tombah instructed one of the mages in his group.

"Now Raamok what have you discovered here?" Tombah said not paying too much heed to Raamok and his state. Raamok stared at Tombah and clenched his sword, anger boiling up in him.

"Relax Raamok, you did good work here and we have a healer that can tend to your wounds." Partaxis said to Raamok.

"I don't care about that, he touched my shoulder, without my permission, secondly and most importantly he killed those orcs and that warlock when I was set to take them down." Partaxis stared at Raamok dumbfounded by what he had said for a few moments before he burst out laughing.

"Now where is that healer so we can move along with this little expedition?" Raamok asked. Within moments he was healed up and the group entered the cavern.

As they entered the cavern again Raamok saw Tombah already there observing the long cord of magick intertwined with each other. Tombah lifted a hand and the cob webs that were in the path dissipated.

"Now see here, these ones are easy but this thicker strand, it would take months to tear apart that strand or years to weave all that magick or, it would take a god that is incredibly knowledgeable in the magick arts. Even then it would take days or weeks." Tombah said to no one person in particular.

"Well, what can you tell us about it master." Shaduuk said as he entered the cavern smoke billowing from his hands. Tombah inclined his head, a look of wisdom settled on his countenance.

"I have an idea but, we should head further in to verify my suspicions." Tombah replied back. Partaxis and Raamok looked at each other curiously before following Tombah and his entourage of casters further in. As the group travelled further in the cavern it got less rough on the walls and started to smooth out, soon becoming something similar to a palace wall. More magick ropes joined the one they were following forming something like a living changing chain link. Soon the ceiling lifted to outstanding heights. Thousands upon thousands of chain links carried farther into the now fully formed palace. Expensive draperies hung from the walls and many exquisite painting adorned the walls as well.

"What is this place? It looks as though it dates back to the age of black. Perhaps older." Partaxis asked his voice echoing among the massive halls.

"These paintings, they are of battles, kings, queens and the kingdom of that time." Partaxis continued on. He suddenly stopped and stared at one particular painting. It was a beautiful piece of a massive battle. The sun raising on the distant horizon its sun beams shedding light on the battlefield. The artist even captured the light gleaming off the armor of the ancient warriors. Standards held high on the field many of them no longer known, bodies scattered the field and in the middle were two massive warriors locked in combat.

"This battle I remember it." Partaxis said in almost a dreamy state. Raamok continued on to the next painting and stopped there.

"I presume Partaxis it was not your finest hour." Raamok said as he looked at another painting that was similar to the other one but it was dreary and darker. A dark storm brewed above the battlefield and there was much death. The battle was obviously over and with the two great warriors only one stood, the other one was in a bloody heap at his feet.

"You didn't win that engagement did you?" Raamok asked as he leaned against the wall with his arms crossed.

"How did you know Raamok?" Partaxis asked.

"I recognize your coat of arms from when we first ran into each other. You try to hide it but you are terrible at doing so. So, once again did you not win that engagement?" Raamok asked.

"No I did not. The battle lasted for days. I and the king of the North, Tahvo, we met each other on the battlefield every day. Never have I met a better warrior or a more sadistic evil one either. We would fight for the whole duration of the battle only to have it end in a draw each day. Thousands of our men died while we were engaged in combat. Now I regret it because I could have saved many of those men had I not such a deep vengeance and hate towards Tahvo. I would track him down every day just to fight him, ignoring any of the other soldier's pleas for help. Finally on the last day we came in contact for the last time. A strong storm brewed above, one that has never been seen before. That battle lasted nearly a whole day and even a little into the night. Both our bodies were sore and tired from the continuous fighting; the field we were in ran red with blood, parts of it flooded from the severe rains. It was only a matter of time before one of us was to make a mistake and it was him at first. He lost his grip on his sword momentarily and I took advantage of it. As I swung my hammer at his head, he chose to have his arm crushed rather than his skull as he put his arm up to take the blow. I thought at that point it was over and I made the second mistake. I assumed it was over. Tahvo had an assassin waiting just in case of him possibly losing. So as I let down my guard I was stabbed in the back. Tahvo recovered his sword and sliced me from left shoulder to right hip before stabbing me in the stomach. He left me for dead at that point. I don't remember much from that point except waking up some time later in a place I did not know and with a person I did not know." His voice teetered off as he thought about the incident. After a brief moment he shook his head clear of the visions and came out of his reverie.

"Anyhow enough of that, our caster entourage has moved on." Partaxis finished with his story and turned to look at the painting again.

"You have a strong ability to survive Partaxis." Raamok said before moving on. As he left Partaxis there he heard a loud bang and a crack spread across the wall next to him. Raamok turned around to see Partaxis leaning against the wall with his hammer planted in it, the painting was a heap at his feet. Raamok went back to Partaxis and threw a bottle of oil onto the painting. He pulled out his flint and with one strike he set the oil on fire which quickly consumed the entirety of it. Raamok turned back again and caught up with the entourage of casters. Within moments Partaxis was next to him with a big smile on his face.

It wasn't too much further before they came to an incredibly massive room which had a colossal throne in it. On the throne sat a colossal giant, one that far surpassed any giant they had seen before in size and stature. All the magickal chain links pierced its skin in many places. As the giant shifted some of the small threads that made the link snapped away and flew down one of the many hundred corridors. As Partaxis entered the room his jaw dropped open.

"TAHVO!" Partaxis yelled at the top of his lungs. Raamok cast Partaxis a quick glance his eyes wide. Raamok's surprise only lasted seconds before he burst out laughing.

"What are you laughing at Raamok?" Partaxis growled.

"His paintings make him look much smaller, or you much bigger." Raamok continued laughing as the giant turned its focus on them.

"Partaxis is that you?! I had thought I killed you." The Giant roared and it stood up to his full height of nearly 150 ft. Many of the chains broke loose but all he could do was stand up and take one small step towards the group before he reached his chains extent. The giant reached a hand towards Partaxis as he did this a massive fire blast blew his hand off spilling blood everywhere. Tombah stood there with fire coating his hand. The giant pulled back and let out a deep rolling laugh that shook the room.

"Wizard I admire your passion but your measly spells cannot slay me." The giant said to Tombah. There was a loud thrum in the air followed by an intense heat. Most of the group had to cover their ears and breathing became difficult. There was a bright flash of light, as the groups eyes adjusted they saw the giant had regained its hand.

"Next time Giant I will melt your head and we shall see if you can regenerate that." Tombah scowled at the giant.

"Tombah give me a boost." Partaxis yelled as he rushed the giant as he leapt in the air a strong air burst boosted him to incredible heights. Partaxis landed on the giant's stomach and punched a fist into it and launch himself higher. At the same time Tombah cast another fire blast that slammed into the knee of the giant forcing him to the ground. At this time Partaxis had reached the giants chest and slammed his hammer into it. A loud crack followed by a pop echoed in the air as the chest broke open. It created a small opening, blood poured out through it. As the giant crashed down to one knee Partaxis grabbed hold of the opening to keep himself from falling off.

As the giant collapsed to one knee Raamok ran at it and jumped up and stabbed his sword into the giants shin just as he had used killing giants before he used his blades to help him get higher with each jump. As he got to the appropriate height he jumped. As he jumped the giant shifted and it sent his jump off course as he started to fall a strong hand grasped him.

"Let's give you a quick boost Raamok." Partaxis said as he swung Raamok up, throwing him towards the giant's face.

"ENOUGH!" The giant yelled releasing a powerful blast that sent everyone flying. His knee healed instantaneous and the wound in his chest closed. Raamok slammed into the wall knocking the wind out of him. As he began to fall the giant cast a spell that slowed his descent. As Raamok's feet settled on the ground a warmth flowed through him and all his fatigue was dissipated, the burning in his chest went away.

"Once again enough, Partaxis even with our history I have no desire to kill you. I did that once already." Tahvo said.

"What are you doing Tahvo and what has happened to you?"

"What do you wish to know? The long story or the short?"

"The short one, giant." Partaxis replied shortly.

"Very well, after the day I had thought to have killed you I grew drunk with power. I wanted to expand my northern kingdom. I fought everyone and anything that threatened that power. I could never seem to conquer the great Fenrir. It stood strong, no matter what I tried I could not destroy it. It was the only thing that kept me from flooding into the southlands. Well, because of this I ran into an interesting proposal from a demon, more precisely, Gullock, the ancient one. He said I could have limitless power; a kingdom forever, a castle forever and I was sold. What I didn't know was the price for accepting a demon's help or in this case an evil god is death in the end or eternal prison. I served one purpose for the dark god and that was to help crush the remaining Holyrage. I know the legends say the Holyrage house was destroyed completely after Uttookari but, the truth is, a small village of them survived. They fought like wild beasts, they repelled our attacks again and again. Our sheer numbers were the only that allowed us to eventually overwhelm them. We suffered enormous casualties. Well after several days of fighting those monsters. We finally slaughtered the last child. I made the mistake of asking when I would get what was promised for me. Well needless to say Gullock was preparing this prison for me even before I agreed to help him; he knew that our battle Partaxis, would have determined who he could use. He took no time to lock me up in here. He did as he promised me, a kingdom forever and a castle forever. So this is my castle and my kingdom is the changing northlands which are tied in with my emotions and thoughts. I feel what is going on up there and right now it is fear and death." Tahvo finished his story with great sadness.

"I have never known you to be a caring person Tahvo, what has changed?" Partaxis asked.

"Remorse, shame, embarrassment, I was used Partaxis it wasn't right. This was not my idea of power. I feel everything up there, recently there was a great love and hurt I felt. It had a profound effect on me. I cannot live this life anymore. I just want to be redeemed and live no more. I know a great evil force is at work and they have intentions on using me. Partaxis, I have been used through my whole life I am done with it." Tahvo said.

"So what do you propose giant?" Partaxis asked.

"It is simple, I will help with this upcoming battle then I wish for you to kill me."

XXVII

Zarron placed his hands upon his ringing ears. He could hear a distant voice calling his name. His head was spinning and a wave of nausea washed upon him. He closed his eyes. When he opened them again he saw a figure approaching him.

"Zarron, Zarron Ra Holyrage are you ok?" The person said to him her voice still sounding distant. He focused and saw The Voice of the Nameless walking towards him with her entourage of High Clerics.

"Yeah….I thinks so. Just a little shaken up is all." He replied in a hoarse voice. The Voice lent him a hand.

"I presume the siege is broken?" He asked his hearing and vision supernaturally restored to normal.

"Indeed it has been broken Zarron. We observed your fight with the witch from the battlements. As soon as we saw you grab hold of her in mid shadow walk we knew it was going to be over, we assembled a counter attack." The Voice finished speaking to him her voice soothing his fatigue and wounds.

"Zarron" Another voice grabbed his attention. He looked towards it and saw Sheen running towards him blood covering her garments. He started, Sheen place a hand up stopping him.

"No Zarron this is not my blood. I am glad to see you safe. Thank you, Lady Voice for leading the counter attack."

"Lady Voice, if you will excuse me I would like to tend to my men and women." Zarron requested of The Voice. She nodded her head towards him. With a clipped movement she turned and took off to examine the rest of the battlefield.

"It is good to see you Sheen. Do you happen to have a status report on my warriors?" he asked.

"Yes Paladin, we lost four, two of the warriors, one Elite and Captain Agrith." Sheen reported sadly. Zarron took a slow breath and rubbed a hand across his face.

"He was a good man. They all were good people." There was a pause as he gathered his thoughts.

"Alright, well let's gather up our dead. We must prepare them for a proper funeral. I will go and visit their families to tell them of their losses. Just do me a favor and recover their pendants of rank for me first. I will be waiting at the citadel for your return with those items." He said to Sheen before giving her a weak smile. Sheen nodded her head and took off to do Zarron's bidding.

It didn't take long for Zarron to reach the Citadel. Once he got there he found Lord Ashen waiting for him.

"Paladin Zarron you did well out there. If it wasn't for your house guard harassing the back lines we would have still been holding off the siege." Lord Ashen commended Zarron.

"Thank you, M'lord. Why is it that such a large force of the Faceless One's people would launch such an attack on the Citadel of the Nameless One?" Zarron asked sternly.

"I could not tell you Zarron, I have my ideas and none of them equal out to anything but trouble." The Hand replied before continuing.

"With further reports these attacks have happened all across Vin Ara Talv, many of the smaller towns didn't last more than a day or two. Already the south eastern provinces have fallen under control of The Faceless One. It would seem that was where they attacked from. Tear Drop keep has been under siege for a week or so longer then we have. Reports from there sound like they are doing well still. Since this siege is broken I am going to lead the Holy Hammerers to Tear Drop keep to lend a hand. If your guard of 20 can help break a siege I am sure 200 can at least do that much." The Hand gave Zarron a smile. Zarron smiled back and took in a breath before asking what he wanted.

"M'lord I need to ask of you a favor. I am hoping you can spare men for the Fenrir. I think the largest force to deal with currently is attacking from there. With the Faceless One's guardian leading the attack we need as much help as possible. I also would like to request Zeth to be transferred to my guard. I lost my captain and I can't think of a better man to replace him." He asked The Hand humbly. The Hand grabbed a passing by Knight and spoke some words with him quickly. Zarron stood back waiting patiently. It wasn't long before The Hand turned back to Zarron.

"Paladin Zarron I will give you 545 brothers and sisters. I wish it could be more but you must understand that it is the most we can spare. As for Zeth to serve as your Captain, I will transfer him under you so long as you ask him first and he comes to me and lets me know he is willing." The Hand instructed.

"Your newest member approaches Zarron, I will take my leave from you and allow you to get to your duties. You have done well today Paladin Holyrage. Don't think anything but that, to have lost the small numbers you have and accomplish what you have is nothing to be ashamed of." The Hand placed a hand on Zarron's shoulder before pressing his forehead against Zarron's before walking away. Zarron took a deep breath in and held back tears for those he lost as Sheen approached.

"Zarron, I have never seen such reverence between a higher ranking and subordinate before. There is a great deal for me to learn of your deity nevertheless, I am yearning to learn more."

"And you shall Sheen, are those the pendants and ranks I have asked for?" Zarron asked while pointing at what Sheen had in her hands.

"Indeed they are Zarron, would you like some company as you deliver the news to their families?" Sheen asked as she handed the pendants and ranks over to him. He took them from Sheen and offered his hand to her.

"It would be nice to have someone with me. Thank you Sheen." Zarron grabbed her hand and pulled her along as he headed off to the first dwelling on his list. It didn't take him long to navigate his way through the housing district before reaching the home of the first warrior he lost.

It was a nice quaint home with a beautiful garden in the front of it. There was a pleasant smell coming from within the home of fresh pastries being baked. Zarron knew that chances were this member's family was making a feast to honor their daughters victory in the field and Zarron's heart sank.

"I don't think I can do this Sheen. I failed this family in not being able to bring their daughter home to them." He turned and spoke with Sheen as a sick feeling rose within his stomach. Sheen looked at Zarron and turned him towards her.

"Zarron you can do this. You are not a failure; you will bring peace to this family doing what you are doing. War is not a pleasant thing Zarron you and I both know this, casualties happen. You are not a failure Zarron." Sheen said to him as she looked deep into his eyes. He knew there was no doubt that what she was saying was true.

"You are right Sheen; forgive me for my moment of weakness. Second time I have had to deliver news to a family that lost a daughter. Mary being my first and even then I sent a rider ahead to give notice to The Hand of his daughter's demise…Let's do this then shall we?" Zarron said as he gained some newfound confidence. They only took another two steps before Zarron stopped briefly and turned to Sheen.

"Thank you Sheen." Zarron said to her as he put a hand lightly upon her arm before continuing to the door step.

The last few steps to the door felt like they took forever. As Zarron got there he lifted his hand up and slowly knocked on the door, the dull thud of his fist seemed to echo in the air. He stood there for some time before an older woman answered the door.

She was shorter than him by several heads, her body was plump and her cheeks were rosy. Deep smile lines etched her face and crow's feet wrinkles adorned her eyes. She was full of joy and energy. He knew without question that she had lived a happy life.

"My, my I don't get many handsome visitors at my door step. Nor Paladins from the church either." The older lady said in a merry tone.

"You are too sweet m'lady; I just wish I was here on better terms."

"Oh? Is that so?" The lady asked still with cheer in her voice. Zarron tried giving her a slight smile but he could not find the strength to do so.

"Ma'am, your daughter Acasia served under my house guard. I sadly did not have a long time to get to know her but in the time I have, she has been incredibly loyal to me and the Nameless One. She helped destroy the supply lines of the enemy in the siege and even participated in the battle today in a surprise attack upon the enemy. She sadly met her end today in the field of battle. I am so sorry for your loss." He choked back tears as he presented her daughters pendent and rank to the mother. The older lady took hold of them as she looked up at him. She gave his hands a squeeze.

"Come now my child and let me get you some tea and pastries." With that the older lady pulled him inside. She signaled for Sheen to follow. She sat them both down on a couch before rushing off to the kitchen. Within moments she came back with tea. She served it along with sweet pastries to both of them.

"What are your names children?" The older lady asked the two of them.

"I am Zarron ra Holyrage and this is my companion Sheen Forestranamas. What is your name kind woman?"

"My name is Thessa. You know Zarron; I have lost 7 sons, 2 daughters and a husband serving under the Nameless One. There has only been one other person to bring me the news of a death of a child that was directly under their command. Many of them don't have the courage or the heart to do it themselves. That one other person that has done that was Lord Ashen before he became The Hand. You have a strong character like him Zarron. You will do well in serving the church." She smiled before continuing on.

"Thank you for giving me peace and doing it personally. I know of you Zarron and this must have been hard for you with your recent loss."

Zarron was shocked.

"How do you cope with losing so many? And cope while still being joyous and not turning away from the Nameless One?" he asked honestly perplexed by this woman.

"Oh it has not always been that easy my child. There are times when it gets hard but, I have never had any desire to turn away from The Nameless One. If given the chance I would not change a thing in my life, my children and husband were strong followers of The Nameless One. I know they are in a better place and I will see them soon. This life is short when compared to an eternity with him. I always remind myself of that when things get hard and it pulls me through while making life bearable." Thessa finished speaking. She remained quiet leaving Zarron and Sheen to ponder what she said.

"Now you two must be off, there are still other families needing to hear word of their loss. And don't worry about me I will be fine. My other children should be arriving soon for dinner and I will let them know what has happened to their sister. May the Nameless One pour out his blessings on you both."

"Thank you Thessa, I shall not forget you and what you have taught me. Your daughter was blessed to have a wonderful mother such as yourself." Zarron gave her a hug before departing, leaving Sheen to her goodbyes.

Sheen's heart was overflowing with emotions, she couldn't believe the joy and love this woman portrayed and her heart yearned to be in her presence more. She never experienced a good mother. However this woman is what she imagined one should be like. Soon tears came to her eyes.

Thessa turned her attention on Sheen who was crying before her. She didn't need any magick to know what was going on with Sheen so she walked up to her and wrapped her arms around Sheen embracing her in a warm hug. The two of them stood together in a motherly daughter embrace for a few moments before Thessa pulled away to get a good look at Sheen.

"You are a beautiful woman Sheen and you have a beautiful heart. I can tell you missed having a mother growing up. I would love to have you stop by when you get the chance to. Now, you have a handsome man out there waiting for you. So how about we get you cleaned up real quick and you two can be on your way." Thessa pulled Sheen to her washbasin. She handed her a cloth to dry her eyes with.

"Thank you Thessa, I am honored you would like to have me over when I can get to it. Zarron was right you are a blessing to your children and I have to add, a blessing to those that come in contact with you. You have so much of the Nameless One's spirit in you from what I understand. Don't lose it and I am so sorry for your loss." Sheen gave Thessa another hug and a kiss on her cheek before stepping out the door. Sheen was startled by the sudden voice of Zarron as she stepped out the door.

"I learned so much from her in those few minutes then I have learned over the many years serving the church. She is a wonderful woman. Come let's move on, I feel a surge of strength and hope after talking with her."

The two of them carried the message to the other men he lost, through it he experienced a little bit of everything. There was one family that was so stricken by their loss they tore their clothes and threw dust on their head. A widow cried on Zarron's shoulder for many minutes and some remained deathly quiet. Despite the strength and hope from Thessa each person they went to wore down their spirit. His heart broke for each one of the families over their loss. He saved Captain Agrith for his last stop. Before long he was standing at his Captains fathers' door. Once again Zarron took a deep breath before he walked up to the door.

As he approached he heard loud laughter and many voices from within. A strong odor of occabot filtered out from the house. He knew of the occabot as a plant that people would grind up and soak in different liquids for flavor. They would dry it out then light it up after it is rolled in thin bark from a pine sapling. It was used for many things, most of the time people would use it as a leisure activity and other times the smell of it would cover up less savory scents. He had smelled it several times after a small skirmish to cover the scent of blood and gore. Not thinking anything of it since most of the town was in celebration he proceeded to knock on the door. As he knocked the noise did not abate any. Within a few moments a man opened the door a little bit and shut it quickly as soon as he saw a Paladin of the church was at his door.

Zarron turned to Sheen, raising an eyebrow curiously. As he listened closely. He could pick up on someone telling everyone else to be quiet and be still. After another minute or two the noise abated and the man answered the door again. He stepped back as the door swung open quickly. The man whisked his way out of the doorway and shut it behind him suddenly. He was an unkempt ugly man who stunk of wine and whiskey.

Despite the oddity of the situation Zarron cleared his throat. He badly wanted to demand what was going on. However he thought it would not be appropriate.

"Sir, would you happen to be the father of Captain Agrith?" As Zarron finished asking the man let out a cackle, his breath reeked of alcohol and the smell of it made Zarron slightly nauseous.

"You mean Aaron, that useless son of mine? Aye I sadly have the liberty of being his father."

Zarron's face darkened at this man's blatant disregard and outright insult towards his son. He was about ready to explode on this man. His intentions were obvious to Sheen but not to the man before him. She acted quickly and placed a gentle hand on his shoulder before whispering to him.

"Zarron be still, this man is but a fool. Loose tongues can cause more harm than good."

"Eh, what is it that pretty lady is saying to you?" The man requested boldly.

"She was merely asking me what might be the name of Captain Agrith's father." Zarron spoke as coolly as he could muster.

"Lyros be my name."

"Well Sir Lyros I bring you grave news of your son's death. He died..."

Before Zarron could continue any further Lyros cut him off.

"Well I can't say I am disappointed, I am surprised the boy even amounted to anything, Bastard killed my beautiful wife at birth. How much money do I make over his loss? You know lady you remind me of my wife, you would look mighty fine laying in my bed at night. I could show you a good time you know?" He winked at Sheen.

"That's it!" Zarron yelled aloud. Before Sheen could attempt to stop him he slammed a foot into Lyros chest sending him flying through his door. A puff of smoke and dust clouded the air as the door slammed down off its hinges. As he followed the man inside the true smell of the house hit his scent. It smelled of sweat, cheap perfume and bodily fluid. As his eyes adjusted to the dim light his stomach sank and righteous fury boiled his blood, threatening to take over his senses.

"You insolent fool; you dare run a whore house in the Nameless One's holy city?" Zarron roared, enraged at this abomination. Lyros whimpered in fear and the rest of the people there cast their heads down in shame. Zarron began to tremble with anger. He reached for his sword, as he attempted to draw Angel Fire he discovered it stuck fast in it's sheathe. He pulled again with more force and still the sword would not be drawn. After one more failed attempt, the voice of his sword entered his mind.

'Zarron I will not have you using me to shed innocent blood. You are better than this, not only to the Nameless One but to yourself and those that look upon you. Remember justice is not for you to take, it is set aside for the Nameless One alone.'

Zarron growled as he spun towards Sheen.

"Sheen, give me your sword." He ordered harshly. Sheen sighed and looked at Zarron seeing his hatred towards this unjust. Her heart hurt for him and the pain he was going through seeing their God's city defiled in such a manner. At the same time she was frightened by his actions. She was also filled with pity for this man before him cowering in his soiled breeches.

'Sheen, my daughter, you have the ability to soothe his nerves. Speak what you feel on your heart and say no more. You cannot force him to give up his free will, but, you can soothe his pain.'

A soft but strong voice entered Sheen's mind. She knew it was none other than the Nameless Ones. She felt nervous about proceeding but she knew she needed to.

"I cannot deny you that Zarron. Just remember that shedding this innocent man's blood will not accomplish anything. It will not sate your taste for this serious unjust act. This man is a fool and the alcohol has not helped him with being any less of a fool. He is still the father of a hero, if you want to see true justice, pray for this man, if you love your enemy it is like pouring hot coals on their head." Sheen spoke with a soft voice as she handed her sword to Zarron. He took the sword from her hand and placed the tip on the man's throat.

"Everyone out! Not you Lyros" Zarron yelled to the rest of the people in the home. The whores and the patrons rushed past him clutching their clothing to their chest in an attempt to hide their nakedness. Not one of them took the time to get dressed properly before rushing out in fear of Zarron. As soon as the last person left Zarron turned his full attention on Lyros. His eyes burned with righteous anger. He took several deep breaths, his eye twitched with anger, his lips curled up slightly and his brow furrowed. He lifted the sword above his head, Lyros whimpered as he curled into the fetal position waiting for the death blow to come. Zarron let out a roar of anger and slammed the sword down narrowly missing Lyros. He kneeled down next to Lyros before pulling him up. He stared at him face to face.

"Lyros, you are here by banished from this city. The money that you would have received from your son's death will go towards the Church to feed and clothe the poor. I would say your house shall be burned to the ground but, that is a decision left to The Hand and The Voice. If I see you again I do hope it will be from a change of heart and mind. I will pray for your soul father of Aaron Agrith." Zarron released his hold on Lyros letting him fall heavily to the ground sobbing.

"Lyros I would suggest you gather what little belonging you can carry and be gone by the time I return." He barked at Lyros. He got up from his knees and retrieved Sheen's weapon.

"Thank you Sheen and thank you Angel Fire for listening to the Nameless One when I was too caught in my rage to do so." He spoke to Sheen as he pushed her sword into her hands trembling. Sheen nodded her head and looked after Zarron for a moment before following him. She felt the strong surge of emotions he was suffering from and she yearned to reach out to him, to hold him, to comfort him. She knew this could not be done yet and possibly not ever, so, with a small sigh she looked over at Lyros again who was still sobbing in a ball. She clicked her tongue at him before falling in beside Zarron.

The two of them walked briskly to the main Citadel feast hall where they knew The Hand and The Voice would be in celebration of the victory. Zarron burst through the doors before the two Soldiers could open the door for him. He looked around briefly to locate where The Hand and The Voice were sitting. Once he found them he directly walked towards them ignoring the cheers, applause, and congratulations from individuals. As he got close to where the leaders of the church were sitting they stood up to meet him realizing the urgent look on his face. They looked towards Sheen for some confirmation of Zarron's emotions and she nodded her head to them.

"My dear Zarron you look flustered." The Voice spoke first her sweet melody calmed Zarron's nerves enough so he could focus.

"My Lord and Lady I have grievous news for you both and seek your wisdom and counsel."

"Very well Zarron, let us take our leave to the courtyard. We can talk there." The Hand replied.

Zarron nodded his head. The small party left the loud noises of the feast hall to the peacefulness of the courtyard. Once there, The Voice cast a veil of silence over them to keep prying ears from hearing something they shouldn't.

"Now what is the grievous news Zarron?" The Voice spoke again.

"My Lord and Lady as I was doing my rounds delivering news to the family of those that were loss from my guard. I came upon an abomination in my captains' fathers' home. Lyros Agrith was running a brothel." Sharp gasps came from The Voice and The Hand.

"I took it upon myself to banish Lyros from this city and his money he would have collected from his sons' death to be donated to the poor for food and clothing. My apologies for not consulting with you firstly on that decision, I also ask for forgiveness for I had planned to kill him where he stood but, Sheen and Angel Fire were listening to the Nameless One more than I was and talked me out of making that mistake. What I need is your wisdom and counsel on what to do with his home."

"Zarron you did well in your decisions and you need not feel guilty about them. Being a Paladin you have that authority to deal with abominations such as that. I am not pleased with your want to slay this man but I sadly cannot blame you for feeling that way. I am pleased to hear that you had a sister and sentinel sword to talk you out of it. As for his house, I am saying that burning it would do the best. It would take far too many hours to banish whatever evil spirits lay in wait within those walls. What might you say Lady Voice?" The Hand finished speaking.

"I agree with what Lord Ashen has said. It would indeed take many hours or days to banish what is inside. Holy fire is the best option for us at this point. Zarron, Sheen and Lord Hand I would like for you to assist me in handling this. There is no reason for me to summon High Clerics and take away any further brothers and sisters from celebrating. It will give you, Zarron and Sheen, a chance to learn something new and understand the procedures of cleansing an area with Holy Fire. It will sap you mentally especially with what you have been through today. I have no doubts that you both can handle it or I wouldn't ask of you this task. Now let us be on our way." The Voice finished speaking and the group of them headed for Lyros' home.

By the time they got there the sun was starting to set and a warm orange glow wrapped its tendrils of colors across the holy city. Voices of sing and praise were heard throughout their walk until they approached the road Lyros lived on. There was no singing or praises nor any dancing. The orange glow seemed to be dulled in this area and life in general seemed to be sapped. A thick aura in the area seemed to suffocate the group. The Voice started to sing a little tune. As she sang the darkness lifted and the air became lively again.

"There was quite the spiritual hold over this place. I am surprised you did not pick up on it when you first approached this area Zarron." The Hand spoke.

"It is odd that I didn't, I wonder why that was." Zarron trailed off in his thoughts.

"Well think nothing of it I am sure you were preoccupied with your grief." The Hand replied back to Zarron. As they approached the house Zarron was stunned to see Lyros in the position they left him in but he was still. The Voice walked up to him and placed a hand on his wrist. She shook her head and looked over at Zarron.

"Zarron he is dead. There is no sign of any trauma or bleeding. He just seemed to have been struck dead." The Voice spoke surprised. At that point a strong wind came over them, dark clouds came from nowhere. Loud thunder and lightning flashed in the sky and the group of them stared up at it confused.

'This man brought an abomination upon my city; he brought down many of my people and led them astray. He caused some of my children to give up their purity. Taught them that beauty is in the flesh only, he is an enemy of mine and Justice was served by my hand.' A loud voice rippled in the air sounding as if the thunder was speaking to them. Lightning flashed again and the house caught fire even with The Voice inside.

The Hand, Sheen and Zarron started to rush inside after her. But, as they did this they saw two figures walk out unscathed, one being The Voice and the other being a divine being of incredible beauty and power. The group blinked their eyes and all that stood before them was The Voice. The Hand let out a sigh of relief and wrapped The Voice up in a loving embrace. Thunder echoed in the air again and the clouds dissipated. The house had been burned to the ground. A beautiful garden grew in its place.

"Where darkness and evil resides he brings the light and beauty." Sheen whispered to herself as she adored the garden. Zarron wrapped an arm around her and gave her a gentle squeeze.

"Well, who's hungry?" Zarron asked feeling peace and joy returned to him.

XXVIII

"Why should we believe that you would dare help us Tahvo? Even with your change of heart now doesn't erase the brutal and evil being you once were?" Partaxis asked his former enemy.

"Partaxis I cannot convince your stubborn bull head of an honest change. But, what I will do is give one of you the secret of slaying me."

"What can you offer me to prove that what you say is true and not a way to release you from this prison?"

"Nothing Partaxis, there is nothing I can offer you that will guarantee what I tell you is the truth, for the dark god that cast me here is the only one that knows how to release me alive from this prison. The grave news of that is he is dead by mine own hands. I am a changed man and a broken man Partaxis I have no desire to live." Tahvo's voice trailed off leaving an eerie silence in its wake. Partaxis stared at Tahvo rubbing his jaw in thought.

"Tahvo, I will not just slay you as you are, chained up with no will to fight. Instead I challenge you to a duel. If death is what you want I can arrange it so that if I shall perish my company here will finish you off. What do you say Tahvo? Do you have one more fight in you?" As Partaxis finished several gasps came from some of his people. Raamok raised an eyebrow at Partaxis intrigued by the change of events.

"Very well Partaxis, I shall do as you request. The chance to fight you again is a thrilling idea. I shall do this, and I shall do it as we fought before. I shall use none of my dark magick. It will be as it was during the Black Wars. If I kill you Partaxis I do expect your people to hold up their end of the bargain and finish me off. I do not want to have them run in fear because their leader is dead."

Partaxis nodded his head towards Tahvo and gave a wicked smile. Before he could say anything further Raamok busted out laughing.

"Run in fear Tahvo? Surely you jest." At Raamok's remark the rest of the group laughed and even Partaxis and Tahvo joined in. It only lasted a few quick moments before Tombah silenced the group with a loud thunderous bang.

"Tahvo how are we to kill you? That is what these dimwits should be wondering and how can Partaxis win in a fight against you? You regenerate instantaneously. I doubt you will be able to keep from using your dark magick as well. I believe this is a ruse to slay Partaxis and nothing more. I demand your secret placed in front of us first before we allow this childish act to happen. Not to mention this may never happen if this dark army led by the Faceless One's guardian wins the day." The group became somber at the mages truth and the joy on Tahvo's face faded.

"Well then mage, you best not lose this fight then. As for my secret I shall grant it to one of you. I will tell them what it is and have it bound in a death stone. Then we can take the stone and position it in such a place on my body that should a sword strike it I will die."

"Well then if it entails a death stone then I shall learn it since I am the head mage here."

"I do not think so Tombah, I do not trust you. I think I shall choose, Raamok."

Raamok raised an eyebrow at his comment. He was about to object but he saw the look of distaste on the mages face. Before Tombah could comment Raamok spoke up.

"Sure thing giant let's do this. Not because I like you any and I don't care for the dealing with magick but I can't pass up an opportunity to annoy the mage."

Partaxis laid a hand on Tombah easing his anger.

"Come now mage, it is nothing to get worked up over. Besides what do you get out of it?" Partaxis inquired of Tombah who was now clenching his fist in anger, fire flashing in his eyes.

"Forgive me for caring Partaxis; dealing with a death stone is something no simpleton should mess with." Tombah replied angrily as he walked away, there was a flash of light and he was gone.

"Good he is gone, it looks as though he teleported a long ways away. Now, Partaxis I am sorry to request this of you but you must also take your leave. I only need Raamok here, I will return him to the Fenrir once we are finished." Partaxis looked towards Raamok as Tahvo finished speaking with a questioning look. Raamok shrugged his shoulder and waved the look away.

"I don't think there will be any trouble Partaxis, I shall be fine. Thank you for your concerns. Now, you best be on your way. Your party seems to be getting anxious." Partaxis gave the orders to his men to file out. Before he joined them he walked up to Raamok and lowered his voice to a whisper.

"He cannot be trusted, be vigilant with him."

"Of course."

"Did you get the stone Tombah?" A demonic voice spoke to Tombah as he exited his teleport point. The mighty Fenrir lay a short ways away, however he was hidden from its watchful stare.

"I wish you to be gone demon; I tire of your constant voice annoying me."

"You were supposed to hold up your end of the deal you fool. Do you not wish for the awesome power I can give you?"

"I am beginning to doubt that demon; if you need control of a useless monster then I doubt you have this awesome power you speak of."

"Don't anger me mage."

"Or what, you will show your-self and teach me a lesson?" There was a shimmer in the air as the demon appeared before Tombah. Poison seeped out from his pores, and dripped from his fangs. The scent of death and sulfur accompanied it. He grabbed a hold of Tombah's robes scorching them where he touched. Tombah gave a wicked smile.

"Not smart demon." Tombah slapped the demon's hands away, cupped his hands and shoved them into the demons chest conjuring a strong magickal blast that sent the demon flying backwards. The demon recovered him-self. He attempted to cloak himself making him invisible to Tombah but found he could not.

"What…what have you done Tombah?"

"For being familiar with magick you don't sense the hex I placed on you? Very disappointing, now, let's do this demon." Fear overwhelmed the demon. He made an effort at running away. Tombah shook his head and tossed up his hand. An invisible wall formed before the demon. He into stunning him momentarily.

"Not so tough when you are cornered and against a truly powerful being? I was never going to give you the death stone even if I did go through with it. In fact I have another purpose for you. Now, shall we fight or are you going to stand there like an idiot and cower in fear of me. You either die fighting or die being a coward, your choice demon." Tombah took a step towards the demon charging an ice blast in his hands. His runes glimmered a light blue with a tint of purple.

"Tombah you don't know what you are doing. You are making a big mistake." The demon said as he started to laugh sadistically.

"You should have run when you had the chance to Tombah." The demon growled as he started to change form. Its legs began to extend; the skin and muscle grew taught then tore away from his body exposing its pale deformed skin. Loud pops accompanied it as his bones broke and reformed. The demon stretched upwards; once again loud pops accompanied him as other bones reformed changing size and shape.

"Good I am glad you finally decided to show your true form. Now, let us do this demon."

****

"Alright giant, show me the way to make these damn death stones."

"Well, we must first have blood in order to create them." Tahvo replied to Raamok. Raamok raised an eyebrow.

"Giant if you plan on me giving up my blood voluntarily you have another thing coming." Raamok drew his blade.

"Nonsense human. I to do not wish to give my blood up so willingly either. Being a warrior myself and you being a warrior how about we duel over it? First blood goes into creating it."

"You are large giant it would be easy for me to win that one. Even when I shed your blood firstly how is it that my blood could be used to create a death stone for you? Don't you need your own blood to create it?"

"Well, there is that, but, there are other ways. Ways that you cannot understand without being magically inclined. So what do you say?"

"You know I love fighting but, what's to say that it won't just imprison me or set you free to do what it is you do?"

"As I said before Raamok I don't know the way to release me from this prison. But, I do understand your concern and I cannot blame you for it. I still wish for a good fight if you are up for it?" As Tahvo finished speaking he took a container and placed it within a rough rune circle. After he placed it there he cut his hand dripping his blood into the container. When he was satisfied with the amount in the container he healed his wound.

"There Raamok my blood is prepared, now shall we fight?"

"Very well giant I don't see the harm in it. Might as well."

"Good, now I must do one more thing." As Tahvo spoke the room they were in began to dull, a strong thrum began. It continued for a few moments before the room became as it was and Tahvo stood at a more humanly height. He still was a massive man one that could match Partaxis's massive size. The chains that held him shrunk with his size but gave him more slack and motion. Tahvo spoke another word and a wicked two handed sword appeared in his hands. The blade came up to his stomach, the hilt extended to his chest. The blade was nearly a foot and a half wide at its thickest point. It had a slight curve yet both side were sharpened. A dark red and black dragon created the focal point on the guard, its claws extending down the blade meant to catch any combatant sword and twist them free, the hilt itself was wrapped in dragon skin. The pommel had a gorgeous red ruby carved to look like a dragon eye. It would shift and change color, sometimes slowly, sometimes quickly. Whatever color it chose did not last long before turning to another color. As Raamok peered at the pommel, inspecting it further he was surprised to see it blink at him. The pupil of the gem moved around taking in the environment with a knowing look.

"That is a sentinel sword?" Raamok asked.

"Indeed it is. I managed to pillage it before anyone else could get to it from a stronghold I conquered." Raamok shook his head at Tahvo then pulled his magickal blade free from the sheathe followed by the broken bottom half of his silver blade.

"Your second weapon is broke Raamok, here allow me to repair it for you. I wouldn't want an unfair advantage on you." Tahvo said as he put his arm forth to take it from Raamok.

"An unfair advantage you say? I will make you pay for those words Tahvo I can fight you just fine with a broken blade. Perhaps after we finish dueling I will take your offer up of repairing the blade. Not until then though. Come now let us do this." Raamok set himself and prepared for the first attack.

Tahvo gave Raamok a smirk then launched the first attack. Tahvo came in with a slower attack at first. Raamok sidestepped out of the way and counterattacked missing Tahvo by a hair. The two of them exchanged a few more blows before stopping for a moment.

"Well now that I am warmed up we can do this for real." Raamok nodded his head towards Tahvo and attacked.

Raamok thrust with a low attack with his magick blade, he recovered quickly as Tahvo parried. He stepped to the side and slashed at Tahvo who brought his arm up blocking the cut with his heavy armor. Tahvo returned with a slash that Raamok caught with his broken weapon. He turned it aside opening Tahvo up for a pierce from his primary weapon. As Raamok drove his primary blade in, Tahvo reached down and caught his arm. He slammed his head into Raamok. Pain exploded from Raamok's head and he was stunned for just a second. However brutal of an attack it was, no blood flowed. Raamok let out an imperceptible sigh of relief. He recovered in time to jump back and parry Tahvo's mighty weapon. Tahvo recovered from the parry. He brought down a mighty two handed swing from above. Raamok crossed his blades catching the massive weapon, pain coursed through his arms almost causing him to lose grip on his weapons. He landed a kick to the stomach forcing him back a step. He took advantage of the situation and attacked Tahvo with a quick high, low and low combo. Tahvo absorbed one blow with his armor and managed to parry the other two attacks. He attacked Raamok with a low blow, he used the momentum of the attack to carry it to a high strike. Once again Raamok parried each blow and the pain seared through his arms. He jumped back a few feet to give him time to assess the situation.

'*His sentinel weapon must have the capabilities of shockwaves. I can't absorb much more of those. I will need to change my plan of attack.*' Raamok thought to himself just before Tahvo came rushing at him.

Tahvo jumped and attacked Raamok. Raamok stepped out of the way delivering his own attack in the process. Tahvo just managed to recover and block the blade. He attacked again with another high attack, Raamok waited till he was coming down with the attack to move in towards Tahvo in an attempt to get within his guard.

The planned attack was largely a success. Raamok managed to thrust his broken weapon into Tahvo's armpit where the armor was weak. Tahvo recognizing the mistake dropped his two-handed weapon. He drew a dagger from a hidden place and at the same time he felt the pain of Raamok's attack he stabbed the dagger into Raamok's stomach.

"Well it appears we have a tie Raamok, both of us drew first blood." Tahvo said wincing in great pain as he stumbled back, the blood quickly draining from him.

"It would appear so Tahvo…Think you can fix us before we both die here." Raamok managed to spout out as his world dimmed a little becoming blurry. Next thing he knew a bright flash went off, his vision cleared up and the wound closed itself.

"Second time I have been stabbed today. I would consider that a bad day." Raamok started laughing.

"That is quite the weapon you have their Tahvo. I have not seen one like it before." Raamok said as he picked up the weapon with some struggle because of the great weight. He handed it over to Tahvo who handled it as a toy. Tahvo thanked him as he set his sword back in its proper place.

"You are incredibly skilled Raamok. Among the best I have ever faced. It was an honor crossing swords with you. Now if you will allow me I would like to repair your broken weapon."

"Sure giant here you go I hope this won't take long." Raamok extended his blade to Tahvo. He took it and looked at it a second before utterly destroying it before Raamok's eyes. Tahvo held out a hand to prevent Raamok from protesting, he passed a hand over his mighty two-hander while speaking some words in an ancient language. The room once again became dark and a deep thrum began. Just as last time it took only a few moments before the room returned to normal and Raamok was surprised to see Tahvo's two-hander shrunk down to a size that was perfect for dual wielding. Tahvo looked at it once more. He caressed it gently before presenting the sword, hilt first to Raamok.

"Here Raamok this weapon has no more purpose for me. I would rather it be put in a warriors hands that would make good use of it and I don't like Partaxis enough to have him take it. The sword goes by the name of Typhoon but you can call it as you will it is no longer a servant to me so that name has been released. I am sad to say it has slain many innocents. I have been working on correcting that, but as you can see I have been imprisoned and have not seen much combat. I think with it being in your hands there may be a chance of redemption for it."

"I am not as good as you think giant. But, I will do my best and I think Typhoon would be a good name for it to keep. It will serve me well as I will serve it well. Thank you Tahvo. I probably will not see you again after this. I do hope the god's find favor in you once you are gone. Oh and just a side note before I take my leave. I have something that may ease your mind since you are so set on redemption. Your crusade against the Holyrage house failed in the end. A single bloodline survived and the dark god Uttookari and Gullock both failed in their conquest. I would say you may have a chance to speak to him before your death because he is actively serving on the Fenrir." Tahvo couldn't contain the smile that formed, nor did he try.

"Thank you Raamok that piece of information does bring me comfort. I do hope to see him before I pass from this life to the next. What is his name?"

"I don't know something like Zarron I think." Raamok gave a little smirk while examining Typhoon lovingly.

"We will still need to complete the whole death stone thing Giant. I mean, I appreciate the weapon, and the fight but."

"You are correct Raamok, I nearly forgot about it with the news you gave me. Forgive me, my mind wandered, now, as for the death stone."

Tahvo turned to the circle which had his blood in the center. He began chanting a phrase in a language unknown to Raamok. As he proceeded he placed a hand slightly above the bucket, fire and lightning arced between his hand and the blood. The room shook with power as he proceeded with the incantation. After a few moments Tahvo stopped with his chanting, the blood had left the bucket and was floating in the air.

Tahvo pressed a hand to both sides of the blood only to be met with a great deal of resistance. He let out a grunt and clamped his teeth together as he fought against the increasing resistance. Sweat started soaking through the clothing he was wearing.

Raamok felt the enormous amount of heat come in a great wave against him. Soon he was slick with perspiration; the air around him began to get thicker. He kept his breathes as even as possible but the pressure, humidity and heat caused those breathes to be labored. As he continued to look upon the ritual his vision became blurred, before he blacked out the air become clear again, the heat and pressure faded. What was before him was a gorgeous glowing dark purple prism. Tahvo grabbed hold of it from the air and handed it to him.

"Now, you must carve my full name into it followed by speaking my name. It will bind the stone to me."

"That's it huh? I just say your name, write it and that gives me the chance to kill you? Seems like something extremely dangerous to know how to create, unless it is your blood that it reacts to."

"No not at all Raamok that is why I said there are ways to do this that don't require a person's blood. It is not for the weak though and had you attempted this you would have died or lost your soul to it. Some say that is how sentinel swords get their spirit. It is from people too weak to create such a magickal device and in turn it swallows their spirit, binding it to the weapon or armor. That is why I wanted you Raamok, a person not versed in such arts to foresee this being done. I do not trust Tombah for something stirs in him I care not for, and he does indeed possess the power to create such an item. Now back to business. Speak my name and write it onto this stone Raamok."

"Well, what is your full name giant I merely know Tahvo nothing more? "

"Tahvo Dragon-Singer." Raamok raised an eyebrow at him.

"So you have among the oldest names in the books. That family has been around since the Lord above Lords created the world. You should be royalty correct?"

"What you say is true Raamok but, I was many sons and daughters down, I had no chance at inheriting the throne." Raamok stood in awe for a moment before writing the name down and speaking it. As Raamok finished speaking his name the stone came to life. The dark purple prism flared a brighter color temporarily then it began to emit a dull glow that beat in time with Tahvo's heart.

"Now, Raamok place the prism here at my heart. It would seem a fair kill spot." As Raamok brought the prism close to Tahvo, dark purple light, much like tendrils reached out and gnawed at Tahvo's chest. When Raamok got mere inches away from Tahvo the tendrils attached themselves to Tahvo's core. They ripped the prism from Raamok's hand, slamming it into his chest. Tahvo let out a sharp gasp of pain as the item pierced his skin before attaching it firmly to his core. Another bright flash of light followed by thunder shook the air before settling down to the dim glow that beat to the heart of Tahvo.

"There Raamok it is done. Ensure Partaxis is aware and if there is time send the Holyrage to me. I must rest now; I thank you for doing this." Tahvo raised a hand to Raamok. He felt a strong sensation of magick engulf him. The physical world around him blurred, but, the magickal world became clear to him. Raamok found him-self travelling quickly by three rivers that twisted and turned, their essence flowed with a clear direction but they were everywhere as well. Different colors flowed back and forth touching everything; some things drew more of it than others. Raamok's sword Typhoon drew a large amount of color that shifted between several dark colors with a light strand mixed in. Raamok's own body had few strands of different color touch him but nothing like that which was in his sword.

Before long a large dark shape loomed before him. It glowed with brilliant colors causing the area around it to seem dim in comparison. All at once the magickal world left Raamok, nausea overwhelmed him and he couldn't help but wretch…into brilliant white snow. As Raamok looked up he found himself in front of the great Fenrir.

XXIX

"Zeth it is good to see you. Thank you for meeting with me this morning. I know I have said it a great deal of times but, my apologies for not meeting with you after Mary's funeral. I was taken immediately into the Paladin test before I could break my fast with you." Zarron spoke to his friend.

"Indeed it is not a problem my friend all is forgiven. I understand you are leaving us this night or on the morn?"

"It is true that I shall be departing soon. I must get back to the Fenrir for I fear there is not much time before those dark armies arrive there. They can use all the brothers and sisters our good Hand has blessed us with. I do have a great favor to ask of you if you are willing."

"Sure Zarron, anything for a friend."

Zarron gave Zeth a smile. "Before you answer that you should hear what I have to ask of you. As you know Zeth I lost some men with this recent assault one of them being my Captain. I don't know if you recall Captain Agrith or not? He was in the class two behind us." Zeth nodded his head. "Well it would seem I am a Captain short and I can't think of a better person to fill that spot then you Zeth." Zeth narrowed his eyes and let out a sigh.

"Why have you asked me of this rather than order it of me? You being a Paladin of the Church now can do that."

"It is because The Hand said the only way he would allow it is if you went and let him know. I don't blame him, you are one of his Holy Hammerers and one of the best he has. The choice is yours."

"Zarron I love you as a brother, but I cannot do as you ask. The Holy Hammerers is where I belong right now; with us getting ready to break the siege on Tear Drop Keep I am afraid I cannot leave them at this time." Zeth said in a dry voice filled with great regret.

"Well, I cannot blame you for that and it is a selfless act on your behalf. I was hoping that you would have agreed but, if the Nameless One needs you for Tear Drop then by all means. I can tell you though that you will miss one heck of a battle at the Fenrir. But, I hardly blame you, it is hard leaving people you have fought beside and served under for so long. Not to mention being a member of the Holy Hammerers is among the elite of the Body of the Nameless. Well, my friend." Zarron held out his hand to Zeth who took it. He pulled Zeth into a brotherly embrace. "May the Nameless One be with you as always my friend. I love thee as a brother and I hope to see you again soon. Kick some Faceless Ones rears for me and break that damned siege in the name of The Nameless. Amen." Zarron released Zeth from the embrace and touched his head to his friends.

"We shall see you soon Zarron. Blessings upon you, May the Nameless One be with you always." Zarron nodded his head and rendered a salute to his friend before departing from him.

It was going to be a lonely ride back to his home in the valley. One he was not looking forward to. As he rode towards his home he was mulling over who to put in the place of his captain when a loud shout pulled him from his thoughts.

"Hail Zarron, how great to see you my friend." He looked up to see a man along with a small team ride up to him; the leader was a head shorter than he was. He had a trimmed red beard which was a sharp contrast to his blondish colored hair giving him an exotic look that few had. The man was well tanned as one would be spending years in the hot sunny lands of the west. His face was slightly weathered from the years many dust storms that the area was renowned for. His build was more slender then his own but, he moved with the grace of an expert swordsman, the kind that needed no shield to protect and defend him-self. Proof of that was the fact that no scars marred his face or body. Very few soldiers that had seen as many conflicts as the one before him could do so while remaining unscathed. Even Zarron himself possessed scars including the most recent one he had received from the barbarian horde in the not so distant past. He winced as he recalled that day before casting the images from his mind, for now. He raised his hand in greetings towards the man while giving him a big smile.

"Elite Jeremiah, how are you? It is good to see you, what pulls you from your duties in the west lands?"

"You mean that sweating hot spot, the armpit of the world as we call it, practically hell on earth over there. Just that I was recalled by the church. It would seem there is far more going on, on this side of the land then where I hail from. They relieved us with some lions from Tyrnith. Not like that took a whole lot, a whole whopping four of us was all they needed to relieve. Good lot they are...I try not to say that too loud around them it goes straight to their heads." Jeremiah smirked as his men chuckled.

"Bah, where is your sense of humbleness." Jeremiah scolded his men in an exaggerated tone laughing.

"I see not much has changed since we parted ways. You are still the same as always perhaps with a bigger head, must be that they left you in the heat to long." Zarron laughed.

"I would say I could say the same thing to you but it would appear much has changed. Paladin Holyrage. I remember leaving you when you were no more than a Knight. Where have they had you these past few years?"

"I was in studies still when you left and upon graduation they titled me with Elite. After that I went to the Fenrir and have been there since about two months ago."

"You must have performed some glorious feats out there to be rewarded with Paladin. Doesn't surprise me I knew you would easily pass me up soon enough. The Nameless One always had a strong calling on you. How is your lovely lady Mary doing? It has been a long time since I have seen her as well." The smile faded on Jeremiah as he saw Zarron's face darken. Zarron shook his head.

"She died about two months' time ago. She was the reason I went to the Fenrir to see about finding details to her whereabouts since she was assigned there. When I found her…it was too late…She died in my arms Jeremiah, and I couldn't save her." Zarron felt tears coming on but held them back. His friends face became saddened for him; he brought his horse in close and placed a hand on Zarron's shoulder giving it a reassuring squeeze.

"I am so sorry to hear about that Zarron, I know you loved her so, I know that you would have done anything you could to have saved her. But, The Nameless One needed her home so he called upon her. If there is anything I can do for you Zarron please tell me."

"I know my friend, but alas I must be taking my leave from you. I have some work to do finding a new captain for my guard along with planning to leave on the morrow to make haste back to the Fenrir. Shall you find time tonight you can call upon me, my home is but a short distance from here." Zarron pointed down the road towards the direction of his home. "It is just around the bend there. Feel free to bring your men I will ensure you are well fed, as you must be tired of field rations by now if you came from the west lands, which I could assume was a hurried ride back."

"Indeed it was, very well Zarron I shall see you tonight so long as The Hand allows it. I am sorry for your precious loss Zarron; once more I am here if you need anything. Alas, tonight you will need to tell me of your adventures as of late. Farewell Zarron." Jeremiah patted Zarron's shoulder once more and gave it a final squeeze before departing towards the Citadel. Zarron spurred his own horse towards his keep when he arrived he was greeted by Frank.

"Good to see you still alive Frank, are my other men back from the Citadel?" Frank shook his head no. "Very well, if you could be so kind Frank, as to bring me the military records of my personal guard to the study that would be appreciative. Also, I could use a nice cup of coffee." Frank nodded his head as he took Thunder from Zarron to stable him.

"I will assume no one is to disturb you m'lord?"

"At least for an hour and Frank if you could please prepare dinner for an extra 4 men tonight. I am expecting some company."

"Of course m'lord." As Zarron walked away Frank called out to him once more. "It is good seeing you again Lord Holyrage." Zarron inclined his head and smiled before walking into his keep. He changed into more comfortable clothing before departing to his study where he found the files he asked for along with a hot cup of coffee waiting for him. He sat down and began thumbing through the files.

Within a couple hours' time a knock came to his door pulling him away from his work. "Please enter." He called out, the door opened revealing two familiar faces to him. They were the two men he sent off to warn people of the siege.

"By the Heavens I thought I wouldn't see you two again for some time. How did your messages get received by the people?" He asked enthusiastically.

"As well as one could hope, most of the Eastern and Northern Kingdoms are in fear of the sudden appearance of such large enemy forces. The ones we did collect seemed to have come here in time to see the siege broken. It is good because a majority have stayed with the church in the meantime to help with recovery operations, along with joining our defensive forces. The Fenrir is gearing up for a large assault upon it from what I could gather so we were unable to gather any men from there. The rest of the land is putting up what defenses they can but, overall the land is in fear." Korbyn reported to Zarron.

"Very well, thank you. Please come in and have some coffee with me."

He motioned them to sit down before continuing.

"Thank you for the reports I will draft up what you said and send it to The Hand the minute I am able. I am aware of the Fenrir situation, The Hand will want to know about the great unrest for the others. I am sure he will want to send some of the Minds of the Nameless to go forth and bring as much peace as one could to the people, perhaps even an Arbiter. Alas, I am sorry to do this to you both but, I would request you gather your things properly for we are heading to the Fenrir tomorrow with 545 of our brothers and sisters to reinforce that front. I know you have served the church so wonderfully and I cannot thank you enough for what you have done. I will be sure to include in my reports the superb work you two have done to The Hand. In the meantime you are released to do as you please until day break tomorrow. If you need anything more please let Frank know or my-self and it will be yours."

"All is well Lord Holyrage, we will enjoy our time but, I will enjoy getting the chance to slay some of the Faceless Ones men. I grew tired of the past few weeks running from them and hiding so I could get the messages where they need to go and I believe, Katareen would agree with me." Katareen nodded her head in agreement. "Thank you m'lord for the concern but, we are quite content with getting the chance to be by your side in the upcoming battle, besides we can rest a little on the way. Travelling with as many brothers and sisters you have for the Fenrir will be a pleasant sanctuary. I don't think there are any bandits or brigands on this side of the Fenrir that would outright attack such a force. We will enjoy our time you have blessed us with, we appreciate it m'lord." Korbyn and Katareen nodded their heads and smiled before they excused themselves to ready for the attack.

Zarron continued to mull over his paperwork for a little more after they left before unrest got the better of him. He got up, stretched himself out and proceeded out the study. After wandering for a little he found himself in the cook house as Frank was preparing dinner.

"Need a hand Frank? I used to be pretty decent finding my way around a cook house. I am restless and sitting still considering papers is bothersome for me as it is." Frank couldn't help but have his mouth drop a little.

"Come now Frank just because you are a help to me doesn't mean I am above working lower jobs. I don't always enjoy fighting you know! So close that mouth of yours and give me something to work on." Zarron jested with Frank. Frank couldn't help but beam a bright smile. He pointed towards some vegetables.

"I need those diced up if you could. The knife is below you. So what troubles you m'lord?" Frank asked as Zarron grabbed the knife and began dicing.

"Please just call me Zarron for now, there is no one here to impress as is. I suppose I am a little disappointed. Well, extremely disappointed at Zeth turning down the offer of being my new Captain. I can't blame him I would do the same if someone asked me to leave the men I have worked so closely with." he let out a sigh as he chopped up the last of the potatoes.

"Well, umm, Zarron, that sounds so odd to say I don't know if I can do that for you m'lord. I figure your feelings are normal. I think given the circumstances I myself would be upset but, we all know the Nameless One has his needs for certain people. Zeth would be one of those that are needed elsewhere is all. Is there none in your guard that are capable of such a position to fill?"

"Well, Frank there is more than enough capable hands. That is what makes is so ridiculous but, despite as I may, none of them have settled in my spirit as the one to fill that spot. I have a hard time acting when I don't feel guided at such things." He paused working on his task and sighed before continuing.

"What about Sheen m'lord? She has been with you longer than any of these even by just a few days; you two also have a knack at saving each other from terrible perils it would appear."

"You are correct with that but, I cannot for she isn't high enough rank in the Church to fill that role. If she was I would more than consider such a thing. Not to mention it would not be fair to those that are her veteran. However much I appreciate this title and rank; I cannot stand the political aspect to things. Alas I should not complain it is a great honor to possess this title." he finished cutting the vegetables. "What is next Frank?" Before Frank could answer a knock on the keep door came. Frank moved to answer the door before he was stopped by Zarron.

"I will get it Frank, thank you. Just finish preparing dinner if you would." Frank nodded his head towards Zarron as he departed the cook house. Zarron reached the door, before opening he looked through the spy-hole, to his delight Jeremiah was there with his 3 companions. He unbolted the door and opened it, welcoming his friends. Jeremiah took two steps in before he stopped to look in wonder at the dining hall. He let out a long whistle.

"Wow, so this is the kind of quarters one gets when they reach the rank of Paladin aye? Tis is nice and well deserved. I pray you don't mind that we arrived a little earlier than anticipated, the Hand released us after a brief debrief and blessing." Zarron raised an eyebrow towards his companion.

"I see you have not even unpacked your steeds. Has that big head of yours caused you all not to receive quarters from the Hand?" Zarron laughed. "Please come in Jeremiah, I will send Frank Roggins to tend to your horses."

"That isn't necessary, there is a reason they give us higher ranks men. It is to have them tend to such simple things." Jeremiah smirked.

"Knight Derth, please go with the warrior and priestess as they tend to the horses. I need to have a moment to speak to Paladin Zarron, alone." Knight Derth saluted Jeremiah before departing to accomplish the task.

"Alone? So is this going to be a good news kind of thing or a bad news kind of thing?" Zarron asked inquisitively. Jeremiah smiled mischievously.

"Depends on how you wish to take it Zarron. I would like to think better news then not but, it depends on how well you enjoy my company because we shall be together often I think after this. So long as you agree to accept what I am about to say. Not like you have much of a choice in it." Jeremiah paused, smiling to himself as Zarron thought through what he was saying. Finally after a few moments recognition settled on Zarron's countenance followed by a smile.

"Yup, you got it right Zarron. The Hand allowed or should I say ordered that I join your personal guard unit. He recognized that my timing couldn't have been more perfect to refill the number of men you lost. I have the orders from him right here." Jeremiah pulled forth a scroll with The Hand's seal upon it. Zarron took it from his hand and read through it quickly.

"Jeremiah this could not have been a clearer answer to my prayers. I will have Frank add you all to the roster but, more importantly I am going to draft up orders for a captain's commission for you Jeremiah. That is of course if you accept this role?"

"Well, who am I to refuse a Paladin, more importantly a friend? Thank you Zarron for this honor, I will ensure to perform my duties to the absolute best of my abilities."

"I know you will my friend. It is good that you came when you did, I see now that the Nameless One was orchestrating this whole affair. Thank you Jeremiah, or shall I say Captain?"

"Captain sounds good to me Zarron. Uh I mean Lord Zarron ra Holyrage." It was Zarron's turn to smirk at him.

"That is an odd thing to hear from you friend, I don't know if I could handle that all the time. Come, we have much to discuss and dinner is just about ready. I must tend to the Captains commission order to The Hand then I will join you. Bring your men in and enjoy some appetizers and a fine drink. I will be back soon. Thank you Jeremiah." He saluted his friend before heading to his study.

By the time Zarron had returned; Jeremiah along with his men and nearly half of Zarron's guards were sitting around the great table enjoying the meal that was prepared by Frank. A great fire burned in the hearth wrapping the chamber in a warm glow. The light from the fire sparked life to the beautiful glass artwork that was set into the roof of the room. Laughter and good cheer filled the room adding to the great joy so many of them had.

Despite all the joy, he struggled to appreciate the full beauty of it. His heart yearned for Mary to be there with him; to laugh with him, smile with him, to appreciate the joy of these people even in the face of an overwhelming darkness. He missed her slight touch to his arm and the smile that sparkled in her eyes when the two of them would laugh together. *She was so beautiful, matchless in every way. Why did things need to end the way they did Mary.* He thought to himself as he let out a sigh. He leaned to the side of the archway out of sight of the great hall. A tender touch on his shoulder pulled him out of his painful memories.

"Zarron, you are troubled my lord." Sheen spoke softly to him.

"I suppose I am Lady Sheen. Too many things were left with no closure. There were so many things. I should have, I needed to do something more." He spoke with his face cast to the ground. Sheen tenderly placed a hand under his chin. She lifted his face up and gave him a weak smile. Her heart felt the overwhelming sadness that was so obvious in his eyes. She bit her lip as she attempted to hold back the sadness that was creeping onto her face as well.

"Zarron, look at me." Sheen asked of Zarron. He brought his eyes up and stared levelly at her tear stained eyes for a long moment, searching her eyes. Sheen caressed his face ever so gently tracing his scar that came from above his brow to just below.

"Zarron, I have only known you for a short time, but, I think I know how much love you have for those that are close to you. I have no doubt you did everything you could possibly do to come out with another outcome. What was set in place beyond the Fenrir was there for a greater purpose that is beyond us. That hole in your heart." Sheen moved her hand down and pressed it into Zarron's chest.

"It will take time to heal, but you must take what joy you can when it comes my lord. If you do not that depression will chase you and consume you. That beautiful caring heart of yours would be at risk becoming hardened and calloused. This world needs all the compassion it can take soon enough. Your men need that compassionate leader; most importantly I need that compassion." A tear slid down her face as she spoke. Her gaze never left his own. He reached up and wiped her tear away. She grabbed his hand and kissed it gently.

"Can I show you something Zarron?" He nodded his head in agreement. Sheen turned herself around. She undid the lacing on her dress unveiling her bare back. He let out a gasp as he saw hundreds of deep wretched scars. The sheer monstrosity of it made his blood boil.

"Wh…what happened Sheen?" Zarron asked through gritted teeth as Sheen laced back up her dress before turning to face him once more.

"I was married once before. Many years ago when I was no older than 16, it was a wonderful point in my life. The man I was wed to was a wealthy nobleman of great stature and respect. He took great care of me but, the timing of it couldn't have been worse. Within a years' time of our marriage the Dead Wars broke out. He didn't need to go, I begged him not to, the wars were hundreds of leagues away but, they happened to take place along the coast where he was born and raised. He felt it was what he needed to do. He went to war and saw it through to the end. I didn't have my husband for 2 years, I never lost faith in the fact I would see him again. I was so joyous when I received word of him returning. I waited for him every day staring out the window at the path that led to our home, and finally one day there he was. I ran out to him and it was a joyous return but, I could tell there was a change in his heart. I knew there was a change in him. It started off as little things, such as losing his temper and yelling at me. It proceeded to develop into throwing things. He would lock himself into seclusions for weeks at a time. Finally one day he struck me. It was only one time at first, he felt terrible after and locked himself away for fear of hurting me again. But, then it happened again and again and again. It was just his bare fist at first, it turned into a mailed fist and ended with him tying me down and whipping my back mercilessly. He whipped my back because he didn't need to look at that when he raped me. I didn't know what to do, I tried so hard to keep having faith that he would get out of it. I convinced myself it was only a temporary setback from the war, which goes to show how naïve I was at the time." Sheen stopped for a moment. She took a deep breath as she wiped tears from her eyes.

"Sheen, you don't need to continue with this." She shook her head vigorously.

"I want to Zarron, I need to. This went on for a year; aside from the abuse and rape he started having dark visitors in the middle of the night, people that I would hardly consider human at all, they were filled with demons and dark spirits. They performed rituals that were not meant to be observed by anyone. I was lucky, if you could consider it that, to never be caught observing these. They spoke to the dead and conjured evils that would disappear into the night. One night they brought with them a woman I knew. I was close to her, we had been friends for years." She paused collecting her thoughts.

"They had her bound and in some form of dark trance. They tied her down in the middle of their ritual, my husband slit her throat and tore out her heart. A great demon emerged from their sacrifice. My husband spoke to it, after that it disappeared into the darkness. I let out a gasp and began sobbing, there was no doubt they heard me, I was in too much pain to run though and I accepted death. Probably would have been another sacrifice for their death magick. They should have found me, it was only a matter of time before they did; the strangest thing happened, the entire group of them ran right by my location as I sobbed there and not one of them saw me, they heard my crying though, I heard them talking about it but they could not locate it and I was kept safe. After a short time they gave up and dispersed. I ran into the house as quick as possible, I locked myself in my room. On daybreak I decided the only thing I could do was…kill my husband. I took a knife and went to him in his bed, I leaned down and gave him a final passionate kiss, which was the last of my love I could offer him, and I drove the knife through his stomach. He reached to my hand that was holding the knife and drove it deeper into himself all while looking into my eyes. That was the first time he looked into my eyes for months. The husband I loved came through in that moment we locked our eyes together. His countenance changed from the dark mask that was there to the pleasant sweet lovely man he was. I remember him saying through his weak quickly fading voice, I love you, thank you. He was gone after that, his final breath left him. I had murdered the man I loved, not the monster I had wanted to kill. I panicked in that moment and left, I knew I would be wanted for murder. The only thing I could think of was how am I going to hide myself? What better way of hiding your identity then becoming something else completely. That is when I joined the shape shifters" She paused for a moment while tears flowed down her face.

"Why tell me these things Sheen? I don't understand." Zarron asked as he wiped away her tears.

"Because, Zarron I want you to understand that you must not get a calloused heart. I have been wounded more deeply from a heart that has become twisted and calloused than anything else. I want you to understand that your compassionate heart cannot become like that."

He conjured up a smile for Sheen before wrapping her up in a warm embrace. "So long as I follow the Nameless One and as long as I know you, I will pray such a thing will never happen. Thank you Sheen you have truly given me a new perspective. We should probably be working on joining our fellow brothers and sisters in arms. If you need more time I will wait with you until you are ready."

"No Zarron, I am feeling much better, just hearing those words from you I feel strengthened and renewed." *I can also feel the comfort in your spirit.* She said in her mind.

"Alright, we will join them, after a few moments of course, we can't go in there with puffy eyes and tear stained cheeks." Zarron let out a deep hearty laugh as he put an arm around Sheen and directed her towards a water basin in the room. After a few minutes the two of them joined the rest of the group in celebration.

"Lord Zarron! What a pleasure to have you join us. Frank makes one outstanding meal and the wine you have here is simply divine." Jeremiah called out to Zarron.

"Indeed he does Captain, I pray that you all haven't drank and ate all the wine and food yet?"

"Well close to it, I would say there just may be enough for you to enjoy it though." Jeremiah winked. He let out a laugh while presenting a wine goblet to the both of them.

"Thank you my friend, and to everyone else, eat until you cannot eat anymore and drink until you are all merry." Zarron raised his goblet to the men before him.

"Tomorrow begins a new adventure for us all, the first steps to stopping an evil force that thinks they can just march onto these fine lands we all love and protect; that they can take what they want, burn what they want, destroy what they will. By the grace of the Nameless One such a thing will not happen while the church stands strong with its mass army of brothers and sisters of the Body and Mind of the church. So enjoy, you all deserve this and we shall do this again God willing in a short time from now celebrating our victories. Amen." Zarron tipped the goblet back draining it to the sound of a great cheer arising from his men. He turned and smiled at Sheen, she returned it with an absolutely stunning smile before draining her own goblet.

"I think we will need a refill Jeremiah and let us get some songs going in here." Jeremiah nodded his head in reply as Zarron slipped into the crowd with his brothers and sisters of the faith. They began singing an ancient battle victory song.

Sheen watched Zarron interact with his people and smiled to herself before lending her voice to the singing.

XXX

A soldier burst into the chambers of Partaxis. "They are here!"

Partaxis stood up from his desk. He turned towards his Lieutenant. "I knew we wouldn't have that much time but, I expected a little more at least. How many of them are there?"

"It looks like a Vanguard force of about 3000. They are attempting to assault the gate."

"Do they have siege equipment with them?"

"Aye, a few catapults, and a couple battering rams, they also have a siege tower of enormous height being built just out of our siege weapons range."

"Alright, get the archers lined up at the top of the Fenrir. I want them to fire only when they have a good shot. No need to waste our arrows on a force that cannot possibly stand a chance of taking the Fenrir, we need to hold onto them for the true threat."

"Already done m'lord, Durakon has taken up the command of the archers."

"Ahh, very well, I can't think of a better person for that job. I need you to wake up our siege engineers and have them go over their checks again. We must be sure our siege equipment is in good working condition. Relay the order to have him load all of them as well."

The Lt. nodded his head. "Is there anything else Lord Partaxis?"

"No not at this time. Thank you lieutenant for the information you provided, you are dismissed." The Lt. rendered a salute to Partaxis before departing his chambers.

"So, they finally showed themselves, I do pray Zarron returns soon

with what men he has gathered." Partaxis thought to himself. He went over to his wardrobe. He dressed in the warm gray and white furs of the Night Wolves before stepping out of the keep into the chilly morning's air. A light snow that happened through the night left the ground covered in a thin layer.

Partaxis stood outside his door for a few moments breathing in the crisp air while listening to the distant noises of commands being shouted throughout Korilith keep as men prepared for battle. After some time of that, he started making his way to the top of the Fenrir where he could see the archers already formed up. A tall slender figure walked up and down the battlements giving hand signals and shouting orders to distant for him to hear at the moment. Their breath could be seen as a white plume against the overcast sky. As he continued his ascent it wasn't long before he could hear the twang of bow strings being let loose and the commands of Durakon were clearly audible.

"Remember men pick those targets carefully, every one of your arrows that miss you will be required in your own time to fletch 2, no matter what hour at night it is or how little rest you got. I will not tolerate wasted shots at this time." Durakon's voice rang out over the battlements.

As Partaxis reached the top he took a moment to look over the battlements at the enemy force that had gathered. His Lt. estimates were close enough to being correct as Partaxis counted the banners and flags of different tribes. The army at the base of the Fenrir seemed so far down, it was a wonder to him how anyone could think they could take this wall. Let alone how we could damage them from so far, but he found that answer quickly as blood splatter drenched the snow at the base, a bright red contrast amidst a sea of white. It was beautiful in its own right he thought. He counted at least 33 dead below, several of them had climbing gear. He shook his head. The other answer to his questions would just need to wait until the main body of the enemy showed up.

Partaxis continued to scan the enemy before him. He spotted the several catapults in the enemy ranks. They were not progressing forward yet, as they were being armored so the army could move them into range and begin their siege. He laughed to himself at the ridiculous notion that they could even do anything. He didn't even think it would be worth wasting ammo on them.

He finally eyed the great siege tower being built far out in the distance and it took his breath away. The tower base was enormous, and the height of it was almost the size of the inner Fenrir from what Partaxis could judge. Partaxis eyes narrowed as his mind drifted to what that tower was capable of if it could get close enough to the Fenrir. But, how were they going to move it once it was made? Before he could continue further Durakon's voice pulled him from his thoughts.

"Hail commander, good morning to you if you wish."

"Well, have we had any losses yet?" Durakon shook his head no. "Good if there are no losses yet then I would say it is a good morning."

"That is a good mindset to have; these men are doing their best at carefully picked shots. I figured I don't see the need to unload all our ammunition quite yet. I pray this is to your liking commander?"

"Absolutely Durakon, I said the same thing to my Lt. What do you make of the siege tower in the distance?"

"To be honest it troubles me. If that tower gets finished and by some form of sorcery it can be moved. We are going to have our work cut out for us. It also depends on how large the main body of this army is. Tombah has been working with our friendly giant Tahvo through mind speech and he can't even pin a number on the army size. This concerns me greatly." Durakon broke off suddenly.

"Tryst you owe me 2 arrows; I heard that shot of yours and the distinct noise of it missing. My apologies commander for the interruption, has there been any word from Zarron and what men he brings?"

"The last I heard from him was from his messenger that showed up a few weeks ago bringing news of the city of the Nameless being under siege."

"Well, I trust Zarron completely; I know he is going to be here and soon. He understands this threat greater than any one of us."

"I hope you are correct Durakon, in the meantime ensure the men get rest as much as possible. No need to work these ones to the ground yet. We will have time for that soon."

"As you wish commander, I will rotate them out as it is needed."

"Good, have you seen Tombah wandering around here anywhere? I am in need of some answers that only a mage could answer."

"I don't know off the top of my head but, I would try checking the library. Those caster types love their books." Partaxis nodded a thanks to Durakon before heading towards the library.

Just as Durakon had advised Partaxis found Tombah in the library studying old tomes. He opened the door, a loud creek echoed into the room, to his surprise Tombah didn't even look up from his books.

"Tombah I have need of your wisdom at this immediate moment."

"Yes Partaxis how can I help you?" Tombah replied without looking up from the tomes he was studying.

"What do you think of looking at me when you answer me?" Partaxis growled.

"I think not Partaxis, how about you speak your mind to me or leave me to my studies." Tombah said unflinching as he continued staring at his book. He wanted to look up to see that look of anger and surprise on Partaxis face, instead he smiled to himself as he awaited Partaxis next action which was likely going to be to wreck the books he was studying. Short tempered people tended to act out in such a manner.

"How dare you speak to me as such mage?" Partaxis growled back and in one swift motion he cleared the desk of all the books. Instead of the books hitting the ground they floated back up and settled to the exact position they were at prior. Partaxis looked at it a moment then proceeded to do it a second time and the exact same effect happened.

"I can do this all day Partaxis, so how about you just settle down and tell me what you need answered." This time Tombah looked up at Partaxis with a fiery gaze that would have caused a lesser man to flinch under it.

"The siege tower being built in the distance, could magick move it at its full height and weight? Can we have Tahvo possibly destroy it also?"

"Ahh so you have two questions not just one, you should learn to count." Tombah let out a wicked laughter and raised his hand to quiet Partaxis who was about ready to explode again.

"That temper of yours should really be controlled Partaxis, it would only help with your leadership. As for the answers, yes magick could move it in theory. It would take a being of immense power though. In particular one that is specialized in telekinesis magick. Or, it could be moved by a bunch of lesser mages exhausting them in the effort but, it could be done. For your second question, the answer is no. They have it built just outside the changing lands. That means the giant cannot touch it. Is there anything else Partaxis?"

"How much is a bunch of lesser mages and could you unravel their magick as it is being used?"

"12, I would say. I could possibly unravel their magick but, they wouldn't approach without some kind of magickal defense. If it is just the one being I think it would even be a testament to my power to stop it."

"What do you mean magickal defense? Shouldn't that be no problem for you or one of your fellow casters?"

"Partaxis you clearly do not understand the magick arts, a magickal defense in this case I would say would consist of a barrier spell in order to stop arrows and other physical forces to get through but, that would require some mage focusing completely on holding up that shield. A few direct hits from a heavy siege weapon would overwhelm the mages ability to hold up that shield. So, I would say they will be hiding within the siege tower and if it is heavily armored our weapons will have some trouble piercing it, so I would venture a guess to say that they would create a very intricate web of magick to cause someone a lot of energy and skill to unravel it. Kind of like a complex spider web that can only be dismantled one strand at a time. I am sure we could unravel it but, there is no chance it will be done in time and if they are really good it would exhaust my brethren and mine ability to do much else."

"So that is it, we are just doomed to deal with that and that is all you can tell me. What useless piece of trash are you Tombah."

"Ah Partaxis, that is where you come in with the mighty warfare strategy. As I said they will not likely have a barrier up that will protect it from physical attacks so find a way to stop it."

"You just said that our weapons would have trouble piercing it. So how is that to help us any?"

"Well, they can't have it completely armored it would pass that threshold of weight to move so there will be weak spots in it and there are other ways to enhance those weapons capabilities. We can have some of our enchanter type casters enhance the ammunition to give it more piercing power. As I said more than likely they will be concentrating on covering up the spell that is moving the giant machine rather than concentrating on a spell that will protect it from things of the physical realm. We can also have one or two of our earth mages create a hell of a battleground to navigate through. I would say with just one maybe two we can stop them. If they have more coming with the main army then we will need to fight and hold that wall. I don't know what more I can tell you Partaxis this will not be an easy fight and should the god's guardian choose to invest his power and talent into moving one of those towers, well we are going to be hard pressed to stop it. I can assure you either way Partaxis we will do what we can. Now, if there is nothing more please leave me be so I can continue studying."

"I cannot stand you Tombah but I at least respect your magickal prowess. I will leave you be for now but, I would suggest you get your mages up to speed on what is expected."

"Well I don't need you to stand me Partaxis, now be gone." Tombah waved a hand towards Partaxis shooing him from the room. Partaxis growled before storming out of the room slamming the door behind him.

"You seem tense Partaxis, care to kill something?" A voice came from the shadows catching Partaxis off guard.

"You know Raamok that might not be a bad idea."

"Good because I was thinking we should make a go at burning that tower down before it is completed. What do you think of that?"

"How do you purpose we do that Raamok? They have an army of men out there; I can't see how this would go well. Unless you know something I do not know." Partaxis raised his eyebrows inquisitively.

"Well, if we take a small enough team we could potentially sneak in there or, there is the option of leading them back a little bit further into the changing lands and have our immortal giant friend do what he does best, change the land so drastically in that section that it kills them off or cuts them off from a team that can get in there and burn the tower."

"You know Raamok you are onto something with that. Alright give me until an hour before sundown to gather together a group. We will meet up at the far western scout gate at that point."

"Partaxis, in order to lure them away we need to have a big enough force where they will be concerned about it enough to send a contingent to attack them. I was thinking maybe have our elite team burn the tower and possibly use the barbarians that we have offered a home to in the shadows of this Fenrir along with some mixture of your men to play as a decoy army. Pack them light so they might be able to move quickly." Partaxis stroked his chin as he thought about Raamok's plan.

"Alright Raamok that sounds like a plan, I think we need to move the meeting time to an hour before sunrise. That will give us time to get our soldiers to their flank and when day break comes we can have them start on their distraction. It will be more of a challenge for us to burn the tower but, I think with the proper camouflage we can get into position. Durakon has been working on some finely crafted suits that blend in perfectly with the environment, if we move slowly we could possibly get right up to the guard line and even possibly past. After that I figured we could just kill some guards and take what they are wearing. Put it on and walk right into the camp from there."

"Yeah, about that Partaxis, I for one and even Durakon are not big enough to pass as one of those barbarians nor do we have the same physique or smell for that matter to even pass as a young one. I do not see that working for us, but, perhaps we can have you bring us into the camp as prisoner's maybe? Tighten the chains about us in such a manner where they look secure but easy enough to loosen. Or we use you to take out a guard as you want and upon taking his place it will give us an unsecured location to sneak through. Upon the guard change you can get into the camp to meet us at some appointed location, we then proceed to burn the tower to the ground." Raamok stated purposefully.

"Perhaps Raamok but what are we going to do about the slain guard? We will have a harder time hiding his body then I would like?"

"That is correct Partaxis but, if we were to approach from the rear guard it would be easy enough to take them out before dragging their body into the changing land. We can have our giant friend cover them for us under a rock or something."

"I like your thinking." Partaxis replied with a glint in his eyes.

"Before you agree you need to hear the part you might not like, and that is we need Tombah or a caster of great pyromancy skill. There is no way we can light a hot enough fire with flint and kindling to burn down that massive structure. We need magick fire or else we can just toss this whole idea aside." Raamok finished, Partaxis gave a snorted in derision. There was a long moment of silence between them, Partaxis rubbed his chin as he thought on the plan.

"No, I think we may not need him at all, casters are not made for stealth, aside from their magick being easily detected should someone be looking, they also don't understand a thing about moving quietly at least the ones we have here. There are spell steal assassins that are proficient in both rogue arts and casting but we do not possess one of those. But, with all that work required for the tower there had to be pitch located somewhere." Partaxis finished with a smile.

"Aye and pitch means a source of fuel to burn down the tower. I suppose all that is left is to gather the team together. I would say we go with the plan of having you take a guards position. Also, instead of dragging him all the way back into the changing lands we can just take your winter suit and place it over him. It should keep him concealed. The smell of his death also shouldn't be too obvious if we were to take a position along the lines of their privies, might smell like crap and piss but, it is a safer bet." Raamok said with a solemn face.

"Then we can be known as the Lord Stink and Vampire Hunter Reek. Perhaps we should bring the wizard along for this one then he can be the High Mage Privy, master of the stench." Partaxis spoke barely as a mighty roll of laughter heaved from deep inside of him that seemed to shake the small room's walls. Raamok let a hint of a smile break his stern solemn face as he watched the big man continue in his uncontrollable laughter.

"Ill gather the people together Lord Stink while you gain control of your composure once more." Raamok left the room to the great sound of

Partaxis continued laughter.

It was nearly day break and Partaxis, Durakon and Raamok had closed to within a spits length from the guard line. They had decided to approach the situation with only their team. They couldn't justify putting together a group of men to play as decoy. They agreed with Raamok's assessment and approached the camp near the privies.

The overwhelming smell of the waste deposit was almost too much to bear but they held on and continued forward. Upon closing the final distance they heard voices, they stopped and buried themselves into the snow as far as they could. The coldness of it sent goose bumps and shivers along their body. The stench of the privy was even greater with their noses pressed to the ground. Durakon had no doubt in his mind that there had been individuals that probably relieved themselves on the ground they were waiting on. The thought of that caused him to nearly gag.

Upon observation the party determined the man talking was the watch commander. The two guards seemed to look their way multiple times and the party could not help but hold their breath for fear of their position being given away. The camouflage had done its part of concealing their advance to the last few feet from the privies walls. They laid in wait, to their relief there was no sign that either of the men saw the three of them laying there. Eagerly they waited until the guard finished speaking with the watch commander.

Once the man had left, Partaxis pulled forth a fine dagger from within his suit. Before he could progress he was stopped by a gentle touch from Durakon, he lipped "no blood" to Partaxis who immediately slid the blade back to its hidden compartment with a disgruntled look. They inched a small distance further, and waited for their opportunity. Once the guard turned his back to the party Partaxis struck.

With one fluid and seamless motion Partaxis flung off his camouflaged cloak. He wrapped his great arms around the guard's neck cupping a hand around his mouth. He began crushing the wind pipe with his forearm drowning out any screams or grunts the man could make, that was if he had time to make the noise. With a quick motion Partaxis snapped the neck of the smaller barbarian. He hoisted his body up and carried it a few steps away before placing it down gently.

As soon as the body hit the ground Durakon and Raamok tossed Partaxis camouflage over the body before pressing back into the ground blending seamlessly with the snow once more. Partaxis quickly took up his post again just as a warrior left the privy. The warrior eyed the guard suspiciously for a moment before making his way over to him. Durakon and Raamok held their breath as the warrior came over and exchanged some words with Partaxis in a barbarian tongue.

Durakon kept his eyes fixed on Partaxis as he thumbed the spear carefully, he would have guessed that Partaxis was contemplating using it or not. Durakon prayed to the gods that would not happen. After what felt like a lifetime the warrior turned and left. All three of them breathed a sigh of relief.

"Good thing the man was more drunk then naught, or else we may have had a serious issue. The man happened to be my relief and he thought it was Krolluck he was to replace not me. He mentioned there were too many new faces and soon everyone blended in with one another. He went on about something about slaying the Fenrir men and drinking their blood. He is anxious to get back to his "Mightiest Fortress" with the spoils of Fenrir enslaved. He was sick of this coldness and said that at the very least the changing lands brought warmth from time to time. So I asked him where the pitch was so that we could sneak a keg of one ignite it, and warm ourselves all night with a mighty blaze. I offered him to join me and tell me about his "Mightiest Fortress" and we can talk about what we will do with our enslaved Fenrir men. He liked that idea and agreed to it so long as I take the blame should the captain find out. I agreed, and he pointed it out to me."

"Brilliant Partaxis, we can get there and await your presence. Come Raamok, this is going to be a cold hour of waiting to be sure for us." The two of them carefully picked their way toward the direction the drunk man spoke of. Partaxis watched for a moment until they slipped behind a tent and out of his view.

After too many close calls with bored camp troops Durakon and Raamok finally got to the small clearing that held the pitch. Thankfully a snow had covered the barren lands around it with a fresh coat of snow deep enough where they could make use of their camouflage. If they determined a need they could drop immediately into the snow to disappear from any unwanted attention.

The two of them peered around the clearing before they moved further, movement caught their attention on the far side of the clearing. They pressed back into the shadow of the tent they were hiding. Raamok took a moment to peek his head around the edge of the tent and smiled.

"It is our friend Partaxis, seemed guard change took place quicker than we had thought." Raamok whispered.

"Well, let's go say hi to our giant friend." As the two entered the clearing they raised a hand at Partaxis who returned it. He had just entered the pitch storage and stopped abruptly, lifting one foot up followed by the other pitch dripped off his boots. Durakon narrowed his eyes, his gut twisted and turned awashing him in an uneasy nausea.

"Something is wrong." Raamok spoke first confirming Durakon's feelings, before he could voice his concern. The air became still and warm in that moment. Their breathing seemed to echo in the air and fill every corner of the field. Just then a single twang of a bow string loosed somewhere. They heard the arrow screaming through the still air. Partaxis eyed it first and began sprinting trying to get out of the pitch pit trap that had been laid. He nearly made it out when the arrow hit the pitch, it seemed to go out and sizzle, only to burst to life again as a mighty fireball that consumed Partaxis. A second later an explosion took place from hidden fire powder within the field, the sheer power of it lifted Durakon and Raamok dropping them flat on their back, Durakon's head hit the ground with such velocity he bounced twice before biting his tongue hard, the taste of blood filled his mouth.

Raamok felt the sting of a blow to his leg followed by a sharp crack as another piece of shrapnel collided with his arm. He let out a gasp of pain and another loud crash came from close by drowning out his roar of anger as a massive fiery figure smashed into a tent causing it to collapse into a fiery heap.

Raamok worked his good arm free from the debris. He reached for a potion he had tucked away in his cloak, as he did his arm started shaking nearly uncontrollably making it almost impossible to grasp hold of the potion. He managed to feebly pull it free, it slipped from his grip and rolled a small distance away putting it just out of his reach.

Raamok cursed and attempted to roll his body towards it. He stopped a few times as his vision became darkened and blurred as pain coursed through his body from his smashed arm and damaged leg. Raamok made another reach for the potion but he was stopped just short. No matter how hard he tried he could not pull his leg free to move the few more inches that he needed to. He rolled to his back again to take a look at his leg, a haft of wood stuck out from his leg, stuck deep into the ground pinning it. He made one attempt at removing it but the pain was too much to bare, it forced him to settle back down.

He stared at the sky for what felt like an eternity each blink seeming to last longer than the former. His head spun, he blinked his eyes one more time, it was a long drawn out blink, far too long, he knew he must keep them open, when he snapped them open again Durakon was over him.

Durakon shook his head clear as quickly as he could, the ringing in his head was nearly insufferable. He shook his head once more before pulling himself to his knees, he spit out a gob of blood. He quickly assessed his joints and body. To his surprise the only wounds he managed to sustain were minor. He looked at the chaotic scene around him, one of the tents had been completely collapsed, and it remained on fire. He remembered the fiery figure that had smashed into there and guessed it had to have been Partaxis. But, if Partaxis was there and even alive where was, "ah there he is" Durakon spotted Raamok a few feet away from him reaching for the potion before collapsing to his back.

Durakon slowly crawled over to Raamok on his hands and knees. Once there he looked him. He knew he was fading fast. His leg was stuck on a gnarled piece of wood that pinned him to the ground. It had hit his knee and smashed the knee to a mush. His arm was in even worse shape, Durakon was amazed that it was even there still. All that held his arm in place was the cloth he wore along with the muscle fibers and sinew. It was a gruesome site. As Durakon was observing Raamok he saw his eyes flitter open again.

"Good Raamok, keep those open, I am going to pull this haft of wood out of you. It will hurt but you have this." Durakon unstopped the potion and shoved it into Raamok's hand.

"Ok Raamok here we go." It was easier than Durakon was expecting to pull it free. The lack of muscle and bone structure that remained helped him in his task. Raamok howled in pain, Durakon pulled the potion from his hands and put the potion to his lips. He waited patiently as Raamok finished the last drop of the concoction. Satisfied with that, Durakon patted him on his chest and pulled himself to his feet to begin his search for Partaxis.

As he put weight on his leg he swayed once nearly falling over, but managed to recover his balance. He wobbled over to the collapsed tent on unsteady legs, stopping to clear his dizziness once. The fires were still hot and burning in little patches here and there. Through the smoke Durakon eyed Partaxis, his big form still. Without giving it any more thought Durakon lurched to his side.

The smoke and smell of burned flesh and hair staggered him momentarily. He had to put out several small fires that were burning away the few remaining pieces of clothing that were still on Partaxis. Durakon put his arms underneath Partaxis pits, he lost his grip as the clothing sloughed away with some skin in tow. Durakon put his hands behind him to brace for impact as he fell backwards, as he pressed them into the earth he felt a mighty bolt of pain shoot up his arms. His hands became balls of fire as the fire greedily consumed the pitch on his hands. Durakon cursed and moved to a nearby snow pile. He drove his hands into it putting out the fire. As he removed them from the snow pile he found them to be tender, red and swollen, every joint and finger hurt to bend. "I don't have time for this crap I need to get Partaxis out of there."

Durakon quickly moved back to Partaxis and this time he wrapped his arms as far around the big man as he could and slowly with great pain and agony he pulled Partaxis out of the collapsed tent without another slip or fall. Once he had him a safe enough distance he dropped him to his side. He gasped as he observed the blackened remains of his back.

Nearly every bit of his back was blackened, the back of his head had no hair left on it, and in addition one ear was burned off. Durakon rubbed hands across his face and stared emptily at Partaxis. He didn't know how long he was standing there before he felt a hand on his shoulder. Durakon was expecting it to be the hand of the enemy pulling him away to be thrown into the torture chamber or, if he was lucky be sentenced to death. It wasn't an enemy this time though. Durakon looked up at Raamok who was standing on his feet as good as new.

"Durakon, thank you. I have one more potion left to offer to one of you. That one has got to be you Durakon, without Partaxis being conscious and so far burned, I am not sure if this will work for him."

"I don't care Raamok, give it to him."

"If I do this, with the condition of those burns on your hand you will never be able to handle a bow or spear again. You will not be able to hunt for the rest of your days."

"Without us making it back to Fenrir I fear I wouldn't be able to do that anyways, Partaxis is still alive albeit a slow heart beat and fading fast. We need him for the Fenrir defense. So give him the potion. Then we need to make haste. If the god's are good we shall make it back to the Fenrir soon and I can seek the aid of a healer. Partaxis will not get that chance if you don't give him that potion." Raamok tossed his hands up in defeat.

"Very well ranger, I will give him the potion." Raamok knelt down beside Partaxis. He tipped the potion down his throat. They both eyed Partaxis carefully along with the camp around them.

"Raamok where are the enemy combatants? They should have been on us by now?" Raamok peered around the camp while Durakon listened carefully to the sounds around him. It was as if the entire camp had been swallowed up in a queer and quiet calm. That sent chills down his spine.

"Perhaps, they chose to run away in fear as they realized their trap had failed." Partaxis voice broke into the eerie silence pulling his companions attentions back to him.

"About time you wake up giant, you should have been awake minutes ago, it was just a little sunburn." Partaxis smiled at Raamok's comment.

"I would love to hug and make up and talk about our feelings but, we should probably be moving and moving now." Partaxis said in a voice that seemed too weak for him. He pulled his large frame from the ground. Durakon and Raamok helped him to his feet. They helped him regain his balance as he staggered under the weight of his body on legs almost too weak to stand on. The skin and tissue on his back had healed into a crude scab momentarily before being replaced by new plush skin. The back of his head had grown meaty once more, the hair remained missing leaving a humorous bald spot.

Partaxis stomped his feet a couple times to get the blood flowing. He grabbed part of the tent that was unburned, tore it free and tossed it over his back to give some protection from the cold. They began departing from the camp in haste.

They smelled it before it came into view. A strong sulfuric smell mingled with the smell of blood and gore. The air became stuffy and still causing breathing to become seemingly toxic. The three of them coughed vehemently as they continued pressing forward as quick as they could. The air around them becoming poisonous, Durakon was the first to heave and stumble to the ground. Raamok followed shortly, Partaxis tore a piece of cloth from the tent cloak, tied it around his head to cover his mouth and ran to his companion's side. He shouted at them with unheard words, his attempts to pull them to their feet were only brief successes, a step here and a step there before falling to the ground again, wrenching up what little contents remained in their stomach. Partaxis head spun forcing him to sit down hard on his rump. The world spun around him in a rapid motion. Partaxis shook his head clear and pulled himself to his feet. He turned and lifted Raamok to his feet, Raamok came to his senses suddenly. With a burst of speed he shoved Partaxis out of his way and in a swift motion yanked Typhoon free.

The magickal blast slammed into the sword, the blast was so large though that part of the magickal bolt burst through his stomach. Raamok's eyes went wide as he stumbled backwards dropping his sword in the process in order to clench his stomach in an attempt to staunch the blood flow. Partaxis watched his friend fall and whirled around to face the attacker.

His attacker was a huge man, standing nearly a head taller than Partaxis himself. Dark hair came to a widow's peak on his forehead, it hung to his shoulder, his eyes were black, black as the night's sky, there was no life in those eyes just a cold calculating stare. Dark stubble outlined his narrow jawline and high cheekbones gave him a fierce look. Overall he was a handsome figure though with no scarring marring his cheeks or wear from old age. His arms were thick and body was slender and muscular. He wore a dark ebony chainmail hauberk that seemed to drink in the light around him. The only thing that seemed to shine on that hauberk was dull eerie red symbols that were inlaid so finely that without close observation you would have missed them completely. Under it he wore dark blood red robe etched with black intricate runes around the fringes. Upon his shoulders a tattered cloak wrapped about him. The clasp that held his cloak together had none other than the symbol of the Faceless One, made from a material that was likened to bone yet it had a life of its own, one that twisted and turned to different shades of blacks and reds. The man curled his lips up into what Partaxis guessed as a smile and began to speak.

"Partaxis, oh I have wanted to see you suffer, your return to Fenrir has been such a pain for me. Seeing you here slowly dying from my poison and watching you lose your companions in front of your eyes, brings me such delight though. Shame it had to be this way, if that wretched witch did her job or the barbarians could successfully lay a trap to kill you, well, we wouldn't be having this conversation would we? But, no you seem to keep on living Partaxis, you survived the black wars when you should have died, you survived the time of imprisonment in the barbarian village. Not even the mighty Liche king could slay you. The woman was too weak to kill you herself and you even beat my mutated creatures, the mighty giant and mammoth. The one I sent to that pathetic barbarian village outside your Fenrir. Don't get me even started with your friends here."

He pointed a finger towards Raamok. "Raamok the vampire hunter, my people had killed him back with the fire trap, yet he is here. My vampires sent to the other side of Fenrir could not kill him. Something tells me he will not survive this round though. Durakon the lucky, slayer of my mammoth with all too good of a bow shot. He will be dead soon from the poison and should he survive, well his hands are useless, he will never wield a bow or spear again." The man's voice was sweet and deep, so sweet it made Partaxis stomach twist and turn. He continued.

"So, Partaxis that leaves just you to slay and I will easily take Fenrir with my main opposition destroyed. I should thank you for bringing me all the men that would cause me a slight pause. Shame it was so simple Partaxis, I would have expected more from you."

"Enough from you monster." Partaxis roared as he charged the man. The man danced out of the way with godly speed. He kept up his attack, nearly every blow missed its mark. The ones that managed to land were shaken off as being nothing more than a nuisance.

"Partaxis, you are losing your steam, where is the ferocity that so many see in you? Perhaps the fact that I killed your companions is causing you to not think well enough and fight like a mad man. You are too sloppy with your attacks and I grow weary of this game." Just then the man stopped in his tracks, Partaxis plunged into the opening, only too late to realize the sword that was drawn. Partaxis feebly attempted to twist away from the slash, the blade bit him deeply into the thick of his leg. Another hand reached out, grabbed hold of him and pulled him into a sword thrust. The blade punched through his back and burst out the front, the man twisted the blade and yanked it free. He grabbed ahold of Partaxis, he turned Partaxis to face him and lifted him effortlessly with his hand bringing Partaxis face close to his.

"Who, are you?" Partaxis asked feebly as blood quickly drained from his body. The man formed a twisted smile.

"The death of you, as many have fallen before me. I am Thead the Immortal, Slayer of Angels, High Commander of Demons, Harbinger of Death, and Guardian of the Faceless One."

XXXI

The night was cool and mist filled. The entire group of the Nameless men and women were quieted for the night. The tendrils of the fog ebbed and flowed throughout the camp covering the asleep in a thick layer. Strands coiled around the watchman's boots, were thwarted by the fire of their torches and the remaining fires of the camp. The mist recoiled only a small distance away from the fire, there it loomed like a great predator on the prowl for prey.

Zarron awoke abruptly to a sudden voice that boomed in his head, the words of it unclear, his flurry of motion chased the mist that was clinging to him a small distance away before it returned clinging to him again. He looked about him and saw nothing. There was no person standing around him nor even awake. He listened intently, he only heard the ruffles of a man rolling in his bed roll, coughs and snores from those fast asleep, the slow methodical steps of the watchmen on patrol, nothing unusual. A small fire crackled and sputtered its last breath, the life of it extinguished and surrendered to the mist who devoured it hungrily. His heart was quick and unsettled, his spirit was troubled. There was something deeply foreboding happening or going to happen. He could not seem to put his finger on it. So he pulled himself out of his bed roll, the mist reeling away. He looked about him, small dark mounds dotted the landscape. Some dark shadows moved to and fro along their camp outskirts. He knew them to be the watchmen and he needed to remind himself of that before his mind could wander to unseen terrors. Their torches cast an eerie glow in the fog and night sky, reminiscent of ancient will o' wisps. He picked up his sword belt, he donned it over his heavy woolen arming gambeson. He gathered up his cloak and slung it over his shoulders. He proceeded to the nearest watchman.

It was then that he heard the voice again, this time it was more subtle and pleasant, yet there was a sense of power in it demanding action to be taken. *Fenrir. Fenrir* the voice came again more rushed this time, finally *Thead.* He froze in his tracks, he took several steadying breathes to contain the upheaval in his spirit. He peered around, silence loomed like a great beast. *Go!* The voice boomed again. *Now!* He swallowed hard, he spun around and headed directly to where his Captain slept.

"Jeremiah, up." Zarron spoke in a hushed voice. Jeremiah shifted under his bed roll a little, he fluttered open his eyes and pressed the balls of his hand into his eyes clearing them. He pulled himself to his elbows as he peered around at the darkness.

"Yes it is early, I understand that Captain, we need to move." Zarron paused briefly before speaking again.

"Now. We need to move out now." Zarron finished in a hurried tone.

"Very well Zarron, I guess it was a good thing that we set up camp in haste and had warm weather aye? Easier gathering up bed rolls over breaking down tents." Jeremiah said as he pulled himself to his feet. He quickly dressed himself, saluted Zarron then departed.

Zarron turned to head back to his own bed roll, before he made it there shouts of men started ringing throughout the camp as captains and sergeants alike aroused their men and women from sleep. The whole camp quickly came to life.

He stooped down and gathered up his bed roll along with the few belonging he had laid out. He quickly shoved them into his travel bag. When he rose up from his bag Sheen was standing before him with his armor in hand.

"Thank you Sheen." he smiled at her as he put out his arms. Sheen slipped the breastplate on him. Followed by the vambraces, the pauldrons and finally the helm. As soon as the final piece was put on he flared the armors magick his eye slits burst with a bright blue smoky glow. The armor shined with a dull white light, the runes etched into the cobalt armor glowed a bright gold. The armor was designed to give the bearer an aura of holiness and heroism, it was meant to intimidate evil. It also served a greater purpose of giving light to the bearer in darkness, yet it could be extinguished if the element of surprise was needed. Another purpose behind the glows and the eerie blue eyes was to allow the Paladin to easily detect wickedness and evil no matter where it hid. The elements broke down the wall of deception. He thought the sight the armor offered was similar to his holy rage and he wondered if maybe the church had developed it as a means to mimic the once great house.

As Zarron looked around he saw the one other Paladin assigned with him, her task was to train him on the unique aspects of being a Paladin. Generally a Crusader with amazing talent and skill would be selected for a chance at becoming a Paladin. After selection they would fall under the mentorship of a given Paladin to learn the role as he or she passed a series of tests and challenges, at the end of successful training they would take up the mantle as the newest Paladin in the Nameless Ones church. If they happened to fail, they would still retain the rank of Crusader. Even though they did not become a Paladin they would be honored as a highly favored and skilled combatant, there was no shame if they failed. Being a Paladin was not meant for everyone, Zarron was still humbled at his selection of the rank. His situation was different in the fact that he was receiving partial training now, but, he was selected by the Nameless One to be a Paladin, which made his situation unique. He knew that after this event with Fenrir that the other Paladin would go on her way and his training would be considered complete.

He watched his Paladin companion flare her magick. Her eyes came to life pulsing with a purple glow, it shifted from bright to dull, back to bright again. Another trait of the armor was to alter the color of the eyes. It was common for the 21 Paladins of the church to vary the glow of the eyes to personify their specialty in the Church. Their specialty were given to them the minute they joined the Paladin rank. No one person assigned them their roles, it was more of a thing that just existed. Few of the Paladins actually knew the specialty they would be, some would venture a guess, but once it was given it just kind of happened and it felt like it was always supposed to be.

Violet were Seekers, ones that were skilled at hunting down veiled evil they were the rarest in the Paladin ranks. There was exactly two of them that specialized as Seekers out of the 21. Green were Arbiters, they would go forth to establish and hold new churches until they became independent, among holding churches they would also negotiate pacts and alliances, they were the most unique role in the body where they spent a great deal of time with diplomacy rather than the typical physical force known of the Body. There was 3 of them out of the 21. White were Menders, they were the strongest healers in the body of the Nameless, their healing magick only bested by the High Clerics from the Mind of the Church. He took a moment to remember their number, ahh yes there are 4 of them. Yellow and orange were Purifiers, they possessed extensive offensive combat skills. Finally there was blue who are the Warders, their primary capacity is to hold the front line and support the team. Overall blue, yellow and orange were the most common and fluctuated in their numbers making up the final 12.

He wondered if the numbers selected for each order would vary according to the need of the church, he recalled something in his training where it was written about a time where the vast majority of the Paladins were Arbiters. Another notable thing was that each armor was made unique for the members of the Paladin rank. His own armor was thick and heavy, its metal was so thick that only the mightiest weapons and magick could pierce it. The Seeker with him had armor that was more liken to leather and robes and it flowed like molten metal yet it was made from the same type of metal his armor was made from. It was amazing to him that she could move as quietly and unseen as she could, there were many moments that she easily snuck up on him unnoticed even with his enhanced hearing. Every time she did, it sent a chill down his spine at how easily she had done that, if she was an enemy he would have been dead many times over.

He nodded his head towards the other Paladin. It was her that told him about the hidden potential of the armor. The flaring of the eyes and glow were new to him, he wished he had known the potential when he was breaking the siege. It would have made it easier to see the enchantments and follow the wicked leaders shadow movements. *'I will need to take some more time to speak to her'* he thought to himself. As if she heard his thoughts she approached him.

Her movements were fluid and unnatural, it was as if she was not even touching the ground. Her armor ebbed and flowed with a molten liked quality Zarron observed earlier. She made no noise as she approached him, her glowing violet eyes remained locked on his eyes. He wanted to squirm under her glare but he remained stalwart. The helm she wore was of angular and twisted design, curved horns flanked the sides of the helm shooting backwards before twisting towards the back center. The horns remained close to the helm, a cross covered the front, angel wings sprung out the side of the cross etched into the surface, the symbol of the Nameless One donned all the Paladin's helms. Her design was darkened and was only apparent when light hit it just right creating an eerie effect.

As she came up to Zarron, Sheen observed her with curious eyes and stepped out of the way. She was barely a hand shorter than Zarron, tall for a woman. She extinguished her glow, revealing beautiful gray eyes and dark tanned skin. When she spoke, her voice was filled with charm and the slight trepidation he was feeling before was replaced with an almost affection towards this woman. She is a dangerous woman he thought, he had run into one Seeker before when he was young and the thought of it still caused him to shiver.

There was a reason they were rare and there was a reason why they were truly the most feared of the Paladin ranks by friends and most importantly foes. It was the first Seeker that hunted down the great Demon Abyss, a master of the shadows and bringer of a great darkness that overtook most of the known world. No one was able to locate the source of it and the Church tried multiple times to take over his supposed keep. When they realized their approach wasn't working the Nameless One spoke to one of the high commanders and anointed him as the first Seeker. He proceeded to plan his capture, he endured 3 weeks of torment and torture before he gathered all the Intel he needed to determine where the Demon Abyss sat on his throne. Single handedly the Seeker freed himself, he proceeded to hunt down the Demon, upon finding him he engaged in combat and beat him severely, after interrogating the wicked one he found out there was another Demon that controlled and directed his actions. He slew the Demon Abyss after gathering the information.

Shortly after that the Seeker hunted down the one that was actually directing and controlling the darkness. He assassinated her restoring light to the land. If wicked men knew a Seeker was nearby or on their way many of them decided to quit and turn themselves in or flee the area as far as they could. Only the most wicked and unnatural foes remained to face a Seeker. Their arrogance besting their logic.

"Zarron, what are you feeling right now?" The question was asked sweetly and it caught him unaware.

"Umm, confused, just a moment ago I was almost fearing you as you walked to me then." He flushed as he continued "and now I feel an attraction towards you."

"Yes, that is about right Zarron, protecting your emotions is vital. At least you are able to recognize what emotions I was working on with you. There are too many enemies that take advantage of our "good nature" so to speak. It is good to understand where you stand with your thoughts and give yourself a constant focal point to think on. You need to grab ahold of every thought and reign it in. Is fearing me a normal thought? Is thinking of me as a love interest typical?" He flushed once more.

"No Lady Kadiallias, you are a beautiful woman but I never have had feelings of love towards you for the brief time I have known you, and I have no reason to truly fear you as if you were my enemy. Fear of your Seeker qualities is true though."

"That is where I was able to be most dangerous Zarron, I just took those qualities I possess and magnified them, which created the far end of those emotions. Zarron, when meeting someone new I want you to do something. Empty your mind and focus on something you can truly grasp a hold of. Like your sword, or the Nameless One, perhaps a tree or plant, maybe your armor you wear or clothing you have on. Upon focusing on them think of the basic qualities of them, listen in your mind for anything that pulls away from those thoughts. If something pulls away from that, then you know your emotions are trying to be manipulated. Eventually after practice and training you will no longer need to think of something physical you will just know."

"Thank you Lady Kadiallias, your training is always appreciated. I will keep what you said in mind and put it into practice immediately." She began to walk away to get to her horse, she paused before turning back to him.

"Thanks for the compliment Paladin Zarron." She winked at him. Her violet eyes flared to life. Zarron chuckled to himself.

"Zarron that was strange wasn't it? Why would she do that?" Sheen spoke as Zarron turned back to her.

"Training Sheen, wait, is that jealousy in your voice?" Sheen flushed a bright red causing him to laugh. He placed a hand on her shoulder and gave it a squeeze. She relaxed upon his touch, she almost always did. He released his grip and returned the salute to his captain as he approached.

"The men are packed and ready to depart Lord Zarron."

"Thank you Captain Jeremiah, let us leave with haste." Zarron gathered up his travel bag. He loaded it quickly onto the back of Thunder. Within moments the entire line of Nameless Ones brothers and sisters began a brisk pace towards Fenrir with no questions asked or murmurs whispered for the queer hour departure which Zarron was grateful for.

They made great time through the night. The only problem they started running into was the supply wagons being too slow to keep up with the pace. Zarron decided that a small group of his men will stay behind with the supply wagon as they played catch up.

There was no time to spare as the sense of urgency to get to Fenrir increased through the night. It was getting close to dawn when Korilith keep along with the mighty Fenrir loomed before them.

Zarron was welcomed warmly by the men and women the served with in the Night Wolves as they arrived, it had been nearly 3 months since he last saw them. Commander Froth was among the last to approach him. He gave him a hearty handshake before speaking.

"Well Paladin Zarron. You brought back a small army, it would appear that I owe you some time to hear about your God."

"I suppose that is true Commander, you are a man of your word. Where is Durakon and Partaxis?" he asked inquisitively with a touch of anxiousness as well.

"They are out with Raamok and assaulting the siege tower. Their assault should begin very shortly if all worked out."

Zarron's eyes opened wide, he whispered a curse under his breath.

"Commander Froth, I need the gate opened now." Froth hesitated a moment as he contemplated the command from Zarron, he nodded his head towards him coming to a decision, Froth turned to bark orders for the gate to be opened. Ranks of men filed close to the gate as it swung open. They quickly searched the shadows and the fallen of the defeated vanguard force to confirm none were faking their death or hiding in an attempt to enter Korilith by surprise. Satisfied with their search they made a hole to allow Zarron and his men passage.

Zarron charged out of the gate with his men in tow, they stampeded over remnants of the dead that were left in the shadows of the Fenrir from the archers the day prior. As the gate was close to being shut behind him a massive explosion erupted from the enemy encampment sending a fiery ball into the air. They observed for a moment waiting for the tower to set ablaze. When it did not light, Zarron kicked his heels into Thunder sending him into a fast gallop.

Thead cackled in delight as he felt the breaths of Partaxis become labored and slowed. A flash of light pulled him from his delight. He looked towards it. His eyes snapped wide in horror, he tossed Partaxis off to the side as quickly as he could. He formed a hasty magickal barrier. Despite his efforts the power of the blast shattered the barrier. He felt a searing pain as the attack tore through his shoulder nearly severing his arm. Before him stood Raamok bleeding profusely from his wound, his sword billowed with smoke.

"You fool, you dare pervert my magick and use it against me. It would have been better for you to stay down Raamok. There will be no coming back this time, I will take your head." Thead's wound began to close and heal itself as he stalked towards Raamok.

Raamok mustered every ounce of energy he had left and stood tall in defiance, unconsciousness gnawed at him; the darkness of it flowed like a mighty torrential wave threatening to take him once more. *No, not this time.* Raamok thought to himself. He smiled at Thead, even as the mighty sword of Thead was lifted to strike. He didn't close his eyes, he kept them locked onto Thead's, and he found himself remarkably at peace facing his possible imminent death. *It wouldn't happen though, there was too many vampires to kill still, so many.* He thought to himself even still while smiling at Thead. A thunderous sound in the distance pulled him from his thoughts and stopped Thead for a moment.

That pause gave Raamok the time he needed to act. He let out a shout, shocking his mind awake and commanding his body to move. He drew and attacked Thead with his second weapon.

Thead, though momentarily caught off guard, reacted and knocked the sword away with a casual wave of his good arm. Raamok let him take it, it was only a distraction, and he quickly side stepped to the wounded side of Thead. Thead attempted to react but Raamok was already where he needed to be, with a mighty swing he hamstringed the Guardian nearly severing his leg with the magickal sword Typhoon. Thead fell hard with a cry of pain, as he fell he lashed out with godly speed. The force of the slap sent Raamok flying away with great speed.

He flew 15 feet before landing hard, the pain in his stomach becoming a fire once more. His arm was broke again from his failed attempt to block the blow from Thead and he assumed his ribs had become fractured. The darkness began a new assault on his mind.

There was no smile or laughter from Thead as he pulled himself to his feet, his shoulder being healed completely and his leg healed enough to limp towards Raamok. He growled quietly as he approached the wretched human. He grabbed Typhoon as he approached Raamok, the weapon burned and blazed in his hand, as if it was trying to get the person to surrender their grip on it. The sensation caused his anger to flare. He held on tighter, unwilling to let the pathetic creation win.

"I had not wanted to expend that much energy on healing Raamok, you have truly made me angry." Thead raised Typhoon and drove it towards Raamok. As the weapon was drawing close, an opening in the sky tore open, a massive fist seemed to form and crush into Thead knocking him flat. As he hit the ground hard, Typhoon came loose from his grip. It skittered into the distance.

Thead attempted to stand only to have another fist form and crush him back to the ground. He let out a mighty roar as dark energy erupted from him vertically collapsing the tear in the sky. He stood onto his feet and turned to face…two Paladins of the Nameless leading an impressive sizeable force. Burst of light shot from them. They tore through him causing hundreds of small holes to form before being polluted with his black blood. Thead stumbled back a step before another volley came and collided into him tearing hundreds more holes.

Thead let out a mighty scream, a darkened nova blast erupted around him, and the intensity of it sent Raamok skidding across the ground while also halting the charge of the Nameless soldiers. He held it there for a moment as he attempted to heal the holes in his body. He was not given enough time.

"By the Nameless One." Zarron stated under his breath as the dark nova cloud formed into a massive dome, halting their advance. Zarron let out a shout of frustration.

"We will bring this barrier down. As one, charge!" Zarron shouted to his men. The entire force he brought with him slammed into the barrier. The sheer weight of the group caused the barrier to shutter slightly but, it held. Zarron screamed in rage, his vision heightened as his muscles bulged with a new strength. He jumped from his horse drawing Angel Fire. He slammed the blade into the barrier, the barrier shuttered and stayed strong.

"No!" Zarron screamed again, he felt himself grow stronger with the more enraged he became. He attacked the wall again and again each strike being mightier than the last. He didn't notice that the men with him backed away from him in trepidation.

Finally a crack formed that was wide enough for Zarron to place a hand in it. He grabbed hold and began to tear small pieces of the barrier apart allowing him and others to see inside. The wicked creature was almost finished healing. He was stalking towards Raamok once more.

"Oh no, no!" Zarron cried out his movements became more desperate as he continued to pull the barrier apart with his hands. One of his men dropped from their horse, his desire to help his commander overrode his fear. He soon joined Zarron in his endeavor to destroy the shield. The two of them made progress but, it was not fast enough.

"Zarron, Zarron" a familiar voice shouted to him. "Zarron." This pulled him from his tunneled vision for a moment as Kadiallias approached him. He saw with his rage that she glowed a magnificent white with bright swaths of blue mixed in. There was also something else, a slight dot of darkness, as he focused on it, it appeared to become larger and this enraged him further. He wanted to tear it apart, he wanted to slay it, but something grabbed his attention, the bright colors pulsed wildly distracting him from the darkness, the white and blue once again surged to life, his mind became more aware and clear.

"Throw me Zarron, there is no way we can get to him before he gets to Raamok, throw me." He picked her up with almost no effort, his strength had grown impressively. He spun her around and with a shout he threw her, she helped by launching herself at the same moment in time, his vision returned to normal and his muscles relaxed as he watched her speed away from him, his rage was gone for now.

Kadiallias erupted in a massive fiery white ball, when she hit the barrier she not only broke through a portion but shattered it completely, she hit the ground gracefully and rolled, she used her momentum to carry her through the roll, when she popped up her dual weapons were drawn, the momentum continued launching her forward.

The weapons pierced Thead easily and with her weight behind them it forced the evil Guardian to the ground. She crouched on top of him then launched herself backwards leaving her weapons in place.

As soon as the barrier shattered Zarron along with his companion identified as Char rushed in. Zarron witnessed Kadiallias flip away from Thead leaving her weapons in him. He summoned another celestial fist smashing it into Thead with as much might as he could muster, the force of it drove the weapons further into the evil Guardian, pinning him if even for a moment.

"Get our men out of here and get the healers doing what they can, quickly!" Zarron commanded of his men, they acted without hesitation gathering Durakon, Partaxis and Raamok. All of them were either nearly or were unconscious and unmoving. As they brought Raamok past him, Raamok reached out and laid a bloodied hand on him.

"Make him suffer Holyrage." Raamok spoke softly to him before he lost consciousness.

I intend to Raamok. Zarron thought to himself keeping a cold steely look upon the Guardian. Kadiallias pulled herself to Zarron's side and withdrew another set of weapons from sheathes on her back. Sheen along with Char flanked his other side. The rest of his men drew ranks next to them, they were still a little cautious of their leader going into such a rage but, there was a sense of awe among them as well from the power of it. They had never seen someone tear down a magick barrier of that caliber before them with bare hands it was unheard of and thought to be impossible.

Zarron didn't give Thead the total time he needed to pull free from the blades before they charged.

Thead's eyes widened as he saw the entire group of Nameless One's minions charge him. The pain in him from the righteous weapons burned. He felt the power in him draining far too rapidly and panic struck him. He wasn't ready to engage the entire group before him with two Paladins of the Nameless leading it, one being a Holyrage and the other a Seeker, his energy was spent creating the elaborate illusion that hid his true army from sight and more importantly from Tahvo.

He knew that if he broke that illusion he would lose thousands to that bastard Tahvo and his land shifting. But, he already felt it slipping, in fact some parts already slipped, such as the massive siege tower. It wasn't meant to be exposed until it was too late for the Fenrir to react. It didn't change the fact that there was much more hidden and in the safety of being outside the changing lands. He still had a choice to make, one that he needed to make quickly.

Self-preservation is important I can come back and destroy all of these before me when I am restored. I can't fall here. Thead grabbed the righteous weapons by the hilt and twisted sharply, he let out a great cry of pain as he pulled them out of his body freeing him from the sapping strength of them. He instantly healed the wounds, and jumped to his feet. As he did another volley of light pierced him, he shielded himself from some, but there were still so many that got through. He cast a magickal barrier up no to no avail, the holy warriors barely stumbled as they broke through it. Thead attempted to teleport away, it failed terribly as another volley of light forced him to lose his concentration and shield himself from the tiny bolts of death. *Fine that leaves me no choice.*

Zarron's men were within steps of the wicked Guardian when an intense heat burst forth and a great snapping sound shook the air. A darkness enveloped them so thick it shocked their bodies as all of their senses were blocked, a numbness took over. It caused them to stop momentarily as vertigo and nausea cascaded through them. Within a blink of an eye though it was gone and with it the Guardian, but, before them a short distance was another massive siege tower rumbling into the unchanging lands with it a horde of wicked creatures.

"By the Nameless One." Zarron stood in shock for a moment before looking towards his companions. They all shook their heads and readied themselves for an oncoming slaughter.

"No, not here. Fall back men! Fall back to the Fenrir!" Zarron's voice boomed. His men turned to begin falling back quickly. Zarron backpedaled away from the massive horde of enemies. Sheen and Jeremiah pulled on him forcing him to turn and fall back with his men.

The horde charged his group. They were still a long distance away but they were gaining ground quickly. Zarron finally got to Thunder and began riding back. He was almost half way back to Fenrir when the earth began to shake and the sky darkened. He turned and looked back, a sense of dread fell heavy on him.

XXXII

The land that was moderately bland before, turned into something likened to the maw of some hell. The earth shook so violently that it nearly toppled Zarron from his horse. The enemy horde that was following his group became flattened by the massive shaking. They stumbled to their feet before the earth opened up and dropped the portion in the changing land into a massive tear in the ground. Titanic rocks shot up from the ground and smashed into the siege tower, the wood and metal that held the tower together exploded into a fury of fatal shards. More rock formations formed, they continued the never ending assault upon the tower. They obliterated the tower, turning the once towering machine of death into nothing more than a pile of broken kindling. At once the wrath of the land turned its attention upon the horde of enemies.

The rock formation that jutted to and fro groaned with the massive weight, then at once it collapsed. Colossal boulders crushed the enemy horde below. As they hit the ground the impact threw the force to and fro. Rocks that followed after the initial shattered into thousands of pieces, most of them being larger than a horse. They tore through the ranks of the enemy crushing bones and tearing the ground apart. Zarron shifted a few times to avoid pieces of stone that managed to find their way to him. The cries and shouts of the enemy rang through the air. Watching the force before him obliterate the horde of wicked ones, did not bring comfort to Zarron as he expected it would. The shouts slowly died away as the land continued its relentless assault and just as quick as it began it was over.

The land abruptly turned back to the relative serene landscape it was before. The entire enemy force was nearly destroyed. The only group that survived were the ones fortunate enough to either be in the unchanging lands or those that escaped to the unchanged land.

"Zarron, we need to get back to the Fenrir and tend to your friends that are wounded." A soft voice pulled him from the adjunct horror that was before him. He turned to the voice, he stared blankly at Sheen for a moment before absent mindedly nodding his head in agreement.

"Before we leave, Captain Jeremiah call the cavalry line that is not carrying the wounded to finish off the remaining enemy force. I don't care how horrid of an experience they had, if we don't finish them off now we will have to face the enemy with that many more when the time comes."

His Captain nodded his head and carried out the order. Zarron watched as the cavalry lined wheeled about charging the enemy. With barely no resistance the wicked ones crumpled under the charge, some of them before they could even react. Zarron watched as a handful of the enemy attempted to form something like a battle line only to be crushed by the heavy weight of the horses and sheared apart with the holy warrior's swords and spears. When the cavalry line wheeled about for a second charge there was no enemies left standing. Jeremiah signaled them to form up and fall back to the Fenrir. Jeremiah joined the head of the line to lead them back. Zarron, Sheen and Kadiallias joined the rear line as they trotted past.

When Zarron got back to the Fenrir the gate was opened for him and his men. As they passed under the mighty wall the gate slammed shut behind them. Commander Froth greeted him.

"Zarron, your friends are in the medical bays. Your healers have already began their task of healing them." Zarron nodded his head curtly before jumping off Thunder. He handed the reins to one of Fenrir's soldiers.

"Captain get our men dismounted and settled. I am going to the medical facility. Seeker Kadiallias with me, Sheen assist Captain Jeremiah in his task." With that, Zarron and Kadiallias hurried to the medical facility.

Sheen took a hesitant step towards them before shaking her head and turning her attention to the Captain.

"How can I help Captain Jeremiah?"

As Zarron entered the medical facility it took his eyes a moment to adjust. He was pleased to see that Durakon was on his feet already. The one and only High Cleric that was assigned to him by the church was fervently working on Partaxis. Kadiallias went right to work assisting the healers as they needed it.

Zarron was grateful for the High Cleric that was assigned to him. They were rare to the Mind of Church just as the Paladins were rare for the Body of the Church. He nodded his head towards Durakon before grabbing a cleric for a report.

"Cleric Peter, do you have a report on these men for me?"

"Paladin Zarron, your ranger friend recovered remarkably well after he had a few moments to breathe. He was just about fully conscious by the time we made it to the gates of Fenrir. His hands were some trouble to get them to respond to healing, it was almost too late for them."

Peter grabbed Zarron by the arm and led him a little ways away from Durakon before he lowered his voice, "Truth be told I am not sure he will be able to shoot that bow as well as he could before, I think the nerves were damaged severely with the fire and the time from the injury to the healing was too great." Zarron's shot a quick sympathetic look towards Durakon.

Peter returned to his normal speaking voice before continuing. "Your dark haired companion is in poor shape, the wound to his stomach was very difficult to heal, the wound responded a little slower with holy magick than anticipated. We had one of our earth menders try his healing, the wound closed much faster with that and we were able to heal that wound to his stomach. She was able to heal the cracked ribs as well, that nearly exhausted her so she couldn't get to his arm. We splint it temporarily until the earth mender has time to recoup then she will address his arm. Partaxis is by far in the worse shape, he has little blood for us to work with and we are not entirely positive our High Cleric will be able to sustain the healing effort long enough for him to recover."

"Thank you Peter." Zarron clasped a hand on the cleric shoulder and went over to Kadiallias and the High Cleric as they worked on restoring Partaxis.

"My lady Paladin and High Cleric I am here to assist in easing the burden of restoring Partaxis."

The High Cleric looked up from his work momentarily, weariness was there but it was overshadowed and overwhelmed by a fire of intrigue and excitement. Chances were that he has not had such a challenging healing in some time. Zarron knew in that moment a High Clerics passion in their craft and a healing was similar to that thrill of battle a warrior experiences before a battle or a duelist before a highly anticipated duel.

"Paladin? How amazing, I am El." He rendered a polite bow of his head, Zarron returned the gesture.

"I am Zarron, my apologies for not introducing myself earlier in our trek. How may I help High Cleric El?"

"That is because I wasn't with your retinue Zarron, I came a day before to setup the medical facilities. It proved to be most beneficial indeed. I will need the Lady Paladin and yours help, along with any of the Clerics you have with you. However much I love the challenge I sadly cannot keep up with healing what little of his blood remains for the time it may take for him to recover. I don't usually say this but a blood healer would be most helpful in this situation, despite the insanity that comes from it, one thing they know how to do that we don't know how to do is create blood, and right now Partaxis needs his blood restored more than anything. So basically what we are doing here is keeping a dead man alive long enough for his body to hopefully renew the blood naturally. Which means we need to keep up with healing infections that are setting in, restoring and balancing his oxygen levels, all while willing his blood to stretch itself even thinner in repairing the sustained wounds, along with stretching it to pump through the vital organs. I expect the Clerics to burden most of the weight of this, but, you Paladins have a good enough grasp on how you recover from wounds to assist as well. You all are not blessed as much as the Clerics are in healing but you can do this, I will warn you that it will make you bone tired and weary. You may hallucinate, your blood flow will slow, you will lose nearly all feeling in your appendages, your mouth will get dry and a mighty headache is sure to form. When it feels like you can't do any more you will need to press that much harder. I will expect you Paladins to work until you lose consciousness. Then if need be get up only an hour or two later to do it for another 10 minutes, 5 minutes, then 1 min. If you don't this man will die. Do you understand this?"

Zarron found himself nodding his head in agreement as his stomach roiled from the possibility that he will probably undertake one of the most challenging things in his life to save a person he knew but, knew little and one that absolutely needed to survive this in order for the defense to succeed. His will steeled itself and he nodded his head in confidence to El.

"It will be done El." Zarron saluted sharply, El smiled at Zarron, before speaking once more.

"Finally you can go take a look at the one with the wound to his stomach and broken arm. It will be most helpful to allow our Cleric earth mender to rest fully so she may be able to help. After you finish that, I will set a healing rotation and request you stay close. May the Nameless One be with you, no, with us all." El turned back to his work on repairing Partaxis, Zarron took the hint that there would be no more conversation for now. He had his orders, it was time to get the mission done.

Raamok lay on his cot asleep, the wound on his stomach healed wonderfully with no signs of ever being there before. However many other scars crisscrossed his body which created more questions for him. How little did he know about this strange companion yet, he knew there was something extremely important about their relationship.

He placed a hand on the wounded arm gingerly. He began summoning the healing magick. It was stopped by a slight almost unnoticeable change in the arm. The coloration faded from a deep bruised purple, his normal skin tone returning to normal, the bones twisted, shifted and settled to the original configuration.

Raamok's eyes snapped open in alarm as he started getting up quickly. Zarron placed a calming hand on his chest.

"Be at peace Raamok, you are in safe hands here." He said in a calming voice.

"I, uh…thank you." Zarron raised an eyebrow at his companion.

"How did you heal yourself Raamok? Here I was about to summon forth the healing but, you healed first."

"You must have been mistaken Zarron, perhaps your tie with your God is stronger than one might think and you subconsciously healed me."

"Raamok you know that is utter folly, I know enough to understand when I heal someone or not. How did you do it?" Raamok shifted his eyes around the room noticing the facility he was in for the first time and the people bustling about. He licked his lips before speaking. When he spoke again it was in a nearly inaudible voice.

"Did anyone else see that take place?" Zarron shook his head no.

"Good."

There was a moment of silence between them as Zarron stared at him inquisitively. "You are not going to tell me how you did it are you Raamok?" Raamok nodded his head in agreement.

"Very well, perhaps some point I will have earned your trust enough for such information. Until I earn that from you I will pass onto the clerics that I took care of the healing." he smiled reassuringly at him before patting his shoulder. He left Raamok to take a seat near Partaxis to wait patiently until they needed him for healing.

Night had fallen again, Zarron happened to be on the healing rotation when Partaxis moved a massive hand. Zarron bit down, put aside the massive head ache that he had been fighting with for an hour, his mouth felt like he had been swallowing sand for days, the feelings in his fingers and most of his body had all went out. The only warmth that persisted was the slow trickle of the healing magick. He pressed hard to bring a burst of healing power forth, the slow trickle of healing magick became like a mighty river. Partaxis stirred more still, the motions becoming deliberate in nature. Finally, his eyes snapped open, he blinked a few times with unfocused eyes. Then, as if a spark took to fire his eyes became focused, Partaxis nearly jumped to his feet. Zarron placed a calming hand on him.

"Be still Partaxis, you are safe, the enemy is defeated for now. You are in the medical rooms in Korilith Keep." Zarron spoke with as clear and confident voice he could bring to bear despite his enormous fatigue. He did his best to put in the right kind of emphasis to calm the large man. Partaxis eyes remained wild for a few tense moments before he calmed down. His eyes focused more clearly on Zarron.

"How am I alive? How are you here, did you bring the army that you set out to get? I could have sworn I would be dead, there was light and darkness everywhere. I was in a strange…place." The last words were spoken in a curious tone.

"Well, Partaxis, It took the nonstop healing of a High Cleric, 7 clerics, my fellow Paladin and myself to keep you alive. There was little blood for us to work on when we got you." Zarron's vision swayed slightly, he blinked his eyes and shook his head, he was so tired.

"Blessedly the Nameless One sent us a vision and we marched hard and fast through the night to get to you, in what appears to be the best time that we could have. If you had received your first healing minutes after we got there you would be dead by now, we routed the enemy…and…and mountains, crashed…tremors." As he watched Partaxis he noted a change to his countenance, he reached out a big hand to him, it looked like it was a long ways away.

He tried to reach out to take it, as he did he felt something dripping down from his eyes, was he crying he wondered, he reached his hand up and wiped at it, when he pulled it away fresh blood stained it. He felt it again, a steady stream this time from his eyes, nose and ears. Then he felt as if a mountain crashed into him, overwhelming his senses, he felt air rush by him, he lost sight of Partaxis, there was a sudden bone crushing stop in momentum. He felt strong hands under him, then another wash of air as he rose, flying perhaps? No he can't fly, a face came into his field of vision, Raamok, yes Raamok…He could tell he was speaking, yet no sounds came, the stream of blood seemed to increase…."Zarron" a voice in the distance was yelling his name. The voice sounded familiar, who was it though…memories of his Mother and Father came and went…he could not recall their voice though, he tried again and still he could not recall it. How could he not remember their voices, how could he not remember, tears began to fall he thought, a sob wracked his body. His stomach convulsed once, twice. He lurched off to the side and felt the wind again, the sudden stop came once more…"Zarron" he heard the voice again, hands gathered him up once more he thought, he didn't feel the wind this time and the world became very quiet, very still and so, very, dark.

"The bloody hell did you do, you get that bastard on his feet or there will be hell to pay."

"There is nothing I can do Partaxis."

"The hell you can't! If your God is so mighty then restore him."

"Do not tempt our God, right now he is not responding to healing, as I told you there is nothing I can do, it is up to Zarron to pull himself out." There seemed to be a drawn out moment of silence, heavy footsteps, likely Partaxis stomped away and a door slammed heavily. There was a sigh from the other person, likely High Cleric El. Then unconsciousness took him again.

"They need you, I need you." Something wet plopped onto his face. What was that, he tried to reach up a hand to wipe it away, his body did not respond.

"I love you."

****

Durakon peered over the land that stretched below him. There was an unease in the air, something unsettling and wrong. The weather had been pleasantly warm for the north, there was even an almost warm breeze if anything at all could be considered warm that far north. Something like that would bring out birds and other creatures but not a single thing stirred, the skies were still, the changing land before him remained unchanged which almost frightened him more than the rest. From what he understood the only reason that land wouldn't change is because there is no life for Tahvo to feed off of, which meant in theory that there was no life left remaining there. He looked off towards the keep and was surprised to see Raamok there, not even an arm's length away. He reeled his emotions of shock in and replaced it with a smooth visage, before speaking calmly.

"Raamok, how fare you today?"

"Restless, something isn't right, the scouts they sent out have not returned and on my treks into the lands I was able to detect so many wicked things. The thing is I was not able to determine where and what."

Durakon grunted in reply. It was all he could do to not shudder with the confirmation of what he had come to the conclusion of as well. The enemy was here, it was just a matter of when they would appear. He turned back to the vast northern expanse of Vin Ara Talv. Raamok took a step next to him. They both stared out into the land.

Moments later horns blared from the eastern side of Korilith keep, Raamok and Durakon both turned to stare down that way. They looked at one another with inquisitive eyes before they began to stalk towards that side of Korilith keep. Then a shimmer caught their attention, they froze in their tracks, turned crisply to the shimmer, both their breaths caught in their throat. A siege tower came to full crisp detail from thin air just inside the unchanged lands. Followed by a second, third, fourth and so many more. Along with them a massive hoard of creatures of all sort accompanied them, with untold numbers more in the towers themselves.

Barbarians formed the front line, mixed in with them were deformed yetis and giants of amazing height. They were flanked by wings of mammoth cavalry. Right behind the frontline marched orcs and goblins. Even more than that were hundreds of thousands of demonic dark ones of all shapes and sizes. The most abundant from what they could tell were spider like beasts with 10 legs, their heads were more likened to that of a bear with powerful jaws, and they had two arms that ended in sharp dangerous claws that were more close to daggers. They stood about the height of a 3-4ft at the shoulder. The second most numerous it seemed were tall sinewy humanoid shaped creatures with sharp angular features, spikes protruded from their elbows and knees. They came in shades of crimson, black and dark purple.

Durakon looked away from the grotesque sight and grabbed the sergeant that was standing close by staring at the same horror.

"Sergeant, I need you to sound the call to arms, signal the torchbearers to light the warning fires." He continued to stare out at the massive horde before him. Durakon placed himself in front of the stunned man. He placed a hand on his shoulder, once he turned his focus on him Durakon addressed him in a calm voice.

"Sergeant, you need to focus, send up the call to arms and signal the torchbearers. We will bloody this enemy, in order to do that I need you to sound the alarm though." He nodded his head vigorously in agreement, he rendered a crisp salute before he snapped into motion bawling orders.

Durakon turned back to the wall as the echoes of commands and of horns called the men on the border between hell and the bastion of hope into action. The slow trill of it was oddly comforting. They now knew what they were facing and that unease and quiet of the past three days finally came to pass.

Then a deep resonate tone shook the Fenrir as the mighty horn of Korilith sound filled the air for the first time in nearly 500 years, a call to arms signaling a warning to the men of Korilith, a call of forewarning to the continent of Vin Ara Talv of a force that threatens the entirety of the land. The sounds of that horn blared three times, the noise would travel as far southeast as the Citadel Heights, stronghold and bastion for the Nameless One. With any luck it would bring in defenders from all over the land.

The enemy responded with their own horns, the noise sounded far away but, grew rapidly to enormous levels of noise that slammed into Fenrir shaking the mighty wall. A roar went up from the enemy as the sky darkened as millions of tiny creatures took flight.

As the enemy raised to the sky there was another mighty shaking in the earth....Tahvo had become aware of their presence. The lands changed rapidly to a massive body of water, a tremendous wave went up, crashing into the back lines of the enemies that were fortunate for the men of Fenrir to have not advanced as far as the unchanged land. The wave slammed into the farthest siege towers, the structures groaned, trembled once and collapsed on themselves, bodies exploded out from the towers. The pieces of it slammed into another tower bringing it down as well. A large swath of the flying creatures got caught up and swept away in the wave, temporarily halting their progress. As it continued on its course it swept up mountains of bodies, a large maw opened in the earth, swallowing them up.

Before the maw closed a massive mountain arose in the near distance and it exploded in a burst of fire. Molten rocks rained down among the enemy, it consumed another three towers in fire. Hundreds of thousands of enemies fell to the fiery assault. There was a loud shout from the enemy line and a single figure launched itself into the air. A molten rock came rushing towards the figure, it reached out a hand and the rock shredded away in a sudden furious blast. The thing reached up a hand with an almost casual motion, it flicked its hand in dismissal, the volcanic eruption stopped instantly and the mountain became completely incinerated. The thing moved again but Durakon and Raamok never saw what it did next, their view became obscured once more by the flying creatures.

Raamok gritted his teeth and stared at the incoming assault. He looked to Durakon, he offered a half smile.

"Looks like we get some pay back. Came sooner than I was expecting it to, no complaints here. Needed to kill something soon, was getting tired of sitting idle."

"Agreed." Durakon pulled his bow free from his back. He pulled an arrow free, knocked it and drew it back as far as he could. He held it remarkably still for a few long breaths, his eyes seemed to lose their focus for a second as if he was staring beyond the winged creatures, a single word was spoke in a language unknown then loosed. The arrow took off faster than anyone could follow, there was a sudden heat in the air followed by an unexpected boom. A noticeable ripple formed. It spread out quickly in the center of the flying creatures. Hundreds of the creatures convulsed once as the first wave rippled through them, the second scattered them with explosive fury. They were sent spiraling to their deaths, a large portion collided with the other beings that were in close proximity causing them to fall rapidly. A few managed to recover, the rest crashed into the ground with crushing force killing them instantly. A third wave rolled away from the rest by another 20' or so, tendrils of some near transparent beast reached out and seized any that were in the area, holding them suspended. Durakon reached out his hand with his fingers spread, he reached out as if picking an apple from a tree and with a single motion of great intensity he pulled the "apple" free and yanked it into him. The creatures that were suspended were pulled into the center, they shrieked in pain and agony as they became compressed and crushed to death. He threw out his hand as if throwing away the "apple," the center exploded, creating a vacuum that pulled in another large swath of the creatures that were incinerated by the intense heat.

It left a hideous gap in the enemy line, cheers and shouts went up from the now populated battlements around Durakon. He turned and smiled at Raamok, who in turn shook his head. He was about to say something when another thunderous blast shook the air, followed by a blast of hot air. An even louder shout of cheers came from the western portion of the wall. Durakon and Raamok were able to look out to see the sky burning. A tremendous wall of fire stretched out, it hovered in the air causing any beast not willing to stop to be charred to a crisp.

Power surged in the air a short distance from them. They glanced over to see one of Tombah's wizard apprentice's nearby glow with lightning fury. Sparks and bolts twisted around their body. The apprentice lifted their arms out with their fists turned in, the spark and bolts that were twisting around his body surged and coalesced in his hands causing them to glow so brightly that those nearby had to shield their eyes. Then as if casting a set of dice he threw his hands out, a massive lightning surged forward, and it flew towards the fire wall. The two powers combined in an impressive deadly array, the lightning reached out sending lances of fire and lightning amongst the enemies. Those that were directly hit by the lightning burst in a shower of blood and gore, any that were nearby were incinerated by the fire that surrounded the lances of lightning. Finally the firewall combined with the lightning exploded in a massive nova of arcing lightning and fire, lighting everything in a 50 mile radius in bright dazzling light.

Raamok, looked at Durakon and let out a chuckle.

"So much for your fancy display." Durakon shook his head clear, blinked a few time to focus his eyes, then with as much emphasis as he could he gave Raamok a stare that would melt a lesser man's resolve. Raamok snorted in derision.

They peered at the field of battle once more, the flyers had nearly all been decimated by the powerful attacks from the wizards. That is if you want to consider decimated being less than sun darkening numbers. There was still so many. Another shout went up and down the wall, archers readied themselves and from somewhere deep in the Fenrir stone ground against stone. Several small bangs were heard followed shortly behind by the cranking of siege weapons being drawn to fire.

There was a heavy silence in the air, it was as if the wall itself along with its defenders were holding their breath in anticipation of the start of a holiday festival. Then all at once the defenders and the wall itself erupted in shouts of rage and defiance. The air became heavy with the thrum of mighty machines of war letting loose, accompanied by a thick layer of arrows as the archers released. Massive boulders the size of small buildings and ballistae bolts thicker around then the neck of a mighty war horse tore into the enemy flyers. There was another 2 volleys from the siege weapons before the enemy was upon them.

The wall, now thick with the noise of battle and the screams of the enemies became a background buzz to Raamok as he drew his twin swords. The true battle was about to begin.

XXXIII

A loud boom, followed by a burst of intense daylight brought Zarron from the deep confines of his mind, he sprung awake, stumbled with the blankets wrapped around him, and he nearly landed hard into the ground before firm hands grabbed hold of him, hauling him up.

"Zarron, be still." A stern voice came from somewhere. He stopped struggling, he breathed in a few breaths. His head felt like it was going to explode, a piercing headache surged through his mind demanding him to be still even if he wished to continue the struggle. His eyes hurt, his muscles weren't in much better shape, they felt sore, stiff and an all-around ache encompassed them.

"Why do I hurt so badly?" He asked to the unknown presence in the room.

"Zarron, you hurting badly at least means you are alive. Which is not what I was expecting, perhaps in another few weeks maybe, or maybe never." El moved in front of Zarron stabilizing him as he swayed on his feet, El gently guided him to a sitting position.

"What has happened?" He asked inquisitively, wincing at the sound of his raspy voice. El poured a cup of water and handed it to him, before sitting down at the chair that was at the edge of the bed.

"Enough, we are engaged with the enemy horde now. I am expecting wounded to come streaming in soon. At least the worse wounded, the clerics and anyone with healing power is on the wall currently taking care of the lightly wounded. No heavy losses or fatally wounded thus far." Before El could finish Zarron began standing up again.

"No, you will not, I cannot keep you from the fight nor would I, but, you need to drink, eat and let me check your vitals." Zarron nodded his head in defeat, he settled back and drank in the water greedily. El got up opened the door and spoke to someone unseen. He was back in a moment to pour more water for Zarron.

"I swear Paladin you are an ignorant stubborn ox." The sudden chiding caused him to pause as he drank water.

"Wh…what?"

"You sir are the first person I have met that doesn't listen to their bodies complaints, when I said you will push yourself in healing Partaxis you should have fallen to unconsciousness before bloody well causing a self-induced coma. Yet, here you are awake after a couple days. Not weeks or months which is typical but days. I should hate you for this but, by the Heavens man, I am impressed. I had done that to myself once, I was healing a child that had been beaten to a near pulp from a gang of thugs." Zarron raised an eyebrow, his interest piqued as he recalled a time so long ago.

"Oh, yes right, you were that bloody child, still not knowing what your body tells you. Caused me to drop into a coma for two and a half weeks. I couldn't believe the mess you were in. You gave me little choice but to work that hard, practically a corpse when Lord Ashen brought you to me."

"So you were the hands that repaired me, thank you High Cleric, and my apologies for the ignorance of my youth. I certainly owe you my life then." Zarron reached out a hand, which El grasped by the forearm gladly, he gave it a hearty shake.

"Your vitals are healthy, seems like you truly are blessed and set aside for the Nameless, been in the Church's service for 40 years and only recently acquired High Cleric, yet here you are a child only a few years after graduating promoted to the rank of Paladin. My main surprise is that you are not a Seeker, with that indomitable will you would have made a fine one."

"You are to kind El, thank you." A knock came to the door Zarron released the man's hand.

"Food, I need you to eat, stretch out your legs then how about you wreak some havoc and destroy as many of those evil ones as you can."

****

Raamok cut down two of the imp flyers before the men behind him could adjust. The creatures were likened to bats, with the exception of a few things, one was the stench of them, it was horrendous. A combination of decay and sulfur, the other difference was the needle like mouth they had and the wings that ended in a sharpened tip. They were not impressive on their own, a simple swat with the flat of a blade would knock them out of the sky. Overall they were not more than 2 feet across and weighed little. What made them dangerous was the sheer number of them followed by a bite that burned and caused distractions. Even though they were slight of size, the volume of them was enough to carry a few unsuspecting men over the edge.

He dodged to the left and cut one of the needlers wings off, before the wing fell out of the way he sheathed his sword, grabbed the wing, spun and with perfect practiced precision sent the sharpened tip into another one that was about to pierce an unsuspecting soldiers neck. As he did another three slammed into his chest sending him back a step. Years of training and supernatural reflexes granted to him by his well hidden vampire half allowed him to recover easily. He grabbed hold of one with his empty hand and crushed the skull with a quick squeeze, it was astonishing to him how easily he was able to do it. He swatted another with crushing force on the flat of his blade, his return stroke cleaved the third in half.

He swung the crushed needler with the broken skull at another attacker swatting it from the air. With a quick kick he was able to knock another from the sky, it flung back and crashed into the armor of one of the defenders with such tremendous force that caused the defender to stumble forward towards the edge of the battlements. Raamok moved, he grabbed hold of the cloak of the defender and pulled him away from the edge. The man nodded his head in thanks then squarely knocked another two needlers out of the air with his shield.

That allowed Raamok to have a moment to breathe, he withdrew his second blade as another six needlers swarmed around him. He engaged and once more the calmness of battle settled on him like a thick fog. Needlers died, men around him fell, some rose, some screamed their defiance. The stench of blood, sulfur and death assaulted his senses. None of it really mattered, all that he was concerned with was the pulse and flow of battle. It was as if his talents at killing were blossoming, growing, being fed by some unknown force. Of the six that attacked him he destroyed them before he had time to take a breath. More came, more died. He didn't know how long the fighting was going on for, it didn't matter. They came, he killed. He noticed at one point that the area around him became clear, the defenders moved to the sides, giving him an unobstructed field of death. He recalled a few times that arrows flew by him to take out a foe that came at his blind side, Durakon he knew was responsible.

The air continued to crackle with energy as spells blew apart large swaths of the swarm. Before he knew it a heavy silence fell around them. It drew him out of his trance. Blood poured off his blade, bodies surrounded him up to mid-calf, his armor was soaked in blood, a wind picked up along the wall bringing a slight chill to him, and his hair he felt was flattened against his head, matted with a mixture of sweat, blood and gore. He looked side to side and saw the fighting was still happening but the area around him and out a large radius was quiet. The needlers were still around but, in his area they were wiped out. Men stirred around him, slaying any of the needlers that were still alive. Most of them choosing to stomp on them like an unwanted bug.

Healers waded through the field mending the lightly to moderately wounded, those that were wounded with minor cuts were handed cloth to bandage the wounds. The most severe, which were few were carried off to the medical facility to receive more intense healing. The gap around Raamok closed in as defenders took up a proper defensive position. They took turns with their shields and some with their boot to remove the needler bodies from the wall. They fell away to the dark oblivion that was the ground. He forgot how high they truly were on the main wall. As he looked back towards the keep, the inner walls were a bustle of activity. Siege weapons were being loaded and prepared to support the upper walls, wounded were carefully weaved between the people working, the small connecting bridge had siege engineers working on some device that he didn't recognize. He admired how carefully and expertly they worked at whatever they were doing.

As he watched he saw the other Paladin working her way to the other side of the main wall from the walkway. She walked with a confident feline grace. She flowed through the crowd smoothly, a few times she danced away from defenders that rushed back and forth almost recklessly, with a casual grace. Her hips swayed with a sensual appeal, her molten like armor did very little in the sense of hiding her womanly shape. He stared at her absolute beauty and felt a stirring in him. She stopped mid stride abruptly, her sightless eyes glowing a magnificent violet snapped to him, the gaze piercing, it made him feel exposed, stripped down to his raw core. He wasn't fully ready for the world to know his darker half, he hardly knew it himself. It made him uneasy to be sure but, he was no coward, he returned her sightless gaze defiantly and let a smile form. Her gaze fell forward again as if nothing happened, she continued on her way, he took a step back. He replayed the moment in his head and he wasn't sure if it had truly happened or he just imagined it. Thinking on it sent his mind racing in circles, his vision swam for a moment before clearing.

He felt a sudden jarring impact to his back, he stumbled forward nearly falling from the edge of the wall only to be yanked back with awesome force. He flew through several defenders knocking them aside like a wind would toss aside grass. Each impact against them hardly slowed his rapid acceleration to the other side of the wall.

Then, he was in the air with the wall out of his reach. He began falling away rapidly. He turned his body so he was falling head first facing the wall. It was then he saw the spiderlike beasts rushing up the wall, when they got near enough to the top they spun, shot their web out which arced up and over the wall, they would give it a tug then basically fall to the bottom of the wall allowing the other ground forces an easy way up. He would claim that he was impressed at the accuracy, very few of them actually hit a defender, which to the greater purpose would be useless, the point was to get troops up not bring them down. Not to mention the line would attach the two and both would suffer the same fate, a long drop with an abrupt and deadly end dashed to pieces at the bottom of the wall.

As he was thinking of this an idea came to his head, he watched as he fell past the creature that had attached itself to him. He would use the momentum of the brief but sudden stop in the line when the creature would be yanked from the wall to fully right himself. The slack in the line started to become taught and just as he was about to hit the end of it he began to turn once more to bring his head back up to face the sky rather than the ground. To his surprise it worked, the line became taught, there was a sudden slow and break in falling momentum as the creature tried holding on with all its strength only to be yanked free. Remarkably the web stayed intact instead of bursting with the sudden stop of several hundred pounds of force.

The force of it brought him upright and slammed him roughly into the wall. He felt his nose break under the force, likely his ribs as well. He scrambled with his feet and hands to find purchase on the snow and ice encrusted wall. His forced his fingers into it digging deep grooves in an effort to create a hand hold, after an intense moment his feet finally found purchase on a slight lip he created in the ice, right after one of his hands seized a hole that the spider like creatures had created when climbing up the wall giving him enough surface to have a solid grip. He swiftly drew his blade, in one swift motion he cut the web away from him, he forced his blade into the wall creating a strong point to hold fast to. He moved his body weight to put more weight on the wedged blade then drew his other blade as one of the spider-beasts closed on him.

He winced at the ache in his chest but, to his complete surprise he felt largely healed from the broken ribs he had suffered from. A warm sensation trickled through his body, the wall immediately around him seemed to pulse with a warmth that nearly melted away his hand holds before dissipating. Rejuvenated he attacked the first spider beast fervently. The beast face nearly melted apart as his blade tore into it. He swung above his head in an arc as another beast was falling back down with his rope in tow. Before it could react it was cleaved in two, its body falling to the greedy starving ground below. He risked a look down and noticed hundreds, if not thousands of the spider beast swarming the wall.

He narrowed his eyes then peered above, the top of the wall was closer than he anticipated. He looked around briefly to assess the situation at hand. It wasn't good but, it wasn't impossible. He wasn't falling currently which was a good thing, and the large body of them were making their way up still so he had some time to think. Another spider beast moved in on him. Without thinking, he let his well-trained instincts take over. He grabbed one of the sticky webs that was close, he pressed it firmly into his belt, and then with a shout he launched himself off the wall, one of the beasts claws swept within inches of his chest. He dropped instantly as he anticipated, as he dropped he flung his second blade at the attacker, it pierced its head and stuck fast into the wall. He fell another few feet before he touched the wall, just as his feet touched he danced out of the way of another attacker. It put him into a spin, he used that momentum though and distanced himself away from the beast. As he planted his feet firmly he turned and flicked his blade in a perfect attack that took the beast clawed hands off. He jumped away from the wall and propelled himself over the beast, as he passed by it he lashed out with his blade, finishing the beast off with a slash to the back of the neck. He landed once again with his feet planted firmly then with a burst of strength he swam up the webbing, grabbed his second blade on the way and used the two in conjunction with the jumps to quickly bound up the wall.

He was nearly at the top when he felt a sudden tug on one of his arms as another web grabbed him. He reversed his blade, cut the webbing free then with a final shout he jumped with all his might in an effort to get to the top of the wall. It would have been enough if it wasn't for another web that grabbed his leg mid jump. He felt the awful sensation of a jump gone wrong, and the wonderful sensation of flying as he fell away from the Fenrir.

Zarron sprinted when he saw Raamok get pulled off the top of Fenrir. His armor proved once more to be like a second skin the weight of it nearly nonexistent, which allowed him to sprint at his normal pace, if not a little quicker. As he closed near the place he last spotted Raamok he saw him all of a sudden erupt up from the other side of the wall. It was looking perfect but, another web came up, snagged his leg causing him to be pulled away from the wall.

"No!" Zarron shouted the sound of it carried before him causing the defenders between him and Raamok to move out of the way. He smashed into one he thought, it didn't slow him down. He felt slightly guilty over it but, the desire to get to Raamok compelled him into action. As he came within 7 paces of the edge, he jumped.

As he cleared the wall he created a lashing of light which he attached to the wall as he flew past it. He flew out from the wall pushed by a supernatural strength. He collided with Raamok grabbing hold of him, he spun in the air so he was facing the Fenrir once more and heaved Raamok with all his strength, bolstered by the armor and a blessing from the Nameless. Raamok soared towards the wall, he hit the side of the battlements, with enough force to knock the wind from him, he was able to grab hold of the edge, with his strength and the help of the defenders Raamok got to the top. The sudden change in velocity snapped the lashing taught. He redirected the sudden surge of power that coalesced and commanded it to pull him in. As if being fired from a ballistae he shot towards the wall.

He directed his momentum towards one of the spider beasts, he brought his entire weight to bear to crash into it. The spider beast burst in a shower of blood and gore, painting a beautiful display of carnage as the massive weight of his armor and bulk crushed it to a pulp. His feet cracked the wall, sending out a ripple in the stone, with another surge of strength he jumped to the top of the battlement.

Raamok, felt the cool stone below him. He let a small smile tug at the corner of his mouth. It was stopped as he breathed in, pain in his ribs smothered the smile. As he thought about the ribs he felt a pulse flow through him coming from the wall to him. A warm sensation covered his ribs, followed by relief from the pain. He felt the bones shift slightly, a few pops later he felt whole once more. After a few deep breaths he was able to confirm that his cracked ribs were no more. Zarron approached him and offered a hand, which Raamok grabbed, a slight tug and he was on his feet once more.

"Just so you know Raamok, gravity exists, not sure if you realized that. I mean we all may want to see about flying just to see if we can, but, you should probably test it on a fall you can recover from, not a death drop." He teased Raamok. Raamok could assume the Paladin was smiling but, his helm with the glowing blue eyes covered any facial recognition.

"You don't say Paladin, gravity exists. Here I was thinking this whole time I could just fly away whenever but, bloody hell, gravity." His tone seethed with sarcasm. Zarron barked out a short deep laugh and slapped him on the shoulder.

"I am glad you are alright Raamok, even more thankful you have chosen to stick around still. It is appreciated." Zarron increased the volume of his voice. "How about we get to some killing. There is still a battle upon us I would say." There was a cheer around them as men focused once more on defending the walls.

Zarron lowered his voice, "Might I have a moment Raamok?" Raamok nodded his head, they took a few steps away from the defenders to have some form of privacy.

"You are magick bound, Kadiallias spotted it firstly. Do you know what that means Raamok?" Raamok raised his eyebrow at him.

"You are a magickal being, somewhere in you is a writhing mass of power that is held suspended. It would seem that parts of it escape from time to time to allow you to do amazing feats but, I would say it is largely uncontrollable." Raamok let out a short breath.

"Here, take this." Zarron handed Raamok his helm. "Put it on, take a look, the wall is trying to feed you. I think you have felt some of those effects, for example your healing factor has increased exponentially. You had broken ribs and a broken nose when I grabbed you. You no longer have those anymore."

Raamok slid the helmet on, despite Zarron having a larger head the helm seemed to form and fit on his head in the exact place it should be. As he peered through the eye slits he was amazed by a few things, one was the fact that his vision was not impaired as he thought it would be, it seemed as though the helm wasn't there, he reached up a hand to make an attempt to touch his face. He could see the hand clearly, yet it was stopped short from his face. The helm was indeed there, the second fascinating fact was the world around him transformed. Where the dull gray stone of Fenrir was, a richly colored light pulsed through it now bringing it to life. The blood of the wicked creatures appeared to absorb the light, as he watched though the wall looked as if it was absorbing the darkness, as it faded away the blood was still there staining the wall but, there was no more magick in it. He looked at his hands, a wisp of color played there for a few moments before disappearing. As his gaze went lower he saw the light color of the wall swarm up his feet, as it got nearer to his heart it was repulsed by a dark, nearly black purple light. The two of them collided, as though two great waves smashing into each other. The magick became scattered away from him, the dark falling back on itself in the might of the lighter magick, most of the magick was clearly separated yet wisps of it managed to gain a foot hold and press through, transforming into a gray color that overtook his body, fragments of it coalesced at his chest, it seemed to sit there, pulse several times, parts of it disappeared into his chest the rest scattered to different parts of his body, where some just withered away as the dark purple renewed its assault on the flank of the light consuming the life from it. He pulled the helm off and handed it back to Zarron with a grunt.

"What am I supposed to do with this information Zarron?"

"Well, I don't think I can say much to that effect, the magick to break that bind is unique to each person, so it is something you may need to sort out or perhaps a powerful magick wielder could break it. They would have to be very powerful though, more so then Tombah, who is nearly on par with an arch mage. In reality I am not sure what you can do with that information but, one thing I know is if you can learn to control that, it will only help in your desire to destroy vampires. It would make you a more deadly warrior then you already are, also since you are aware of it, you will have a head start on sorting out what it might be that can break that binding." Raamok stared at Zarron with a face deep in thought.

"Perhaps Paladin, or perhaps it doesn't matter in the end. There is little I can do about it right now anyhow. Thank you for the insight." Raamok held out a hand to Zarron who took it and gave it a hearty shake.

"I appreciate you being here once more Raamok, let us hold this wall and win this battle."

"Indeed."

A shout came up from a short way from the two of them. As they turned to look several defenders flew by them. Zarron was able to reach out and grab one of them, saving him from a certain fall to his death. Another collided with the flank of a defender the two of them fell hard but remained on the top of the wall, one of the thin spiked demonic beings along with a small contingent of spider-beasts had managed to take the section of the wall.

An arrow zipped past Zarron's head sinking deep into the eye socket of one of the spiked demons. It let out an ear piercing screech as it tried to rip the arrow free. Yet as it got a good grip a bright flash of light went off and the head of it melted away. Three more arrows flew past him each one taking a spider-beast in the face. The defenders rallied and closed up the gap, making short work of the remaining spider beasts. He turned to spot Durakon as he turned away rallying the defenders around him before he engaged another unseen enemy.

Zarron nodded at Raamok, they both knew what needed to be done, and they would follow Durakon's lead and support the defenders as needed.

Zarron took a moment to watch Raamok prowl the walls like a caged lion looking to break free. He watched him go for a moment, something in his spirit stirred as he watched him, he said a prayer for the man that was rapidly becoming someone he was sure he could count on. A shout from further down the line commanded him to action, so he took off at a jog looking for the break in the line.

He was proud to see that the majority of the men on the western side of the Fenrir were part of the Night Wolves, he had served with many of them and knew they were honorable men. The Sun Wolves consisted of the second majority. The Night and Sun bears covered the Eastern side of the wall, his people from the Nameless Church were sprinkled along the entirety of the wall, the wizards under command of Tombah were concentrated at the center, it allowed them to react to the situation as needed. They were truly the heavy weapons in the grand scheme of things, the siege weapons could only do so much and concentrate on a limited area, whereas the magick that the wizards wielded could cover vast areas, the strange magick of the Fenrir only enhanced their awesome power. Wild cheers would always go up when a massive firewall or a blizzard of sulfur and brimstone rained down on the enemy destroying vast swaths of them giving the defenders a reprieve from combat.

By the time the sun had gotten to high noon, Zarron had closed 5 breeches. It was on the fourth that Sheen joined with him, she was held up in the armory sorting the final count of the weapons that were available.

She joined in the most magnificent beautiful way, he was having troubles cutting down a large group of the spider-beasts, and they kept pouring over the wall, seemingly endless in number. Eventually one of them got a webbing wrapped around his leg while another pulled back his shield, they were slowly working him over to the edge of the wall. That was when a beautiful golden eagle swooped in, he could recall the sun gleaming brightly off its wings, the sight of it dazzled him and was awe inspiring, then it changed in an instant and Sheen was there at his side. She had swooped one of the beasts off the side, she grabbed hold of the webbing in her beak and snapped the line with such ease, as she turned into her human form her blade was out, there was a flash of sunlight glinting off steel then he was free, there was no more enemy threat there. A wave of relief coursed over him, he thanked her graciously.

His sixth breech was difficult, one of the twisted Yeti's had managed to take the wall. The sheer size of it was unfathomable, it had knocked at least 4 defenders off the wall before he could get there. He interceded as the creature brought a massive club to bear on a fallen defender, he recognized the man to be the Captain that had relieved him from duty on that last night before he ventured into the changing land in search of Mary. He brought his shield up to catch the club, as it hit the shield it knocked him to his knee, the force of it was amazing. His arm went numb, it was the first time that day he truly felt the blows that fell against his shield, with almost inhuman speed it brought its club up again and slammed it into his shield once more. There was a sudden pop in his shoulder, and despite the incredible strength of the armor he felt his bone snap. His entire arm went slack, it was just dead weight. He bit down on the shout that was rising in his throat. As the beast wound up for another attack, which would surely finish him, there was a thrumming and a sword flew past him, striking the beast in the arm. He seized the opportunity and reacted, he threw a low kick connecting hard with the creature's knee, its knee bent then snapped. He lunged from the ground with an upper strike, Angelfire burned to life in a blazing hot fury, and he brought it to bear with what strength he could muster. He struck, the beast was cut open from hip to shoulder, Angelfire easily cutting through the tough hide, parting flesh, muscle and bone with ease. Sheen came flying over his head in a perfect jump kick that sent the beast falling over the edge. She grabbed hold of her thrown blade, pulling it free as it slipped away to the dark oblivion below.

"Zarron, you should really be more careful, those things could cause serious harm to you. Maybe even break a bone or two." Sheen smiled at him, she tried to make it light hearted but he knew that wasn't how she felt at all. She was…frightened for his life. He felt a deep sympathy then, this woman did indeed care for him. A stranger once, but no more. He smiled to himself hidden behind his helm, he took a deep calming breath and responded as light hearted as he could.

"Aye I suppose they could do that, Captain, perhaps it is a bad time but, what do you think of the church sending me here so early? Think it is because I am hated or quite good?" Zarron sheathed his weapon and offered a hand to the captain.

"I haven't decided yet, perhaps a little of both methinks." The man grabbed hold of his offered arm allowing Zarron to help him to his feet.

"I am in your debt Paladin, thank you. Might I suggest you have a cleric look at your arm?"

"Huh?" He looked down at his arm dumbfounded, he had forgotten about the break already. Mainly because it had healed already, the intense magick of the wall pulsed through him enhancing his minor regeneration spell he had cast.

"I will be fine, I must be off though, some other person is probably picking fights with things bigger than them." Zarron saluted, said a quick goodbye and proceeded down the Fenrir looking for another point he could help with, Sheen remained close behind him. He could sense her anger that was boiling just below the surface, her weariness only compounded it. He still didn't quite understand how he could feel her on such an intimate level. He had to do something though.

So he stopped, she nearly ran into him. He removed his helm as he turned to look at her. He wasn't sure what he was doing but he knew it was the right thing. She looked up at him, her eyes were beautiful, he had not truly looked at her, there was times he shared a moment but, never did he look at her, and my god were her eyes beautiful. He all of a sudden had a great urge to wrap his arms around her, to pull her close and embrace her. So he did just that. After a brief moment he pulled her away from him and looked into her eyes.

"Sheen, beautiful Sheen, scars and struggles are on the way but in our heart we know we are not alone. Be still precious daughter of the Nameless, this is all in the hand of the Nameless, you have done a remarkable job here, and I have not praised you for how incredible you have done. You are an honorable woman, one that has blossomed into something utterly amazing, we cannot worry about things we cannot control. I will be with you as long as the

Nameless One allows and when it is time he will take me home, there is little we can do. You will continue to do the amazing task you were given, I believe you will do it to the best capacity you can. Do not fret, be still and know he is God." He looked into her eyes for a moment more, he leaned down and kissed her on the forehead. He pulled away, looked her in the eyes, and then donned his helm once more to face the enemy.

XXXIV

It was getting near evening, the sun was slowly slipping behind the horizon. The battle did not let up throughout the day. The defenders weary as they were continued to repulse wave after wave of attacks. Yet despite the supernatural energy the wall fed them, it could not give them water or food. The cooks, wounded and those that couldn't fight worked tirelessly running water and plates of food to the defenders. It was a peculiar sight to Zarron as he watched them work. They would come running up with food, water or spare weapons nearly exhausted. When their feet touched the Fenrir they came to life. As he watched he saw the magick of the wall flow through them, reaching to all corners of their body. Each time one was restored the wall lost a little bit of the intense color, yet it came back to life as the wicked ones fell. He could only conclude that the magick in their blood restored the vast supply of magick the Fenrir had built up. He had known there was some magick within the wall but, this was so much…more. He rubbed at the ridge of his nose and squinted towards the enemy line.

He could see explosions of molten rock, water and trees. The battle between Tahvo and the unknown lone enemy, likely Thead the Faceless Ones Guardian persisted. The power was amazing. The distant booms of their powers collided, sometimes the sound would sound far off as they fought in some distant part, then they would move closer to the Fenrir, creating a deafening roar. The most terrifying part was that the enemy horde was still in the changing lands, there would be no reason for the fight if Thead had the full might of his horde concentrated in the unchanged lands. All Tahvo could do at that point would cut off a retreat, which was likely not going to happen. He sighed.

"What troubles you Warder?" a voice came from nearby unexpected. He turned to face Kadiallias.

"Hunger I think, need some food." It wasn't the entire truth, he was concerned about the enemy numbers and didn't want to speak of it in front of the defenders. He was concerned about the engagement with Thead that would surely happen. Once again speaking those thoughts in front of the defenders would do no good, and he was hungry.

"Come, let us get some food, these men have got a rhythm now, I think they will be fine for a few moments. We can bring over some of the members of the church to cover for us." He waved down a Knight and requested she find the reinforcements needed for their sections of the wall.

"Sheen would you like to join us?" Zarron offered, she declined respectively. He knew she had a weary concern for Kadiallias, so he let it go and waved to her before heading towards the kitchens.

As they walked down the wall they saw from the Eastern side Partaxis strolling among the men. Loud cheers erupted as he came close. As they walked down one of the two interconnecting walls, they heard the fascination in the defenders of what Partaxis has accomplished. He was indeed a beacon of light and hope that the people rallied behind. His massive form easily towered over the rest of the people and his stature demanded attention, the fact that he was one of the last of the Black Army demanded respect. All in all he was key in rallying the defenders, the wall would keep them energized it would seem but, he brought out the best in their fighting spirit. It wasn't long before they pressed by the wave of servants running food out to the defenders and found themselves in the kitchen. They grabbed some bowls of soup, a piece of bread and some coffee before finding the quietest corner they could find.

They sat in quiet contemplation both of them enjoying the peace before Kadiallias spoke up.

"Zarron, all will be well. Be strong of and good courage. I know you are concerned about the numbers, even more so at what to do with Thead. We cannot worry about those things that are out of our hands. We can only do the best we can do, the rest is up to the Nameless." Kadiallias took a sip of coffee as she finished. She peered over the edge of the cup at Zarron awaiting a reply. His mouth opened and closed a few times unable to form words.

"Let me ask you something, I want you to think about this. I don't know all the details but, when you destroyed Fervver did you think twice about it? Did you even consider once that failure was going to happen?" He shook his head in the negative. "Exactly my point, you are talking about an ancient evil power that you wiped out without a second thought. Remember that your faith is the key to this whole affair, we do what we can and let the pieces fall as they will."

Zarron let out a short breathe. She was right he knew that absolutely. Something still was gnawing at him. Then he remembered Raamok being magick bound.

"I confirmed with Raamok that he is indeed magick bound. I know you had the sense he was. There is also the dark stain on his spirit."

"Yes. I can't quite place a finger on what it is though." She replied inquisitively.

"It is vampiric in nature, but, I don't think he is an enemy. I think there is something more going on that we don't quite know."

Sheen raised an eyebrow. "Vampiric truly? I am impressed that you know that, it has escaped my thoughts on what it could be. How have you come to your conclusions on it?"

"A few things, healing factor being the main. The next that it took an earth mender to heal him properly, holy healing was working slowly. The man is faster, stronger and more durable than any human should be and something in my spirit tugs me in the direction of vampiric."

"Would you consider him a threat to the church or our mission as a whole?" She asked probing.

"He is very much a threat, probably one of the most dangerous in this land, but, I don't think he is against us. When I first met him I saw him take down fine, good soldiers in a matter of seconds yet he didn't kill any of them. He could have, it would have been easy but he didn't. From what I understand from pieces of information I have gathered he has helped out tremendously with the defense of Fenrir. He has also proven that he is willing to put down his life for the defense of the realm. Admittedly I think there is some selfish intent, he is on a path of rage and vengeance, but I don't think it is all selfish." Zarron paused for a moment, he let out a sigh.

"Also I was given a vision, one of great intrigue, he was a key part. I will not speak more on it because I am not sure what it means yet." After he finished speaking there was a moment of silence that seemed to stretch between the two of them. Kadi kept her piercing gray eyes on him, he shifted his shoulders uneasily.

"Very well Zarron, we will leave that be. We must report him to the Hand and Voice, I will not accept anything else. But, you are right, he is dangerous. We can use that for this conflict." She got up from her seat, her gaze never left his.

"You have a knack for finding the good in people; Sheen, Raamok. Who else will you come upon? I'll see you on the wall Warder and may the Nameless One be with you." She touched his shoulder lightly as she went by. He watched her step into the growing darkness, and disappear from sight.

He let out a brief sigh before rubbing his temples. Even amidst the noise around him he felt he could close his eyes and sleep. He was not recovered fully from his encounter with death, the pain and fatigue that coursed through him confirmed that. There was no time for resting though, or was there? What would a few moments of closing his eyes matter, they were holding the wall well after all.

A heavy, all-encompassing silence shocked him awake. The weight of it bearing down on him felt like he could reach out and remove it like a blanket. He was still in the kitchen, he cursed under his breath as he looked about trying to gain some understanding of time that passed. Outside was consumed by the shroud of night now, his coffee was still in front of him. He gulped down the last bit and a sigh of relief coursed through his body as he found it to be warm still. As he rose from his seat the chair fell, the noise of it filled the area and it sounded louder than it should have. The kitchen was still operating, the smells of the cooking rose up to meet him.

Something was off still, as he went outside the full weight of it was understood. As he looked at the defenders he saw that many were still. They were staring off into the changing lands. He sprinted up the stairs, when he got to the top he pressed past a few of the defenders and what he saw caused his stomach to clench.

There was no more bright flashes of light or the booms of great magick in the sky as the two colossal powers fought. In their place though was something more terrifying, the entire enemy host was in battle formation. The amount of siege towers were so vast that he couldn't see the first or last in the line. The heaviest concentration was focused in the middle. There lines were lit by an eerie green glow coming off the siege towers.

"Turns out the wizard might know a thing or two." Zarron suppressed the urge to jump as the big voice boomed. "He had suspected magick would be used to move the towers rather than shield them. I don't know much but judging where the heaviest concentration of that sickly pallor is I would say it is moving the towers along." Partaxis finished. Zarron stared off for a few moments before speaking.

"It is shockingly similar to Fervver when we first spotted him floating on the sickly red glow. I would say you are correct. How long has it been like this?" Partaxis peered up to the sky, he assumed, to think about the time that has passed.

"Not long." Partaxis scratched his beard. "Perhaps half hour. The fighting stopped about that time frame. I think, the entire enemy force is concentrated now. Attack will come soon I am sure of it. This is not over yet, we still have some tricks up our sleeves." He stood by Zarron's side for another few moments the two of them staring in wonder and awe at the force before them. "I must see to the defenses now, hold this wall Zarron. Perhaps speak with your God on our behalf, we could use any blessings he can spare." He placed a massive hand on Zarron's shoulder before departing.

Zarron shook his head clear. He looked around and found Jeremiah, he pressed his way through the defenders to speak to him. He was pleased to see Raamok with him as well. As he got closer both of them turned and cracked a tired weary smile at him.

"Well Zarron, it looks like the fun part is about to start." Jeremiah spoke with a tired voice.

"Bloody hell, this looks like it requires the big boy, I'll be back." Raamok shouldered past them and left to two of them with bewildered looks.

"What do you suppose that means?" Jeremiah asked.

"Like I understand the man, I would venture to guess he is off to get something that will kill things faster." Almost as if on cue Raamok returned with a beautiful blade that he had never seen before. Angelfire reacted almost instantly to it. She flared to light as if in warning or greeting, he couldn't quite sort out the emotions of the weapon yet, the shock of it caused Zarron to pause for a moment. He placed a tentative hand on the pommel of the weapon, to his surprise there was no obvious lingering sensation of what had happened. It was quiet and calm, the familiar warmth of it persisted. Yet, something seemed off, it was as if Angelfire was saddened by something he ventured a guess at.

"Let me guess a sentinel weapon of some sort?" He asked as if he already knew the answer.

"No, just magick from what I can tell. No words have been formed from it. It is a powerful weapon though. To be honest it was called a sentinel weapon by the previous owner. I am not sure if he was wrong or maybe something changed with ownership." Raamok looked at it lovingly one more time before sheathing it.

"What do you call it Raamok?"

"Typhoon, I kept the name from the previous owner." Zarron looked at him with a curious look. "Who had it before?"

"Oh yes, I am glad you asked. It came from a giant of a man named Tahvo, he is the one behind the lands changing. It was him that was battling Thead. He was hoping to meet with you, to ask for forgiveness for his part in waging wars on the Holyrage house."

"What!?" Zarron's eyes opened wide.

"Yeah, he said a lot of things back there, to be honest Zarron you might as well hear it from him. I understand that your teachings within the church teach forgiveness. So I would say you have a perfect opportunity to practice it with him. Now, if you will excuse me I have business to tend to. Best of luck to you Paladin." With that, Raamok turned and left a bewildered Zarron behind.

That sword was once alive, I knew it well. Angelfire spoke to him after Raamok left. It drew him back, the initial shock of the situation passed away, he would deal with it after this battle is finished. He was about to speak to her but was stopped as she continued. *He will restore its life, just needs time. You cannot allow him to be imprisoned or held up. You know just as much as I do that the Church will declare him dangerous and want to pull him in for questions.*

"I know Angelfire, it is not my intent for him to ever appear before the Hand or Voice. I will of course report him, it is my duty but I will also lay down my life if need be to keep him free. There is a greater purpose in him, thank you for confirming my insight. You are a most excellent companion Angelfire. Come now, we have a battle to win."

"Jeremiah, gather the Nameless Ones people together, we are going to pray together and seek the favor of the Nameless. After we finish with that, grab my guard and stay with me."

It wasn't long before the members of the Nameless came together. El opened the prayer. "Lord, you are mighty, yet the enemy gathers round us and you remain silent. Please don't let your people go down without your presence, we gather before you as humbled servants facing a titan that is fierce and hungry. Let the wicked be disgraced and lie silent in the grave. Let their roars and cries fall on deaf ears. You are mightier than the mightiest titan, you are vaster then the oceans, protect us. Let your fire fall down on the enemy, may your righteous anger fall on our enemy."

As he finished the prayer, there was a mighty boom of thunder, followed by a tearing noise that caused many to drop to their knees to cover their ears. Then the night sky seemed to become tight as if stretching out a hide for skinning, the stars became stretched and pulled obfuscating the beauty that was there, then another loud crack went through the air, the night sky snapped together and rolled up as a scroll. The Heavens were opened if only for a moment. In that moment many Angels and Winged demons were seen fighting one another, war had touched the Heavens and Hells, then the fire poured down as water flows from a water fall. A mighty wind picked up it struck the fire and turned it into a mighty torrent. It took a more solid defined shape. As it closed in on the enemy line a dark mass formed that was darker than the night sky, it struck the fire and the two presences fought to a standstill. The enemy was not consumed by the mighty torrent but, they were held in place. There would be no getting past that torrent of fire, the Heavens were no longer visible as the fire poured out, and there was no denying that the weight of that conflict was still felt.

"It would seem there will be no more battle tonight. Those of you that can, rest. For those that feel fresh and wish to not rest, you will be posted as watchmen. If you see something you know what to do, should the fire fade before morning report to Partaxis immediately, he will get the garrison roused. Men of the Nameless, remember that your God has responded to your request and has found favor in us. Remember this, be willing to answer any questions that come your way and after this is done, remember." Zarron finished speaking, his last words seemed to echo up and down the wall. Murmurs of praise and thanksgiving travelled through the crowds. As he departed he took his own advice and laid down to rest.

XXXV

True to the Nameless One there was no battle the night prior. Zarron woke refreshed the following morning. As soon as the sleep was chased from his muscles and his head became clear once more, he got up to grab a cup of coffee and breakfast. It was a beautiful morning despite the situation at hand and there was some pep in his walk. It felt good sleeping, his muscles ached from the fighting the day before but, it wasn't a deep ache. The Fenrir did well in keeping muscle fatigue and energy levels high. It wasn't long before he found himself on top of that mighty wall peering over the battleground. The fire still poured from the heavens, suspended in place by the dark mass. There was a tenseness in the air that was not unexpected, but there was a calmness as well. It was a queer feeling to be certain, all these individuals facing an enemy that the world has not seen in such mass and power yet they remained calmed. He could not have asked to serve among more noble people. Many of these being farmers and local towns people who answered the call of the mighty horn. He had discovered in the morning meal that there was a large influx of individuals through the night. Enough to fill out their numbers by a legions worth. It was quite the busy night for the logistics department in finding places for these people to rest and food for them to eat.

On the wall he spotted Sheen a short distance away. He waved to her as he moved closer. The two of them stood staring at the holy fire. His guard showed up shortly after, there was an eagerness in them that was not there before. He chalked it up to a renewed hope and fervor.

As he was standing there he felt a sudden pulse of power emanate from the flame, it shook his core. The vibration of it was so powerful that he took a step back to stabilize himself. As fast as it came it went still just as fast.

He peered around at the men and women around him, none of them seemed to feel what he felt. Any of them except Kadiallias. She stopped as he did in her tracks as she was walking up to him. Her eyes widened momentarily, it was only a flash but it spoke volumes to him. He knew what was coming next.

"Men and woman of the Fenrir it is time! Prepare for battle!" His voice boomed, it echoed up and down the wall. Many others picked up the call to arms and relayed it. He could still hear the echo of the line when the fire suddenly dispersed. It wasn't done spectacular, creating a spectacle for all. It merely rolled up like a scroll and disappeared without a noise. The enemy machines of war began to move.

As the machines began to move there was a terrible ear piercing grating sound as if stone was sliding against stone, followed by a loud bang. He peered around and looked up and down the wall. He smiled to himself as he realized they opened the compartments up to deploy their siege weapons. He stepped away from the wall once more and breathed calmly. He took the time to look up and down the wall, the thought that many of these men would die saddened him. He peered at his own bodyguards and knew the risk was there with them as well. He may not have known them long but in that short time with them he had grown incredibly fond of them. After all they had stopped a siege already. This was different though, this was saving the world.

His stomach fluttered as he turned to look at them. He did not want to see any of them die. The ridiculousness of the situation played over and over in his head. Anger roiled and boiled in him. *How dare the Faceless One bring a war from the heaven and hells to this earth? How dare he. Damn him.* The thoughts were like acid eating away something within him. He clenched his fist tightly, then released. He repeated the gesture a few times while he took a couple deep breaths. His world blurred slightly, the anger continued to rise.

Finally something in him snapped and he snarled, he let out a bellowing shout of rage. The air around him became a haze, heat sweltered and several of his men backed away before lending their voice to the shouting. It wasn't long before the entire wall of men shouted and screamed at this enemy that had taken so much already. Fenrir vibrated with anticipation, the wall seem to come to life and let out a deep slow rumble. In reality he figured the walls mystical properties amplified their voices, carrying them out to the awaiting army. The enemy assault seemed to stutter a step as their voices hit them with all the power it carried.

Just as their voices seemed to fade out there was a resounding boom. Following it came several more booms, their siege weapons had begun the assault. The cheering and hollering was brought back to life as the Fenrir released a massive volley of ballistae bolts and boulders. The massive boulders smashed into the enemy line, direct hits left massive holes in the line leaving behind puffs of red and black mist where enemies once were. The weight of the boulders carried them far and the damage to the enemy numbers were devastating. However effective they were against the ground troops the ones that hit the tower merely bounced off as if they were a child running into a wall. However there was one or two that hit the towers in such a manner that they dropped directly in front of the massive machines causing them to stop in their tracks giving the men on the wall a few more precious minutes.

The ballistae's on the other hand shone with an array of colors. Many of them hit the tower to little effect but any that were red or white easily smashed through the towers. The ones that shone black or orange were repelled easily. As the next round of volleys shot forth he realized many more shone with red and white. The rest of the colors were still present but not to the large amount as before. However something amazing happened when the new round smashed through the towers. As they collided an eye blink later massive magickal chains attached to the projectiles. They attached loose and slack then they became rigid as if they were being pulled taught. The towers lurched and shuttered. Many of them being pulled off balance slightly. The chains became slightly loose once more than they were yanked taught again. This time there was a loud crack, the towers that were hit the most stuttered once then exploded to pieces. The power of it sent a massive shockwave that knocked down and killed many that were near it.

A roar of excitement went up as several more towers fell to the attack. It would seem that short of the magick moving them there was still something there that protected them. It was amazing to him the amount of power needed to sustain such a thing. At the same time though he was talking about an evil Guardian imbued with powers from his great god. As far as he was concerned that power was near limitless and being surrounded by such wickedness would only aid that resource.

The beautiful chaos reigned for moments longer before the siege weapons stopped. The towers and the army were now close enough that the danger to the wall and the people manning those weapons was too great. Already he saw several of their siege engineers fall from their nook in the wall, arrows protruding from them. There was another noise of stone grinding against stone as the passages began to close. One by one they closed with a resounding boom. Soon silence filled the air once more.

The defenders took on faces of stone as the enemy closed in. The field of battle was a mess of shrapnel and corpses of the slain demonic army. However there was still so many. The numbers were nearly unfathomable. Overall the attacks on the siege towers were largely successful, they had destroyed nearly half of them before they had to stop their attacks. The mages were all but spent he imagined. The amount of magickal energy needed to pull those towers apart was awesome. He was proud of Tombah and his small contingent of wizards. The rest of the work would be on the defenders shoulders. He looked around at the men around him, smiled then donned his helm.

He moved his guard to be the first line of defense for one of the approaching towers. It would be a brutal few moments of fighting that they had to hold their ground for. If only for a few moments until the rest of the defenders could organize and assault. He made note that Kadiallias took up the front at another nearby location. Before a few others he could make out Durakon and Raamok on one. Partaxis stood ready at another. However farther down the line he saw there was no one immediately there in front of the towers. It was strange to him, it didn't make sense. That was not his problem at this time what he needed to do was focus on the one in front of him.

He took a deep breath as the tower slowly creaked towards him. He could hear the battle drums and war horns of the enemy host. Inside the tower there was a loud banging noise and chains rattling. A low deep growl filled the air. The air was thick with a tenseness that could be sliced, cooked up and served for dinner. He took another deep breath. *Be strong and of good courage, there is no darkness where light resides. Be strong and of good courage.* He repeated the mantra a few times in his head before his mind relaxed and he was able to focus. He looked side to side at the stony grim faced looks of the men and women beside him. He lingered for a moment on Sheen taking in her stern face, her eyes focused and zeroed in on the tower looming before them. She was more focused and clearer than he had ever seen her before. As he thought about that he felt her emotions flow through him, the calm he had thought was there was nothing compared to the calm she exuded. She turned then and winked at him before donning her helm. He chuckled to himself and returned his attention to the tower.

XXXVI

The door slammed down in front of Raamok, a massive war mammoth came charging out. He managed to dodge out of the way just barely as it barreled out. The few soldiers behind him didn't move fast enough, they were tossed effortlessly off the battlement.

"Holy hell, shoot the damn thing. Lines form up, spears up front." One of the sergeants bellowed nearby. The men on the wall moved forward and pressed the beast. It reared up on its hind legs and let out a loud bellow. Several arrows zipped in sinking deep in the beasts hide. It stepped back once then came crashing down crushing the soldiers that tried to close in and slay it. The step back was enough to stop the tide of enemy soldiers from pouring forth from the tower. It was a moment that Raamok seized rapidly.

He jumped up and stabbed the beast, the strength of the attack drove in the blade just enough for him to grab hold and fling himself on top of its writhing mass. He pulled his blade free just in time to steady himself as it lurched forward. Its massive hulking head driving at the Fenrir defenders. Once he felt his balance returned he dashed forward a few steps. He drove his blade deep into the back of its skull. It hurt the beast tremendously however the sword was not long enough to deal the fatal blow. *Damn.* He was suddenly jerked forward, he kept his balance for only a moment before an arrow slammed into his back. The armor had stopped it from biting to deep, he was also sure the beast lurching as it did made it a weaker attack then it could have been. He turned to the sight of several enemies bounding up the beasts back. As he turned to view them he missed the trunk of the mammoth as it reached up to grab hold of him.

He felt a sudden crushing force wrap around him. He felt it tug him, he turned with the momentum and drove a hard kick at his blade that was stuck fast in the skull of the creature. As it drove deeper into the beast, he felt the constricting force let loose. His momentum continued him forward, he turned in time to grab his blade stopping his momentum. All of a sudden he felt a rush of air as the beast rose again on its hind legs. He tightened his grip on the weapon which saved him from falling into the horde of excited enemies.

There was a sudden jarring impact, the beast let out a trumpet of pain. Then another impact came, inches from his feet burst forth the tip of a ballistae bolt. He settled his feet on it as he grabbed his blade. He twisted it before yanking it free. He reached up and grabbed hold of the ear of the beast. He propelled himself forward with what momentum he could, he used his blade to stab into the creature's mouth giving him the grip point he needed to free himself from the falling beast. He launched off the beast landing safely in the care of the defenders below. As his feet touched the ground he pressed his attack forward. He figured the least he could do was give the beast a push to send it on its way. His strength combined with the men on the wall were able to give the beast the push it sorely needed. He watched it crash into the bridge, the weight of the creature causing it to groan with exertion. To his chagrin the bridge held. However it did take a large swath of creatures with it. Most importantly it gave the defenders a few precious minutes to regroup and close the gap the mammoth had created. He drew Typhoon before joining the fight.

Partaxis smiled to himself as he watched his plan unfold around him. The flanks were left unprotected to allow the siege machine to clear the first wave of attackers and in essence put the towers out of the picture forcing the attack to be pushed to the center where he knew he was strongest. Thankfully the arrogant Thead helped play into the plan by sending the majority of his troops at the center. To some extent he could understand the reason for it. There was no other way down to the next level and access to the keep except by the middle bridges. The enemy force would have taken insane casualties running towards those bridge points. The entire wall would have been exposed and opened to the siege weapons stationed at the lower wall. He watched as the bridges dropped, a thrum of strings let loose. The first waves were obliterated on sight. The few that were able to make it through found a swift death at the flanking defenders of Fenrir.

The next volley came with a wonderful surprise he was sure they wouldn't have appreciated. As they crashed into the tower powerful explosions ripped through the air. The fireball having very little locations to escape to, quickly blasted through the stairway of the tower greedily eating what oxygen remained. It wasn't long before the first one collapsed under the intensely hot flames. However successful some were there were others that were not as much so. He tossed it up to the protection on the towers not being worn down enough. Those would be a problem but, he was confident between the defenders and the siege weapons they could wear down those number to manageable levels. A loud crash brought him to the front as the bridge fell into place from the tower before him.

A giant came swarming out of the entrance unfolding itself. However he was not going to allow the beast to get to its feet first. That was not an option. He attacked.

He brought down his mighty hammer smashing the elbow of the giant. It crashed into the ground hard. When it let out a roar of defiance its spit was tinged heavily with blood. He guessed that it had bit its tongue on the fall. He quickly jumped over to the other side of it and smashed that elbow. Finally he grabbed hold of its neck, he hugged it with crushing strength. The giant almost broke free of his grip a few times. However the injuries to its arm didn't allow it to gain as much leverage as it needed. So Partaxis squeezed tighter and slowly he pulled the giant to the edge. With a mighty shout along with a grunt of effort he heaved once more. He threw as much of its size and weight as possible over the edge. It was not its whole body but he did get enough of it to the edge that it fell forward. Nearly unconscious there was little the giant could do to stop the fall. As its head and shoulder fell over the side it pulled the rest of his body with it. It smashed into the wall once or twice on its fall cracking the stone work before settling at the bottom with a resounding thud.

The fighting continued in a fierce tug of war for some time. Zarron, after finishing off the monstrosity that came charging out of the siege tower held the ground with his men for some time until they got the foothold they needed to fully employ their disciplined combat maneuvers. After a short while he stepped away from the front line to grab a drink of water and eat a bit of food. His body and mind ached from the continuous flow of magick and combat. He admired the defenders, he decided he was very proud of his troops, the cohesion they displayed was near flawless. They would hold for a while he was confident of that. However he knew others were probably not so. It was then a messenger boy ran up to him.

"Paladin Holyrage, I have an urgent request from the Eastern flank they have lost their section of Fenrir, It wasn't the farthest tower either so our force over there is split in two. Without assistance they will surely die. You are to retake Fenrir and shut down the towers. We are consolidating our forces to the middle."

Why are we consolidating our forces is it truly that terrible. How long have we been fighting for? Zarron thought to himself. It doesn't make sense. He looked around trying to get some feeling of time that had passed. The sun was nowhere to be seen, a thick cloud cover rolled in at some point. The mountains of bodies seemed to be his only recognition of time, they were stacked high on both sides. He was astonished at the carnage of the scene. Both sides had truly bloodied each other, however his side held the upper hand as there were far fewer of the defenders of Fenrir lying dead.

The Fenrir had continued to work its mystical properties as the blood was absorbed into the stone. He was thankful for that once more, truth be told the blood should have been running thick and heavy causing terrible footing. Yet it remained largely dry. He pulled Jeremiah back from the front along with Sheen.

"Hold this position, I need to go support our other forces that are not doing so well. I am leaving this in your capable hands. If you need me, break this, I will come as quickly as I am able." He slipped a small runic stone into his captain's hand. The captain nodded his head and rendered a quick salute. Zarron returned the salute, he turned to address Sheen.

"Sheen you are with me I could use a hand. You have done well and I would love to have you by my side. We will grab whoever else we can as we move along as well." She smiled at him as she gave a nod. His stomach flipped with that small gesture, it was such a beautiful site after observing the twisted faces of demons. Without any further delay they took off at a jog towards the East.

It wasn't long before they were at the breach. Along the way he had grabbed Raamok to assist along with Durakon. As they got closer the desperation of the men fighting was palpable, he could almost feel their emotional anxiety as they fought a losing battle. He picked up his speed to a sheer sprint. The rest fell into place creating a wedge.

"Move, clear the way!" Durakon shouted as they ran through the haggard defenders. Despite the confusion they were able to get through the defenders with minimal interference. As they cleared the last defender they smashed into the enemy front.

Zarron with his bulky armor hit the enemies with tremendous force. He brought to bear his entire weight, focusing it into his shield. The effect was devastating, he knocked down the first unit he came upon, and they fell in front of him before being trampled to death. As he pressed through the group he cast a spell, tendrils of blue and white light reached out, they grabbed any enemy that he pressed through and forced them to fall in. All in all the majority burst to flame as the tendrils touched them the few that were strong enough to resist came crashing in around him. He was able to penetrate 20 feet into the group before the weight of the enemies in front of him and those that were in tow slowed him down. He gave a final push with his shield creating an explosive blast that sheered through the dark ones in front of him as if he was cutting butter with a hot knife. There was a 30' cone of destruction in front of him. He then brought in the tendrils releasing their grasp on the enemy, he focused their energy into a concentrated ball then willed it to explode. The excess energy erupted in a mighty bang that evaporated the dark ones that were close. He reached up a hand and summoned forth a beam of silver blue light, he willed it to stretch out 15' around him. The light of it provided protection and regeneration for his companions while causing holy damage to any of those that were evil. He had hoped Raamok would be able to resist the effects.

He risked a glance back at his companions, they held their formation perfectly. They made quick work of the remaining dark ones that were not pulled in by his tendrils or evaporated from the spell. As they came within the light of his aura all of them began to glow with the same silver blue light. However the light was duller on Raamok but he did not seem to be hurt by the effects. Probably reduced protection on him. He made a mental note to provide a little more cover for him if he was able to. As he was about to turn around he noticed Raamok's sword began to gain a brighter color, the sword greedily ate in the light and there was a slight change to the weapon. He stowed away that knowledge for another day. For now, it was time to save some lives.

As he was about to turn around several rapid fire arrows zipped by him. He turned his attention to the front only to see the enemy force had managed to regroup and were beginning to swarm. Durakon had killed two that were unbelievably close. The enemy returned fire with archers of their own. Zarron caught two arrows in his shield another one bounced off his chest plate with little effect. It appeared all their attention was on him, the hate for the holy warrior before them was enough to drive them mad with a desire to kill him. He smirked to himself, what foolish creatures these were.

He began to charge the line, he cast the tendril of lights spell once more, this time however he cast it in front of him pulling in all he could around him. He didn't think he had the energy to evaporate them. But, he could give them all a nice push. So he concentrated the tendrils upon him, he took the excess energy and converted it to a powerful explosion that sent a large swath of the enemy flying. Many of them flew right off the edge of the mighty Fenrir.

The rest of the force hit him at once. Next thing he knew he was swarmed by enemies. He cut and slashed where he could. His companions joined the fray. When he saw one of his companions begin to be pressed he cast the tendrils of light on the foe, forcing it to fight him. Keeping the focus of all the enemies was difficult, but, it felt right. It was what he was meant to do. It almost seemed like his armor and willpower helped highlight the enemies that were no longer focused on him so he could cast his spell and pull them in on him. Also the constant holy damage was enough to anger many of them so much they couldn't help but attempt to claw and destroy the monster that was causing them the pain. Between his defensive fighting and Angelfire's constant guidance he stood his ground well. Despite it though a few stabs and slashes from the enemy made it through his defense. His armor did remarkably well at holding up to the attacks. He certainly felt a few crushing blows though, some also managed to pierce through his armor, nothing that the aura couldn't heal away though.

They had been fighting for a few moments when a loud cheering and roar arose from behind them. The defenders that were pressed moments before snapped out of their shock and charged the enemy. The effect of that raw emotion caused the small group of companions to press harder. Zarron meticulously kept about his business pulling in those enemies that had decided to focus elsewhere. Raamok, charged into them his twin blades cutting down enemies almost faster than one could process. Occasionally a loud boom came from him as Typhoon's power came to life. Durakon sped arrow after arrow into the enemy, they fell away like water around a rock. Sheen herself stayed closer to Zarron, she stabbed in and finished enemies that were wounded by his attacks and turned the tides in their favor if he became overwhelmed. His blindside was her other point of focus. If any one of the dark ones came remotely close to the blind side of him she brought down her wrath upon them with great fury.

Almost as fast as it started it was over. The sheer power and rage of Zarron and his companions obliterated the force. They retook the defensive point in front of the tower. There they made one final stand.

"Durakon, please stay with them and hold this place up as long as you are able. The rest of us are going to rescue the trapped defenders." Durakon nodded his head in agreement. Zarron signaled the rest of his team forward.

Between the points there was little resistance to encounter. Most of the threat that came were dealt with quickly and violently by Raamok who mercilessly jumped on the enemy. It wasn't long before they came upon the swarm of the enemy at the next tower. Needless to say it wasn't good. Bodies littered the area, many of them the defenders of Fenrir. Zarron caught a brief site of the area a little ways away from the tower. There a few defenders held their ground against the waves of enemies. They were in terrible shape, probably down 90% of the initial numbers.

"Come, they don't have much time." Zarron growled. His vision narrowed, the world fuzzed a little. His rage was coming on he knew it. He smiled, he was glad, he was not able to get it to ignite in himself for some time. It was so easy before he felt, yet even still he realized he didn't understand it. His smile descended to a frown as he became frustrated with himself over the ignorance of his blood line. He had no clue how to use this amazing weapon, it made him furious. He let out a shout and rushed forward quicker. The enemy became a mass of black light. Their evil enraged him further.

As he was about to smash into the line there was a sudden whoosh of air and an enormous tremor. The ground beneath him lurched upward before dropping him to the ground. As he watched he saw several bright blue glows go flying to the dark abyss below. They were the defenders he knew. A sudden shockwave sent him flat on his back. Several more blue glows flung by him then there was an explosion and something wet and sticky blotted out his field of vision. His vision returned to normal, his muscles relaxed as he wiped away the substance from the helm. He pulled away his hand and looked at a mix of bright red and black blood. As he peered at the enemy before him all that stood there was one being, he emanated with dark magick, it fell away from him like magma. He had enormous skeletal wings that stretched out and moved casually. In his hand was the last of the defenders. He picked up the man and licked his face. Then casually he crushed the head of the defender. Blood and gore gushed out of his hand, he threw the body off to the side unceremoniously. He licked his hand clean.

"Did you know you can taste fear Paladin? It has a unique taste one that stands out from the rest." He stared at Zarron for a moment, watching him closely. Zarron's hand twitched. He clenched it into a fist. Power began to coalesce there.

"Tsk tsk pathetic creature, you cannot stand against a Guardian. You may have got one up on me last time but I assure you it will not happen again." In an eye blink Thead stood above Zarron, he lifted his foot and smashed it down onto Zarron's sword arm. There was a screeching noise followed by a crumpling effect that ended with a spectacular snap.

Zarron let out a grunt of pain, the spell faded from his hand, his concentration broken. He breathed out a ragged breath. His arm was broke, no not broke smashed. He had a second to react as Thead prepared another assault. He loosed his shield then summoned Angelfire to his other hand. As the foot came down the sword pierced through it easily. He twisted the blade sending the evil guardian off balanced.

Raamok not missing a beat came flying by him Typhoon striking the leg of the guardian with a mighty boom. Surprisingly Thead kept his footing. Raamok spun back and away from Thead. He was rewarded with the guardian turning to face him exposing his back to his companions. Raamok came in with a feint, Thead dropped to a low guard which left his upper body open. He seized upon that opening, bringing his second weapon around him he stabbed at the guardian and was rewarded with a wet thunk as his weapon pierced Thead's stomach. As he was yanking his blade free another blade punched out his chest. Magic pulsed through the blade then it exploded opening the whole a few inches. He could see Sheen on the other side pulling the blade free. Thead plopped to the ground unmoving.

A thick silence filled the air, despite the victory it did not feel that way. Zarron grunted in pain as he pulled himself up. The combined healing efforts of the Fenrir helped restore his arm, the ache dissipating slightly. Before he could heal it completely he had to pull his armor off. If he didn't then the arm would not heal correctly. As it was the piece was useless anyhow. As he tugged at the straps pain coursed through his arm once more, removing armor seemed to hurt more than the actual breakage. He attached the piece of armor to his belt. He would tend to it later.

A sudden noise began to emanate through the air. It started off almost like a whispering breeze then it roared to life before forming into a terrible cackle.

"You fools think you can handle me. That was a mere shadow of me, a beautiful shadow illusion. Hard to master but, once you do it." His voice trailed off in ecstasy. The laughter continued then duplicated itself, once, twice, and then a hundred times. They were soon surrounded by hundreds of cackling Theads.

"Oh you all look so sad, this will be easy killing you one by one. I think I will start with the lady. After all I am a gentlemen and ladies should always be first."

Zarron winced in pain as he listened to Thead's threats. He had to do something, but what could he do. A solid hit to the back of his head broke his thoughts. Behind him stood one of the shadow clones, or Thead there was no way to tell. He parried the next attack and thrust forward. The clone didn't even attempt to dodge the attack. It pierced its shoulder, as he pulled his blade free the wound instantly healed, it attacked again. Before he could respond he was grabbed from behind and thrown. He flew out of the group of them landing hard on stone. His momentum was too great and he found himself sliding off the edge.

As he felt the Fenrir give way under him he slammed his weapon into the wall, there was a pulse of light and a tremor from it as Angelfire pierced it. The impact jerked him tight, his arm strained from the effort. The muscles had not fully healed themselves. He knew he could not hold long.

He gazed at his friends, they were amazing. The speed and ferocity they fought with was glorious. They had killed several of the clones, no easy feat to be certain. He would imagine that if there were fewer perhaps the odds would have shifted. The chaos though was what Thead sought after. It was working as well. He needed to do something. With an exertion of effort he was able to secure another hand hold. He began to pull himself up relieved that it was over. Then there was a shimmer in the air before him and Thead stood there. He wagged his finger at him before reaching down and with casual strength he lifted him up.

"You are finished Paladin." He felt the cold hard steel of Thead pierce his chest. The colors around him seemed to fade. He stared up at Thead with cool calm eyes. Darkness encroaching around him. Then the colors seemed to crash in on him and a sudden enormous pain erupted in his chest. Anger flared up and the rage took over.

He grabbed Thead's hands and pried them away. He pulled the blade free, as he did it disappeared in a cloud of smoke. He heard and even felt his blood drip to the stone below. It was a strange sound, it seemed to echo then crackle like a fire. The wound quickly healed as his body erupted in fire.

The Thead before him melted away, it proved to be another shadow clone. His aura flared to life as a new power erupted within him. He felt a connection to the wall as if it was a living entity. He commanded it to grow. The aura swiftly enveloped his companions. All the clones burned away until all that was left was one. Except it wasn't a clone was it? It reeled in pain feet from Sheen. He reached forward in an attempt to grab her. *NO! Attack Fenrir!* A sudden surge of power flew through his body, the magick that flowed through the wall dimmed around him. All of it condensed in his hand. He pointed a finger at Thead.

"Bang."

The air shimmered and vibrated around him, the power shot forward followed by an enormous boom. The stone below it melted under the intensity, following the blast the wall exploded in a powerful shockwave sending waves through the stone. The blast shot through Sheen, she let out a gasp, her body quickly healed from any wounds. Her strength surged and for a moment she felt invulnerable, those moments proved vital as the shockwave of stone crashed into her, she dropped to the ground covering her head, it threw her and Raamok into the air, she came crashing down on her face but the healing power surged through her from the aura, rapidly healed the wounds. Raamok, kept on his feet as he fell back to the ground. The impact had the exact opposite on Thead. The blast temporarily halted a few inches before his outstretched hands. It wavered there for a moment trying to press through the defense. The air became incredibly hot, then the shockwave hit, Thead managed to stop the stone wave causing it to separate around him. However the thousands of stone that came behind it was too much. His concentration faltered. He made the choice to jump off the side of the Fenrir, the power that had settled in his hand a moment before exploded in a brilliant white light. He may have jumped off the side but the blast sent him into a near uncontrollable spin. However to his dismay he survived. He hovered out of reach bloodied, burnt and haggard, he had a fierce scowl on his face. Zarron took off his helm and smiled at him.

Thead took off at a great speed into the darkness. Zarron let out a sigh as his vision returned to normal. His control and connection with Fenrir was gone. The aura flickered briefly before going dark. He recast it again at the original level.

"Come we have to condense our forces, I fear this was a one trick and done. I understand what this wall is and I can guess what he will do next." There was a pause as Zarron stared after the guardian. "He is going to kill Fenrir."

XXXVII

Partaxis spun to the side avoiding a strike meant to impale him. A sword burst through the attacker as one of the defenders came to his aid. It wasn't needed to be certain he was already formulating a plan to kill the creature but, it did improve morale whenever one of his men got the honor of defending him. Since he took command of the defenses people were always flocking around him. He didn't understand it fully, part of it was the fact that he rescued so many in the barbarian raid a month or two ago. The other more probable fact was the point in which his name was known. He did come from a line of ancient royalty, it didn't mean much to him since the split in the kingdoms but it was present. Names still carried a great weight. Finally with his history with Tahvo being out in the open now it brought a hero alive. Many of the people there had heard the story of the Black Wars passed on over the years. Since he was such a pivotal role in it, those stories they heard of the legendary warriors became a reality.

His status pretty much made him untouchable, he could do anything he liked and what would someone say? It still made things difficult to choose at times. He knew when he formulated the plan to funnel the enemy to the middle was basically going to throw away lives. The fact that the flanks held out as long as they did was better than he was hoping for. However it made the decision even more difficult. Those men signed their death warrant when they went to the flanks with blind loyalty. He stepped back from the front and peered towards the East.

His eyes widened as he saw a winged demon land and utterly annihilate the defenders. It suddenly shifted and there were hundreds of them. There was a golden light that filled the air, he watched it flicker then dim to nothing. He scowled deeply, then looking away he gave a knowing look to Tombah. Tombah nodded his head as he scurried away to put in place the next move. He peered back to the East just in time to see a sudden bright flash of light, the wall seemed to groan under the stress of it and the color in it seemed to dim. He wouldn't have noticed if it wasn't for the sudden contrast. He shook his head. *That makes no sense, stone doesn't change just to change.* He turned and found another one of the wizards in Tombah's entourage.

"You there, what is happening on the Eastern wall?" The wizards golden eyes looked towards the Eastern side. He narrowed them briefly before returning his focus on Partaxis.

"The magick has been drained from it. That is why it is dimmer in comparison. The fact that you noticed it means you have some capacity for spells yourself Partaxis, if it weren't so you wouldn't have seen that." Partaxis thanked the wizard. Then a thought formed in his mind, primarily who was there.

"Wizard, what kind of magick is that? Is it one of yours or is it demonic? Can you tell?" The wizard peered back at the location.

"Well that much magick being pulled leaves behind a noticeable shadow we will say. I would say you are looking at light magick with a twist of something…ancient along with small remnants of demonic. Very curious spell if you ask me and cast by someone not experienced in using it. There is far too much fallout from the light and ancient side, any mage hunter would easily be able to pick up on the trail of it. So it can't be one of Master Tombah's apprentices or of the Voice of the Nameless. They are all trained and practiced in the hiding of magick since they began training. One of the first things taught to a new caster." The wizard continued rambling on but Partaxis was far away. He knew who that was over there now, it was Zarron. Before he could move there was a sudden shockwave followed by an enormous boom. The top of the Fenrir to the East and West flanks burst into a dazzling inferno.

The effects were devastating, the entire flanks were destroyed in an eye blink. He was assured something spectacular was going to happen when Tombah and himself went over the plan. He just didn't expect something so spectacular. He focused his mind and told himself to snap out of it. He had just killed many good men, the weight of their sacrifice weighed heavy on his soul and he knew it wouldn't go away anytime soon. However deep down he knew that if given another opportunity he would have repeated the same task, perhaps he would have given more time to clear the walls but the loss to the enemy was a thousand times worse than his own.

****

"We need to get out of here quickly, to warn the others. We can't have Thead succeed." Zarron growled as he began to sprint.

"What do you mean that he will kill Fenrir? It is just a wall." Raamok asked inquisitively.

"It is more than that this is a living entity, an ancient power that…" Zarron faded out, he slowed his pace for a step or two. He felt a pulse of heat zip by him. He looked at the wall as runes began to show themselves. It was very faint at first, another heat pulse zipped by him and the runes began to glow brighter. He looked up to view the initial group of men they had rescued. They were holding the horde off with renewed energy and spirit. Durakon was glowing with primal fury, the wall feeding him copious amounts of energy. He killed one after another after another, if there was a small break he pushed the enemy back with a barrage of arrows until the rest of the group could stop the hole. He was a titan standing against waves of darkness.

Another pulse, this time he could feel the heat begin to rise. *By the Nameless they are going to die.* He put his head down and began sprinting as fast as he could towards them. The sudden speed and ferocity of his advance took a moment for the others to process. They looked to one another with curious glances before hauling after him.

As he ran he began to cast a shield. The pulses picked up speed they zipped by faster and faster. The heat was getting near unbearable, another pulse his head began to hurt, and it caused his concentration to falter for a second. However it was a second he couldn't afford. The wall before him began exploding in a brilliant, intense inferno.

He fell to his knees and collapsed on top of the Fenrir in a heap. His head hung low, it had become so heavy. He somehow found the strength to lift his head towards the men. He saw Durakon look towards him then back towards the explosions. Durakon looked back once more and nodded his head towards him. He formed a crooked smile, fire in his eyes.

Zarron watched as the explosions disintegrated Durakon and the men they had worked so hard to protect, Durakon who he left in charge to protect them, he didn't expect to say good bye to his brother, his rescuer, he knew at that moment he would probably never erase that final image of him being consumed by the fire. It came so suddenly and they were gone. The enemy with them but, he didn't care. They had preserved those men, many of them he had served with only a few months ago. They were going to survive this, not all but some. Now they were no more. The explosions continued accelerating towards him. He felt the presence of his small party come near. The intensity of the explosion forced him to look away. He felt the presence of the explosions drawing ever close. He lifted his gaze towards the fire once more and spoke a word.

The fire peeled away rapidly, it soared over them and around them. The ferocity of it scorched their lungs as they breathed in. The fires raged around them melting the stone. He began to rise then he felt Fenrir scream, the intensity of it drove him to his knees once more, the shield around them flickered, the inferno that seeped in for those brief heart beats scorched their clothes. Another scream came from Fenrir, he braced for a third one but it never came. He felt hands pull him up from his knees. He looked and saw

Sheen and Raamok looking at him in wonder.

"Apologies, come we need to move I don't know how long I can hold this shield." Zarron croaked, his voice hoarse and haggard. That was all the motivation the team needed. They began moving forward quickly. As they passed the burnt out wreckage of where Durakon was moments before he said a silent prayer for his fallen companion and the men with him. The siege tower itself was no more, it had collapsed onto itself and was still a raging inferno. It would burn for a while to be certain. As far as they were concerned any tower caught in that blast was utterly destroyed, the enemy could no longer make use of them.

After a few more moments they finally left the hellish firewall. However they were not out of the fire yet. The center of Fenrir was in absolute chaos. The enemy doubled their efforts and struck with rage and zeal at the defenders of the Fenrir. They were pressed hard. Zarron looked around trying to decide what to do when Kadiallias appeared before him as if from nowhere. He took a step back at her sudden appearance.

"Zarron, you are ok, by the Nameless I had thought you were done, I saw Thead fly towards you then the sudden blast of light. I tried to get to you but this damned firewall erupted in front of me. Stopped me in my tracks, knowing I couldn't go any further I hunted down who caused it. Turns out Partaxis used it as a surprise attack against the enemy in an effort to control the battlefield, plans backfired though and the enemy swarmed the center with numbers that we did not account for. We had to evacuate the West side, currently the bridge is holding, our defenders here on the East side have been pressed on all sides. We are holding the influx from the West and the enemies on our side, thank the Nameless for your house guard, they are stopping up holes and prowling like wild men supporting weak points, turning away mighty beasts and overall controlling the flow as best they can. They can't last forever though. It just isn't possible. There is just too many currently." She opened her mouth to continue when a sudden boom came from the West interrupting her.

They all turned to look and saw an enormous fire burst leap several hundred feet into the air, it spewed forth fireballs and large stones. Kadiallias reacted first, she tossed up a shield just in time to catch the first mighty hit from the debris. It nearly knocked her on her back yet she managed to hold. Zarron jumped in to reinforce it with his own. They managed to stop the majority of it. Except one piece which was so unbelievably heavy it destroyed their shield with almost no effort. The only thing that saved them was it was high enough that their party was able to drop prone to miss the behemoth of a stone. Finally the smoke drifted away enough to show that the western bridge had been destroyed. They only got a few moments to stare in shock at it before the smoke clouded their vision once more.

There was almost a heavy silence that fell on the entire field of battle. The dins of steel on steel, shouts of men dying and those of absolute rage faded into the background. Zarron looked at his companions who blinked the dust and soot out of their eyes. They shook their heads clear of the ringing. He could almost hear their heart beats, feel their breathing. He felt as if he was in a state in between his rage, the colors began shifting around him, his vision pulsated smoothly between tunnel and normal. He reached into himself to try to bring the rage out, bring it to the front so he could crush the enemy. Then it all came crashing in on him. Mighty horns blared out their calls, men shouted orders. The sounds of battle returned. He lost his peace and the rage subsided.

It didn't take them long to get to an area they could be useful at. Zarron's men shouted with renewed energy as they saw him alive. He had chosen to place himself at the western side of their flank to help hold the influx of enemies that were routed directly to them with the destruction of the western bridge.

He was fighting off a particular tough press of enemies when the defenders around him erupted in a sudden violent cheer. It distracted him momentarily and he lost his focus. The dark ones he was controlling lost their focus on him and wrought out several brutal wounds before they were finished off with the line of defenders. Zarron cursed, with a heave he used every ounce of remaining energy he had to throw the line of enemies off the wall. It gave his men enough time to close the gap and gain another foot of precious land. He backed up to see what caused the ruckus only to see that Partaxis had made an appearance.

His eyes became slits as he stared at this man that he once respected whole heartedly. He stalked towards him quickly with a dangerous look in his eyes. The men that were guarding him stepped between the giant of a man and Zarron. They placed their hands on their weapons getting ready to draw. He stared at them icily his glowing eyes fixed on both of them. They hesitated a moment before Partaxis spoke.

"Zarron, I..." He paused for a moment. Before he could talk again Zarron interrupted him.

"A word in private Partaxis." He fixed his eyes on him icily. Partaxis raised his hands in surrender and led the way back towards the keep. It took them a few minutes to get there. As he opened the door, he turned to look at Zarron he felt a sudden pain explode in his head, he hit the ground hard, stars erupted, and he was only just able to keep conscience.

"That was for Durakon, you are lucky I don't kill you for such a disgusting arrogant choice throwing away good people's lives for what? A little gain to make you feel like you had the upper hand? You never had it, those men died for nothing. We are in a worse situation because of your poor insane planning. I really should kill you Partaxis, but despite all your asinine tactics the men adore and love you. That is the reason I didn't embarrass you in front of them. I am not sure what happened between the events of the barbarian camp and now. But, you are not the same person as you were before.

These people might think you walk on water, they may fear you but your little dog and pony show does not work on me. I am going to finish this battle, then I can assure you we are done Partaxis. I will not stand by someone so willing to toss away good people's lives, no toss away is too mild, butcher would be more appropriate." With that Zarron turned and left focusing his attention to the defense of the Fenrir.

He was pleased to find that Raamok had taken to battle in full ferocious might. The foothold Zarron had given the men was used by Raamok to expand their footing. Where he had given the defenders maybe a few feet Raamok had taken that to nearly 50 feet. It gave them room to maneuver which was sorely needed. Zarron joined the fight and the two of them fell into a rhythm, they weaved a path of death and destruction amidst the foe. Several times they became surrounded, cut off from the front line. That is where Sheen came in, she was always there to clear a path to Zarron once more. It was with one of these pushes that everything changed.

A sudden chain of explosions rocked the wall. Zarron managed to get over to the edge and his eyes widened as he looked at a chain of suicide towers smashing into the Fenrir. The power of each one sent a rippling shockwave that shattered ice encrusted walls. They kept coming, there was little he could do. They came quicker and quicker. He desperately looked for a way to stop them but, there was nothing they could do. The enemy had taken that part of the wall. Their siege equipment was all but useless against such things. He stared in horror at the rate the ice departed. Soon they would be at the wall, the real wall, not the ice encrusted monstrosity it had become but the actual stone. *No, no this can't be.* His heart raced as he thought of Fenrir and knew that Thead wanted it destroyed. The memory of the screams he felt replayed in his mind, panic began to swell in him. He said a prayer and began to just breathe. This was all in the Nameless Ones hands, he focused his thoughts on that.

Once more the battlefield became quiet, the noises drifted into the background. Peace settled on him. His vision pulsed sporadically at first, or he thought it was. Then he found the rhythm, a soothing presence drifted over him. He wanted to move, destroy this enemy. The rhythm became sporadic once more. He breathed a few more times than peace settled.

His rage exploded in him. He felt his power increase, then the noise returned, Fenrir called to him, he purposely directed his mind on that, and his rage became focused. This rage was controlled he found, it wasn't the unhindered anger that was always there before but focused. He turned to look towards his friend, the darkness in Raamok called out to him, he wanted to destroy it. However the light in him glowed brightly, more bright then he had ever seen. Fenrir called out to him once more and his thoughts settled.

"Raamok, you need to fall back. Gather the defenders and retreat to the secondary wall. Fenrir is lost."

XXXVIII

There was something dangerous in Zarron's eyes, Raamok knew better than to push it. However he also knew he wasn't done. He would do what the Paladin requested but then return immediately. Another explosion rocked the wall, he stumbled but kept on his feet. The explosions were getting more violent. He was able to take a couple more steps before another explosions burst to life. Half step, boom, three steps, boom. At this rate it would take ages to, boom, it would take ages to walk the short distance to the defenders. Boom, another explosion ripped through the air. However this time a nearly impossible to perceive crack formed below his feet. There was a great shudder as if the wall heaved in pain. Boom, another one. He found the farther he got away from the center the less the impact was on his footing. *Finally*, he sighed a great sigh of relief and began sprinting. Within just a few moments he was in front of Partaxis. His face was purpled from a blow, it was new. He didn't see it before Zarron took him aside. He suppressed a chuckle as he thought about it.

"Partaxis, it is time to fall back. According to the paladin Fenrir is lost." There was a grim expression on Partaxis face, it turned into a deep scowl.

"We are holding for now why would we give this up?" He growled.

"Look Partaxis, I am not one to run from a fight so how about you look at it as repositioning your men to a better fighting point. The Fenrir can't hold up, we have been lucky to stop them so far. It wouldn't be long before they regroup. Once one flank fails they will be able to roll us up and finish us off. However if we move back to the bridge, we are only defending one point, however I think we need to send a team to the last stand. I think Zarron knows this wall is going to fall apart any minute. No way can it sustain that many explosions in a row. Not to mention the siege weapons can't touch the enemy. It is just a matter of time. When that wall falls there needs to be a welcoming party there to welcome them to the lands and ensure they pay the proper taxes for entry."

Partaxis gave a weak smile before his mask dropped in place relaying no further information on his thoughts. He opened his mouth a couple times to speak before catching himself. He breathed in a great breath before calmly breathing out.

"I have made one bad call for the day, I see wisdom in what the paladin says. We will fall back in order. Bringing in the flanks at the same time and rolling onto ourselves. We will hold our front on the keep side of the bridge. So if need be we can blow it at any time and stop the flow of enemies. We will swap the frontline defenders with the rear and send the front to the last stand to get a few moments of rest. They have been fighting without the aid of the Fenrir so they are tired. It is at this point that our task becomes dire." He paused for a moment in contemplation before turning his attention to Raamok.

"What are you planning on doing slayer?" Before Raamok could respond there was a great buzz in the air followed by torrent of wind leaving him short on breath. He looked over to the breach point and an enormous mass of black and green slammed into the wall. The explosions was deafening, it scattered hundreds of green globules along the wall. As those globules came into contact with the enemy they melted away in brief moments. A few of them managed to reach their defensive line. The unfortunate souls that weren't hidden by a shield began to melt immediately, body parts melted away leaving a string of limbless defenders writhing in pain. Those that had a shield dropped them immediately as the acid ate through them. Those of the Mind of the church and a few wizard types that were left quickly reacted containing the acid and stopping the effects of the substance. Within a few moments the attack was under control.

The buzzing and torrent of wind came again, the defenders cringed and some even backed away as another mass of black and green arced towards the Fenrir. There was a pop followed by a great heat, not painful nor comforting, it was somewhere in the uncomfortable field. A magnificent shield flared to life glowing with a brilliant blue and silver. It met with the projectile, the two powers collided with a stunning boom sending out a massive shockwave. The shield pulsed momentarily before solidifying then it did something unexpected, it melded around the remnants of the projectile and consumed it.

Raamok peered towards the wall and saw Zarron there forced to a knee, he could make out Sheen next to him helping him to his feet. The enemy began to surge towards them once more. Most being stopped short of the target due to the acid field. However a few who he guessed were immune to the poison made haste to them, Sheen moved to intercept them and to his surprise Zarron was back on his feet. He looked away and gave his attention to Partaxis once more.

"I am going to cover Zarron as he does whatever he plans on doing. I figure a little help won't be so bad. Not to mention if he was the cause of that shield I can't imagine that power persisting very long. He will need a hand. I would suggest you make haste Partaxis, let's not make his sacrifice be in vain. I don't know how many more precious moments you will have to get the defenders out of here. Take them all, any one that stays will likely die. I am only going to cover him for another shield pulse or two before falling back myself." Partaxis gave a short nod to him before turning and shouting orders to the defenders.

The explosions picked back up to Raamok's dismay slowing his progress as he moved towards Zarron. The wall seemed to shudder more with each impact, it gave a clear picture of the amount of damage that it had sustained. After a few more minutes he was in the fray of combat once more.

The retreat went as well as one could hope for. Partaxis managed to pull back nearly all of the defenders. The few that remained he made perfectly clear to them they would likely die. They chose to stay, however they were few and he checked it off in his mind as an allowable loss. The loss of Raamok however would be terrible and Kadiallias as well but he knew there was little he could do to convince them otherwise. Especially Kadiallias with her piercing stare, he shook off a shutter as he thought about her. Out of respect for the sacrifice that those that stayed he made a note of each of their names. Char, one of the house guards of Zarron, Corwin a Night Wolf scout, Jubilee a member of the Mind of the Nameless, Lylith a wizard apprentice, Ghost another Night Wolf member and finally the brothers Blake and Tendra. Those two came from the round of reinforcements after the horn was sounded. He had almost lost the rest of Zarron's house guard but after some persistent and difficult persuasion he was able to convince them they were needed at the breach point in the last stand more than here.

Another enormous boom drew his attention to the top of the wall where he could make out the shimmer of silver and blue from the shield. However it was duller in color then he remembered. That was not a good sign he knew. He also saw that the Fenrir itself was a muted color. Very little of the vibrancy was there any more. He had taken the liberty to blow the inner tunnels that ran along the length for siege equipment to deny them another access point. There was another amazing boom. He looked towards the top of the wall and did not see any sign of the shield. Another massive explosion erupted and the Fenrir groaned, a sharp crack resounded in the air followed by the wall rippling before snapping taught and shattering. A raw, emotional scream echoed in the air. The colors of Fenrir flared once, twice, and finally flickered out of existence.

The defenders stared open mouthed and eyes wide in shock at the enormous gaping hole. Dread filled the air, so thick that you could taste it. As

Partaxis looked around he noted that most of the defenders had lost the color in their face. The dread and fear settled itself heavily in his stomach, he swallowed down the bile that was rising. He breathed a moment or two bringing in his fear and stared in shock once more at the remains of the Fenrir.

The men finally coming to, became restless, and aware of the fear and dread that was oh so real, it wasn't long before one of them chose to run. The movement brought Partaxis out of his stupor. He came to and with several great long strides he caught up with the man. He lifted the man as if he was a child and dragged/carried him to the front before setting him down next to him.

The man's desire to run was replaced with a new fear and wonder, he stood there next to the towering man whimpering softly. Partaxis looked down at him and rested a big hand on his shoulder. Then he grabbed the man's weapon and placed it in his hand, he turned him towards the enemy.

"The enemy is that way boy, not the other way. You will find no peace in that land if you run from this nor will you find it in your life knowing you ran from a battle of intense magnitude that none has seen. The mighty Fenrir has fallen, she has protected our lands for many many years, and it is now on us to return the favor. Stand and fight boy, I will watch out for you, and you watch out for me."

It was at that point the sounds of the enemy war horns could be heard. The defenders froze as they watched the breach. Within moments the first enemy combatant came into view, then another and another, as if releasing a dam the rest of the enemy force came bursting forward, their numbers flooding the killing grounds of the last stand.

The siege equipment of the second wall came to life once more. Their powerful ballistae and stones crushed hordes of the enemy. Archery fire poured down on them, yet they came. Fire burst forth from the fields as the traps stirred to life. They still came. There was so many, finally it was the defenders turn the two great forces collided in a grand battle. The defenders fear and dread replaced with rage and anger. They attacked the enemy host with great zeal and vigor.

****

Zarron got up as a new burst of energy flowed through him. His rage continued as he felt Fenrir stirring. It was an odd sensation having such a connection with what appeared to be a wall. He didn't understand it completely, he drew the conclusion that it was something to deal with his Holyrage, since that was the only time he felt the wall and could command it. *Just add that to my long list of questions.*

He went to Sheens side immediately and casually slew several of the poison walkers. They were not particularly amazing is stature or strength but immunity to poison and a bite that displayed the same characteristics of the poison made them dangerous. He had watched Sheen replace several blades as she fought off the creature. Thankfully there was no risk of running out of weapons anytime soon as the wall was crowded with the dead. He felt a sting as one managed to bite down on him a small drop of the poison managed to burn a hole through the less protected joints. He flung it to the ground and was about ready to stomp on it when Raamok showed up and slew it with his Typhoon. He risked a glance towards the defensive line and saw that Partaxis was pulling back.

"Thank you Raamok, for carrying the warning to them. However I can't have you stay. This is not going to hold. There is no point in throwing away lives."

"Don't you worry about that, I wasn't planning on staying for long. Just enough for you to do what you think you are doing. Then off we go."

"We?" Zarron asked.

"Indeed, we, there were a few of us that couldn't let you have all the fun on your own. So we will guard you, do what you need to do." Zarron slapped Raamok on the shoulder cheerfully. He quickly greeted the rest of the group. After a brief exchange of greetings and some talks they fell into positions they felt were most fitting and he would have to confess they did well. It took little to no effort for them to fall into a rhythm. He was appreciating the work of it all when Fenrir shouted out a warning to him once more.

Zarron peered into the distance and saw another blob of black and green arcing towards the wall. He reached down to Fenrir and felt the strong presence once more. He drew upon that pool of power and formed it into another barrier. The projectile smashed into the shield with even more force. Thead had been pouring more power into it. He let out a grunt of exertion as the impact drove him back several feet. He slid dangerously close to the edge before the projectile was rebounded. The sheer ferocity of the attack didn't allow him to manipulate it to absorb the energy. He could feel Fenrir cry out as the energy was taken away. *I am sorry Fenrir, I didn't expect that at all.*

"We cannot stand against many more attacks child of rage. My force is weakening. You cannot allow Thead to destroy me. You cannot!" The enormous voice dropped Zarron to his knees. He removed his helm and flung it to the side. He moved a hand up to his ears and felt blood. He winced in pain before he cast a healing spell to restore the damage. He stumbled forward a few steps to get away from the edge. He donned his helm one more. *How about we control the mind speak unless you wish to kill me.*

"Very well, my apologies child of rage. We are in grave danger. I am losing energy faster than I am gaining it. The battle being pressed back to the other wall has weakened me...I must feed on the essence of the dark ones. Come now to your feet child, another one is incoming."

Zarron barely formed the shield in time as another one smashed into it. It wasn't enough though. The power of the attack shattered his concentration and a portion of it got through, he fell flat on his back pressed down by the weight of the attack. He felt Fenrir cry out in pain as it collided with her.

"Another is coming Zarron, be strong young one." Zarron held out his hands feebly, they were shaking fiercely. He slowly pulled himself to his feet. He gathered together energy and formed a shield as the projectile came in. There was a sudden gasp from his companions as he felt an incredible burst of pain shoot through him as something hit him in the side hard. The shield fell apart, he attempted to bring life to it before another strike smashed into his side. He turned to see Thead on top of him, his eyes went wide, not at the presence of the evil Guardian but of the missile that smashed into the wall unhindered.

He felt Fenrir cry out in pain. "It is getting dark, cloudy…I am dying. I don't want to die child, where are the colors, what happened to them? Please, I don't want to die." He heard Fenrir's deep wretched cries as the voice faded.

Her voice came back again in a moment, clear and serious "I see the ancient one, he is gaining power you must stop him before he breaks another seal. I am through my child, arise. Take what I have left and awaken. Do not forget me Zarron." The voice faded to nonexistence.

The light of the wall pulsed once, he felt a surge of power and strength it was enough to send Thead away from him. The wall pulsed once more, he felt his energy restored then the great and mighty Fenrir went dark. Thead began laughing triumphantly a short distance away from him. It took Zarron a moment to track where he was.

"The seal is nearly broken Zarron, just need to extinguish the last portion. Then on to the other seal you so willingly brought to me." Zarron stared in confusion and followed Thead's gaze which landed heavily on Sheen. He got to his feet placing himself between her and Thead. He began to laugh once more.

"Oh yes Zarron, she is one of those mighty seals. Kind of pathetic that they gave such a task to a woman as this. Doesn't matter though, Uttookari will rise again. You can be certain of that. This time with a bit more success, the seal will be destroyed and I will have killed the only force that has stopped him so far, House Holyrage. How pleased he will be. Enough with this chatter it is time to finish this."

He attacked quickly, his foot connected with Zarron's chest before he could even react. Zarron went flying backwards narrowly missing Sheen, the force of the blow dented his armor. He crashed hard into one of the battlements shattering it.

Corwin was the first to come awake and he attacked. Zarron watched him pierce Thead's side, but with a flash of light and a burst of magick he was nothing more than a red mist. Thead turned his attention on Lylith, he was attempting the same magick on her. She was a little more prepared and was able to get up a magick shield in time. Her concentration was gone after the savage burst of magick. She would have fallen shortly behind if not for Char who intervened. He lashed out at Thead forcing him to falter in his attention for a moment.

Lylith took advantage of that moment, she sent a lightning bolt at him. It tore through his shoulder nearly taking the arm with it. However with one smooth move he knocked aside Char with a fierce kick, summoned a bone spear and flung it at her. The force of it hit her so hard that she flung back into Zarron, the two of them collided. He felt pain explode in his side as the spear punctured him as well. He pulled the spear free and healed the wound as he laid Lylith onto her side. He looked over her and seeing no life left in her he let out a desperate cry. His companions were dying, it wouldn't be long until all of them were gone. The rest of the team were fully engaged in combat. Kadiallias led the front attempting to keep Thead's attention on her.

It was when Zarron moved to engage that he noticed Char's absence. He scanned the field quickly and spotted him hanging onto the edge of the Fenrir trying not to fall. He rushed over to him and reached down to pull him up. It was then he noticed the battle raging below and how desperate of situation they were in. The enemy swarmed through the opening, there numbers were astounding, the defenders looking like nothing more than a small stone trying to hold back the power of the ocean. With a small tug he pulled Char up.

"I need you to protect the others, reinforce the last stand they will need all the warriors they can and you are the mightiest of my house guard. Go, grab Sheen and get out of here she cannot fall into the enemy hands. I don't understand what her role is or what these seals are but you need to save her. Take the others as well, I cannot risk your lives any further. Please don't argue just go." Zarron commanded him. Char looked at him for a moment or two longer before nodding his head in agreement. Comfortable knowing he would do what was asked Zarron turned and entered the fight.

As he charged towards Thead, Raamok got sent flying towards him and Thead jumped into to the air on his mighty wings flattening the attackers. It was then he got an idea.

"Raamok, I need you to welcome Thead to the ground once more." Zarron shouted at Raamok as he grabbed hold of him with white tendrils of light. He attempted to put more earthly magick into it over holy for fear of damaging the vampire side in him. He didn't have time to perfect it nor the skill, so he continued to do what he could. When he got enough lashings onto him he flung him towards Thead.

Raamok had just a brief second to process the information yelled at him by Zarron, it didn't make sense initially as he was flying away from his target but then an unpleasant warmth grabbed hold of him at several places and with a burst of speed he found himself flying quickly towards Thead. It all made sense in that moment, he just hoped Zarron had a way of getting him back to the earth. He felt the lashing slacken as he approached his target. He readied his weapon and with practiced expert precision he brought Typhoon around severing one of the guardian's wings. He then felt another unpleasant warm sensation as the lashing grabbed him from the front and yanked him full force back towards the ground, or more appropriate Thead. He brought his blades to position once more as he collided with the guardian, it felt as if he had run into a solid brick wall. He slashed out with his blades, at the last moment Thead twisted and instead of taking a whole wing with him he took half of one. However the damage was done. He was entangled with the guardian as they plummeted back to Fenrir. He adjusted his weight and managed to turn at the last moment so Thead would take the brunt of the fall. However before he hit the ground with him he felt the tug relieve itself from his front and move towards his back. He kicked out with his feet to give Thead a final courtesy push. The sudden momentum shift slowed him enough, soon the tendrils of magick disappeared and he felt himself under the comfortable constant flow of gravity once more.

As Thead smashed into the ground the companions charged him taking full advantage of the downed guardian. They all attacked with great fury. Zarron took a quick second to recover from the intense exertion of moving Raamok around. A sudden burst of energy forced him to pause in his charge. Thead let out a mighty roar as he gained his feet once more his companions sent off balance.

"Enough! I have toyed with you all long enough! Now, prepare to face the true power of a guardian of a god!" Thead shouted with an intensity that shook the core of their souls. He flung into action taking advantage of the brief space he gave himself. Within a near eye blink the group that was engaged with him were suddenly impaled with shadow tendrils. The only ones that weren't effected was Sheen, Raamok and himself who must have been outside the radius of the spell effect. Rapid dark red pulses fed into them. Their screams of pain awakened something in Zarron once again, he felt the surge of power pulse through him again, however it was not the same as Fenrir but similar.

He threw Angelfire towards him, the power of the sword formed a fiery shield around Thead enveloping him in holy fire, severing the dark tendrils powers.

His companions fell to the ground limply. He scanned them all briefly his vision showing him essences of life still flowed through him. He grabbed hold of each of their life essences and pulled them together before sending them as far away as he could. Which to his disgust was no further than the Korilith barracks, in particular his barrack room.

Each one became wrapped in a holy light, their bodies broke down into the magick that formed them and he sent them on their way. They disappeared from sight to be reformed in his barracks room. The force of moving them drained him of his new found power quickly. As he turned to face Sheen he noticed her essence had begun to drastically fade, she swooned on her feet before collapsing. The alien power in him flickered out of existence.

Zarron walked over to Raamok. Maintaining his connection with Angelfire as best as he could. The fire shield was soon to break but he needed to get Sheen clear. Raamok was his last resort to accomplish this. He knew he didn't have the power left to teleport them as he did the others. Raamok was just beginning to engage when Zarron laid a hand on him.

"Raamok, thank you for your aid in this fight. You have dealt the near death blow to this wicked creature. I cannot thank you enough for that. Despite that, I fear I have one more favor to ask of you. I need you to save Sheen, rescue her. Do what you can to get her as far away as possible and hide her. If I fail I need to know she is safe. Can you do this for me?" Zarron pleaded with him. Raamok looked at him quizzically.

"I don't think so Zarron, she can get off on her own I owe this guy some pay back. I will not be running away like some coward." Raamok spat in disgust before resuming his walk towards Thead once more. Zarron placed a hand on his chest.

"Please Raamok, this fight is no longer yours, you have your own to deal with. This fight is mine and he has much to pay for." Zarron's eyes flared to life, a righteous fire settling there. One Raamok couldn't dismiss. They stared at each other for a moment, Raamok shifted his eyes between Zarron, Thead and Sheen. He looked off to the side for a moment before swallowing hard and returning his gaze to Zarron.

"Very well Paladin, however I will not take her all the way away from here. I will only take her to where you sent the other fighters and then I will return to assist." Zarron considered this for a moment before agreeing and telling Raamok where he sent them. Zarron returned his focus to Thead.

"Go now Raamok, I will hold him back as long as it takes." he breathed in and out a few times before fully reconnecting with Angelfire who was still holding Thead in place just barely. It wasn't long before Thead's power overwhelmed Angelfire.

Thead, shattered the fiery shield and let out a roar of frustration as he realized the attackers were gone. He regained control as he realized that the ones that were left were the ones he needed. He let out a grunt and healed the majority of his wounds. However to his dismay his wings were not healing back. He began to stalk towards Sheen, he still had to finish her off, however the seal of Fenrir he realized had become shattered the last of the required energy was gone. A little remained still but not enough to make a difference. He smiled to himself, all things considered it was a good start.

Raamok was only able to take a few steps before Thead began stalking towards them. As the guardian lunged at Raamok he was suddenly stopped in his tracks. Massive light hooks grabbed him by the mouth and turned him away. Thead attempted to fight them but he was not strong enough apparently. Raamok peered over and saw Zarron glowing with a magnificent aura of blue and silver his eyes ablaze with a blue fire. He turned and quickly began to move Sheen away with haste.

Zarron pulled with all his strength and yanked Thead towards him. He nearly lost control of the powerful being the first few tries but noticed with each effort it got easier to pull him in. Thead let out a growl as he tried to pull free once more. Not having any success he turned his full attention on Zarron and charged.

Zarron let go of the hooks as Thead rushed him, he dodged out of the way just barely of the first strike. The second strike he had to jump back to give him the space he needed to summon Angelfire once more. As he did though Thead turned towards Sheen and Raamok once more. He formed the hook and chain again and grabbed hold of Thead, this time he yanked with enough force to pull the guardian right to him. As he came towards him he kicked him in the stomach causing the guardian to double over. He brought his sword down which was parried by the guardian who returned with his own strike aiming to disembowel him. He turned the strike to the side causing Thead to stumble forward a step.

Zarron used that momentum to carry him to the flank of the enemy and finally behind him. He was now successfully between Thead and the retreating members. As he settled there he brought his shield up and caught a powerful blow that sent him sliding back a few steps. However he kept to his feet and prepared for the follow up strike. It came as he anticipated, he turned it aside then slammed the pommel of Angelfire into Thead's nose. There was a sickening crack and a burst of black blood poured forth.

Thead recovered quickly and drove a solid hit knocking him flat. He felt another blow as a kick followed sending him skidding terribly close to the edge. He stopped just barely, his shield came free and went falling to the earth below.

Once more he saw the group of defenders fighting below, they were fully engaged at this time, and he could make out Partaxis mighty form at the front. However there was so many dead, he guessed their numbers at this point were well below half of what they started with at the last stand. The banners of the Nameless One were scattered and snapping in the wind, his men and women were still in the fight. An eruption of pain brought him back to his senses as Thead landed heavily on his back.

He was forced to turn around and several savage punches fell onto his head. His helm was suddenly violently ripped off and more savage punches crushed his face. He felt his eyes begin to swell shut and he tasted blood. His vision began to swim. Then he heard a voice reach out to him. It was the Nameless One.

"My Son, rise. His power is weakened for he has sworn off his god the Faceless One. He is now the enemy to the heavens and hells. Stop him."

The presence of his God gave him renewed vigor he began to rise to his feet. Thead knocked him down with a few more punches before he felt the strength of them recede to the point where he was able to pull together a defense. He was able to land a solid kick that sent the guardian back a few steps giving him the much needed space he required. The two of them breathed heavily recovering.

"Your god has left you Thead, you gave up your sacred duty when you declared Uttookari as your god. You are destroyed Thead. Used up, nothing more. Let me help you by sending you on your way." Zarron charged forward. A sudden laughter erupted from Thead and he began to glow with a darkness that was ancient and old.

"You fool, I don't need the Faceless One when I have the might of an Ancient God that took the three mightiest to stop. Even then the combined force of the Nameless, Shapeless and Faceless couldn't kill him. They could only lock him up for all eternity. Thanks to you failing in preventing the rupture of this seal his power has only grown." A dark globule of energy formed in his hand dark purple ebbed and flowed throughout it. It suddenly became a solid form of a spear. Zarron tried to avoid it but he was committed to his attack, the power of it punched through his armor, he felt it rupture his inside and burst forth out his back. His world instantly dimmed, his rage was the only thing keeping him from dying he knew. However the darkness was still there.

He needed to extinguish that darkness, the hate for it grew. He coughed up a heavy glob of blood. He spat it out, the pain caused his head to swim once more. He concentrated on the darkness. The ancient evil swirled from the spear to Thead. The power of it intimately connected with the host. He gave a weak laugh.

"That power is going to be the death of you. That ancient magick requires a deep intimate connection with its host. Such a strength, for the most part. Unless you encounter a truly terrible force against evil, one designed uniquely to kill your kind. A Holyrage. Then it becomes your weakness. That power sustains you just as much as you sustain it, extinguish one and they both die." He reached down and grabbed that ancient magick with his own and began to pour in as much of his righteous anger he could, the light in him feeding and twisting the darkness. Erasing it bit by bit. By the time Thead realized what was happening it was too late. He tried to wrestle free from the grasp however he could not. The more he struggled and tapped into his magick the faster the holy magick consumed it. He couldn't release the spear either, the intimate connection with the corrupted dark matter didn't allow him to. His attempts at physically harming him failed as well. His dark magick that coursed through him caused it to phase through the light and greedily be consumed. As far as he could tell Zarron was no longer physical, he was a manifestation of light. Agony tore through him, he felt his mind slipping away. Before it was gone he had to do something, it was then that he saw Sheen.

"You have taken all from me Holyrage, so I am going to take something from you. I may not be able to kill the other seal but I can keep you from ever getting to her." He reached out with the last of his power from the Faceless One and summoned forth a dark light, it struck Sheen and in an eye blink she was gone. Zarron attempted to reach out and stop the power but he was not able to, the concentration he had left was focused clearly on destroying Thead.

"What have you done evil one?" Zarron demanded through gritted bloody teeth.

"I sent her to somewhere that you will never find her." He smiled at Zarron briefly before he released all the dark energy he could. He forced it all against the small weak point in Zarron break in concentration.

Zarron felt the loss happen just as Thead surged his power forward, he attempted to contain it. But, the sudden instability of it backfired and a brilliant explosion of light and darkness erupted. He saw Thead fly away from him disintegrating in a black and purple haze tinged with silver and blue, there was a sudden ear shattering boom and he saw the top of the Fenrir bow, flex and snap then spring apart to thousands of pieces. He felt a gust of wind and the force of the explosion threw him off his feet and away, Fenrir continued to crumble away the pieces becoming distant. His vision flickered, then there was a sudden jarring stop and his world went black.

EPILOGUE

Jubilee watched the explosion rock Fenrir. Her pace quickened and ears buzzed as she looked for any signs of Zarron. It wasn't long before she noticed a bright white light go flying from the top. It collided with the top of the bridge sending chipped stone in every which way. Then disappeared beyond her sight falling to the far side of the last stand. She made note of the direction and began to move that way until a firm hand grabbed hold of her. She attempted to get free but the incredible strength of the person held her in place. She felt someone yelling something at her. She turned and looked into the face of Tendra whose countenance was twisted with emotional anguish. It took her a moment for his voice to become a reality.

"We need to help the front, we will find him after we repel the enemy we need you there. There is little we can do for him now, he is in the Nameless Ones grasp." She stood there dumbfounded for another moment before her training pulled her free. She went with Tendra and joined the front in their battle.

The battle raged on, chaos was the dominant force on the field. The explosion that sent Zarron flying also began a chain of events that could not be stopped. As the defenders were reaching the sheer exhaustion point the great wall of Fenrir burst to mighty pieces. It crushed the enemy caught in the last stand, the bridges forced the debris into the area. It wasn't long before most of the enemy horde was crushed. The defenders were blessedly far enough away to miss the amazing monstrous debris.

The enemy that were fortunate enough to survive could be seen retreating through the mighty dust cloud. A few of them rushed forward trying to break the defenders. However they did not break and they stopped the enemy while taking incredible casualties as a result.

As soon as the enemy was routed and order was restored Jubilee along with Tendra and Blake began their search of Zarron. Char joined the search shortly after. It took them several hours of back breaking labor removing stone and rock before there was a shout from Char. The rest of the team hustled over to him where he was attacking the rocks like a mad man. They all joined along and within a few minutes they uncovered the bloody crumpled body of Zarron. They carefully removed his body and placed it aside. Jubilee frantically began to assess him for any sign of life. There was none that she could find. So she began to do the only thing she knew to do in desperate situations, she began to pray to the Nameless One. Char quickly took his place by her side and lifted his prayers as well. Tendra and Blake looked to one another, shrugged their shoulders and took up positions around Zarron bowing their head in prayer as well.

"This is an outrage, how did you not know your guardian was trying to revive the ancient one Uttookari!" the booming voice of the Nameless echoed through the council chambers.

"I swear he acted on his own accord I had no knowledge of these actions, must have been the dark powers of him that covered his intentions." The Faceless One sneered back. The sincerity in his voice was noted by the Nameless.

"What say you to this Shapeless One?" The Shapeless One scratched what he assumed was his chin. He peered down at the Fenrir deep in thought. There was a long silence before he spoke.

"I think the Faceless One was not aware of the intentions of Thead. We all fought tooth and nail as the mortals say, to contain the ancient one, there would be no gain for us to release him. We all knew the power he possessed. My concern is there is at least 2 more seals we need to watch carefully and your little pets are nonexistent. The last of them fell this day! He gestured towards Zarron's body surrounded by his companions. We also need to worry about containing the power struggle that is beginning at this very moment. Before it was just between the two of you, now it has stretched across the entire Heavens and Hells realms. All those pathetic young gods seek their fame and fortune in joining the ancient one. Very few of them understand the nature of that wicked one. What can we do?"

The Faceless One let out a shudder "It sickens me to say such a thing but we need the Holyrage line at this time. However I will not let him go free forever. This blood debt will be paid."

The Nameless One peered at the Faceless his lips curling in disgust at him but also the fact that he was right. He could not expect one of his greatest assets to be revived without recompense. The painful sacrifice that would be sure to come sickened his stomach and settled wrong on his mind. However there was little else he could think of at this time. For now they needed Zarron.

"Very well Faceless One it shall be done, we will negotiate the blood debt at another time. Shapeless One mark my words on this, you shall be the witness of the meeting. I will not spend our time bickering over the details now Faceless One, you either take my word at this time or we watch our world crumble."

"Very well Nameless One, it will be done with the Shapeless One as our witness. However much I hate you I know you are a God of your word." The two great Gods shook each other's hands. The Nameless One looked down at Zarron who was now laying on top of the ruins, his companions around him. There was a great sadness in him as he watched, his life would be short he knew. However he could turn this to his advantage, he smiled a great smile as he reached down and touched Zarron.

"Awaken chosen champion, my child of rage." Air rushed into Zarron and his eyes snapped open.

ABOUT THE AUTHOR

Jonathan Socha is a USAF Veteran and father of two. His passion for writing fantasy began at a young age as an outlet for his overactive imagination, also as a means to bring his love for video games to life. Jonathan currently resides in New Hampshire with his beautiful wife and 2 boys.